ALSO BY
DIA REEVES

Bleeding Violet

Slice of Cherry

Dia Reeves

SIMON PULSE

NEW YORK   LONDON   TORONTO   SYDNEY

SIMON PULSE
An imprint of Simon & Schuster Children's Publishing Division
1230 Avenue of the Americas, New York, NY 10020
First Simon Pulse hardcover edition January 2011
Copyright © 2011 by Dia Reeves
All rights reserved, including the right of reproduction in whole or in part in any form.
SIMON PULSE and colophon are registered trademarks of Simon & Schuster, Inc.
For information about special discounts for bulk purchases, please contact
Simon & Schuster Special Sales at 1-866-506-1949 or business@simonandschuster.com.
The Simon & Schuster Speakers Bureau can bring authors to your live event. For more
information or to book an event contact the Simon & Schuster Speakers Bureau
at 1-866-248-3049 or visit our website at www.simonspeakers.com.
Designed by Mike Rosamilia
The text of this book was set in Adobe Caslon Pro.
Manufactured in the United States of America
4 6 8 10 9 7 5 3
Library of Congress Cataloging-in-Publication Data
Reeves, Dia.
Slice of cherry / by Dia Reeves.
p. cm.
Summary: Portero, Texas, teens Kit and Fancy Cordelle share
their infamous father's fascination with killing, and despite their tendency
to shun others they bring two boys with similar tendencies to a world
of endless possibilities they have discovered behind a mysterious door.
ISBN 978-1-4169-8620-1 (hardcover)
[1. Sisters—Fiction. 2. Murder—Fiction. 3. Supernatural—Fiction.
4. Dating (Social customs)—Fiction. 5. African Americans—Fiction.
6. Texas—Fiction.] I. Title.
PZ7.R25583Sli 2011
[Fic]—dc22
2010021805
ISBN 978-1-4169-8968-4 (eBook)

For Ruby Lee Woodson . . .
and all the family history I never got to hear

FROM FANCY'S DREAM DIARY:

Daddy stood at the front door screaming for Kit and me to let him in. Kit told me to run and get Madda, so I tried, but Madda wasn't in her room. Her bed was unmade and spits of blood stained her sheets. I ran back to the front door, but now Kit was gone, and the door was wide open. And Daddy was dragging her down into the storm cellar by her feet.

CHAPTER ONE

Fancy only allowed three people in the whole world to get close to her: Daddy, who was on death row; Madda, who was working the graveyard shift; and Kit, who was dead to the world in the bed next to hers. And so when she awoke to find a prowler hanging over her, violating her personal space, her first instinct was to jab her dream-diary pencil into his eye.

But even in the dark of night with a stranger in her room, Fancy wasn't one to behave rashly. Daddy had been rash, and now he was going to be killed. No, Fancy would be calm and think of a nonlethal way to teach the prowler why it was important not to disturb a young girl in her bed late at night.

She breathed in the yellow smell of the prowler's beery

exhalations. He was panting, as though from nervousness or excitement. The heat of his hand whispered across Fancy's cheek, and she felt a tug on her scalp. A pair of scissors flashed in the dark, and then a lock of Fancy's hair fell against her half-closed eyes, much shorter than it had been.

As soon as the prowler turned his attention toward Kit in the next bed, Fancy slipped quietly to the floor.

Because Fancy and her sister slept in the sleeping porch at the back of the house, a room with screens instead of proper walls, they relied on numerous paperweights to keep their papers from scattering in the constant breeze. Fancy plucked one such paperweight from the desk at the far end of the room, her eyes never leaving the prowler's back.

While he hung vampirically over her sister's sleeping form, Fancy crept closer, the paperweight cocked back, cool, smooth, and heavy in her hand, the prowler's head growing larger in her sight. But before she could swing her fist forward, the prowler screamed and staggered backward, pinwheeling past Fancy and then crashing into the vanity.

The light clicked on. Fancy blinked in the glare and dropped the paperweight; she heard it rolling away. The light brought her back to herself, back to reality—the white summer linens on the beds; the broken-spined medical books along the only real wall, behind Fancy; the old black phonograph near the tea table. The jars full of various animal organs lining the shelves.

The prowler was the only unfamiliar thing, harmless and weaponless now that his scissors lay abandoned on the floor between the sisters' beds. He sprawled before the vanity, paper white, young, and sweaty; the golden hilt of Kit's switchblade curled ornately from his side like a strange doorknob to another world.

"Help!" he screamed, his hands fluttering over the hilt of the switchblade, afraid to pull it out.

Kit, in her pink satin slip, knelt beside the prowler, as awake and merry as if she'd been dancing all night. "Who you yelling for, Buttercup?" she asked with her usual zeal, despite the late hour and odd circumstances. "Nobody here but Fancy and me."

She yanked her knife free, and the prowler jerked back against the vanity, blood soaking his white T-shirt and spreading like an electric-red bruise. One of Kit's lipsticks dropped into his lap, a mute suggestion from the universe, perhaps, to fix himself up—he certainly wasn't looking his best.

Before retracting the blade, Kit wiped it clean on the

prowler's jeans, and then scanned her younger sister for damage. "I thought you were asleep."

"I thought you were," said Fancy.

"I saw him leaning over your bed. What was he doing to you?" Kit asked the question brightly, but the look she gave the prowler was anything but.

Fancy touched the shorn black lock dangling in front of her eyes. "He cut my hair." He'd left plenty behind. Unlike Kit's pixie-short hair, Fancy's hair fell past her shoulders in a fluffy waterfall.

"Well, he didn't come all the way out here to give you a haircut," said Kit as she frisked the prowler. "Better check the loot."

Fancy searched under Kit's bed, but the treasure chest they stored their allowance in was still locked and untouched. "It's all there," she said, and returned to the foot of her own bed.

Kit's search had turned up her charm bracelet and Fancy's missing hair in a baggie. "I get why you'd want a gold bracelet," she told the prowler gently, "but hair?" She slapped the bag against his runny nose, ungently. "What do you want with my sister's hair?"

"Please. Call an ambulance." The prowler was shocky, confused, as if he didn't understand that the girl whose question he wasn't answering was the reason he needed an ambulance.

"Ambulance schmambulance," said Kit, and poked him in his hurt side. She smiled when he screamed.

"I'm bleeding!"

"I know," Kit said with exaggerated slowness, as though the prowler were feeble. "I *stabbed* you." She rescued her lipstick from the prowler's crotch in a way that made him wince.

"You wouldn't be the first person to die in here," Kit told him. "Our great-uncle died in Fancy's bed from influenza when he was eight. I'll put you in my bed." Kit shot a questioning look at Fancy. "Seems only fair, right?"

Fancy had pressed her cheek against the cool brass bedpost, her eyes half closed as if she wished she were still asleep. "We can't let him die in here."

"I guess not. You tell us," Kit said to the prowler. "Where *do* you wanna die?"

The prowler lurched to his feet and scrambled for the screen door. Before he could get it open, Kit snatched a paperweight from the vanity, one with Fancy's baby teeth inside it, and rapped him on the back of the head. After he crumpled to the floor, Kit said, "Interesting choice."

The prowler looked much younger in his unconscious state, but still older than Fancy and Kit. College age, at least.

"You think he came as a prank?" said Kit, prodding him with her bare toe. "A college prank, or a hazing? Somebody ordered him to come to the Bonesaw Killer's house and get proof that—"

"Who cares why he came?" said Fancy, sliding her heated cheek along the post, seeking another cool spot. "Only thing I care about is getting rid of him."

"You're right." Kit propped open the screen door. A dust-colored moth fluttered inside and alighted on Kit's bare shoulder, as though she were the brightest thing in the room. "Madda would lose her shit if she came home and found the place drenched in blood."

"Don't say 'shit,'" said Fancy as Kit flipped the prowler onto his back and hoisted his legs. "Where're you taking him?"

"To the cellar."

The ground shifted under Fancy. She abandoned the bed-post, sweat beading beneath her pink sleep romper.

"What's wrong?" Kit had paused in the doorway, leggy and boy thin in her slip; nothing like Fancy, who had begun to develop at an alarming rate since her fifteenth birthday a few months before.

Fancy felt as though she were experiencing another symptom of that unwanted development, something like a menstrual cramp, only in her chest instead of her belly. She thought of Daddy, and the last time she'd seen him in that courtroom three years ago. She didn't want this to be the last time she saw Kit.

"Madda'll find out."

"Madda's scared of the cellar," said Kit, dragging the prowler halfway out the door, carefully navigating her backward descent down the porch steps. "Not enough loot in the world to make her go near it."

"What if he screams?"

"You ever hear Daddy's people when they were in the cellar?"

Fancy grabbed the prowler's trailing arms and yanked him back into the room and away from Kit. "You're not Daddy."

The sisters' dark, deceptively innocent eyes flashed as they squared off on either side of the threshold, the prowler lying bonelessly between them.

"And this ain't a squirrel or a deer," said Fancy. "This is a person."

"No, *this* is a piece of shit who broke into our house." Kit snatched up the prowler's legs again and yanked him through the door, rucking his bloody shirt up to his chest. She blinked at the display of flesh. "Nice body, though."

When Fancy had lain in bed thinking of how to punish the prowler for invading her space, never once had she considered taking him down into the cellar. Well, maybe she'd *considered* it, but it simply wasn't an option.

She said, "You aim to get busted like Daddy did?"

Kit looked at Fancy as though she wanted to scoop her up and drop her into the nearest cradle. "Before Daddy went to jail, did he somehow make you the boss of me? Did Madda come home while we were asleep, shove us back up her womb, and then give birth to *you* first?"

"You know they didn't."

"Well, until they do, stop ordering me around! And in the meantime, why don't you act like my sister and help me?"

Fancy wavered, but only for a moment, before she took the prowler by the arms, struggling with his weight as she helped Kit lug him from the house. Kit was elder, after all, and as hardheaded as a statue—once she set herself on a path, dynamite couldn't blow her off it.

But a nuke might.

Fancy racked her brain for something nuclear as they crossed the backyard to the cellar, confident like every baby of the family that she would get her own way in the end.

The only section of Portero that could support a storm cellar like the one on the sisters' property was the upsquare area with its red hills and sprawling forests—the rest of the town was too low and prone to flooding. The towering hardwoods that characterized not only Portero, but all of deep East Texas, dwarfed the sisters' one-story house and blotted out much of the moonless sky. The light from their sleeping porch spilled into the yard and picked out the cellar doors angling up from the ground several feet away.

Madda had eradicated all traces of Daddy in the house, and the cellar where he had tortured and killed at least fifteen people held no physical trace of him either. The tiny, windowless gray room had nothing to do with the man the sisters had known, a man who'd taught them how to make kites and teepees, who had taken them fishing and mushroom-picking.

The sisters carried the prowler into the cellar and lashed him to the metal cot the way they'd read in the papers their father had done to so many others. Except for the cot and a tall metal shelving unit lined with boxes of nonperishable foods and supplies, the only item in the cellar was the kineto-scope, a pretty wooden device that seemed almost as out of place as the prowler.

Kit sat on the cot with him and gave him a slap to hurry him out of his stupor. "Wake up, Buttercup."

His eyes fluttered open, blue and startled. He tried to jerk upright, but the rope restricted him.

"What're you doing?" He looked around, disoriented. "What is this place?"

"You mean you don't know about Daddy?" said Kit, surprised. "About the room where he did everything? You're in it. Don't you feel special? You should, so take your shoes off and set a spell." Kit laughed. "You're gone be here awhile."

The prowler looked like he wanted to laugh too, like he wanted to believe it was all a big joke, but then Kit flicked her gold switchblade and the laughter curdled.

"This is a mistake!"

"You got that right," said Kit, smiling at him. "You picked the wrong house."

"I just wanted some things! Just . . . Bonesaw Killer things. I wasn't gone hurt y'all. I swear!"

"A few things for what?" asked Kit.

The prowler hesitated, shamed. "To sell online."

"Craigslist or eBay?"

"It didn't matter."

"Don't matter to me, either," said Kit, as if revealing a secret.

"I figured I could make extra money for school, just—"

Kit touched the switchblade to the prowler's mouth, silencing him. His mouth trembled beneath the press of the blade. "School's out, Buttercup."

Fancy moved closer to the cot. "Kit, listen—"

"What do you think?" Kit asked as she tapped the blade against the prowler's mouth. "Throat? Heart? His eyes would be the obvious choice, but I want to look into 'em while he dies."

"Why? Think you'll see Daddy stamped in his corneas, giving you a thumbs-up?" Fancy regretted her sharp words when Kit looked at her with tears shivering in her eyes.

"Sounds good to me."

And like that, Kit handed Fancy the nuke she'd been looking for. "If you wanna see Daddy, I'll show you."

For a long moment Kit simply stared at her sister, unable to speak, and when she did, her voice was unusually soft. "You said you couldn't see him anymore."

"I ain't even tried," Fancy admitted. "Not for a long time. But I will if you promise not to kill him."

"You'd do that?"

"I'll try."

Kit swung off the cot, her eyes shining as before, but not with tears—with excitement. "Try now!"

Fancy scanned the metal shelves but knew it was hopeless. "There ain't anything in here to look through."

"The kinetoscope?"

Kit pushed Fancy in front of the small cherrywood box with a round lens on the front that sat atop a brass stand. It was what had passed for television about a hundred years ago—people would turn the crank and watch images unfurl through the lens. Daddy had fixed the kinetoscope but hadn't been able to find the right kind of film or the crank that would make it work. But even though the machine was empty and crankless, it was still possible to see moving images inside of it.

It was for Fancy.

She had far-sight. That's what Daddy called it, an ability to see what was happening in the next room or miles away. All she needed was something reflective to look at and she could see anything: She could even make up things. Like the happy place, a world she'd invented after Daddy had gone away, a world she needed. The real world had stopped being fun a long time ago.

"I only ever see the happy place in the kinetoscope," Fancy protested, already sorry she'd offered. It hurt too much to think about Daddy. "I've never seen anything real in this thing."

"You said you'd try."

So Fancy tried.

She only had to think of what she wanted to see—real or imaginary—and she would see it. So she knew right away, when the lens of the kinetoscope remained black, that it wasn't working, but she furrowed her brow and clenched her fists so that Kit would feel she'd at least—

A scream sent her whirling in time to see Kit's gold switchblade slice across the prowler's chest. A second slice crossed the first cut, forming a large red X.

"*Kit!*"

"Don't mind me," she said cheerily. "Just keeping myself entertained."

"You promised you wouldn't kill him!"

"He look dead to you?" Kit pointed the dripping blade at the writhing, wild-eyed prowler. "Cuz he looks real spry to me. I'm just gone play with him until you bring Daddy up on the screen." She drew back her switchblade, and Fancy quickly turned her gaze back to the kinetoscope. The happy place bloomed bright and large in the round lens, a mostly sepia-toned panorama straight out of *Better Homes and Gardens*. It did that sometimes without her having to think about it consciously.

The Headless Garden was in view on the screen, the area in the happy place she most liked to watch because it had the most calming effect on her. Fancy knew the place well, down to the sundial and the fountains, the animal topiaries and the carefully sculpted hedges.

At the very center of the garden stood a circle of headless, winsomely proportioned statues that gave the garden its name. Fancy loved looking at the statues, mostly because she could look at them as long as she wanted and they couldn't look at her with disgust in their eyes or ask snide questions about Daddy and whether it was true that he ate all his victims.

But watching the statues wasn't calming her. Because they were bleeding. Slashes appeared randomly on their golden skin as though from invisible whips, their blood a golden glitter that dusted the air like pollen, vibrant against the sepia landscape. The golden blood beckoned Fancy to run and play in it, to catch it on her tongue like snow.

"Fancy!"

Fancy jerked away from the screen, blinking, trying not to notice the whimpering mess on the cot and failing. "What?"

"I asked you if you want a turn." Kit noticed the beige glow of the screen and rushed to the kinetoscope, beaming. "I told you to tell me when Daddy—" The hope in her face faded at the sight of the oddly bleeding statues. "Try again."

But as soon as Fancy thought about Daddy, the screen went black.

"Damn it!" Kit kicked the bowed brass legs of the stand, nearly knocking the kinetoscope to the floor. She visibly reined herself in at Fancy's disapproving look and took a deep breath. "Tell you what, why don't you take this"—she held out the gory switchblade—"and put a few hash marks on Buttercup over there. That'll help clear your mind."

Fancy looked at the prowler, shirtless now and covered in myriad bleeding cuts. Some of them looked deep, possibly as deep as the one in his side. His blood wasn't golden like the statues . . . yet still it glittered and beckoned in a similar way. She turned away from the knife and wiped her sweaty hands on the short legs of her romper. "You'll have to stitch all those cuts," she said, and her voice only shook a little.

"Says you."

"He's gone bleed to death otherwise!"

"So? Death by a thousand cuts." Kit looked at the blank kinetoscope screen, defeated. "You think Daddy ever killed anybody that way?"

"You promised."

Kit snatched the first-aid kit from the shelf and tossed it to Fancy, who almost fumbled it in surprise. "*You* stitch him up."

Fancy opened the kit and noted the sutures and hooked needles, trying not to be excited at the thought of poking holes into the prowler's skin. She kicked away the bloody rags of his shirt and knelt by the cot, but Kit followed her down.

"First things first." She put the switchblade in Fancy's hand and wrapped her own around it, insistent. "Not until you take a turn. It's only fair. We do everything together."

Fancy's hands began to sweat again, the prowler spread out before her like an oddly iced pastry, begging to be sliced. "I don't want to."

Kit guided her sister's hand; the knife slid teasingly down the underside of the prowler's bare arm as he strained against the rope. He flinched from the touch of the blade so near his armpit, as though he were ticklish, even in his fright.

"We're practically the same person," Kit said, like a cartoon devil whispering enticements into Fancy's ear. "You think I don't know what you want?"

Fancy quickly nicked the prowler's underarm, and just as quickly elbowed Kit away. "There, I did it. I'm done." She freed her hand from the knife, from Kit, from temptation. "Now go get me some peroxide. I don't see any on the shelf."

Kit refused to be shooed. She stood and set her hands on her hips. "What did I tell you about ordering me?"

"I'm not ordering. I'm asking. Now go on!"

Kit blinked at Fancy's tone, one she almost never heard. "Fine, spoilsport."

As soon as the cellar doors closed behind Kit, the prowler went to work on Fancy. "Please," he said, his voice ruined by tears and blood loss. "While she's gone. Please let me go. I won't say anything."

Fancy kept silent, carefully threading one of the needles from the kit.

"I know you're a good person. You didn't let her kill me. I know you're good. Please?"

Fancy looked him in his eyes until he stopped babbling and really focused on her, really saw her. When he was quiet, she said:

"Daddy's locked up, so we never see him. Madda had to start working twelve-hour shifts to support us, so we never see her, either. If Kit kills you, they'll lock her up too, and then I won't have anybody. That's the only reason you're alive. Because if I thought I could do it and not get busted, I'd kill you myself."

Fancy looked away from the prowler's horrified stare and finished threading the needle.

"I'm the Bonesaw Killer's daughter," she whispered, almost to herself. "Why would you ever think I was good?"

FROM FANCY'S DREAM DIARY:

A DOCTOR EXAMINED ME AND KIT AND SAID THE REASON WE WERE SICK WAS BECAUSE KIT HAD MY HEART AND I HAD HERS. BUT WHEN HE SWITCHED OUR HEARTS, THEY STOPPED BEATING.

CHAPTER TWO

"After breakfast," said Fancy, setting the table while Kit sliced fruit at the counter, "let's go to Bony Creek. We ain't been in a while."

"Alas, we cannot, Fancy Pants," said Kit, the blade flashing in the early morning light that streamed in through the kitchen window. "We gotta bathe Franken."

Thanks to Kit, the prowler was now covered in so many stitches that she had laughingly renamed him, like a pet. Kit cared for him like a pet too, feeding him, cleaning up his filth. Franken seemed to flourish under her care and rarely screamed anymore, even when she cut him.

Fancy admired her sister's knife skills and wondered

whether Kit had always been so adept or if her time with her cellar playmate had honed her abilities. Fancy herself had developed such first-rate suturing techniques that she could probably get a job at a hospital. She wished Kit would leave Franken alone, though. It was stupid to constantly slice up a guy you were never going to kill. It just created a lot of blood that had to be cleaned up, and Fancy had enough chores to do.

"Don't gimme that face," said Kit. She dumped all the fruit into a bowl and handed it to Fancy. "You're the one who wanted to keep him alive."

"Keep him alive, not keep him *forever*. We spend half the day fooling with him. We never hang out anymore."

"We always hang out," said Kit, keeping watch over the bacon and eggs. "Sometimes we hang out on a train, sometimes we hang out on a plane. We often hang out in the sun, and sometimes even in the rain."

"Not at Bony Creek," said Fancy, ignoring her sister's poetic exaggerations. "Not since school let out. I wanna look for fairy rings."

Kit actually laughed at her. "You don't still believe in that stuff, do you? That's just make-believe."

"Doors aren't make-believe." And they weren't. It wasn't

a coincidence that Portero meant "doorkeeper." Portero was full of doors, and not all of them had four sides and a doorknob. Many were much more subtle than that, and sometimes people would pass through one not realizing what it was and end up on a desert with four moons and purple sand and creatures that thought human beings tasted like chicken. "People disappear through doors all the time."

"I know that, but not through *fairy* doors. Fairy rings are just mushrooms, Fancy. I can't believe you'd rather play with mushrooms than a real-life boy in our cellar."

Kit had become disturbingly boy crazy over the past year. She pranced around in tight T-shirts and leggings that instead of emphasizing her skinniness showed off her curves, slight though they were. She wore lipstick and nail polish and rubbed blackberry-scented cream into her skin and hair, as if she wanted some boy to mistake her for a pie and eat her.

"It ain't about the mushrooms," Fancy said, setting the fruit bowl on the table. "It's about the doorway inside the mushrooms. Wouldn't it be neat if—" Fancy froze, realizing she'd set a place for Daddy, something she hadn't done in a long time. She lifted the plate she'd set for him and caught a flash of his face on the porcelain surface, but she couldn't hold on to the image.

"What're you looking at?" Kit was watching her closely.

"Nothing." Fancy thought briefly about telling Kit that she'd seen Daddy, even if only for a second, but decided against it. Kit would only get upset, and if she got too upset, she might take it out on Franken. "I'll figure out how to open a fairy door one day. And just cuz something's a fairy tale doesn't mean it's not true." Fancy cleared away the extra setting. "And Franken won't be 'real-life' much longer. Not if you don't stop cutting him so much. At least give him time to heal. He'll get infected otherwise."

"I *should* be more careful with him. Do you know what he said yesterday?" Kit emptied the bacon and eggs onto a serving dish, her eyes dreamy and faraway. "He said, 'The cellar is brighter with you here. You radiate light.'" She held the metal serving spoon to her face and smiled at her reflection. "'You radiate light.' Isn't that pretty?"

"Gorgeous." Fancy bumped Kit with her hip as she passed by to set the eggs and bacon on the table. "But he'd say anything to get you to stop cutting on him."

Kit gripped the spoon to her chest and swooned against the counter. "You don't mean to say you think he was lying?"

"Yup."

Kit unswooned and glared at her sister. "You know, you could at least humor me, for Christ's sake."

"Boys always lie." Fancy shrugged. "The sooner you face that, the better."

"How would you know?" Kit threw the spoon at her, but Fancy, used to Kit's moods, caught it without even looking and set it gently on the table.

"Yeah, Fancy, how *would* you know?"

The sisters jumped as Madda kicked the back door shut behind her, her arms full of groceries from Alcide's Cajun Market. She was wearing her black work Dickies with her name, Lynne, stitched over her bosom. She looked sweaty and tired and happy to be home.

Fancy felt the same grateful thrill to see her mother that she always felt, as though Madda had somehow been tricked into caring for them and any minute would realize the truth and flee. However, there was no mistaking the sisters' maternity; Madda shared their looks: the whisky eyes and ballerina necks, the Cadbury-smooth skin and rolling gait that made a dance of every step. Once Madda's hair had been swingingly long like Fancy's, but working all night at the factory had robbed her of the time and energy needed to maintain such vanities, and so she'd shaved her head. That was Madda's way: When something became inconvenient, she scrapped it.

"Y'all got any boyfriends I don't know about?" she asked, grinning.

"Puke," said Fancy as she dropped into her chair at the table.

"Not me," said Kit, when Madda looked at her. "To my eternal shame." She took one of the grocery bags and helped put the food away.

"It's not shameful," Fancy exclaimed, watching them work. "Virgins automatically go to heaven."

"Heaven schmeaven. I don't wanna get saved that bad."

Madda smacked the back of Kit's head on the way to the bread box. "Don't talk like that. And if you want a boyfriend, go out there and get one. How you expect to meet anybody if you never leave the house?"

Since it was Friday, Madda gave the sisters their allowance— a generous one since they took care of the house and did most of the cooking and all the chores. It paid not to inconvenience Madda.

When Kit squeezed into Fancy's chair, butting her with her sharp hip bones, Fancy gave Kit her share of their allowance for safekeeping.

Kit fanned the money. "You keep paying us like this," she said as Madda joined them at the table, "we gone fly away in a private jet, and you won't ever see us again."

"Everybody flies the coop sometime. Kit, sit in your own chair."

When they were settled properly around the table, Madda said, "I'm fixing to be dead to the world in a short while, so I wanna remind y'all to get new dresses. Especially you," she added, shooing Fancy away from her plate. "I swear there ain't one thing in that closet of yours that fits anymore."

"Why we need new dresses?" said Fancy, her mouth full of Madda's bacon.

Madda smoothed Fancy's hair away from her mouth, where she'd crammed it in along with the bacon. "For Juneteenth. You're fifteen now—more than old enough to participate."

The bacon stuck in Fancy's throat.

Kit, seeing Fancy's distress, said, "I been old enough for two years, but you never made *me* go."

"You would've gone without Fancy?"

"Of course not!"

Madda spread her hands as if to say *there you go*, and then proceeded as if the matter had been settled. "So new dresses. Something real nice for the bottle ceremony."

Dresses? Ceremonies? *Socializing?* Fancy said, "I don't wanna go to Cherry Glade."

"Why not?" Madda asked, though she sounded as if she had been expecting Fancy's reaction.

Fancy exchanged a helpless look with Kit, who answered for her. "Same reason *I* don't wanna go. We hate it when people *look* at us and *say* things. Forget that. Summer vacation means we don't have to put up with other people's crap."

Madda said, "Everybody goes to Cherry Glade on Juneteenth."

"But—"

"And that's that." Like Kit, when Madda made up her mind, it stayed made up—only more so. "I know how shy you girls are," she said gently, "but Juneteenth means something, especially in our family. You girls are direct descendants of Cherry du Haven. She—"

"We know, we know," said Kit. The sisters had heard the Cherry du Haven bit of trivia a million times. "Once upon a time there lived a famous slave who died and then came back as a ghost or whatever to grant wishes for all the good black children in town." She tapped Fancy on the head with an imaginary wand. "Bippety, boppety, boo!"

Madda scraped her spoon against her plate, annoyed. "One of these days, you girls are gone wish y'all had paid more attention to the family history. Cherry was *special*. She passed that on through the years, maybe even to y'all. Big Mama used to tell me all these stories about—"

Kit pretended to snore, and Madda finally gave up. On any other day Kit would have been interested, but Fancy guessed that her sister wanted to win at least one battle.

Fancy made herself calm down. It was just one day, and they had plenty of time to mentally prepare to be around so many people. Just one day, and then they could have the rest of the summer to themselves.

"What're y'all planning today?" Madda asked Fancy.

"We're going to Bony Creek." She shot a defiant look at Kit. "After breakfast."

"Not right after," Kit shot back. "Maybe later in the day."

"Y'all know to be careful?" said Madda. "There's cacklers roaming the woods. Used to be they all stayed around the dark park." Madda shook her head. "These days they're just making themselves at home all over town."

Kit said, "We can handle cacklers. One good kick to the head and they're toast. Hi-ya!"

"Not just cacklers," Madda continued, as Kit karate-skewered several strawberry and banana slices from the fruit bowl. "Wild hogs, too. And corpses."

"Corpses?" Kit snorted. "What could they do, besides stink us to death?"

Madda was silent for so long the sisters stopped eating and stared at her. She said, "I guess y'all don't have to worry about it, old as you are."

"Worry about what?" asked Kit.

"Nothing." Madda wiped her mouth. "Just boring family stuff. So." She leaned back in her chair and gave her daughters a considering look that immediately put them on edge. "Y'all aim to spend the whole summer at Bony Creek?"

"And the music store," said Kit. "We need some more records for our collection. They had this one record from 1910, and I hope hope hope it's still there!"

"And the bookstore," Fancy added, wondering why Madda was so interested in their summer activities. They always did the same things. "What else is there?"

"Classes." Madda drew a deep breath. *The kind you take before diving into deep and possibly shark-infested waters.* "I signed y'all up for summer classes."

Fancy had the strangest sensation that Madda had just spoken Chinese. She turned to Kit, but Kit looked just as bewildered as Fancy felt.

Kit said, "You did what?"

"I don't mean for the two of you to sit around all summer watching grass grow. Not this year."

Madda *was* speaking English, and yet Fancy still couldn't process it. Kit, fortunately, was much quicker.

"Why would you put us in summer school when you know we passed everything?"

"I know how smart y'all are and how much you like science and . . . anatomy." Madda knew about the jars in the sleeping porch and could never hide the disgust in her voice whenever she had to refer to the sisters' love of dissecting animals. Of course, she thought they were doing the work for school and extra credit. She had no idea the dissections had been off the clock and unsupervised.

"I'm not talking about school," she continued. "These are just fun little classes. Nothing heavy. You in music at Gracie"—Madda turned to Fancy—"and you in art at the Standard. It's only three days a week: Mondays, Wednesdays, and Fridays."

"You didn't even put us in the same class?" Kit in a fury

wasn't a pretty sight, but Madda held her ground, even when Kit screamed, "We're not going!"

"Think of it as a cultural experience," Madda continued, ignoring Kit's outburst. "You won't even be graded. And remember what you said, Kit. If you want a boyfriend, this is how you get one. You go where people are, and you mingle."

"We don't *want* to mingle." Kit left her seat and once again sat with Fancy in her chair. "Not if it means being ripped from the side of my only sister!"

Madda huffed. "Stop being so dramatic; nobody's trying to rip you apart."

"Then why can't we be in the same class?"

"This ain't a discussion between me and you, Kit. This has already been decided. Classes start next Monday, but since Juneteenth's on Monday, both your teachers said y'all can start Wednesday."

"*Next* Wednesday?" Kit picked up the pitcher of orange juice and cocked back her arm.

"Christianne," said Madda, her voice full of danger. "Throw my good pitcher, and I'm gone throw you right after it."

Kit put the pitcher down.

"Look at me." When Madda had Kit's attention, she said,

"I love that you and Fancy are so close. But it's okay to be close to other people, too."

"There *are* no other people! Are there, Fancy?"

Fancy, who had been watching in stunned silence, said, "People?" as though she'd never heard of such a thing. "They're like dolls. Plastic and shiny and fake."

"Like if you took out their batteries," Kit said, "they'd fall over."

"Exactly! Who cares about people? It's not like they matter."

It was Madda's turn to stare at her daughters in disbelief. "*Everybody* matters. People aren't toys. You can't just . . ." She trailed off, and looked away from whatever she saw in Kit and Fancy's eyes. "The people in this town matter as much as you or me. And the sooner y'all learn that, the better."

FROM FANCY'S DREAM DIARY:

MADDA BROUGHT A YOUNG MAN HOME AND TOLD KIT AND ME THAT HE WOULD BE TAKING CARE OF US FROM NOW ON. THE MAN CLIPPED A LEASH TO KIT'S NECK AND TOOK HER OUT FOR A WALK. A FEW MINUTES LATER, KIT CAME BACK ALONE AND WHEN MADDA ASKED HER WHAT HAPPENED, KIT GAVE HER THE LEASH WITH THE MAN'S SEVERED HAND DANGLING FROM THE END.

CHAPTER THREE

The sisters sat alone in the dark, shuttered living room, crammed together in a huge rocking chair. After bathing Franken, Kit hadn't wanted to go to Bony Creek, and neither had Fancy, who felt much too raw.

"*Classes*, Fancy!" said Kit, rocking them violently. "Our whole summer ruined over two classes *that we don't even need!*"

Fancy elbowed her sister in the ribs. "Hush." It would take a lot to wake Madda, who was asleep in the back room, but Kit had a lot.

"Don't tell me 'hush.'"

"Did you put our allowances in the treasure chest?"

"The hell with money! Why am I the only one freaking out?"

A few bars of slanted light came through the shutters and glanced off the fish tank across the room, where a two-foot silver dragon fish cut through the water. It belonged to Madda, who'd named it Merlin and liked to watch it chase down and eat the live fish she fed it. Fancy understood that side of Madda, that small morbid streak. But she didn't understand Madda's desire to separate her and Kit. Fancy closed her eyes. "It's not real to me. I can't think about it."

"You better think about it. Madda's serious! She—"

Fancy's eyes flew open. "Shh. Listen."

The rocking stopped, and the sisters' ears pricked at the sound they'd been waiting for: the telltale squeak of the mailbox opening.

They waited until they heard the mail truck roar to life and then fade in the distance before they burst out onto the front porch and into the summer heat.

Fancy quickly weeded out the bills and junk mail, placing them back into the rusty black box beneath the porch light. What was left over was the only thing that could have distracted the sisters from Madda's summer-killing news: a bunch of handwritten envelopes with no return addresses.

They hurried into their room with the letters, and after

Kit got the sun tea from the porch steps, they sat at the pink, flower-shaped tea table that overlooked the garden. Kit played an old record on the phonograph, which crackled and popped as some woman sang about another woman named Dinah Lee.

As Fancy added ice and sugar to the tea, Kit began to read:

"'What I love about Guthrie Cordelle is that not only is he one of the few black serial killers, he's one of the best ever. I am glad that black people are finally representing because the world needs to know that black people can be just as crazy if not crazier than white people.'"

The sisters looked at each other and giggled into their teacups. "*That's* what 'the world' needs to know?" said Fancy.

"*And* she misspelled 'representing.' What a bozo. Oh, wait. This one has an address from Canada! 'My uncle shot my aunt in the face. I'm sending you a piece from the shirt she was wearing that day. If you could send me something from one of Guthrie's victims, that would be awesome. Best wishes, Albert. P.S. It doesn't have to be bloody.' How cool is that?" Kit studied the enclosed square of yellow fabric and sniffed the rusty brown splotches staining it. "Foreign fan mail, Fancy, and he wasn't mean or crazy or anything."

"Sane people don't send bloody clothes through the mail."
Fancy tore off the Canadian postage stamp and placed it in the
keepsake box on their desk filled with other such stamps from
Algeria and Israel and Nepal. Daddy's crime spree had made
news all over the world.

"*Would* we have sent something to him?" Kit asked as Fancy
came back to the table.

"Nope." Fancy opened another letter. "Probably he's just
looking for something to sell. Like Franken was."

"Maybe Albert's lonely," said Kit, almost stubbornly.
"Maybe he wants to be friends."

"You think people wanna be friends with us? Listen: 'Your
father is the devil himself and you girls are the devil's spawn.
He should have killed you instead of innocent God-fearing
Christians.'"

Fancy showed Kit the letter, the angry dark slashes gouged
into the notebook paper. "*This* is what people think of us. And
Madda wants us to think they matter. What's wrong?"

Kit was toying with the gold switchblade again, hitting it
against the table. "You think Daddy did want to kill us?"

"Trying to understand Daddy is like trying to nail jelly to
a tree." Fancy turned away and swapped "Dinah Lee" for Cole

Porter's "Anything Goes." She hated when Kit started obsessing over Daddy's possible motives—you could talk and wonder for hours and never get anywhere. Daddy was a mystery.

"He couldn't've wanted to," Kit said, almost to herself. "It would've been easy as pie. Deep down he must've known that we're just like him, and that's why he let us live."

"He let Madda live. *She's* not like us."

"She's not like us and she *doesn't* like us; otherwise she wouldn't be trying to split us up."

Fancy grabbed Kit's fidgeting hands, forced them to be still. "Don't talk like that, Kit."

"Even if Madda does like us, she don't like the *real* us. If she knew what we were really like, she'd turn on us like she turned on Daddy." Fancy felt the tension ease from Kit's hands. "At least I have you and Franken."

Fancy dropped Kit's hands as if they had suddenly become radioactive. *"Franken?"*

"I can be myself around him, too." Kit gave her a surprised look. "What's not to love about that?"

"You don't love him," said Fancy sharply. "You love *cutting* on him. Don't confuse it."

Kit put her switchblade away and poured herself more tea.

"Well I ain't confused about one thing: Nothing'll ever split you and me up. Not classes, not Madda, not boys."

"Not death," Fancy added, relieved to hear Kit speaking sensibly.

Kit raised her pink cup to Fancy in salute. "Not even death. Not even Franken's death."

Fancy groaned. "Don't start that again."

"You said yourself we can't keep Franken forever," Kit insisted. "Sooner or later we're gone have to get rid of him."

Fancy sipped her tea thoughtfully, fascinated by the way Kit could speak of loving and killing someone in the same breath. But not fascinated enough to let her do anything stupid. "We got all these medical books, right? Maybe we can study up on how to cut out the part of Franken's brain that remembers stuff. He won't remember he was here. And we won't go to jail."

"A lobotomy?" Kit gave Fancy a surprised and admiring look. "Why can't you think of awesome stuff like that all the time?"

"Bring me some more hostages," said Fancy, "and I'll make a list of fun things to do to them."

"Oh, boy!" Kit jumped to her feet.

"I'm *kidding*."

Kit dropped back onto her stool and opened another letter. "Spoilsport."

A few days later Fancy finally convinced Kit to go to Bony Creek with her. The sisters parked their bikes near the slow-moving snake of water, which ran deep in the woods about a quarter of a mile from their house. The thick cover of leaves filtered the harsh afternoon sun, and so the light that made it to the forest floor was cool and green and harmless.

The sisters, in their swim clothes, weaved in and out of the trees. They seemed to have sprouted from the forest floor, with their reddish-brown skin the color of autumn leaves, as doe-eyed as the deer that occasionally wandered into their kitchen garden to snack.

"See anything?" asked Fancy over the trickle of water and birdsong.

"Sure." Kit slapped a mosquito against her neck. "Poison ivy and deer crap and rocks. Oh, my!"

A scream of laughter shrilled from the forest, one ungodly yipping laugh . . . and then a chorus.

Fancy stopped dead, her skin rough with goose bumps, her

peaceful slumbering forest now awake and heavy with malice. She whispered, "Cacklers? This far upsquare?"

Kit didn't say anything, but as the laughter crescendoed, her frown grew darker.

Fancy had once overheard Big Mama speak of a man she'd lived next door to when she was a child, back in the fifties, a neighbor who had caught a cackler and kept it chained in his front yard like a pet for weeks. It had scared Big Mama to death to have to walk by it on her way to school. She'd said the worst part was how human it had looked, a slimy white mannequin with a pumpkin-sized head and pink eyes. It never barked or laughed or made any sound like cacklers normally do, but every time Big Mama passed her neighbor's yard, the cackler followed her with its eyes and seemed to grin at her with a white, needle-toothed mouth that split its face ear to ear.

But one day on her way to school, Big Mama noticed that the cackler was gone. Instead her *neighbor* was chained in the yard by his throat, and the lower half of his body was simply gone. Eaten.

Fancy pulled on her sister's arm. "Let's go back."

"Screw that." Kit shook her off. "I ain't letting some trespassing cackler run me outta my own woods."

She turned slowly, as if she wanted the cacklers to get a good look at what they were laughing at.

"It's two o'clock in the afternoon, creeps!" she shrieked, startling not only Fancy but the entire forest. "Does that sound like dinnertime? You think you can come into our woods and make a meal outta *us*? These are our woods! You hear me? THESE ARE OUR WOODS!"

Silence.

Kit waited, scanning the dappled trees, animal-still, waiting for any excuse to strike. Fancy imagined the cacklers gathering their young and slinking away into a safer stretch of forest. Fancy couldn't help but smile at her sister—Kit was such a badass.

When the silence continued unabated, Kit relaxed and said, "There's one."

Fancy grabbed Kit. *"A cackler?"*

"No, stupid girl, a fairy ring."

Fancy followed Kit's pointing finger to a circle of mushrooms, at least two feet in diameter, nearly hidden in a copse of dogwood trees. The mushrooms that formed the circle weren't storybook-friendly red caps, but pig's ears—slimy brown mushrooms that looked like the flesh of a creature had been scratched off and left to rot on the ground.

When Fancy curled her lip, Kit said, "Beggars can't be choosers. Come on and let's get this idiocy over with." They made their way to the pig's ears, and as they stood before the circle of mushrooms, a hawk screamed somewhere above them. Otherwise the woods were unnaturally silent, as though simply being near the fairy ring had moved the sisters at least halfway out of the world. Fancy could feel the laces of time and space wanting to unravel. She just had to find the right place to tug.

Fancy marked the starting point with a photo of Daddy taken a month before he'd been sent away. He was doing a muscleman pose with his shirt off, which was hilarious, because Daddy was almost as skinny as Kit.

"What's the picture for?" Kit asked, watching Fancy position the photo just so against one of the mushrooms.

"To help me focus. Shh!" She looked at the picture for a long time, until she could almost see Daddy's blood pumping through his biceps. She held the image in her mind, willing a door to open to him the way she'd tried to will herself to see him in the kinetoscope. Hopefully, today she'd have better luck.

"Ready?"

Kit rolled her eyes, which Fancy took as an affirmative.

"One, two, three, *go*."

The sisters began walking in opposite directions around the outside of the fairy ring.

Fancy grabbed her sister. "Not that way. Counterclockwise."

"We *never* go counterclockwise."

"Maybe that's why it's *never* worked. Now come on."

After a few minutes of circuitous walking, Kit said, "I feel like a dork." She scowled at the hawk screeching in the treetop. "Like all the birds are laughing at us. How many times we gotta go around this thing?"

Fancy thought it over. "Thirty-six."

"Thirty-six?"

"That's how long it's been since we last saw Daddy. Besides, three is a magic number, and thirty-six is a multiple of three."

"There's no such thing as magic."

"Just do it, Kit."

"What did I tell you about ordering me?"

Fancy looked over her shoulder. "You said somebody's gotta do it, so it might as well be me."

"Wow, is it Smart-ass Day?" Kit took a swipe at the back of Fancy's head and only just missed. "You shoulda told me; I'd've brought you a present."

Fancy squealed as Kit chased her around the fairy ring,

managing to stay just ahead of her. "Just curtsy every time I walk by. That'll be present enough."

"Oooh, you think you bad?" Kit sang. "Huh? You think you bad?"

"Bad enough to make you mad," Fancy sang back, laughing, then squealing as Kit grabbed at the middle of her back.

But the old playground rhyme came to an abrupt end as a storm-gray hawk swept out of the dogwood tree and attacked Fancy.

She shrieked and dropped to the ground, batting the hawk away with one arm, the other shielding her face from its vicious yellow talons.

"Come on, bird," said Kit, yelling over the screeching hawk. "Everybody likes street rhymes. How about this one? Down down, baby, down down the roller coaster—"

"*Kit!*"

"Lemme sing to it." Kit grabbed the bird under its long, pointed wings and flung it high into the air. "Music has charms to soothe the savage beast. Miss Mary Mack, Mack, Mack. All dressed in—"

"You are *not* charming that bird," Fancy yelled as the hawk wheeled above the trees.

Instead of going back to its nest, the hawk zeroed in on the sisters again. But this time it dived for Kit, its hell-red eyes full of rage.

"Maybe it's deaf," said Kit, waiting patiently for the hawk, her switchblade in hand, but the hawk's flight halted in midair.

The sisters gaped at the motionless bird in silence. It could have been stuffed and mounted, it was so unnaturally frozen, and centered directly over the fairy ring.

The fairy ring!

"It worked!" cried Fancy. She grabbed Kit. "We opened a door!"

Kit circled the hawk, careful to stay far from the mushrooms lest she get trapped as well. By the time she reached her sister's side once again, she was frowning. "If that's a door, why didn't the bird disappear? It's just stuck up there."

"Maybe this is all we can see from our side. And where the bird is, it's actually flying around and having a great time."

"I don't think so, Fancy." Kit's dubiousness had given way to shock. "*Look* at it."

The hawk molted, shedding feathers as quickly as an ill-used feather duster. In no time it was nude, like a plucked chicken, its skin nubby and goose-pimply, as though without its feathers it had caught a chill. Seeing the hawk in this new, pathetic state made Fancy want to help, even though it had tried to kill her. She began to reach into the fairy ring—

"No!" Kit snatched her back. "You want me to stand here and watch that happen to you?"

What was happening was that the hawk was losing its flesh and bone the same way it had lost its feathers—huge chunks of it were simply falling away and hitting the ground inside the ring like rain. But the pieces weren't staying on the ground. The flesh rapidly decomposed as soon as it touched the soil, until it had disappeared into the earth . . . and into the pig's ears. The mushrooms were no longer slimy folds, but baseball-sized balloons.

"I bet those ain't even mushrooms. Just something disguised as mushrooms, something carnivorous." Kit pulled Fancy back until Fancy was half hidden behind her, well away from the pig's ears. "Whatever it is, it ain't a door." Kit turned to face her. "And even if it was, Fancy, what's the big plan? Run away to fairyland like the Lost Boys?"

Fancy crossed her arms. "Not fairyland."

"Where then? Where the hell are you trying to go?"

"I don't know!" Fancy slumped against a tree. "Fairy rings

are just doors. Doors open and close in Portero all the time. If we found the right door, we could do anything: get rid of Franken, rescue Daddy—"

"What?"

"It's not like I don't know it's a long shot. But it happens. Remember that story about the boy who played hide-and-seek with his little brother? He hid inside the broom closet under the stairs, and when he came out, like, five minutes later, he was *five years younger*."

"Lemme get this straight. You wanna go back in time to stop Daddy from killing?"

"I know it's a long shot," she whispered, and looked away from the incredulity in Kit's face, trying not to feel like an idiot and failing.

Kit pulled Fancy away from the tree and into a loose embrace. "He wouldn't've stopped. It's like with me and Franken—once you get a taste for blood, nothing else satisfies." Kit kissed her fingers like a gourmand.

"Stop joking." She hid her face in her sister's neck. "Sometimes I feel like he's dead already."

"Everybody dies, Fancy Pants." Kit steered her sister back toward the creek. "Now I'll tell you a story. Do you know what

Uncle Miles did before he died in our room, all feverish and snotty? He opened a door."

Fancy lifted her head and looked her sister in the eye and still couldn't believe it. "Shut up."

"Big Mama told me! Well, she didn't tell *me*. I heard her talking about it with Aunt Sybelline one day, a long time ago. The door that leads from our sleeping porch to the inner room isn't the original door. The door that used to be there had a keyhole. Uncle Miles put his key into that keyhole and twisted it and twisted it until he unlocked a door."

Fancy's hand dropped unconsciously to touch the silver skeleton key dangling from the silver necklace she always wore. Kit and Madda carried their keys on key chains, and Daddy had kept his inside his shoe. All Porterenes had such keys. The Mayor, an ageless mysterious woman with mirrors for eyes, gifted them to all Porterenes on the day of their birth. Porterenes would sooner part with an arm than with their keys. It was as much a part of them as their skin and bones: They were doorkeepers, stranger, braver, and more badass than anyone else in the world.

"What was on the other side of the door?" Fancy asked.

"Death," said Kit, as though it should have been obvious.

Fancy tried to picture it. "What did Death look like?"

"Not the person. The *place*. Uncle Miles opened a door, not to another world, but to his own grave. A big hole in the cemetery waiting for him to fill it, and the sight of it freaked him the hell out. He slammed that door and locked it and never opened it again. Anybody who wanted to get into his room had to go outside and circle the house and come in through the porch door. Nobody could open that inner door, even after he died. That's why they had to tear the whole thing out and put in a new door."

"But it's not like Uncle Miles locked out death. He died anyway."

"That's what I said! Nobody can escape death, not even Daddy. If you did go back in time and warn him, he'd probably get hit by a bus or something. Daddy made his bed, and now he's gotta die in it." Kit squeezed Fancy's shoulders. "I'm not saying it doesn't suck, but sometimes you just gotta face facts."

Fancy, who had zero interest in facing facts, pulled out of Kit's grip and plopped down next to some shrubbery near the creek. "I don't wanna talk about death anymore." She reached in her pocket and removed a worn leather pouch. "You wanna play marbles? I found a cat's-eye the other day. It's pink." She fished it from the pouch. "See?"

"Forget that." Kit sat next to her. "All this talk about death has me in the mood to see Daddy. Show me."

"In what?"

"One of those marbles?"

"They're too small."

"In the creek?"

"Too big."

"I know." Kit went to their bikes, leaning tiredly against two pine trees, and retrieved her water bottle. She then kicked off her flats and pulled off her leggings and waded into the creek in her black bikini, navigating the skeletal river stones that gave Bony Creek its name. She splashed the clear, sunny water on the back of her neck as she filled the bottle.

"How's this, Goldilocks?" she asked after she'd returned to her sister.

"Just right," said Fancy, glumly.

She took the bottle from Kit and stared at the clear water, and after a short time it darkened.

It was like watching a wee film. A grim one featuring a slight man in an orange prison jumpsuit swinging gently from an improvised noose made of bedsheets that dangled from the ceiling of a narrow gray cell.

Kit gasped. *"Daddy?"*

The man's legs twitched at the sound of Kit's voice, then kicked up and out, high kicks like a Rockette as Fancy hummed the cancan song under her breath.

Kit looked away from the dancing man in the bottle and scowled at her sister. "That's not funny."

Fancy abandoned the cancan for the *Charlie Brown* theme song. Immediately the man performed the Snoopy dance, twisting violently on the rope.

"I said that's not funny! Stop it!"

Fancy stopped humming and squirted the bottled water at Kit, destroying the image inside. "You're the one who wanted to see him."

"Him. Not one of your weirdo fantasies." She wrested the bottle from Fancy and squirted her back.

"I can't." Fancy scrambled away from the water and sat near a shrub overrun with mustang grapes.

Kit followed her. "You could if you wanted to."

"I don't want to."

"You promised!"

Fancy picked a grape and popped it into Kit's mouth; Kit accepted it in surprise, then puckered her mouth as though it was sour.

"What if he's getting raped?" Fancy asked. "You wanna see that?"

"Nobody gets raped on death row," said Kit, like she knew anything about it. "They're all isolated from each other and lonely. Maybe Daddy's just lying around, thinking about us and missing us terribly. Why don't you fantasize about that? Or, I know! Show the day he took us fishing on the Sabine. That was the best day ever."

Fancy tried a grape. They were *very* sour. "I can't see the past. Or the future. Unless I make it up. I can only see the present."

Kit shoved Fancy aside so she could reach the grapes herself. "You're so useless sometimes." She unscrewed the cap from the bottle, emptied the creek water, and began to fill it with grapes. "You think Franken'll like these? They might be too sour for him."

Fancy, who cared nothing for Franken's likes or dislikes, said, "People might be looking for him by now. We should probably do that lobotomy soon."

"What's the hurry? There's only him and his drunk mother, and she won't even notice he's gone."

Fancy slipped off her cover-up, revealing a black one-piece suit dotted with pink teddy bears. She was frowning. "How do you know that?"

"He told me. His home life is *extremely* tawdry."

"You been going down to the cellar without me?"

Kit paused in the act of picking grapes, seemingly surprised by the upset in Fancy's voice. "You make him nervous."

"Me? You're the one slicing him up every night."

"Well that's just it, Fancy Pants. I know him inside and out. Literally. So he feels like he can talk to me. And I didn't cut on him at all yesterday. I decided to let him heal like you suggested, and since I couldn't play with him, we talked. I told him about our classes, and he thinks they're a good idea."

"Who cares what he thinks?"

"It's just conversation, Fancy," Kit said calmly, the way Madda would have, refusing to argue when that was what you most wanted to do. "Let's go sit in the creek."

The sisters settled themselves in the middle of the creek. The jolt of cold water up to their hips made the idea of summer bearable again. Odd but harmless blue fish with forward-facing eyes swam fearlessly around the sisters' legs.

The sisters fell silent, listening to the woodpeckers jackhammer the trees. After some time Fancy asked, "You think it's true? What they say about Cherry? That she can grant wishes?"

"Madda swears it's true. My problem is, I have no idea what to wish for."

"I'll probably ask for tickets on a steamer ship."

Kit crinkled her nose and let the fish swim between her fingers. "Nobody travels by steamboat anymore, stupid girl. Not around the world they don't."

"Fine, then," said Fancy, disappointed. "Plane tickets."

"To where?"

"The South Seas. Some island nobody's ever been and could never find."

"How you gone get tickets to a place nobody's ever been to and could never—?"

Fancy splashed water at Kit. "Don't bug me with details." She thought some more. "I'll wish for Madda to get promoted. Then she won't have to work double shifts and we can all be together."

Kit splashed Fancy back. "If we could make wishes like

that, I'd wish for Daddy to get a 'get outta jail free' card, but Madda says that at Cherry Glade you can only make a wish for yourself. It's too bad I don't know myself that well."

"What's that supposed to mean?"

The blue fish huddled in Kit's lap, as if their weird, sad eyes could see her distress. But Kit didn't want to be comforted. Not by fish. She shooed them away. "Something's missing, but I don't know what it is. Ever since Daddy left, there's this hole."

"*I'm* here," Fancy said, and hugged her sister as tight as she could.

Kit hugged back, squeezing hard enough to hurt Fancy's spine, but when Fancy let go, Kit slumped like an overwatered flower. "That didn't fill it." She pressed her hand to her chest. "That's what I'll wish for, I guess. Something to fill this emptiness."

FROM FANCY'S DREAM DIARY:

A SHIRTLESS WOMAN LAY FACEDOWN ON THE CELLAR FLOOR. DADDY WAS STRADDLING HER AND YANKING BIG, SILVER BATTERIES OUT OF HER BACK. WHILE HE WORKED, HE WHISTLED A SONG. I THINK IT WAS "HAPPINESS IS A WARM GUN."

CHAPTER FOUR

The sisters biked along the road that led into town, on their way to buy new dresses for Juneteenth. Even though summer hadn't officially begun, the sun was brutally hot, burning the high grass and nourishing the virulent sunflowers that overran the fields.

"Music for you makes sense," Fancy was saying, longing for a heat rash or sunstroke so that she would have a reason not to go to Cherry Glade. "But me and art? I can barely draw stick figures."

"I'm not going to that class." Kit removed her black newsboy cap and splashed water over her head from her water bottle, gasping as if it were freezing.

Fancy was surprised into silence; the pink ribbons on her black sun hat flapped in the wind. Not even Kit would defy Madda. Would she?

"What could Madda do?" said Kit, reading Fancy's mind. "Put us on punishment? And if she did, how could she enforce it? She's never home!"

"I don't want her to be mad at us," said Fancy hesitantly.

"Who cares if she gets mad!" Kit yelled, startling a flock of oil-colored grackles from the sunflower fields. The birds spun like a blue-black dust devil before resettling out of sight. "Why should I have to go to some phony-baloney class just to make Madda happy? How come nobody ever tries to make *me* happy? Why can't I ever do what *I* want?"

For once Fancy didn't feel that Kit was being a drama queen. Madda acted as though they never saw other people. The sisters saw plenty of *other* at school, where they were in not only different classes but different grades. Fancy knew exactly how to deal with people: stay away from them, and when that was impossible, ignore them. People inspired too many unhealthy urges.

The sisters coasted along in silence for a while, the trees thinning as they rode into downtown Portero, or the square, as everyone called it, after Fountain Square, a landmark in the middle of town that Porterenes used to orient themselves. Upsquare was north of Fountain Square, and downsquare was south. Anything north of upsquare or south of downsquare was way upsquare or way downsquare. Anything farther away than that was outside the borders of Portero and therefore of no interest to anyone but outsiders.

Fancy and Kit jounced along redbrick streets past low, colorful buildings. The docile trees lining the medians had cute little cages around them and nothing in common with their cousins in the wild forests upsquare. The whole town generally smelled pine fresh or, when the wind was right, like freshly baked bread, thanks to the bread factory in the warehouse district. Many days, however, Portero smelled like blood.

The sisters turned at the light onto Claudine Street and skidded to a stop.

Claudine Street looked as though it had been unzipped, bricks scattered everywhere. Cars and trucks were flipped over or teetering at weird angles; hard, white water from a burst hydrant swept past the sisters' tires in a flood.

The sisters pedaled onto the dry, deserted sidewalk and parked their bikes at the nearest bike rail. Kit took Fancy's hand and led her up the street, deftly maneuvering around the pools of blood on the sidewalk.

"What do you think did all this?" Fancy asked, clinging to Kit's hand, passing shop windows where wide-eyed people watched them go by.

Kit only shrugged. That was the problem with living in Portero—it could have been *anything*.

"Don't be scared, Fancy Pants. Look." Kit pointed out the sun-bright green trucks lining the street. "The Mortmaine are here. Whatever it is, they're already on it."

If Porterenes were badass simply for surviving daily life in Portero, the Mortmaine were beyond badass, an elite group of men and women who wore only green, like a uniform, and whose only job was to prevent monsters from swallowing the town whole.

But just because the Mortmaine were out in force was no reason to be incautious. The sisters hurried into a dress shop midway up the block, a cool oasis with "Summertime Blues" thumping from a hidden speaker. A shopgirl in a slim dress with a mandarin collar stood behind the counter leisurely munching her way through a bag of pork rinds while flipping through *Vogue*.

"Hey," Kit called. "What the hell happened outside?"

"Monster," said the shopgirl, not looking up from her magazine. "Came up from under the ground. Usual shit."

Slightly disappointed that an exciting tale wasn't to be had, the sisters set themselves to the task of dress hunting, rummaging through the clothes racks for something ruffly and refined enough to pass muster at Cherry Glade. When they'd narrowed it down to two dresses, Kit sought the opinion of the shopgirl.

"What do you think of us in these?" Kit held up the black seersucker halter dress with white dots for herself and the black lace cotton pinafore for Fancy.

The shopgirl sucked pork-rind crumbs from her fingers, studying not the dresses but the sisters. "Ain't y'all those Cordelle girls?"

The sisters sighed. It had only been a matter of time. "Yeah, we're those girls. So what?" said Kit.

"Too bad they don't still hang people," said the shopgirl. "That's what. Y'all's daddy was purely evil. Lethal injection's too good for him. After what he did, *hanging's* too good for him." She didn't even say it in a mean way, as though Daddy's "evilness" were such a foregone conclusion that it didn't even bear getting upset about.

Kit took the dresses to the shopgirl, her friendly smile poison red. "Forget hanging," she said as the shopgirl rang up the dresses. "*I* think they should peel all the skin from Daddy's body with a fruit knife, fry it, and then *make him eat it*. Like . . . well, like pork rinds." Kit helped herself to a handful from the bag on the counter. "Think of it! A pound of Guthrie Cordelle flesh, all crispy and delicious. Mm-mmm!"

The shopgirl turned pale at the sight of Kit's bared teeth, so pale she was nearly invisible. "Th-that'll be seventy-eight seventy-three."

Kit swept the bag of pork rinds to the floor and then flung four twenties into the shopgirl's face, making her flinch. "Keep the change," she said sweetly.

Once they were outside, Kit's friendly smile melted in the fervid sunlight as they stormed up the broken street. "Hanging's too good for him?" she yelled, flinging the dress bag backward to Fancy. "What does *she* know from hanging?"

"The bike rack's back that way," said Fancy, running to keep up with her sister's longer legs.

"You know what we should do? We should hang *her* and then ask how good it is. Get her expert fucking opinion."

"Don't say 'fucking.' And you can't kill someone for being

rude. If we did that, we'd have to kill everyone in Portero."

"So no downside, right?"

Kit detoured down a shaded alley and then another. Fancy realized they were behind the dress shop. A few of the bricks from Claudine Street had made their way back here—whatever had exploded out of the ground had done so with great force. Water from a leaky pipe sticking out of the building had created several tiny puddles that wet Fancy's pink bobby socks and attracted thirsty clouds of mosquitoes.

Fancy looked around, uneasy. "Why're we back here?"

"We're gone wait for that shopgirl," said Kit, her long spider hands picking carefully over the Claudine Street bricks, testing the heft of each one.

"Why would she leave the shop?"

Kit settled against the building opposite the side door of the dress shop, her cap pulled low over her eyes so that her poison mouth was the most visible part of her, the same shade of red as the brick in her fist.

"She smelled like an ashtray," said Kit, "so she'll take a cigarette break. And she'll come back here because going out front and blowing smoke in the customers' faces ain't exactly good customer service."

"We don't *have* to hurt her. We could just . . ."

She had Kit's full attention, but Fancy had no idea what normal people did when someone insulted them.

Fancy swung the dress bag a few times and then stood near her sister against the wall. "We can't really hang her, Kit."

Kit stared unblinkingly at the blank metal door of the shop. "Why don't you go get us some snow cones?"

"You trying to get rid of me?"

"I'm trying to get a damn snow cone. Here." Kit dug a few bills from the pocket of her leggings. "Now go on."

Fancy crumpled the money in her fist and set the dress bag on the driest bit of the ground she could find. "Promise you won't—"

"I'm not gone kill her," Kit yelled, exasperated. "Now would you *leave*? Jesus. You act like you think I don't have any self-control at all."

You don't, Fancy could have said, but Kit was the oldest, and Franken had used up all of Fancy's bargaining chips. The best Fancy could do was try to hurry back before any real damage was done.

On her way back to the alley with the snow cones, as she carefully crossed back to Claudine at the corner away from the wreckage farther down the street, she saw Gabriel Turner. He was a tall, skinny boy with butterscotch-colored skin and long black braids that curled girlishly against his shoulders. Fancy usually didn't notice boys the way Kit did, let alone remember their names, but even she knew who Gabriel was. His father had been Daddy's last victim.

Gabriel was standing in an empty parking space in front of a music store, the kind that sold instruments, with his black shirt tied around his bare shoulders like a cape. A line of golden saxophones gleamed in a display window behind him that was streaked with blood. Fancy wondered if Gabriel had put the blood on the window, since a similar streak decorated his bare chest. And because he was prodding a severed human head at his feet with a stick.

"You don't want any kisses from me, do you?"

Fancy faltered, thinking he was talking to her. But Gabriel was staring down at the head, frowning at it. He startled her when he jabbed the stick through its eye—it made an unforgettably wet sound.

"It's too bad," said Gabriel. He used the stick to raise the head to his face; he spoke into its ear. "Real monsters eat you from the inside out."

She edged around the bright blue car that was in her way so that she could get a better look at what insanity looked like, but before she could get close enough, Gabriel's older brother, Ilan, came out of the store. He froze when he saw what Gabriel was holding, and then he grabbed his brother and slapped him across the face. Fancy was sure she saw pearls of blood arc through the air, it was that hard of a slap.

Gabriel staggered back into the blue car and clapped his hand over his mouth. "What was that for?" he cried, his words muffled.

Ilan kicked the severed head and sent it flying into the ruined street before he turned to glare at his brother. "It happened again!" He had a gravelly voice, like he spent all day screaming at the top of his lungs. At Gabriel, from the looks of it.

Fancy got a good look at Gabriel then and saw not insanity, but fear and confusion in his eyes.

And then pain as Ilan slapped him again, this time on the ear.

Ilan was much darker than his brother, with none of his brother's immature softness, but they both had the same light brown eyes. If not for the resemblance Fancy wouldn't have believed they were really related. Kit would never have treated Fancy the way Ilan was treating his brother. "It's gotta stop, Gabe," he said.

Gabriel pushed Ilan in the chest. "I don't know how to make it stop! You act like there's a switch I can turn on and off." Gabriel crouched and hid his head in his hands. A customer walking out with a violin case nearly tripped over him.

"I don't wanna be like this," Gabriel muttered, rubbing his thumb against the gold cross dangling from his neck like it was a lucky rabbit's foot. "I'm trying so hard not to be like this."

"Try harder." Ilan hauled Gabriel to his feet and gave him a shake. "You think I wanna chase after you my whole life? Cover for you?" Ilan let him go and looked up and down the street as if he wanted a taxi to drive by so he could hail it and take off, but taxis weren't thick on the ground in Portero. Ilan turned to his brother, his face dark with resentment. "I shoulda strangled you the day Ma brought you home—we'd all be better off."

Gabriel stilled at Ilan's words, his fist tightening around his cross as if he wanted to rip it off and whip Ilan across the face with it. Instead, Gabriel let go of the cross, unknotted his shirt, and pulled it on over his bloody chest.

Both brothers wore tight, punk-rock clothes, but they didn't really look the part—they seemed more wretched than rebellious. Ilan caught sight of Fancy standing and gaping at him and his brother, and the resentfulness seemed to leave him all at once. He wiped his hands on his jeans and sidled in front of Gabriel, as if hiding him from sight. "Got any wet wipes?" he asked her.

Fancy's reply was to run away from Ilan and his weirdo brother as fast as she could. When she made it back to the alley, bursting with gossip, the sight of the shopgirl sprawled on the ground at Kit's feet—the puddles ruining her black silk dress—killed Fancy's urge to speak.

"Finally!" Kit yelled, grinning. Her face was spattered in blood; not much, but Fancy could have played connect-the-dots on it. "Is that pineapple?"

"I knew it," said Fancy as Kit took the snow cone from her. "All that talk about trust so you can stand out here in *broad daylight* and kill some stupid girl—"

"She's not dead."

Fancy checked the shopgirl's pulse and, upon finding a strong, steady beat, released a huge breath she hadn't known she'd been holding.

"I just smacked her upside the head a little." Kit flipped the brick and caught it behind her back with one hand. "Kit Cordelle aka the Bludgeoner."

"Bludgeoner. Bonesaw Killer." Fancy fished a wet wipe from her pocket, pushed back the newsboy cap, and cleaned Kit's face, scrubbing harder than necessary. "I ain't gone let you follow in Daddy's footsteps."

Kit dodged the wet wipe long enough to take a bite of her snow cone. "I guess I am too pretty for jail."

"You didn't have to send me away like that."

"I thought . . . maybe you didn't like seeing me go to work on people." Kit looked down. "Like maybe you don't like that side of me."

Fancy studied Kit's blood-free face and shoved the wet wipe back in her pocket.

"Don't be ridiculous, Kit. I like violence just as much as the next person." She thought of the Turner brothers and their horrible relationship and hugged Kit tight.

"And I like *you*. Just the way you are."

FROM FANCY'S DREAM DIARY:

That chubby-cheeked boy I had a crush on in kindergarten asked me and Kit if we wanted to go on a date; he didn't care which one of us. We said we'd both go out with him but we had to change first. So he followed us home and waited while we went in the house and changed, but when we met him outside in the garden wearing nothing but our skeletons, he ran away screaming.

CHAPTER FIVE

The sisters sat in Madda's car on Seventh Street before one of the tall, skinny houses that adorned the streets near Fountain Square, a white one with an orange-sorbet trim.

Madda craned her neck and frowned at her daughters slumped miserably in the backseat of her Honda. "What're y'all waiting for?"

"You to come to your senses," Kit cried, "and rescue us from this scam!"

"What this is," Madda said, "is a sweet, elderly woman named Annice who's gone blind and needs help. Not a scam."

"Why do we have to do some old lady's chores? Nobody ever does *our* chores."

"Yeah," said Fancy. "Can't we just chip in and buy her a maid?"

"This is about being a good neighbor, not throwing money at a problem to make it go away."

"She ain't *my* neighbor."

"She's a fellow Porterene, Kit, and that makes her your neighbor. Look!" Madda pointed out of the car window. "Everybody's pitching in." The old lady herself sat in a rocking chair on her stoop as people filed into her house or worked industriously outside of it weeding flower beds, painting the shutters, and washing the windows.

"This is how people behave in a community," Madda said, staring gravely at her daughters. "They help each other."

"Help schmelp. Just because they're all jumping off a bridge doesn't mean we—"

The stern expression on Madda's face silenced the rest of Kit's griping and sent the sisters scrambling out of the car. The heat was miserable after the coolness of Madda's Honda.

"I'll be at the Super Seven," she said. "While I'm in there, I'll pick us up some empty bottles for the ceremony. Pink ones, if they have any."

"You're not coming in with us?"

"You can't hide behind me your whole life, Fancy. Now go on. And be nice!"

After Madda drove off, Kit took Fancy's hand and led her up the old woman's stoop. Fancy couldn't remember what Madda had called her. She smelled unpleasantly fruity, like the statice Madda grew in the backyard, straddling the thin line between overripe and rotten.

"Hey, Miz Annice," said Kit. Kit always remembered people.

"Hay is for horses, child," croaked Miz Annice, but she was smiling. She wore a muumuu and slippers and thick black sunglasses like she secretly wanted to be cool. "You here to help ole Miz Annice?"

"Yes, ma'am," said Kit. "Just tell us what you need, because we *live* to serve others."

"That refrigerator of mine needs a good cleaning."

"Then will you make us the happiest children in creation and allow us to clean it for you?"

Miz Annice reached out, and when she happened upon Kit's thigh, she gave her a good swat. "You're a real cutup. And a real sweetie to help out an ole lady like me."

"I know it," Kit agreed, so exuberantly that Miz Annice laughed.

After they'd escaped into the house, Kit said, "She was all right, huh?"

"She didn't even say anything to me."

"She's blind, stupid girl. She probably didn't know you were there."

The sisters went into the kitchen, hoping they'd have it to themselves, but a boy and girl were at the sink, washing dishes. At least they were supposed to be washing dishes. Mostly they were splashing each other with suds and giggling and stealing kisses from each other.

Fancy ignored them and opened the refrigerator, which was disgusting, the shelves grimy and full of expired food. The sisters trashed everything and then scrubbed the refrigerator from top to bottom. When they were done, the fridge was spotless but empty.

"Maybe she doesn't eat," Fancy said. "Maybe now that she's blind, she can live off her sense of smell."

But Kit wasn't paying attention to her. She was frowning at the dishwashers.

"Hey, lovebirds!" Kit yelled. "Y'all think Miz Annice wants your sweaty passion leaking all over her fine china? Go get sweaty someplace the hell else."

The dishwashers looked like they wanted to comment, but when Kit narrowed her eyes at them, they decided to do as she said.

When they had gone, Kit turned to Fancy, pouting. "Why can't I find a boy to make out with me while I do the dishes? How dare they stand there and rub my face in their love?"

"*I'll* find you a boy."

Kit perked up. "You will?"

"Lemme just get my boydar." Fancy pulled out her imaginary boy radar device, and scanned it around the kitchen. "I'm registering activity in the garbage can."

"Garbage can, my ass."

"Wait. I'm getting something."

Kit squealed. "*Who?*"

"Tall, dark, handsome. Enjoys good food, walks on the beach, and"—Fancy double-checked the boydar—"evisceration."

"Me too!"

Fancy put the boydar away. "You never even been to the beach."

"I never eviscerated anything either, but I can tell it's something I'd like. So where is he?"

"I'm expecting him any second."

Almost as soon as the last word left Fancy's mouth, the Turner brothers came in through the back door.

"Great timing," Kit whispered, while Fancy stood there, dumbstruck.

"Hey, Kit," said Gabriel, the sunlight following him inside and glinting off his teeth as he smiled at her and set his plastic bags on the counter. He looked much less crazed than he had outside the music store, and there was no sign of blood or severed heads, which was promising. "Maybe you don't remember me, but I'm Gabe. That's Ilan."

"We know who you are," said Kit cheerfully. "Our dad killed your dad."

"Yeah," said Ilan in his gravelly voice. The sunlight bathing his brother seemed to have shunned him. "That *was* kinda memorable."

Kit leaned against the counter as the Turners put away the groceries, chatting with them, in full social mode. She was very good at it. So bubbly you could almost believe she was that girl. She usually only got like that before she went to work on someone: the shopgirl, Franken. Maybe she wanted to kill the Turners and finish the job Daddy had started. Fancy had to admit that the symmetry of such an act had some appeal, but Madda would be coming for them soon. They didn't have time for poetic justice.

"Wanna help me carry stuff to the pantry?" Gabriel asked Kit, waving a jar of beets at her.

"No, she doesn't." Ilan gave his brother a hard look, before addressing Kit. "Best not to leave him alone with young girls."

"Is he dangerous?" asked Kit, intrigued.

"He's just joking," Gabriel said, and then looked to Ilan to back him up, but Ilan wouldn't.

"The last girlfriend he had," Ilan explained, "he locked in his room and wouldn't let her leave."

"I didn't lock her in! I was locking things out."

"What things?" asked Kit.

Gabriel stared at the jar of beets in his hand, shamefaced. "I used to think things were following me. Trying to get me. But I don't think like that anymore. Hardly ever. I'm much better now." He said this to Ilan. "Penny forgave me. We even go to Bible study together. Everything's cool."

Nothing's cool, Ilan's face seemed to shout, but he said nothing.

Fancy almost felt bad for Gabriel, having a brother who didn't seem to trust him, or even like him.

Kit touched the cross hanging around Gabriel's neck. "You got religion?"

"Yeah."

"That work for you?"

"So far." He sidled closer to Kit, no longer ashamed. "That and being in the right place at the right time."

Fancy stopped feeling sorry for him. Instead she inched toward the back door, but Kit wasn't paying attention.

"Pig Liquor?" Kit squealed, laughing at Gabriel's black T-shirt, which had a decal on the front of a fat pink pig floating inside a liquor bottle.

"That's our band name," Gabriel said. "Stop laughing. We spent two weeks coming up with that name. You're required by law to be impressed."

"Well, I do pride myself on being a law-abiding citizen," Kit said as she picked lint off Gabriel's impressive T-shirt, some teasing thing in her eyes, which turned to laughter when Gabriel slumped next to her against the counter, as if her touch had drained the strength from his legs. "Y'all going to Cherry Glade?"

"Yeah." Gabriel was scant inches from her, close enough to do who knew what, and yet Kit didn't back away. "Had my fifteenth birthday last week."

"Fancy's old enough too this year. We had to go shopping for new dresses and everything."

Gabriel studied Kit's leggings. "Have I ever seen you in a dress?"

"I haven't worn one in years."

"This is why I believe in karma," Gabriel told his brother. "We buy Miz Annice groceries, and now I get to see Kit in a dress."

"I'm your reward?" The hard tease in Kit's eyes was replaced with simple surprise, and like Gabriel she slumped against the counter. "I never been anybody's reward before."

"What do you think, man?" Gabriel asked his brother without taking his eyes off Kit, as though her sudden bonelessness were . . . appetizing.

Ilan glanced at Kit. "She wouldn't fit in the trophy case."

Fancy found herself smirking at Ilan's ironic tone, glad she wasn't the only one who found Kit and Gabriel's behavior irritating.

"I mean about seeing Kit in a dress."

Ilan looked at Fancy. "Not if it's anything like what her sister's wearing."

He lacked Gabriel's artful hair, instead sporting a joyless buzz cut with ruler-straight sideburns. He lacked his brother's height, as well, as if his own growth were happening more insidiously, not in a great spurt but in stages, slow and relentless as the Himalayas. He bent his craggy attention on Fancy. "You're fifteen?"

"Yeah," Kit answered when Fancy wouldn't.

"You look it," he said, ignoring Kit. "If you think a skimpy little-kid dress is gone hide all that," he waved a hand at her body, "you're wrong."

Fancy crossed her arms over her chest. He was long-boned like Kit, as if he'd been fashioned to spend his days chasing things through fields. He looked like he wanted to chase Fancy—something predatory and unsettling filled his eyes as he watched her.

Ilan turned his disturbing gaze on Kit. "Y'all should have a family intervention about the way she dresses. It's criminal."

"Don't talk to us about family," Fancy told him. "The way you treat your own family is what's criminal."

Everyone gaped. The jar of beets Gabriel had been holding dropped to the floor and exploded like brains.

"Am I dreaming," Ilan said, "or did you just talk?"

"She did, man!" Gabriel exclaimed. "I heard it too."

"People kept saying she could talk," Ilan told his brother, "but I always thought it was, like, an urban legend."

Fancy, who couldn't believe she'd allowed herself to be goaded into talking to strangers, ran out the back door.

Kit chased after her, calling:

"Fancy's got a boyfriend, Fancy's got a—"

"Shut up!"

Kit caught up to her, laughing. "Where're you going?"

When Fancy realized her headlong dash down the street was attracting attention, she slowed to a fast walk. "To the Super Seven. We can meet Madda up there. I'm *not* waiting in that house another second."

"Why? You in a hurry to tell Madda about your new *boyfriend*?"

"Stop saying that!"

"Well you must like him, or else why would you talk to him?" Kit was so giddy she was nearly screaming. "You *never* talk to people."

"I wasn't talking to him," Fancy said. "I was just pointing out that . . . oh, shut up. Like I would ever be interested in a boy who could be so mean to his own brother. Even if his brother is a weirdo."

"What're you talking about?"

As the sisters hurried down Seventh Street, Fancy told Kit how Gabriel had behaved outside the music store.

Kit shrugged it off. "Who hasn't picked up a stray head? Remember that time when we were little, back when people still liked us? A whole bunch of us found this severed head in a field and played kickball with it? And you—"

"Don't make excuses for him," said Fancy in her sternest tone. "It's one thing to use somebody's skull as a ball; it's a whole nother thing to be whispering secrets into its ears. A person's gotta draw the line somewhere, Kit. I mean, you should have *seen* him. It was so weird."

"You wanna know what's weird? You having a conversation with a boy."

"I did not!" she hissed, since she couldn't scream it the way she wanted to. The residential part of Seventh Street had given way to the business part and more people were crowding the sidewalks, and the last thing Fancy wanted was to attract any more attention. "One sentence ain't a conversation."

"For you it's more like the Gettysburg Address. Why didn't you tell me you ran into them before now?"

"I don't know. After I saw you with the shopgirl, it didn't seem important."

"I understand. Crushes are more fun when they're secret."

Fancy couldn't tell if it was the heat or Kit's teasing, but her head felt hot enough to explode. "Ilan is *not* my secret crush. Ilan." Fancy said it again. "EE-lan. What kinda stupid name is that, anyway? French?"

"We're more French than he is. *We're* descended from the du Havens."

"We were *owned* by the du Havens. Slight difference."

"Spoilsport." The bustle on the street came to a stop momentarily, as everyone, the sisters included, stopped to watch a funeral procession drive past. Fancy wondered, as she always did whenever a hearse drove by, how much such a car would cost. She was convinced it would be kick-ass to drive around in a hearse—as a person, of course; not as a corpse.

After the procession passed, the sisters continued on, and Kit said, "Gabriel's cute, isn't he?"

"No."

"He is, liar. So's Ilan, I guess. But Gabriel . . ."The boneless-ness from the kitchen hadn't faded; Kit was wobbling all over the sidewalk, grinning.

Fancy smacked Kit upside the head, knocking her cap into her eyes.

"Hey!" Kit righted her cap and barely avoided crashing into a parking meter.

"Don't lose your head just because he was flirting with you. Our dad killed his dad. The only thing that boy could possibly want from you is revenge."

Kit's giddiness drained away, and she was silent a long moment before she admitted, "That's what I'd want."

"Exactly!"

"But the rest of the world ain't like us, Fancy."

"You say that like it's a good thing. At least we're honest about being the bad guys."

"Honest to who? Nobody knows what we're really like. Except Franken."

"Yeah, and *he's* tied up in our cellar, so I guess that's just as well, Kit."

FROM FANCY'S DREAM DIARY:

A man came up to me fussing because I was alone in the woods. I told him I lived just down the trail, but he insisted on walking me home, going on and on about weirdos and serial killers. I told him killers are charming and attractive, nothing like me. He said, that's not true and that I was very pretty, and so I smashed a paperweight into his face. The whole time I beat him, he kept telling me how pretty I was, even when his broken teeth made it hard to speak.

CHAPTER SIX

"Ereway inhay the oneymay! Ereway inhay the oneymay!"

"Stop *singing* that." Fancy stood on the pedals of her bike in a vain attempt to outpace Kit's irritating rendition of "We're in the Money."

Kit, however, easily kept pace. "But the pig Latin part is the best part! I'm glad Esme let us listen to it at the store; otherwise I never would have bought it. I hate all that Depression-era crap, usually, but just listen to what I've been missing!"

Kit started singing again, and even the birds seemed annoyed by the song, fleeing high over the shady road.

Since Fancy liked "all that Depression-era crap," normally she would have been glad to see Kit being so broad-minded, but she was still upset over how Kit had behaved with the Turners yesterday. And to make it even worse, Kit had told Madda everything that had happened, and the two of them had wasted their whole dinner talking about boys in general and Gabriel in particular until Fancy had been ready to burst her eardrums with her fork.

"Who's Esme?" Fancy asked. Anything to keep the singing at bay.

"The lady who owns the record store that we've been going to for the past four years. God, Fancy, don't you *ever* pay attention to people?"

"Why should I?"

"They're not always boring. Remember that girl we saw in the square playing 'Heart and Soul' on a recorder? *With her nose?* It was the coolest, freakiest thing ever."

"I've done cooler, freakier things than that. And so have you. Remember that time you made that squirrel eat its own liver?"

Kit shrugged off her sister's praise, unimpressed with herself. "What's the point of being freaky if you can't show off like the recorder girl? Picture me on the street: 'Hey, mister, is that your dog? Wanna see me make him eat his own liver?'

I can't really see anybody giving me a standing ovation for that."

"Since when do you care what other people think?"

"I don't," said Kit, quickly. "I'm not saying that people don't suck. I'm just saying maybe they don't suck *all the time*."

Before Fancy could rebut, the sisters came upon a man standing by his truck with the hood up, and Fancy's urge to speak shriveled.

He was old and bald beneath his trucker hat, which was dirty white like his truck. He wore a white T-shirt and blue jeans that rode low beneath his formidable beer gut. Obviously he was from out of town. Porterenes always wore black, except in church on Sundays. It was a cultural thing, an acknowledgment that death, like the monsters, was all around them.

"Hey, girls!"

The sisters slowed their bikes but didn't stop.

The quiet two-lane road the sisters were biking along was part of historic El Camino Real. It cut through the woods right past their house and hardly ever got traffic since the highway had been built.

"Y'all got a cell phone?" He was trying to flag them down with his hat. "I gotta call for a tow or something! This truck . . ."

He paused, as if having to describe how his truck had let him down was more than he could bear.

"I got a cell," yelled Kit, doing her bubbly thing.

"You do not," hissed Fancy, coming to a halt beside her sister, across from the old man and his truck.

Kit hopped off her bike and retrieved a cell from the bag with the records and whispered, "I swiped it from that shopgirl. I been using up all her anytime minutes calling people in Houston and Miami. And Japan."

"No good deed goes unpunished," Fancy warned.

But Kit ignored her and crossed the road, wiggling the cell at the old man. "Here you go! And if you wanna download some games and songs while you're at it, feel f—"

The old man snatched the phone from Kit's hand and threw it into the woods. Before either sister could react, he hooked his arm around Kit's throat and held a grimy screwdriver to her cheek.

"You!"

Fancy flinched from the harshness of his voice, how it had devolved so quickly from harmless to beastly. "Get over here. Stop right there! Close the hood. Good, now get in the truck."

Fancy did everything the old man said, and then mouthed

Told you so at Kit while he nervously scanned the road for traffic. Kit made a moue of annoyance.

The old man shut Fancy inside the backseat of the hot, stale-smelling truck, where there were no handles to get out; a mesh partition kept her from crawling into the front seat. "You sit there," he said through the rolled-up window, calm now that he had control of the situation. "You sit there till I come for you. Meantime, your sister and me can get better acquainted." When he nuzzled his veiny nose into Kit's cheek, her annoyed look intensified.

The old man shoved Kit ahead of him into the woods, and they soon disappeared into the thick foliage. Fancy began to count, and when she reached fifty, an agonized scream silenced the forest.

Fancy heard the scream again just as Kit burst from the trees, grinning as she opened the truck door to free Fancy.

The air outside felt almost cool compared to the inside of the truck. Fancy fanned herself with her hat and glared at Kit. "*Told* you not to talk to strangers."

The grin vanished. "Okay. You were right. I admit it." Kit threw open her arms to embrace the surrounding forest. "Hear that, bats and bunnies? Fancy was right and I was wrong!"

The only answer was another scream.

"What'd you do to him?" She gave Kit an admiring stare. "And in only fifty seconds?"

"Come see."

The sisters hurried back into the woods, tramping single file along a deer trail. They found the old man lying motionless just off the path on a bed of cloverleafs and . . .

Fancy laughed. "Ghoul's delight?"

"Yep." Kit pointed to the fuzzy ivory flowers clustering over the solid ground cover beneath the old man.

"He pushed me to my knees and told me to eat him. So while I was on the ground, I plucked one of the flowers and then shot up and stuck the pistil into the moist little ball of his eye, and down he went. Then I stabbed him with his own screwdriver, because if there's one thing I can appreciate, it's irony."

The old man's muddy right eye was as glassy and motionless as a doll's; his left, however, glared daggers at the sisters as he screamed at them, the screwdriver poking tumorously from his shoulder.

Kit dropped next to the old man, careful of the ghoul's delight. "Obviously you ain't from here and don't know about all the crazy plants that grow in Portero. These flowers you were so eager to do me on cause paralysis."

Not that he was completely paralyzed; he could shrug his shoulders a bit and wiggle his knees.

"You wouldn't have minded if *I'd* been paralyzed, though, right?" said Kit. She produced her switchblade and waggled it in the old man's face. "Would've made raping me way easier. But not funner."

Fancy rapped Kit on the back of the head. "Don't say 'funner.'"

"Lemme alone." Kit swatted her back. "It's playtime."

Fancy didn't feel the reluctance to harm that she'd felt with Franken. Or even the shopgirl. For the old man, twitching on his back like a dying cockroach, she felt nothing.

"You said you didn't mind violence," said Kit, misreading her hesitation. "And anyway, he tried to hurt me."

"I know." When Kit looked at her with disappointed eyes, Fancy realized she felt something after all. "That's why we're gone kill him."

Kit jumped to her feet and grabbed Fancy by the shoulders, face shining brighter than the sun burning along the trail. "Really?"

Fancy took Kit's switchblade and lifted the old man's

T-shirt. She jabbed the knife into the left-hand side of the old man's enormous gut. He screamed when the knife went in. He couldn't feel it, of course, but he could still see.

"There." Fancy stood and made an *after you* gesture to Kit. "Now you can unzip him and see if you really do like evisceration."

Kit squealed and hopped in place like a kid on Christmas Day, and when she finally reached for the knife, her hands were shaking. She rolled him onto his side as she yanked up on the hilt of the switchblade, which parted his belly as easily as Moses had parted the Red Sea, and then laughed when Fancy squealed and skipped back with the old man's guts decorating her Mary Janes. "Look what you did to my sister's shoes!"

But the old man didn't want to see; his one working eye swirled every which way except down at his intestines.

"I wanna unzip something else," Kit exclaimed, pulling the switchblade free. "Maybe his liver?"

"No, he needs that," said Fancy. "People can live a long time with their guts hanging out. But livers are important. Cut out his eyes, or sever his fingers. He doesn't need those."

"What does it matter if I cut out his liver and it kills him? We *are* killing him, right?"

"Yes, but I want him alive when the animals come."

"Animals?"

Fancy grimaced at her shoes and cleaned them as best she could in the grass. "All this offal is sure to attract 'em." She leaned over the old man's face, forcing him to look at her. "You said you wanna be eaten? Let's see if you get your wish."

An hour later the sisters sat in a tree, legs dangling, watching the pack of hogs through the waxy magnolia leaves as they feasted on the old man. His flat eyes stared blankly at the sky. His paunch had deflated, empty of all the stuff that had fallen out of him. His bloodstained cap was turned to the side on his head as though he had become a B-boy in the afterlife.

"We should go," said Fancy nervously, as the hogs fought over the old man's scraps.

"Why?" Kit watched the scene below as raptly as some women watched soap operas. "This is great! Besides, you're the one who wanted to wait and watch him get eaten."

"But what if *monsters* come?"

"Fancy." Kit looked away from the drama to stare at her sister, surprised. "We *are* the monsters."

FROM FANCY'S DREAM DIARY:

WE CAME HOME AND SAW MADDA IN THE LIVING ROOM CROUCHED ON THE FLOOR EATING RAW STEAK. SHE HAD FANGS. WE RAN TO HER AND HUGGED HER. WE SAID, YOU'RE JUST LIKE US. MADDA TOOK THE TEETH OUT—THEY WERE SHINY AND PLASTIC—AND SAID, NO I'M NOT.

CHAPTER SEVEN

Kit burst into the cellar. "Look what I have, Franken!"

She hopped onto the cot where Franken lay pale and still, as if Kit had pulled him out of a drawer at the morgue.

He studied the jar she held to his face, the ear that flopped against the glass as she shook it. "Who's that?"

"Some guy we met on the road who wanted to commit ungentlemanly acts upon my person. We ripped out his guts and let the hogs eat him. But this!" Kit tapped her red fingernail against the jar. "This is mine."

Franken looked away from the jar and frowned at the ceiling. "Is that why you didn't come see me?"

Kit stopped smiling. "I wanted to come, but"—she shot

a quick look at Fancy, who was scowling at her—"Fancy wanted to shop for records. And then the old man showed up and—"

"Sometimes I think you'll never come back," Franken whispered. "That you'll leave me down here to rot till I'm just a pile of stitches and bones."

"I wouldn't do that!" Kit stroked his pale hair. "I wouldn't be taking such good care of you if I meant for you to r—Jesus, is that lice?" Kit peered at the bug she'd picked out of Franken's hair.

"Is it?" Fancy asked, backing away toward the shelves.

"Nah," Kit decided, crushing the bug between her fingers. "Just a mite. I'd better bathe him again, though."

"You bathed him yesterday," Fancy complained, as Kit filled a bowl with bottled water and hand soap from the shelves. "He just lays there all day. How could he get dirty?"

"I don't know," Kit said, kneeling by the cot. "Dead skin cells? Sweat? Mites? Go play with something and don't bother me." Franken didn't have a shirt, not since Kit had cut it off him, so she just pulled down his pants. "And don't look at his junk! You know how shy Franken is."

Fancy huffed as far away from them as she could, which in

the small space wasn't as far as she would have liked. She sat on the floor near the cellar steps and played jacks and wondered for the millionth time why Kit had to get so involved with people.

"You girls down there?"

Fancy jerked and looked toward the stairs before she realized it was just the intercom on the wall above her head. Kit made a shushing gesture to Franken as Fancy pressed the button.

"Yes, ma'am."

"Well, come on up and help me with dinner. It's getting late."

"We're on our way." Fancy let go of the button and turned to Kit. "She wants us to help with dinner."

"I can hear."

"So come on!"

"In a minute." Kit wrung out the washcloth and gently rubbed Franken's legs.

"This is ridiculous!"

"Cleanliness is next to godliness, Fancy. Besides, the constant washing also helps prevent infection."

"You just like seeing him naked."

"I'm not even looking at him! I feel sad when I look at him." Kit ran her hand over all the scars she'd put on his body. "I feel sad because *he's* so sad. You really should let me put him outta his misery."

"No."

"You can't blame her for wanting me dead," Franken said to Fancy, startling her. He always acted as though she weren't in the room. Even now, though he was talking to Fancy, he was looking at Kit. "I'm all cut up and hideous now. She can't stand the sight of me."

"That's not true," Kit exclaimed. "You're not hideous. I swear." She held her hand to her chest, over the empty space she was always complaining about. "You're like a doll I had when I was a kid. She was all stitched together and her head kept falling off, but I loved that doll. That's what you look like. Like somebody just loved you to death."

"Isn't that the doll you ripped to pieces?" said Fancy. "After Daddy got arrested? Classic misplaced aggression, Franken; she really wanted to rip *Daddy* to pieces."

Kit shot her an outraged look. "I did not!"

"But it's too hard, ripping a grown man apart."

"Not *that* hard." Kit got off her knees and ran her eyes

down Franken's body. "Not with the right tools. The hard part would be finding the right-size jars for all the pieces."

When Fancy saw a wash of terror chase away the mushy, lovelorn expression on Franken's face, something tight in her chest relaxed, and with relaxation came enlightenment. She knew now what she would wish for—the ability to kill whenever she wanted without getting caught.

Because if Kit thought Franken could fill the emptiness inside her, she was sadly mistaken.

"Evisceration is so fucking *cool*!"

Fancy winced and smacked Kit on her ear. "You want Madda to hear you talking like that?" Madda was out in the garden picking green tomatoes to fry, while the sisters set the table.

But Fancy didn't feel near as disapproving as she sounded. Kit was right.

Evisceration *was* cool.

Kit rubbed her ear absently, still grinning. Franken was right about one thing. Kit really did radiate light, especially when she was happy. Fancy turned away from her; sometimes that brightness was too hard to face.

"After we kill Franken," said Kit, "I'm gone put *his* ear in a jar too. Just like that old man's. I'll start a collection!"

"I hope you hid that thing real good," Fancy hissed when Madda came back to the kitchen. "Last thing we need is Madda finding it."

"She won't. Madda'll never notice it among all the jars full of squirrel spleens and whatnot."

"And we are not gone kill Franken. How many times I gotta tell you?"

"You don't even like Franken; all you do is complain about him, and you can't still be worried about the police." Kit pinched Fancy's cheek. "Not after what you did to that old man."

Fancy slapped her hand away. "That was different. Besides, you did all the work. I just watched."

"Don't try to distance yourself from what happened. Voyeurism is participation."

"What're you girls whispering about?" asked Madda, eyeing her daughters expectantly as she fried the tomatoes.

"Nothing," the sisters trilled in unison, smiling their brightest good-girl smiles. And then Kit turned to Fancy and whispered, "And what's the difference between Franken and the old man?"

"Franken's a thief, but he never tried to hurt us."

"I don't think that'd matter in a court of law."

"*Of course it would matter.* There's no legal reason to take a hostage. But with the old man, that was self-defense."

"No, *that* was self-indulgence."

Fancy couldn't deny how she'd felt: relief and a slippery pleasure at having taken such ultimate control over someone. "Maybe a little," she admitted.

Kit grinned. "You were right, you know, you and your boy-dar. I *do* enjoy evisceration, and so do you. We're learning all kinds of things about ourselves today."

"Be serious, Kit."

"I am," she said. "For the first time in my life I felt like myself. No pretending, no hiding. Just me, warts and all. Too bad it was wasted on that old man. I wish I could drop my guard like that with somebody I loved."

"Hello."

"I mean besides you. You think Madda would ever . . . ?"

"Wanna watch us eviscerate someone?" The idea was so insane that it was no wonder Kit couldn't even get the words out. "What do you think?"

"Think about what?" asked Madda, bringing the tomatoes to the table.

"Nothing," said the sisters, again.

After Madda said grace, she gave her daughters a long look. "What y'all been up to all day?"

Fancy said, "Just went to the record store and—"

"We saw a corpse on the road home!"

Fancy kicked Kit under the table, but it was too late. Madda gasped, and Fancy's serving of tomatoes hit the table instead of her plate. "A corpse? What did it want?"

"It was dead," Fancy said quickly. "Already dead when we saw it."

"Yeah, Madda," said Kit, still grimacing from Fancy's kick. "The dead can't talk."

"But they can," said Madda. "They can ask you things."

The sisters waited for the punchline, but there was none, and Madda didn't look like she was joking.

"It didn't speak to you, did it?"

"Speak?" Kit looked as shocked as if Madda had cursed at her. "What're you saying?"

She smirked and said, "Nothing." Just to irritate her daughters. "It still might not happen. It never happened to me. It did happen to Big Mama, but she was twelve. You girls are way too old to—"

"What?" The sisters leaned toward Madda, breathless.

"To speak to the dead." Madda paused, gauging her daughters' reaction, perhaps expecting them to laugh or otherwise dismiss what she'd said. When they remained silent and wide-eyed, she continued. "Sometimes, corpses like to speak to certain people in our family. Like Big Mama. Big Mama wouldn't set foot in a cemetery. Cuz sometimes when she'd step on a grave, the body would rise. And speak to her."

Fancy's weirdness threshold, which like any Porterene's was extremely high, stretched painfully into the stratosphere. *"Big Mama was a witch?"*

Madda waved her hand dismissively. "I don't think it had to do with witchcraft—everybody knows there's no such thing as magic. It's just that sometimes, some people get born with a gift. Like being born with double-jointed thumbs or a birthmark. Something you either have or you don't. Does that make sense? It'd be nice if y'all did inherit something from my side. I know y'all can see things, the way Guthrie could—"

"Fancy can," said Kit, matter-of-factly. "Not me."

Madda looked at Fancy and sighed. "I just wish y'all had more of my blood in you than your daddy's. It's nice to be different, but he was different in too many wrong ways."

"But why are we"—Fancy hesitated—"why is *our* family different at all?"

"It's always been like that. Your daddy's people have far-sight. On my side people can settle the dead—all the way back to Cherry du Haven, and Lord knows where she got it from. But Cherry's gifts were strong, so strong they lasted beyond death."

"It's one thing for somebody like Cherry to talk to dead people," said Kit, "but . . . *Big Mama?*"

Big Mama had been a tough woman, tall and quick to slap any kid dumb enough to back-talk her, but she had always been merry, too, and full of funny, inappropriate stories. She laughed a lot. Daddy had said it was because she drank a lot. Anybody who drank that much oughta be in a good mood, he'd often said. Peach schnapps had been Big Mama's liquor of choice; her pores had always been sweet with the stuff. And though she had been full of stories, mostly about other people, the most exciting thing the sisters had ever seen her do was chase one of her ex-husbands out of the house with a broom. And now they were supposed to believe that Big Mama could reanimate corpses?

Kit asked, "What would the corpses say to her?"

"She said"—Madda frowned in remembrance—"that they'd always ask something like will you hear me or will you grant my plea, and Big Mama'd say yes, and then she'd give them whatever they needed to be at peace."

"What would a corpse need?" asked Fancy.

"To apologize. To confess. To accuse. To be heard. Big Mama listened. So did Cherry."

Kit brought out her switchblade—she'd remembered to clean it, thank God—and began tapping it against the table. "Why is it that only certain people can do things?"

"Why is it that you can sing and play that piano," Madda said, "and Fancy and I can't?"

"Because I don't suck the way y'all do."

Fancy thought about kicking her again. "Way to be lady-like, Kit."

"It's as good an answer as any." Madda brushed her hand against Kit's cheek. "Nobody knows, baby."

Kit leaned into Madda's touch. "How come you only ever tell us the boring stuff about our family history? About slavery and stuff. You never told us Big Mama was a witch!"

"Don't call Big Mama a witch."

"But she was . . . special," Kit insisted. "So if our family's special, does that mean we get an extra wish at Cherry Glade? There's gotta be *some* perks, right?"

"We only get one wish, like everybody else, greedy girl. That reminds me." Madda left the kitchen briefly and returned with two pink glass bottles, round and squat and stoppered like they'd been made to hold perfume. She gave them to her daughters. "I was lucky to find pink ones," she said. Some families had good-luck charms; some had good-luck mottos. The Cordelles had a good-luck color.

"What're you gone wish for, Madda?" Fancy asked.

"To be able to spend more time with y'all," she said, settling back in her chair. "See if I can keep the two of you outta trouble."

Kit gave her a big-eyed stare. "We don't get into trouble."

Madda huffed. "Maybe you don't get *caught*." She eyed her daughters with exaggerated suspicion. "I'd love to be able to see what y'all get up to when I ain't here."

"We ain't interesting, Madda," said Fancy in her most reassuring tone.

"I doubt that," said Madda, who didn't seem at all reassured.

Much later, after Madda left for work, the sisters sat in mismatched chairs at their desk in front of the wisteria-eaten porch screen. The rate at which the vine was creeping into the room was disturbing, especially to Fancy, who often expected to wake up with it growing into her mouth, choking her. The room was lit with hurricane lamps, which the sisters favored. Electric light was too piercing and chased the shadows away—the sisters liked shadows.

"You think somebody could raise that old man from the dead?" Kit asked, doing an elaborate twirl routine with the switchblade as "It's Your Thang" played on the phonograph. "Not that there's much left to raise."

"Who?" Fancy was busy writing down her wish to Cherry, what Kit should have been doing instead of obsessing over a corpse. "Big Mama's been dead a long time. And if *we* could, it would've happened by now. Big Mama was twelve when it happened to her."

"What if it happened to somebody else?" Kit grabbed Fancy's shoulder, causing her to scratch a line down her formerly pristine note. "Some bastard member of our family who we don't even know about? Some person who goes for a walk in the woods and stumbles across his animal-ravaged carcass and raises him—"

Fancy balled up the ruined note. "Calm down."

"You calm down!" Kit dropped her head to the desk. "I know what that old man's dearest wish is—it's to get laid by young girls. To get laid by me! What if he comes back for me?"

"Well." Fancy rewrote the note and slipped it into the bottle. "You keep saying you don't wanna die a virgin."

"My life is going up in flames, and you're joking?"

"I don't joke; I quip. It's much more refined." She pushed away from the desk and Kit's phony paranoia and went into the inner room's bathroom to brush her teeth.

When she went back to the sleeping porch, stepping over the wet footprints she and Kit had tracked in earlier after their bath, Kit was scribbling her own note. "'Dear Cherry,'" she said as she wrote. "'Please help me avoid . . . losing my virginity . . . to a corpse. Your friend, Kit.'"

Fancy had to laugh at Kit's theatrics. They both knew that if that corpse was dumb enough to come back from the dead, Kit would simply "play" with it until it begged to go back to hell.

"Don't waste your wish on nonsense," Fancy said, pulling back the sheet on her bed. "I gotta waste my wish on us not getting caught for killing that old man *and* for what we've done to Franken. So *you* need to wish for us to stay together."

Kit paused in the act of putting her silly note into the bottle. "I'll wish for that if you promise me something."

"What?"

Kit leaned forward, her gaze darkly intense. "If that old man comes back wanting to get laid, then we do him the way we do everything—together. You with me?"

"Nope." Fancy flopped back onto her pillows.

"You mean you won't have sex with one measly old corpse?" Kit balled up her note and hurled it at Fancy. "Not even for me?"

Fancy caught the note in one hand and set it calmly on the nightstand. "Kit," she said gravely, "a girl's gotta have some things just for herself."

She expected Kit to pretend to faint or something equally ridiculous, but Kit only stared into her empty pink bottle, a thoughtful expression on her face.

"Just for herself," she whispered.

A whisper, but it resonated in the hot, narrow room like a curse.

FROM FANCY'S DREAM DIARY:

ME AND KIT SAT IN BIG MAMA'S LAP WHILE SHE TOLD US A
BORING STORY ABOUT THE OLDEN DAYS. BIG MAMA TOLD KIT
TO RUN AND GET THE PEACH SCHNAPPS BECAUSE IT WOULD
PUT US IN A LISTENING MOOD. BUT WHAT KIT BROUGHT BACK
WAS CHERRY SCHNAPPS SO BIG MAMA SLAPPED HER AND
WOULDN'T LET US DRINK IT. SHE SAID CHERRIES WERE
BAD FOR GROWING GIRLS.

CHAPTER EIGHT

Cherry Glade wasn't much to look at: several acres of flat green land surrounded by elm and maple and pine with a single dead moontree at its center. But people who set foot on the land could feel its power; their bodies would tingle as if they were waking after a long sleep. Only five such places existed in Portero, places Porterenes called Keys because doors to other worlds often appeared near them. All Porterenes could recite dozens of tales of people who had vanished near Cherry Glade and were never heard from again.

But Porterenes were used to such mysteries, and not even the possibility of disappearing off the skin of the world was enough to keep the crowd from having a good time. The

Crayola-green glade was dotted with sun-hatted picnickers and flocks of children in ties and kneesocks chasing each other. The older kids played subdued games of Frisbee and touch football, mindful of their party clothes. The older people sat in the shade of the encircling forest, either playing cards or keeping a sharp eye on everyone. They also had control of the music, much to the dismay of the younger crowd. Teens begging for Jay-Z and Mary J. Blige had to settle for Lenny White and Chaka Khan.

The only spot devoid of any people was the moontree, which stood in the center of the glade, its tall, blackened limbs curling upward like a candelabra.

The sisters, who rarely went to public gatherings, were reminded of the family reunions they'd gone to on Madda's side of the family when Big Mama had still been alive. That was before Daddy's actions had made their family persona non grata. Unfortunately, the Cordelles were just as non grata at Cherry Glade. As they scouted for an empty picnic table, Madda called out to several people, who either returned her greetings with chill, short replies or pretended not to see her at all.

"Bitches," Kit muttered.

Madda smacked her on the back of the head. "Why you wanna talk ugly on a day like today?"

"They got no call being mean to you," said Kit, rubbing her head. "*You* never did anything. That's why I hate stuff like this!"

"This ain't a day to be hateful, Kit." Madda tilted her head toward the sun. She looked less tired than usual, more like Kit on her bubbliest day, and Southern-belle pretty in her flowery sun hat. She'd spent her day off sleeping at night like a normal person, and it had done her a world of good. "We're here to pay our respects to Cherry, and to think about how things've changed since the Civil War. Nothing else matters."

The Cordelles claimed an empty table in the shade, the forest at their backs. They unpacked the food they'd made, not just for themselves, but for the other families. It was a custom to go to different tables and take a plate of whatever looked appetizing, but the generous array of food at their table was clearly being shunned. Fancy didn't even want to think about what would happen when it was their turn to go table-hopping, how the experience might drive Kit to drown some rude person in a bowl of potato salad. Killing the old man had quieted the sisters' inner murderers, but Fancy wasn't sure how long it would last.

Kit didn't look murderous just then, though; her face lit like a Fourth of July sparkler. "There's Gabriel and Ilan!" she cried.

The brothers were way on the other side of the glade, in the midst of the touch footballers, waving at them. *Gabriel* was waving. Ilan just stared at Fancy and rolled up the sleeves of his black dress shirt, as if he intended to go to work on her.

Fancy harrumphed and picked a strawberry off Madda's slice of cheesecake. "I don't care."

"You don't, huh?" Madda gave her a sly look. "Ilan's a nice boy."

"You don't know that," Fancy said around a mouthful of strawberry.

"I *do* know that." Madda scooted the slice of cheesecake closer to Fancy so they could share it more easily. "He used to deliver my lunch when I worked the day shift. Know what Ilan told me once? He told me he didn't blame me for what Guthrie did to his family." She smiled in Ilan's direction. "If that's not nice, what is?"

Fancy found herself interested, despite her better judgment. "Did y'all ever talk about what happened the night his dad—?"

Madda wiped cheesecake from Fancy's mouth. "Only thing he wanted to talk about when he came around was *you*."

Fancy laughed but then stopped when she noticed how hysterical she sounded. "Me?"

"He asked about you all the time," said Madda, as though it was something to be proud of.

"Puke." Fancy watched Ilan play touch football, watched him run down the other boys on his dangerously quick legs. "He asked about *me?*"

"Yes indeed."

"You never told me that."

"You never seemed interested in boys."

"I'm *not.*"

Madda nodded wisely. "That's what I told him. I guess he listened. Otherwise he'd've been trying to talk to you all last year."

Kit, who had been listening to this exchange with some interest, sang, "Fancy's got a boyfriend!"

"Shut up, you." Fancy elbowed her sister, her face burning and not because of the sun.

"Fancy and Ilan sitting in a—"

"*Shut* it."

"Both of you shut it," said Madda, "and eat."

"Madda," Kit said after some time, "will our wishes really come true?"

"Yes," said Madda with zero enthusiasm. It was as though Kit had asked whether the sun would set that night. "Wishes aren't everything, you know," she continued. "The worst thing you can do is rest all your hopes on a wish. A granted wish doesn't equal a perfect life. My great-aunt Mary once wished for a child. She had been trying and trying, but she just couldn't get pregnant. No one knew why. So she came here and asked Cherry, and the next month Mary was pregnant. But when she gave birth, the baby was dead.

"Mary cried and cried about it. She wouldn't stop crying. And one day, while she was cursing Cherry for giving her a baby just to have it die on her, Mary's tears turned to cherries. They rolled down her face and onto the floor, a flood of them, and spelled out the words 'You asked for this.'"

Madda regarded her daughters, who were listening silently. "It's okay to wish for things, but wishes are fragile, and the world we live in is very hard."

After they finished eating, Madda shooed her daughters away from the safety of their picnic table. "Y'all go on and mingle."

"With these losers?"

"Don't start with me today, Christianne. You can either

come table-hopping with me, or you can mingle by yourselves. Choose."

"By ourselves," said the sisters in unison.

Madda smiled at them. "Good choice."

The sisters wandered away, hand in hand. They stayed in the shadow of the forest circling the glade until they found an empty picnic table out of Madda's sight.

Fancy kept Kit entertained with the bubble solution she'd brought along in her pocket. Projected in the clear, fragile bubbles she blew were images of genteel Madda body-slamming all the mean, unyielding women not worth the polish on her little toe. When the stereo began to play "Kung Fu Fighting," Madda stopped body-slamming the women and began to drop-kick them instead. The sisters found this hilarious.

"What're y'all laughing at?"

The bubbles burst. A line of kids stood before their table, eyeing the sisters.

The tall, no-neck boy who'd spoken stepped forward. "If my daddy was a murderer, I wouldn't sit around laughing all day."

"Maybe they're too ignorant to know any better." This from a girl as dark and treacherous as black ice. "We're taking up a collection for y'all, you know."

"For what?" said Kit breezily, even though her hands had clenched into fists.

"So y'all can go to the hospital and get neutered. The last thing the world needs is the two of y'all breeding more murderers."

Fancy said such things to Kit all the time, but hearing it from a stranger made her want to run out and have a baby right now. How dare they tell her she shouldn't have babies?

"First of all," said Kit slowly, taking time to look everyone in the eye, "girls get spayed, not neutered. And second of all, the last thing the world needs is *y'all* breeding more victims."

"*I'm* a victim?" said the boy. He leaned over the table and got in Kit's face. The whites of his eyes were as yellow and sour as the pit stains on his shirt. "You think you can take me? You got your daddy's blood in you?" When he opened his mouth again, Kit reached across the table and grabbed his tongue between her fingernails and yanked on it.

His head slammed to the table, allowing Kit to brace her other hand on his face while she pulled and pulled. "Quite a lot of his blood, actually," said Kit as the other kids backed away. "The curiosity I get from my mother, though. You know what I'm curious about?" she asked the squealing boy in her grip. "I'm curious about how hard I'd have to pull to rip your tongue out of your fucking face."

Fancy slapped at Kit's hands, but Kit shrugged her off. "Lemme alone. It's playtime."

Gabriel approached the table. He was as fresh and cool as if he'd stepped down off a cloud. He certainly didn't have pit stains. He reminded Fancy of the statues she'd seen in the happy place, golden and perfect. If she chopped his head off, he'd fit right in. *Oh, if only,* Fancy thought as he moved in on her sister, her hands itching for an ax.

"What game is this?" he asked lightly, as if he watched girls rip out people's tongues every day.

Kit said, "This is called watch-a-young-punk-get-his-ass-kicked."

"Ripping out a guy's tongue doesn't count as an ass-kicking."

"No?" Not that Kit had managed the ripping part yet; she couldn't seem to get a good enough grip.

"Maybe try," Gabriel began. "I don't know, actually kicking him in the ass?"

Kit thought about it; the boy squealing around her grip on his tongue didn't seem to affect her concentration one bit. Finally she climbed over the table, pulling the boy by the tongue to his feet. Then she spun him around and kicked his ass. The guy hit the ground, and his friends immediately circled him, protecting him. Kit faced them with her hands on her hips, smiling her poison-red smile. "Now what?"

"Now," Gabriel answered, "you let him live with the shame of getting beat up by a girl."

"I can't believe you're taking their side," yelled the black-ice girl.

Gabriel looked at the crowd of kids and said calmly, "Y'all don't have any reason to be mad at them. They didn't do anything."

The black-ice girl pointed at Kit. "She pulled Robert's tongue out!"

"Tried to," Gabriel reminded her, and then addressed the group. "But even if she had pulled it out, if you step on a rattle-snake and get bit, whose fault is that? Do I really need to tell you what it says in the Bible about loving your neighbors? Like it or not, the Cordelles are our neighbors, and if *I* can forgive and forget, that's the very least y'all can do."

The crowd slunk off, chastened, carrying their shamed friend with them.

"See?" Gabriel smiled at Kit. "You win, and no one gets dismembered." He pulled out a wet wipe and cleaned her bloody hand.

"So . . . you *don't* like dismembering?"

"No."

"Evisceration?"

"Not so much." He laughed like he thought she was joking. "I'm a dull sorta guy."

"Yeah, kinda." She didn't seem alarmed that he had yet to let go of her hand, even though it was now spotlessly clean. "But that's okay."

Someone rang a bell. A tiny bell with a hellishly bright peal that caused everyone in the glade to wince simultaneously. Someone shouted, "It's time!"

Fancy yanked her sister from Gabriel's sanctimonious clutches and dragged her back to their picnic table to get their pink bottles.

The bottle ceremony began soon after, and the whole mood changed. The dead moontree became the center of attention as everyone gathered around it. Porterenes brought out brightly colored glass bottles containing slips of paper with wishes scribbled on them, and tied them by the neck to the naked branches of the tree. People stood on stepladders or rode piggyback on each other's shoulders to reach the highest limbs, and soon every branch was full of bottles flashing in the sunlight. The kids under fifteen stood well away from the crowd at the tree, watching closely and eager for the day it would be their turn.

When the last bottle was hung, the tree looked as though a rainbow had crashed into it and become entangled. People crowded together around the tree, even crowded around the Cordelles, marveling at the tree's sparkling beauty. In that moment Fancy didn't hate everybody. A calm clarity settled over the world and made it simple and lovely. The wasp buzzing past her face had a fairy shimmer; the sun didn't burn but rather fed her skin. She hummed with energy—everyone did—and no one seemed hateful, but rather like big-eyed children, regardless of age.

The only sound was of dragonflies buzzing low in the grass and the distant scream of a hawk in the woods. A soft breeze tickled the bottles and set them swaying. The wind hooted over the bottle necks, low and mournful like a voice.

"Fancy . . ."

The voice didn't surprise Fancy. It was almost as though she had been expecting it. No one else seemed to hear it, though. Not

Madda. Not even Kit. She touched her sister's shoulder, but Kit seemed half asleep, staring at the tree with the same awestruck contemplation as everyone else. Everyone was so still, asleep with open eyes. It felt like one of her dreams, like Fancy had stepped out of time, like the rules had all changed. The sensation wasn't jarring; Fancy had always felt at home in her dreams.

"Fancy . . ."

The crowd parted, gliding away from Fancy as if on rollers, until she stood alone, her pinafore fluttering in the warm breeze. Even Kit had left her side. A glittering pink path materialized at Fancy's feet, stretching narrowly across the green glade and disappearing into the woods.

"Come to me. . . ."

Fancy stepped onto the path, which clicked under her Mary Janes, and left everyone behind. She had a distant thought of whether this was how people disappeared from the world: They followed the path that came to them just to see where it led. It wasn't horrifying, but exciting. To be called. To be chosen.

Fancy felt that inevitable tug as the dreamworld exerted its authority over her, entering the dark coolness of woods that didn't feel like woods. She could have been anywhere or nowhere, alone in a way she'd never been before, perhaps on the edge of the universe, where even the stars were strange.

The longer she walked, the darker and less defined things became, until the only clear thing was the glittering path. The more she walked, the more excited and sure she became that something singular and glorious awaited her.

In the darkness the path widened to form a pink circle that twinkled as though mixed with starlight. In the center stood a barefoot woman wrapped togalike in silver cloth. Her hair was wrapped in silver as well. She gleamed like a fallen star made flesh. Otherworldly . . . but familiar. Fancy knew that nose and those cheekbones. The woman looked the way Madda had when she was younger and less factory worn.

The woman held out her arms. "It's been long since one of my own has seen me."

"Miz Cherry?" Fancy had to fight an insane urge to curtsy.

Cherry shocked Fancy by taking her by the shoulders and kissing her cheek. Her touch was inhuman, cold and glassy like a porcelain doll, but after her initial flinch Fancy relaxed into her grandcestor's embrace.

"You found me," said Cherry. "I wondered if you had the strength to seek me out." She had a strange accent Fancy couldn't place—the *r*'s and *a*'s were all wrong.

"Ma'am," Fancy began hesitantly, reluctant to contradict. "I *didn't* seek you out. You called me."

"And you came. You didn't have to." Cherry released her. "No one else did."

Fancy scuffed her shoe on the path, feeling the burden of conversation.

"Are you shy?"

"I never do the talking."

"You should. People would listen." She brushed the backs of her fingers against Fancy's throat. Fancy felt a tingle, as though Cherry had soaked her fingers in menthol.

"What is this place?"

When Cherry smiled, she looked so much like Madda it was creepy. "What would you like it to be?"

Fancy thought about it, and between one blink and the next she and Cherry were in the cellar.

"I'm sorry." Fancy chewed her finger, her words muffled and ashamed. "I don't know why I chose here."

"Don't you?" Cherry didn't seem upset to find herself in the Bonesaw Killer's lair. "You're more in control here. Happier."

A moontree sprouted painlessly between Cherry and the cot, shooting up and then spreading quickly, like a beach umbrella. Unlike the moontree at Cherry Glade this one was alive. It had deep purple leaves and tight white buds like pursed mouths that would only open in the moonlight. Fancy was amazed that such a huge tree could fit in her small cellar, but somehow it did.

"Now we're both at home," said Cherry, satisfied, descending gracefully to the floor. She patted the space beside her, and so Fancy sat next to her and marveled at the way Cherry glowed, even in the shade of the tree.

"If you lie beneath a moontree, you'll die in thirty days," she added, quoting a well-known Porterene superstition. The moonflower buds hung quivering over Fancy's head, like fat acid drops waiting to drip and burn her.

"The reason people die in thirty days is cuz those flowers are poisonous."

Cherry reached up without looking and plucked one of the flower buds. "So are lies." The plucked bud bloomed in Cherry's hand, fragrant and intoxicating. And toxic. Cherry pressed the flower into Fancy's hands.

"I want to talk about what you wished for," said Cherry. "And I want you to be honest."

"I want me and Kit and Madda to stay together. I don't

want anything to split us up." The flower seemed to draw the words from her. "And I keep thinking, for that to happen me and Kit need to be able to get rid of people without getting caught. People like the old man."

"You already got rid of the old man. You won't get caught."

"But it's not just him. I'm thinking about the future, too. Kit and me, we are who we are. That won't change. And then there's Franken."

"You want to get rid of Franken?" Cherry said, disapprovingly. "You saved his life—that makes you responsible for him."

"I *have* been responsible. He's still alive. So far. We decided to give him a lobotomy, but that might accidentally kill him. Or it might not work the way we need it to. I'd feel better if I had something more certain. Like a doorway to shove him through."

"If you want a door to open, all you need is a key."

"This?" She showed Cherry the silver Porterene key she always carried on her necklace.

"That's the wrong kind. For what you need you'll have to go into the dark park."

"The dark park?" Fancy's stomach dropped to her feet, and she wondered briefly if that was what evisceration felt like. "No way. I'm not going in the *dark park*."

"If you want to get rid of Franken without 'getting rid' of him, it's the only way. I'll help you as much as I'm able, because we're kin. But if you want this, you'll have to earn it."

Fancy remembered all the stories she'd heard about the dark park—*hundreds* of stories—about people who had entered it and were never seen again.

"Maybe Kit and me should just be satisfied with a trip to the South Seas."

"*You* want to go to the South Seas. Not your sister."

"Kit likes what I like. And we like to do things together. She even made a wish for us to be together forever."

"Did she?" Cherry stood and crossed the room toward a kinetoscope exactly like the one in Fancy's cellar. She knew it wasn't her kinetoscope, though, because this one had the crank that hers was missing. Cherry waved Fancy over and cranked the kinetoscope, but instead of an image appearing on the screen, the image projected around them, so that Fancy felt like she was standing in the middle of a film. A film starring her sister, whose flickering, sepia image sat at their desk in the sleeping porch writing "true love" in large red letters on a piece of paper. She even drew a heart around the words before putting the paper into her pink bottle.

Fancy stood in shock as the image disappeared. Cherry had released the crank and simply watched her.

"True love? She wasted a wish on *true love*?"

"That's what she wants."

"It is not! Besides, who's there for her to fall in love with? Everybody in town hates us."

"They wouldn't if you and Kit were less selfish. Gifts are meant to be shared."

"What gifts?"

Cherry turned the crank again. The kinetoscope projected an image of Fancy and Kit giggling at the images in the bubbles of Madda fighting the mean women. The image vanished almost as quickly as it had arrived.

"That's no gift," said Fancy. "Well . . . I guess having the sight is sort of a gift, but it's mostly useless except for eavesdropping. Or make-believe."

"Because that's all you use it for." Cherry stroked the kinetoscope. "Finding the key will expand your ability."

"Which one? The sight or killing?"

"Either one."

Fancy studied Cherry carefully, heart thumping. "You don't mind? About us being killers?"

"Why should I mind? I'm not your judge. I'm your kin—I only want you to be happy."

"Killing doesn't make me—" Fancy rethought the wisdom of lying under the moontree. "Maybe it makes me a *little* happy. But Kit talked about having a hole inside her. I have it too." Fancy hadn't known that was true until she heard the words pouring out of her mouth. "And not even killing can really fill it."

"Maybe because you don't use it to make others happy. A world of people could use your help."

"Helping people." Fancy took out her bubble solution. "You sound like Kit."

"More than you do. Strange that two girls who swear they are the same person have so little in common."

"We *are* the same," she said, filling the cellar with bubbles. "We share everything."

"Then why are you here without her?"

Cherry extended her palm, and one of Fancy's bubbles settled into it and expanded until it was so large, Fancy could no longer see Cherry behind it. Because Kit was inside it, wandering away from the bottle-filled moontree, stretching as if waking from a deep sleep. She looked around, confused, as if she'd lost something.

"She's looking for me," said Fancy, feeling a twinge of guilt as she put her toy away. "How do I get back?"

But she couldn't see Cherry around the huge bubble, and not through it. She reached out to Kit, and the bubble exploded.

Fancy gasped, all the breath knocked out of her. She blinked to find not only the bubble gone, but the cellar and Cherry gone as well. There was only the dark and the path, glittering pinkly but dimming like a guttering candle flame.

Fancy raced back the way she had come, frightened of what would happen if the path vanished before she could return to her family. And it had taken such a long time to reach Cherry. The path would probably fade before she was even halfway—

Fancy rushed out of the dark, otherworldly woods and into the glade, blinking at the brightness, wincing at the loud voices surrounding her even as she welcomed the noise. She'd never been so glad to be among people.

"Fancy, what's wrong?"

It was Madda. Fancy, blinded by so much light after so much darkness, stumbled and fell. Into someone's lap.

"Man. I didn't think Cherry'd grant my wish *this* fast."

Fancy's eyes adjusted and narrowed on Ilan, grinning at her in extreme close-up. She shoved him into a plate of corn on the cob in her hurry to flee his grip. She ran to Madda, who was sitting across from him.

"Why are you sweating like that? And shaking?" Madda felt her forehead. "You getting heatstroke?" She poured Fancy a cup of lemonade. "Drink this, and stay out of the sun for the rest of the day."

Fancy leaned against Madda's side and drank the lemonade, glaring at Ilan the whole time. He was still just sitting there, dabbing at the smears of butter on his dress shirt. "What's *he* doing here?"

"He came to keep me company." Madda smiled at him. "I told you, we're old friends."

He seemed a lot more relaxed than the last time she'd seen him, less tense. Maybe because his brother wasn't around.

"That's the second time I heard you talk in public," he said, smiling at Fancy. "Your ma said you could, but I didn't believe it."

"Whyn't you go talk to your *own* mother?"

"Fancy!"

"I can't." He gave her a brittle smile. "She pissed off when I was ten."

Madda reached over and smacked Ilan upside the head. "Don't say 'pissed.'"

He rubbed his ear good-naturedly. "Sorry. You might be wrong about her not being ready to socialize, though. She looks ready enough for me."

"I don't mean physically. Stop leering at her."

"I'm not leering. I'm *appreciating*."

"Oh, well, that's different, then."

The familiarity between them was infuriating. Fancy backed away from it, out of Madda's arms. "Where's Kit?"

Madda's jaw dropped. "Don't you know?"

"She's with Gabe," said Ilan, still appreciating her. "I can see through your dress."

Madda groaned, staring at Fancy as if she'd never seen her before. "What did I tell you about wearing a slip? And a bra! Good Lord."

Fancy crossed her arms over her chest and hid behind Madda. Ilan, unable to look through her clothes, was forced to make eye contact.

"They're over there in the trees," he said. "Near the girls playing jump rope."

Madda grinned. "*They?*"

Fancy bolted from the table, past the girls singing "Shimmy, shimmy, cocoa pop!" and glimpsed Kit and Gabriel through the trees. They were slow-dancing to "Signed, Sealed, Delivered," which was *not* a slow song, and sharing an ice-cream cone. Gabriel was almost a head taller than Kit, and it was strange to see him towering over her—Kit had always seemed so much bigger than everyone else.

"Why're you being so nice to me?" Gabe asked.

Kit took a lick of the vanilla ice cream—Kit didn't even like vanilla ice cream!—and then held the cone to Gabriel's mouth. "You think I'm nice?" She was surprised and open, letting him see her.

"A nice change." He seemed to like what he saw.

"From what?" When she held the cone out of reach, he tickled her until she lowered her arm.

"People who don't know how to act around me," he said. "People who think I need to be patted on the head or something. Because of what happened to my pop. You know?"

"I know."

He let her go long enough to unfasten his necklace. "Take this."

She hesitated, staring at the cross dangling from the end of it. "I'm not religious. Not really."

"That's not why I'm giving it to you." Since she wouldn't

take it, he fastened it around her neck himself. "Look. It's got my name carved on it. So now you get to carry me close to your heart."

"And between my boobs."

"I told you"—he wrapped her in his arms—"I'm always at the right place at the right time."

They leaned in close.

"Kit!"

Fancy charged forward as they jerked away from each other guiltily.

"That's . . . *unsanitary*." She pointed to the ice-cream cone in Kit's hand.

"You should feel honored," Kit told Gabriel. "Fancy only talks around people she likes."

"I wasn't talking to him!" Fancy grabbed Kit by the hand and pulled her away so sharply her ice-cream cone tumbled into the grass.

"Damn it, Fancy."

"Why ain't you with your brother?" she asked Gabriel, ignoring Kit. "He don't care enough about you, so you gotta come over and bother my sister?"

Gabriel jerked as if he'd been pushed in the back.

"Stay away from my sister!" Fancy grabbed Kit's hand and stalked off, dragging Kit behind her.

But Kit didn't want to be dragged. She jerked free of Fancy's grip. "What's your problem?"

"Don't act like *I* did something wrong, when you're the one who didn't even notice I was gone."

"Gone where?"

"I was off in the woods. Cherry called me."

"*Our* Cherry?" said Kit, first stunned, then disbelieving. "Were you dreaming? I didn't hear anything except bottles tinkling." A faraway look clouded Kit's eyes. "Like a woman laughing."

"I didn't hear any laughter. Just a voice. Cherry's voice."

"You met Cherry?" Kit saw the truth in Fancy's eyes and met it with awe. "Holy shit, Fancy! What did she say?"

"You didn't notice I was gone. Or is it that you didn't care cuz you were too busy making kissy-face at that holy-rolling weirdo?"

Kit looked back at Gabriel guiltily. He stared at her, too, like he wanted to come over but didn't dare. Fancy poked out her tongue at him.

"Maybe Cherry put a spell on me," Kit said.

But Fancy wasn't ready to let Kit off that easily. "She said you wished for true love. Even though you were *supposed* to wish for us to be together forever. How could you do that to me? For a boy you don't even know. And who doesn't know you. He called you *nice*. Not only is he a weirdo, he's brain-dead."

"I could be nice if I wanted," Kit snapped. "It's easy when you hang around with nice people."

"So go be nice to him!"

Fancy stormed away, and even though she was angry—Kit thought that weirdo was nicer than her?—it pleased her to see Kit's shadow intermingling with hers as Kit hurried to keep up.

At their isolated picnic table Fancy was glad to note that Ilan had joined the long list of people who had abandoned their family.

Fancy came up behind Madda, who was clearing away the food, and hugged her. "I'm tired. Can we go home now?"

"We sure can." She squeezed Fancy back. "I don't know about you two, but I had enough socializing for a year."

"Two years," said Fancy. She looked at Kit, expecting her to say, "Three years." Any other time she would have.

But Kit was too busy staring at Gabriel.

FROM FANCY'S DREAM DIARY:

I saw CHERRY hanging out at FOUNTAIN SQUARE. I said hi, but she tried to pretend like she didn't know me. WHEN I finally got her to speak, she called me FRANNIE. BITCH.

CHAPTER NINE

Fancy snatched "Singin' in the Rain" off the phonograph and whirled it like a Frisbee across the room.

"Hey! I was listening to that."

"You got no business listening to something that cheerful," said Fancy. She abandoned her losing hand of solitaire to rifle through the crate below the phonograph stand for a more acceptable record.

Madda had long since left for work, and both Fancy and Kit were at the tea table with only the dim orange glow of a hurricane lamp to keep back the darkness. The sisters, fresh from their cold-water baths, had stripped down to their sleep clothes. They could have been haunts, so still and somber-eyed in the half-dark.

Fancy put "My True Story" by the Jive Five on the phonograph, a depressing song completely in synch with her mood.

"Wanna play beauty shop?" Kit asked, waving her gooey nail brush practically under Fancy's nose.

"I don't wanna play with you." Fancy dealt herself a new hand. "And why you gotta do your nails right next to me? You know I hate that smell."

"I have a bottle of polish that smells like violets. I could paint your—"

"No." She felt Kit's gaze on her but ignored it.

"If it's just the smell that's bothering you—"

"Nail polish is *not* what's bothering me."

"Fine." Kit disappeared under the tea table and then laughed when Fancy squealed at the touch of Kit's mouth on her bare foot. "I'm sorry. Sorrysorrysorry." Every time she said "sorry," she kissed Fancy's foot. "I'm sorry. How many is that? A hundred? Is that enough?"

"No. Ow!" Fancy snatched her foot away from Kit and rubbed the bite mark her sister had left on her instep.

Kit crawled out from beneath the table, frowning, and slumped on the stool. "It's not my fault my hormones keep getting in the way."

"It is your fault. You don't have to give in to it. Especially over a guy like *Gabriel*."

Over the sound of the music Fancy heard the ping of bugs bouncing off the screens. The lamps drew them. Sometimes, especially on moonless nights, the light in the sisters' room was the only light for miles.

"Why don't you like him, Fancy?"

"Cuz he's a big phony. Fussing at you for trying to rip out a guy's tongue. Meantime he's going around shoving sticks into people's eye sockets."

"It was just a severed head."

"That's not the point! Besides you already have one man. Isn't that enough for you?"

"What man? Franken?" Kit laughed. "I can't exactly take him home to mother. I can't take him anywhere. Except on Halloween." She clapped her photo-shoot-ready hands together. "You know what? If you take a hostage, we could double-date!"

Fancy shoved her finger into her mouth and pretended to gag.

Kit grabbed her hand. "Look at those nails. You need a manicure even more than you need polish."

Fancy snatched her hand back. "I said no."

Kit looked so dejected that the last of Fancy's anger sloughed away. "I forgive you, Kit. Okay? Let's just forget about what happened today." She reshuffled her cards. "But I like my nails the way they are. I like *everything* the way it is."

Kit looked at her own blood-colored nails and seemed more dejected than ever, yet she smiled. "Let's just do what you wanna do, then." She took the cards from Fancy and began to deal. "Whatever you want. Like we always do."

"Fancy . . ."

Fancy awoke in Kit's bed with Kit's breath in her hair, their chests rising and falling as one.

"Fancy . . ."

Fancy rolled over, rubbing her eyes and shoving Kit's knee out of the way. "What?"

But Kit was fast asleep.

"Fancy."

Fancy shot up, squeezing the sheets to her chest. The voice had come from across the room, from the phonograph Kit had forgotten to turn off; it hissed and crackled her name from the dark throat of its horn, darker even than the night surrounding it. She knew that voice.

Fancy shivered as the leaves washed against the screens. "Cherry?"

"You have an appointment to keep," hissed the voice, "in the dark park."

Fancy threw the covers over her head.

"Fancy." The voice was reproachful, but Fancy didn't budge. "Remember what's at stake, Fancy. Your future. Your sister's."

Fancy lowered the covers and got out of bed.

"Come here."

Fancy went forward and stopped before the phonograph.

"Reach inside."

Fancy reached into the icy throat of the horn, skin crawling, expecting it to clamp on her arm at any second. She flinched when her fingers bumped something.

"Take it."

Fancy grabbed the object and ripped free of the phonograph horn, her arm as numb as if it had spent thirty minutes inside a refrigerator.

"That will lead you where you need to go."

The object in her hand was a piece of paper, but in the dark she couldn't make out what was on it.

"Remember, you have to go alone. If you can't get it on your own, you don't deserve it."

"Get what?"

"The key. Good luck."

A sharp snap resounded in the room as the phonograph shut itself off.

Fancy chained her bike in the parking lot of St. Mike's, which was across the street from the dark park. The sun floated just over the horizon, the sky streaked with red as though God had killed someone and hadn't bothered to clean it up. But the dark park seemed to shun the light. Just the sight of those sunless, tangled trees, tall as skyscrapers and stretching wider than her eyes could see, had Fancy ready to hop back on her bike and pedal off. She lived in the woods and felt at home there, but the dark park was something else entirely—a creaking ancient forest full of doors and the monsters that had come through them. The only thing that made what she was about to do even remotely bearable was that the parking lot of St. Mike's was packed with shiny green trucks. Mortmaine trucks. They often patrolled the dark park, keeping the monsters that lived inside in check.

If things got out of hand, Fancy could just scream for help, and if the Mortmaine weren't too busy or too far away or too indifferent (as they sometimes were), they might come to her rescue. Maybe the Mortmaine presence in the dark park had sent all the monsters into hiding; maybe Fancy wouldn't even see one grotesquerie the whole time she was inside.

Thus comforted, Fancy crossed the street and entered the dark park.

To her surprise and relief she spied a sunlit trail and quickly began to follow it. She unfolded the paper she'd gotten from the phonograph as she walked along. It was as blank as it had been all morning. She had no idea why—

As Fancy watched, a pink dot appeared at the bottom of the paper, while at the very top appeared a thick black X. The dot was moving, inching turtle slow up toward the X. When Fancy stopped moving, so did the dot. When Fancy walked backward, the dot disappeared. But when she walked forward, the dot reappeared.

Assured that she was on the right track, Fancy hurried on.

Though the line on the map was perfectly straight, Fancy's

way was not. But no matter how she swerved, the dot kept straight on the map. When she chose the wrong fork in the road, whenever she went in the wrong direction, the dot vanished. Fancy panicked every time it happened, as though she herself had vanished, but she always managed to get herself turned in the right direction.

The dark park was normal at first, similar to the woods surrounding her home. But the deeper she went in, the weirder it got. The leaves seemed to reach out to her and trail along her arms and hair. Fancy pretended that the wind was doing it, even though there was no wind.

At one point Fancy passed a giant cobweb just off the path, with large bones stuck to it. Animal bones, Fancy thought, even though the partial rib cage and femur looked disturbingly human. Just old animal bones in a web that had been abandoned a long, long time.

"Hey!"

Fancy shrieked and broke into a run.

"Hey!"

The voice was human. Mortmaine?

Fancy slowed and looked back, startled to hear a human

voice after what seemed an eternity, but there was no one on the path.

"Hey!"

She peered through the dark trees to her left and saw it.

Fancy knew right away it wasn't human, no matter what it sounded like. It had a head, but the rest of it was some kind of yellow jelly. The nose it had given itself kept sliding into its mouth. As she watched, the jelly morphed itself into a human-ish shape and began to walk toward her. "Hey!" A bit of its yellow blob stretched from the center of its chest and made something that looked like a hand. "Hey!"

It reached for her, and when the hand it had made came into contact with the sun beaming along the path Fancy stood on, it caught fire. The thing shrieked and lost whatever human-ness it had tried to give itself. It shrank into a ball of goo and squished out of sight through the dark trees.

"Sunstroke," Fancy said, shaking so hard that her teeth were chattering. She then checked the map. "I've been in this sun forever; that's why I saw that."

She was three fourths along the line, almost at the X. It would be ridiculous to run screaming out of the woods when she had come so far. It was just sunstroke and animal bones and the wind. After Fancy got the key, she and Kit could both do whatever they wanted and there would never be any consequences, and for that Fancy could put up with anything.

Fancy squared her shoulders and continued forward along the path, and the dot on the map disappeared.

She backtracked until the dot reappeared and then scouted about but found no alternate trails, as she had the other times the dot had vanished. There was just the sunny path and the dark woods pressing malevolently on either side of her. She sidled to the right, and the dot disappeared, so she sidled left . . . and the dot stayed. She had to keep going left. Off the path. Into darkness. Where that slugboy thing was waiting for her.

Fancy stared horrified into the woods. She had to do it. For Kit she would do it. If she quit now, she'd never have the guts to come in again, not after what she'd seen. She took a deep breath and plunged into the trees at such a high speed she was sure her feet didn't touch the ground for at least five yards. As soon as they did, she stumbled and crashed head over heels right out of the trees and down an embankment. After a swift, stomach-churning free fall she landed on her butt in a green, piss-warm stream.

After several moments spent shaking and assuring herself that nothing was broken, Fancy stood and consulted the map that she'd still managed to hang on to through all her long fall. The pink dot was there and—thank God—closer than ever to the *X*. She tested possible directions and determined that she had to go upstream in the flowing water toward a bridge. She moved quickly; the sunlight was strong on the stream and made her feel safe, but the sooner this quest was over, the happier she'd be.

Before too long Fancy found herself standing beneath the bridge. As soon as she unfolded the map, the pink dot, which had moved directly over the *X*, floated off the page. Fancy gasped and flinched as it drifted up past her face to the bridge's underside, which someone—a crazy someone, obviously—had decorated with junk.

The pink dot rolled along the shiny pieces of randomness overhead—cracked CDs, wine bottles, a toy submarine, stained glass, tinfoil—and then came to a stop over a long brass . . . something.

Fancy jumped up and grabbed the thing by its wooden handle and struggled to pull it free. It was difficult, and the more she pulled on the handle, the more she saw what was holding all the junk to the bridge—slime. When she yanked the brass object free, a big drop of slime, pink slime, fell on her map. The line and *X* that had sustained her along the sunny trail had disappeared, replaced by one word in pink script: *RUN*.

Fancy looked up. Several amphibious creatures hung above her, hiding the shiny junk from sight, leering down at her. The slime attached to her map had dripped from the mouth of the creature directly above her. When the map jerked from her hand and into the creature's wide, wet mouth, Fancy realized it hadn't been slime, but a tongue.

Fancy took the map's advice and ran.

She raced along the stream and then up the embankment, going back the way she'd come. But the frogmen were quicker than she was, leaping over her head and catching hold of the trees, waiting for her to pass by, like it was some game. They were greenish-brown, blending so well with the trees that she didn't see them until they whipped their tongues at her, at her skin, stripping bits of it off. Snacking on her.

She made it back to the path, but she was no longer safe, assuming she had ever been safe. The frogmen were right behind her. Unlike the slugboy they had no fear of sunlight. A tongue on her leg tripped her up. She hit the ground on her back and watched the frogman greedily swallow a good bit of her shin. Fancy screamed and ran on mindlessly.

Straight into a green wall.

She bounced off a Mortmaine woman dressed all in green. With her were two companions: a Mortmaine boy, also in head-to-toe green, and a girl in purple—a Porterene, judging from the silver key dangling from her purple bracelet, though Fancy had never heard of a Porterene who wore color outside of church. And she had never heard of a Mortmaine wearing anything but green.

Fancy decided she was hallucinating, that her mind was trying to distract her from the fact that she was being eaten alive by frogmen.

"Look out!"

As the frogman's tongue came whipping at Fancy, the girl in purple snatched it in one gloved hand and used it to yank the creature forward. The frogman landed at her feet in a sprawl, and she stomped on it, grinding it beneath the heel of her purple boot like it was no more than a cockroach.

The other frogmen hesitated in the treetops, glancing at one another as if they knew the Mortmaine were nothing to tangle with. They leaped back the way they had come.

The first Mortmaine flipped her long black hair and said to the purple girl, "Don't go thinking you're a badass ninja. Toadies don't weigh much is all. That's why they're so easy to yank around."

The other Mortmaine whispered into the purple girl's ear, "You're my badass ninja."

She giggled and whispered back, "No, you're *my* badass ninja."

"Neither one of you is a badass ninja!" the first Mortmaine shrieked.

"That's not true, Shoko," said the purple girl, with some strange accent. "Poppa says I'm very definitely a ninja."

Shoko and the boy looked uneasily around the woods, like the purple girl's dad was going to jump down on them from the treetops. Shoko shoved Fancy toward the boy. "Wyatt, take her outta here so I can have at least a small break from you and Hanna playing kissy-face all day."

"Don't be such a hardass, Shoko," Wyatt said. "You're not fooling anybody." He walked Fancy out of the dark park, holding her hand the whole way because Fancy refused to let it go.

They left the dark park behind, and Fancy saw the sun shining, saw cars speeding by, felt a breeze on her skin, and started to believe that maybe she *wasn't* being eaten. That maybe she had survived.

"You okay, kid?" Wyatt asked her.

Fancy shook her head.

"Good. Maybe now you won't think you can go in and out of the dark park like it's the frigging mall. And if you do go in there again, for Christ's sake, don't run. You run, you might as well tattoo 'prey' on your forehead. Humans are predators, not prey. Always remember that."

Back at the parking lot of St. Mike's the Mortmaine sprayed her with something that he said would heal her stripped skin and then gave her a long hug until she stopped shaking enough to actually operate her bike. He nodded to the brass object still clutched in her fist.

"Was that worth it?"

Normally she wouldn't talk to anyone except for Kit, but it seemed rude when he had just come to her rescue in such a huge way.

Fancy said, "If it's not, I'm gone come back here and burn down this whole forest!"

He smiled. "Now you're thinking like a predator. A psychotic predator, but still an improvement."

* * *

Fancy rolled her bike into the garage and limped to the back of the house, her muscles sore from her romp through the dark park, her skin itching from the stuff the Mortmaine had sprayed on her arms and leg to heal them. Her hand hurt from her death grip on the brass object, which was the only bright spot. Despite her cowardly behavior, she had gotten what she'd gone into the dark park for. Now all she had to do was figure out what she was supposed to do with it.

She went into her room and saw Franken sitting at her tea table. In her chair. Drinking her tea. With her sister.

"There you are!" Kit jumped up to greet her. "I got your note about a quest. What happened? You look like two miles of rough road."

Fancy pulled away from Kit, feeling like she was hallucinating again. "What is he *doing* in here?"

"I just brought him up for some fresh air." Kit lowered her voice. "You were right about being greedy. It's like Dorothy said in *The Wizard of Oz*—you have to look for your heart's desire in your own backyard." She pointed to the brass object in Fancy's hand. "What's that?"

Fancy shoved Kit out of the way and stalked toward Franken,

who hurriedly offered her a cup of tea as though that would keep her off him. "I can go back to my room. I don't mind."

Fancy slapped the cup out of his hand. "Our cellar is not your room!" The cup hadn't made a satisfying enough crash, so she grabbed him and yanked him outdoors and down into the cellar, screaming the whole time. "You are *not* our guest! You are *not* our heart's desire! All you are is a *corpse* waiting to happen!"

She pushed him onto the cot, and Kit hurried to his side.

"This is my fault," Kit told him. "I should have talked to her first. Fancy doesn't handle change well. Or at all, really."

But Fancy wasn't paying attention to Kit. In the kinetoscope she'd caught a glimpse of Cherry standing in the happy place.

A flash of anger swept over her as she remembered the dark park ordeal she'd been forced to suffer through, but then Cherry dipped out of sight of the screen and returned holding a parrot-sized Franken in a canary cage.

When Cherry opened the door, shook Franken out, and let him scamper at her feet, Fancy wondered if Cherry knew she was mad and was doing funny tricks to make her laugh. But there was nothing clownlike about Cherry, who seemed a bit impatient, the way people got when they were trying to explain something to a person who just wasn't getting it.

Cherry pointed to something offscreen, and Fancy followed her finger and came to rest on the brass object in her own hand. Now that she saw it so close to the kinetoscope, she understood what it was.

"Holy smokes." Fancy brought it close to her face. "*That's* what this is?"

Cherry smiled, and the screen went black.

"What're you talking about?" Kit asked, snuggling with the life-size version of Franken on the cot.

"This is the missing crank to the kinetoscope." Fancy showed her. "The key Cherry wanted me to find. The key to the happy place. It's the *kinetoscope!*"

Fancy finally shared the story of what had happened to her at Cherry Glade, and how Cherry had helped her find the key to getting away with murder in the dark park.

"We use the scope to send people to the happy place," Fancy explained. "No body, no evidence."

"Send them how?" asked Kit, eyeing the crank dubiously, joining her sister so she could get a closer look at the crank.

"Like this."

Fancy ran her hand over the kinetoscope, and her fingers dipped into a hole on the side that was full of dust. Kit stood by uncertainly as Fancy affixed the crank into the hole where it fastened with a satisfying click.

"Here we go." The crank clicked as Fancy turned it, like a jack-in-the-box, only instead of hearing music, they saw the image of the happy place on the screen projected onto the four walls, and then the ceiling and the floor. The cellar was no longer around them.

"Fancy, what the hell?"

"Not hell," said Fancy, fitting into her happy place as surely as the crank had fit the kinetoscope. "Home."

FROM FANCY'S DREAM DIARY:

I called 911 to report Kit missing, but the dispatcher said that Kit wasn't missing. She put Kit on the phone, and I listened to her cry for a long time. When I asked Kit why she wouldn't come home, she said I had to first promise not to kill her if she told the truth. She kept asking, but I never gave her my word.

CHAPTER TEN

The sisters stood on the platform in the center of the garden, which was ringed by eight gigantic faceless golden statues in varying poses facing the garden. Between each statue sat a large elevated plot of earth that was bricked in stone in the shape of a circle. The sun glinted off the statues so brightly, it made Fancy's eyes water. She was so used to seeing this place through the lens of the kinetoscope that all the color had her head spinning. When Kit grabbed her and twirled her in a circle, that didn't help.

The platform was the centerpiece, surrounded by a green-scape dotted with fountains and flocks of pink flamingos that stared at the sisters as if to ask how they had gotten there. Animal topiaries lined the path that led from the platform and through the giant hedges that enclosed the garden.

Fancy pulled away from her gawping sister and looked for the kinetoscope, but it hadn't come over with them. Nothing in the cellar had. Except Franken.

He stared wide-eyed at the sky, lying on his back at the center of the platform as if he were still tied up on the cot, and Fancy felt a flash of irritation that she was sharing this moment with him and not just with Kit.

Kit danced over to him and dropped to her knees beside him. "You came over too!"

"Of course he came over," said Fancy. "I asked Cherry specifically for a way to get rid of Franken."

"Get *rid* of him?" Kit drew her finger across her throat.

Fancy tried not to roll her eyes, but it was hard. "Not like that. I mean get him out of our hair. Out of our cellar. And especially out of our sleeping porch."

"I can't believe you went into the frigging dark park. Alone. You must really not like Franken."

He lay still as death, his eyes closed, shirtless, his stitches like skinny zippers all over a tacky suit from the eighties. Tears were rolling down his face, which was also tacky. How dare he ruin her fun with his tears?

Kit put her hand on his shoulder. "Franken, it's okay."

"He doesn't realize he's free yet; that's all. It'll sink in." Fancy kicked Franken's feet out of her way and circled one of the statues so she could see it from the front. She had to tilt her head way back and squint her eyes to see all of it, it was that tall and bright.

"Maybe we should take him back."

"So you can cut on him some more?"

"At least then he'll show some life. This just seems cruel."

"He needs to learn to live without us. Without *you*. He's way too attached. Like hostages who get Helsinki syndrome or whatever and fall in love with their kidnappers. It's unhealthy."

Kit lit up. "You think he's in love with me?"

"Everybody flies the coop sometime," said Fancy, ignoring the question.

But Franken refused to fly away. He just lay there sniveling like a two-year-old.

Kit said, "Franken, don't be like that. This is good news. You're free now."

"Okay."

"No, I mean it this time." She smoothed Franken's mite-free hair.

"You're really letting me go?" His face was full of some odd emotion.

"Yep." Kit smiled, trying to be happy for him.

"I can go home?" Nervousness—that's what it was. Reluctance.

"Forget about home," Kit said. "That's over. This is your home now. It's really great here. Fancy and me used to sit in front of the kinetoscope for hours watching the happy-place people running around and having fun all the time like we used to before Daddy got arrested. You'll have fun here too, and if anybody gives you any lip, tell 'em Fancy sent you. It's her place."

"*Our* place," Fancy corrected her.

Franken leaned heavily against Kit as she helped him sit up. He stared all around and then winced as if the happy place had punched him in the face.

He whispered, "You killed me, didn't you? That's why I'm seeing all this—because I'm dead."

"If I had killed you," Kit whispered back, "you would know it. Believe me." She pulled him to his feet and held him up, their arms around each other. "And you sure don't feel like a corpse."

He was taller and, even ragged as he was, still bigger than Kit. He could have knocked her over the head if he'd wanted, but he didn't want to fight. He didn't want to be free. He wanted Kit.

Fancy wanted to puke. She left the statues and pulled Kit away from Franken. "I wanna see what's beyond the garden," she said. But when they hopped off the platform and onto the grass, frightening the flamingos into an awkward run, Franken tried to tag along.

"Not you." Fancy shoved him back toward the platform. "We don't want *you*."

The sisters left him sitting forlornly among the headless statues and ran beyond the gap in the hedges, exiting onto a hill overlooking a rustic village nestled in a green valley by the sea.

People milled about, sailing on the ocean in big white ships, frolicking on the beach, talking and laughing together on the streets of their village.

"It's just like in the scope," Kit breathed. "How weird is this?"

"Not just like," Fancy said, frowning. "There should be a hill."

"You mean this one we're standing on?"

"Another one. Just beyond the village."

A lush, green hill materialized in the distance, just small enough that a person could run up it without getting winded. Several children did just that, dragging their kites behind them like unruly dogs.

"There," Fancy said. "That's better. What?" she asked when Kit kept staring at her.

"How did you do that, witch?"

"Do what?"

"That hill just appeared out of nowhere, that's what. Out of *nothing*."

"Yeah?"

Fancy didn't understand Kit's astonishment. Being inside the kinetoscope was no different from being outside it, and she had been arranging and rearranging things inside the happy place for years.

Kit stood behind Fancy and wrapped her arms around Fancy's shoulders. "Do you have any idea how amazing you are? I wish I could do even half of what you can do."

"If it's in me, it has to be in you." She leaned back into Kit's embrace. "We're practically the same person."

"No, we're not. I feel it now, the difference between us. I never felt that before."

Fancy felt as if all the air had been squeezed from her lungs. "We're not different! Don't say that. You just have to concentrate."

Kit tried. She let go of Fancy and furrowed her brow at the village below.

"What're you thinking about?"

Kit unfurrowed and sighed. "Franken. He should be here, seeing all this, since he's gone live here now."

"We're in paradise, where we can make anything happen, and all you can think about is *Franken*?" She said his name so loudly, the happy-place people stopped everything and looked their way, attentive as meerkats.

"You brought him here," Kit reminded her quietly, as if she were trying to make a point about how loud Fancy was being.

"I brought him here to get rid of him."

"And you did, Fancy. So why can't we all have some fun now?"

"You wanna have fun with Franken? Fine. Let's *all* have some fun."

Fancy stormed back through the hedges to the Headless Garden, ignoring Kit's cries for her to wait and to calm down. Fancy did neither. Instead she jumped onto the platform where Franken was sitting looking glad to see them, to see Kit. And then she threaded her fingers through Franken's hair and twisted off the top of his head.

"Fancy!" Kit came to a stop before Franken, whose eyes had gone wide.

"What just happened?" he asked her.

"Hold this." Fancy dropped the top of his head to his lap, and he grabbed it, reflexively, then froze when he realized what he was holding.

Franken's brain was shiny and throbbing and bluish-gray.

"It's wrinkled like the old man's intestines!" Fancy exclaimed. It was almost beautiful to see a brain at work in its natural habitat, instead of floating in a liquid-filled jar, totally out of context. "Do you remember which part we have to cut out?" she asked her sister, who just gaped at her like a fish.

"Me neither," said Fancy. "I'll just cut it all out." She snapped her fingers at Kit. "Gimme your knife."

"Are you crazy?" Kit screeched, finally finding her voice. "You can't give him a lobotomy *now*. There's no point. Put his head back on."

"But you said—"

"Put it back!"

Fancy wrestled the top of Franken's head away from him—he didn't seem to want to let go of it—and twisted it back over his brain, feeling inordinately put out. "All you been talking about since you took him hostage is killing him."

"I changed my mind."

"Change it back! We can do anything here."

"I don't want to hurt Franken."

"No one would know."

"I'd know!" Giant pink wings sprouted from Kit's back.

It was Fancy's turn to gape as Kit spread her wings to their farthest point and squealed joyously.

"Holy shit, Fancy, are you seeing this?" Kit flapped her wings and knocked Fancy onto her butt as she shot six feet in the air, laughing until she thumped into something, feeling the air above her like a mime.

Fancy said nothing, but Kit wasn't bothered by her flight limitation, holding herself aloft on feathers as fluffy as goose down. With her black leggings and camisole she looked like a punk angel.

"You were right, Fancy. It *is* in me. I can change things too. We *are* the same. Isn't that great?"

The fluffy pink wings burst into flames.

Kit yelped and crashed to the ground, rolling and choking on the burned feathers fluttering about her face as the cellar reappeared around the sisters, shutting them out of the happy place.

"That's not who I am," said Fancy, almost conversationally, as she watched her sister burn.

FROM FANCY'S DREAM DIARY:

The sun beat so strongly on everything and was so oppressive that I decided to pluck it from the sky. I swallowed it and floated up, rising over the world, scorching everything in my path.

CHAPTER ELEVEN

Kit picked herself off the cellar floor, her arms wrapped around her body as curls of smoke arose from what was left of her camisole. Fancy stood before the kinetoscope, watching the screen so she wouldn't have to look at Kit, avoiding her sister's gaze as if they were strangers in a cold, claustrophobic elevator. As she watched Franken sift through the pile of ash and feathers on the ground below the platform, Kit moved in close and Fancy couldn't resist peeking at her sister, if only to reassure herself that Kit wasn't hurt. She wasn't, at least not physically.

The light from the screen made Kit's face look ghastly. "You set me on fire," she said, her words as pallid as her face.

"I didn't mean to," said Fancy, but Kit was already talking over her.

"You go on and on about how it's our place, and then as soon as I make one little change—"

"Who asked you to change anything?" The words tore out of Fancy, so big and loud they scared her. But not Kit.

"Don't yell at me, you little shit! You set me on fire!"

"Don't talk to me like that." Fancy stared into the kinetoscope, wishing fiercely that she were back in the happy place.

Kit grabbed her and spun her around so they were face to face. "Look around, Fancy. You're not in your imaginary kingdom anymore." She shoved Fancy to the floor and stood over her. "So now what?"

When Fancy tried to stand, Kit pushed her down again, harder than before, so Fancy decided to stay low—the position matched her mood. "I'm sorry." She spoke the words into her knees, not wanting to see the anger in Kit's eyes. When Kit didn't respond, Fancy looked up. Kit was no longer standing over her, but sitting on the cot.

She removed her switchblade and fooled with it like she always did when she was upset.

"Why'd you do it?" Kit said, her voice soft.

"I wanted the *wings* to go away. Not you. You weren't even hurt."

"Don't tell me I wasn't hurt!" She jabbed the knife at Fancy, who winced as though it had entered her flesh. "Those were *my* wings on *my* back. You don't even wanna know what that felt like."

Fancy squeezed her knees tighter. "Next time we go back, I'll let you set me on fire."

"Set yourself on fire. I ain't going back there."

"Don't talk crazy, Kit. We have to go back. Where else can we hide the evidence?"

"Evidence?"

"I told you what Cherry said. About how we need to help people. I figure she means we should protect them from pervs like the old man. Criminal types."

Kit put the knife away, a sure sign she was starting to come around. Kit never could stay mad for very long.

"How're we supposed to be able to tell? 'Excuse me, sir, we're thinking about cutting your throat, so could you tell us, are you a good witch or a bad witch?' People don't advertise themselves that way."

"Advertise!" Fancy sprang to her feet. "That's it!"

"What's it?"

Fancy ran up to the sleeping porch, Kit on her heels demanding to know what the big deal was.

Fancy knelt beside her bed and, from beneath it, pulled out the stash of fan letters stuffed in a Fanta carton.

"Them?" Kit sat on the floor near Fancy, her long legs cramped in the narrow space between their beds. "They hate us. And they're insane."

"Not all of them." Fancy settled against the nightstand and shuffled through the letters she'd dumped into her lap and started reading. "'I know people who need to be killed.'" Shuffle. "'I don't get why Guthrie killed nice people when there's so many jerks out there who deserve it way more.'" Shuffle. "'I wish I had it in me to do what he did.'" Fancy looked at Kit, a breeze rippling through the letters in her hand. "Know who does have it in 'em?"

Kit was all smiles. "Us?"

"Exactly!" They went through the letters, and when they had a list of people they felt good about, they wrote a letter to each one of them, choosing their words carefully.

"'So if you have a problem,'" said Fancy, scribbling furiously on their pink stationery, "'we'd love to hear about it.

Sincerely, the Cordelle sisters.'" Fancy finished the last letter with a flourish, and after shoving it into an envelope, she gave Kit a big hug.

Kit's halfhearted embrace worried Fancy, but when she looked into her sister's face, it wasn't lingering anger over the wing incident she saw, but thoughtfulness. "You think . . ." Kit paused, unusually hesitant. "When people find out what we're doing . . . when they realize we want to help . . . you think they'll like us?"

Fancy pushed out of her sister's embrace, laughing. "Who cares if people like us? *We* like us. Besides, nobody knows about the happy place but you and me. How could they find out? Even if someone tried to use the letters against us, where's the proof? No body, no crime."

Kit shoved the carton of letters under the bed, her hesitancy gone as if it had never been. "Franken knows."

Fancy scooped up the stack of envelopes and went in search of stamps. "Well, he's gone now."

She put the letters in the mailbox, and when she came back into the room, Kit was still leaning against the screen door. "I miss him."

Fancy stood next to her. "You'll get over it."

"Easy for you to say. You hate everybody." Kit reached back and rubbed her shoulders over the spot where her wings had been. The back of her camisole was almost completely burned away, though the skin beneath was smooth and untouched. "I felt like him and me were really starting to understand each other."

"The only thing a wolf understands about a rabbit is that it tastes good."

"Franken does taste good." Kit's face took on a gleam of sublime hunger. "His blood splashed on my face one time, so I licked it off. It was like V8. You sure we had to let him go?"

Fancy opened the porch door and hustled Kit out. "Positive. Come help me clean out the cellar."

They stripped the linens from the cot and scrubbed the cellar with bleach, eradicating all traces of Franken's temporary stay.

"There," Fancy said, satisfied with their thorough cleansing. "That's done."

"Good." Kit stretched the kinks out of her shoulders. "I gotta practice my scales. I wanna be tip-top for class tomorrow."

She threw the rag at Fancy, trusting her to catch it as she always did. Instead it smacked her in the face.

"I thought we weren't going."

Kit stared at the cot, thoughtful again. "I changed my mind."

"Why?" Fancy had a sudden urge to bleach the inside of Kit's skull, scour away the annoying bouts of thoughtfulness that kept gunking it up.

"You said it yourself," said Kit as she stomped up the cellar steps. "Everybody's gotta fly the coop sometime."

"I didn't mean you," Fancy said, but Kit was already gone.

Since Kit had decided to go to her music class, Fancy saw no reason to stay home getting dumber and dumber while Kit became advanced and sophisticated. So she rode her bike down to the square, to the Standard, an old movie palace with curtains and a balcony.

The art class, however, was not held in the pretty part of the theater, but in the attic, which could only be accessed by a narrow metal staircase that spiraled like a slide at a water park. Numerous fans blew in the cavernous room, yet it was still just short of sweltering. Sweat beads formed on Fancy's face almost immediately. The smell of paint and sour pickles crinkled her nose as she made her way past student work on the walls to the pairs of chairs and easels arranged in a circle. The room was large, but the class was small, consisting of a handful of kids roughly Fancy's age: a few she vaguely recognized from Portero High, but only one whose name she actually knew.

"Hey, Fancy."

Fancy took the chair next to Ilan's. She had to, since it was the only empty one in the room.

He looked like a work of art himself, like he had been purposely sculpted to look good from every angle. No matter how he turned his body, the light hit him in startling ways. His fingernails were stained with phthalo green. She tried to imagine his nails stained with blood like hers sometimes were, but she decided that green suited him better.

He leaned in and said, "I had a dream about you."

He smelled like a mountain. Fancy had no idea what mountains smelled like, but a mix of sun-baked rock and piney woods seemed about right. He leaned back and took his smell with him, leaving her with sour pickles.

Since they were in pairs, the teacher, Mr. Hofstram, had them draw a picture for each other that would serve as an introduction. An artistic business card, he had said.

Ilan drew quickly, finishing before the time was up. Fancy

gazed at the paper he'd given her, a skillful drawing of them kissing.

"That's what I dreamed about." He rested his arm against the back of her chair. Fancy thought about stabbing it with one of the X-Acto knives strewn irresponsibly around the room. But, unlike Kit, she was used to ignoring such urges.

"My dreams always come true. Did you know that?"

She decided not to look him in the eyes ever again. It was too much like being shoved over the edge of a ravine.

Instead of answering, Fancy drew on her own paper. She used the same colored pencils and took even less time with her drawing than Ilan had. She handed the paper to him.

"'Drop. Dead.'" Ilan turned the the paper this way and that, studying the letters. "It's not really a *drawing*." But he smiled as he spoke, a smile that hit her in the chest like a rock.

It was really unfair, this ability he had to attack her without even touching her. Fancy knew she'd have to be on guard around Ilan; he was tricky.

The "drop dead" drawing was the best work Fancy did for the next two weeks. She was painfully inartistic, as Mr. Hofstram was happy to constantly point out to her.

She went home to find Kit at the piano, practicing. Fancy flopped next to her on the bench and threw her arms around her, making Kit laugh.

"How was class?" she asked, as if she couldn't guess the answer.

"I still suck. The room is still too hot. Everybody still ignores me." Not *everybody*, but in addition to not looking at him, she refused say anything about Ilan, refused to even speak his name. His interest in her was so inexplicable Fancy had no words for it.

"Want me to go to your class and beat everybody up?"

Fancy thought about it. "Not right yet." She straightened and picked out a few notes on the piano that vaguely resembled "Three Blind Mice." "How was your class?"

"Awesome." Kit's face lit up. "We're learning 'Beyond the Sea.' It reminded me of you, how you always wanna sail away. Listen."

Kit played it for her, singing the words jauntily. She had a nice voice when she wasn't screeching at the top of her lungs.

"You think he kept his word and went home to his girl?" said Fancy as the last notes died away. "Or you think she's still waiting for him?"

"If he did leave her, she probably moved on." Kit replayed the song in a different key. "That's what happens when people split. They get over it."

"If you left, I wouldn't get over it."

"Sure you would. I'd write to you. Eventually. Ow!"

Fancy pinched her sister again for good measure. "That reminds me: Did you get the mail?"

The music came to a halt. "Oops."

"Oops?" Fancy shot off the bench. "You can't be forgetting like that, Kit," she said, hurrying out to the front porch. When she came back inside holding a stack of letters, she was still grumbling. "Madda would freak if she knew about all this."

"She wouldn't," said Kit. "It's not like she doesn't know people hate us."

"But if she saw the *other* mail," Fancy insisted. "If she knew people wanted us to kill for them—"

"Do they?" Kit looked at the mail in Fancy's hands. "Has anyone written back asking for our services?"

Fancy sat on the bench, and together the sisters went through the mail, but it was the same old hateful tirades.

"I knew advertising would be a waste of time," Kit said, dumping her share of the letters into Fancy's lap.

"It's only been a couple of weeks."

"Only? It's been forever since we killed that old man. And now that Franken's gone, I don't have anybody to cut on. Not that that was particularly satisfying, but at least it was something. You know how when you stab people, it's like plugging into them? You feel their hearts beating; you feel their blood flowing. You see their struggle for life, and in that moment they start to seem real and not like windup toys. I miss that. That realness. You know what we should do?"

"What?"

"Hunt."

"Hunt what?"

"Whales, you stupid girl—what do you think? Bad guys! If people won't ask for our help, let's just volunteer it."

"So now you think you can just spot 'em on the street, easy-peasy?"

"We're predators, Fancy. Predators can always sniff out prey." Kit shot up from the piano bench and grabbed Fancy, nearly making her spill the letters all over the floor. "Let's go catch some bad guys!"

Fancy pulled away from Kit, wondering why her sister had to be so antsy about everything. "We can't just *go*. We have to think this through."

"What's to think about? The great thing about having a killer instinct is that it negates the need to think."

"We can't just go club people on the street and drag 'em back to the cellar."

"The cellar." Some of Kit's enthusiasm cooled a bit. "Right."

"Right. We need to test whether the kinetoscope works outside the cellar. Otherwise, we can't cover our tracks. Go wait for me in the backyard."

A few moments later Fancy joined Kit in the kitchen garden with the kinetoscope. Without the stand, it was just big enough to be a pain to carry any great distance, but small enough to cart on Fancy's bike or rest in her lap. Kit sat, absently picking snails off the tomato plants as Fancy cranked the kinetoscope . . . but nothing happened.

"See?" said Fancy. "Maybe it *does* only work in the cellar. There's no way we can convince all the bad guys to come home with us."

"Don't give up just yet. You know how you can only see things inside small spaces: a puddle, or a cup—"

"Of course!" Fancy shot up, surveying the expanse of forested land. "There's just too much space!"

The sisters hurried into the house and cranked the kinetoscope in the shuttered living room. The walls flickered slightly, but that was all.

"Well, this is the biggest room in the house," Fancy said, looking at the high ceilings and the tall shuttered windows they supported.

They next tried their inner room, one of the smallest rooms in the house aside from the bathrooms. Fancy turned the crank once and then joined Kit's laughter when the happy place immediately projected on the walls. She felt the kinetoscope vanishing in her hands, so she stopped cranking before the happy place could fully form around them, and the walls returned to normal.

"Well, that settles that." Fancy flopped onto the bed.

"So we have to be somewhere small and enclosed or it won't work. Which means that instead of people coming to our cellar, we'll have to convince them to let us into their homes. So that we can slaughter them."

"You're good at talking to people," Fancy said, surprised to hear the uncertainty in her normally confident sister's voice.

"I know, but . . . sometimes when you talk to people, it turns out they're kinda interesting. Interesting people might be harder to kill than, you know, dullards."

"If they're bad enough, it won't matter how interesting they are." She stood and balanced the kinetoscope on her hip. "Go get the old man's ear. And a steak knife."

"Why?"

"It'll be safer in the happy place than here where Madda can find it."

"And the knife?"

"For stabbing. Der."

Kit ducked into the kitchen and came back minutes later with a steak knife and the jar holding the severed ear. "How many ears do you think this thing can hold?" Kit asked.

Fancy put the jar and the knife in her pocket. "Let's find out, shall we?"

FROM FANCY'S DREAM DIARY:

ILAN RAN UP TO ME IN CLASS AND GAVE ME A BIG HUG. I TOLD HIM TO GET OFF ME BUT HE SHOWED ME A DRAWING OF US HUGGING AND SAID I HAD TO LET HIM. I TOLD HIM THAT WAS A FAKE DRAWING CUZ IN THE REAL ONE WE WERE KISSING, AND HE SAID, SO KISS ME THEN! BUT INSTEAD OF KISSING HIS LIPS, I BIT THEM. HARD.

CHAPTER TWELVE

The sisters had to bike around their upsquare neighborhood for two hours before they finally happened upon a villainous situation: Five boys, just a few years older than Kit, were beating up another boy in the parking lot of Wyverly Park, a few miles from their home.

The boys were transies, transients, which was how Porterenes thought of the outsiders who wandered into their town, because they almost never stayed long. Transies lacked Porterene fortitude and tended to end up fleeing town in terror or getting eaten by monsters in a relatively short amount of time. There were, of course, a few special individuals who moved into town and were able to tough it out.

These boys, however, were not special.

The sisters stopped at the edge of the parking lot and watched, but the boys, intent on their victim, didn't notice them.

"You know how rare it is to get one of these freaks alone?" said one boy wearing smoky aviator glasses. He and the boy in the orange Longhorns T-shirt he was speaking to weren't involved in the beating but were instead sitting in the shade on the hood of a red Escalade, drinking beer.

"I know," said Longhorn. "Why're you alone, freak?" he yelled. "Are you such a freak that even in a town full of freaks nobody wants anything to do with you?"

"Or did the *monsters* eat all your friends," said the aviator boy, "and you're the only survivor?" All the boys laughed at this.

"Why're you wasting your aggression on him?" said Kit.

The boys jumped and turned to see the sisters behind them on the other side of their truck. The silence was so deep Fancy could hear the whack of a ball from the tennis court nearby.

"Why beat him up?" Kit continued, eyeing the scrawny, bleeding boy curled up in a handicapped parking space. He seemed even scrawnier compared to his attackers, who were fit, like they spent all day baling hay or something vigorous and outdoorsy like that. "There's barely enough of him to make it worth your while. If you really wanna take out your frustrations on someone, you should go find a crowd and have a good old-fashioned rumble!"

"Is that what we should do?" asked aviator boy.

Kit nodded. "There's a party at the water tower teeming with huge, strapping guys who can take a much better beating than him. Me and my sister can show you where it is."

The aviator boy looked her over. "I see all that black, so I know you gotta be from here. Why would you help us out?"

"Because I know that if y'all start any shit at the water tower," Kit admitted cheerfully, "you will get toasted. And I wanna see it. Is that a good enough reason?"

The boys laughed and piled into the truck, leaving the scrawny boy motionless on the ground.

The car was large, but then so were the boys. Fancy had to climb into one guy's lap in the backseat in order to fit, a boy wearing green Bermuda shorts, which Fancy resented. Only the Mortmaine wore green, and this bully was as far from a Mortmaine as a person could be and still be human.

"*They're* gonna get toasted," said the green-clad boy, squeezing Fancy too tightly. She wanted to smack at his wandering hands, but she had a death grip on the kinetoscope, peering into the round screen and letting the view of the happy place settle her nerves. "And after we rumble with them, maybe we'll rumble with the two of you." More laughter.

"You hear that, Fancy?" Kit was crammed in between the aviator boy and Longhorn in the front seat. "We get to be the spoils of war. But that's only if you losers win. What're the odds of that happening, Fancy?"

Fancy was already turning the crank. "Zero percent."

Almost immediately the view inside the kinetoscope appeared outside, creeping along the interior of the truck until the world beyond the windows was hidden from view.

"Dude?" The boy sitting farthest from Fancy in the back-seat had a tattoo of a girl on his arm and was pointing at the pink flamingo staring at him through the window. "Are you seeing this?"

The only answer was a collective gasp as the window, along with the entire truck, disappeared. They hit the headless statue platform on their butts, flamingos scurrying from the com-motion. The aviator boy scrambled to his knees, gawking at the ring of statues as if he thought they might come alive and crush him underfoot. "This isn't possible," he whispered, and then looked to Kit for confirmation.

"Sure it is." She leaned toward him like a black mamba ready to strike. "Anything is possible here, even that rumble you wanted to have. Remember?" She snapped open her switchblade. "So okay. Here we go!" Kit removed the aviator boy's sunglasses and jammed her switchblade into his left eye. As the aviator boy fell over dead, Kit put on his shades and chuckled.

"Look at me!" she yelled to Fancy. "I'm a pilot!"

But Fancy was busy with her own boy. The kinetoscope had vanished, leaving Fancy's hands free to grab the steak knife she had hidden in the deep pocket of her shorts. She used it to stab the boy with the green shorts in the chest. She had to try a couple of times because the knife kept glancing off his ribs. The third time was the charm, however, and before he managed to knock her off his lap, she sank the blade into his heart. She had a hell of a time trying to pull the knife free, though. Stupid ribs.

The bullies had wanted a rumble, but now that they'd gotten their wish, they were almost completely paralyzed. That's why transies were so easy to kill—they wasted so much time gaping and questioning every little thing, they didn't notice important things like the fact that they were being slaughtered.

Longhorn, for instance, had scooted past Kit and was shaking the aviator boy's shoulder, completely ignoring the hole Kit had put in the boy's head by way of his eye. "John? *John?*" He gaped at Kit. "What did you do to him, bitch?"

"I stabbed him!" she exclaimed, flicking eye and brain matter from her switchblade. "God! Why am I always having to explain that to people?" She slashed her knife at Longhorn, but he jerked back and up, so instead of slashing his throat, she only nicked his chest.

Longhorn took off, leaping from the platform down to the garden. His flight broke the others' paralysis, and the remaining two boys also scrambled away. The sisters took off after them—Kit went after Longhorn, and Fancy, after she finally got her knife free, went after the boy who had sat in the middle with her in the backseat. She chased him across the greenscape, past quacking flamingos and topiaries shaped like butterflies. Her boy was as swift as an antelope, and Fancy knew she'd never be able to catch up. If only she had a way to block his path—

Two men, huge and burly and dressed in white like orderlies at an insane asylum, stepped out of the hedges. Their coveralls roared like an angry sea as they darted forward and caught the antelope boy by the arms, one on either side. The antelope boy was huge, but between the two men in white, he looked like a gnat.

Fancy, startled by their sudden appearance, had frozen, but they didn't do anything or even speak. They simply hauled the boy back toward her and then stood, as though awaiting instruction.

Fancy looked around for Kit and saw her riding Longhorn's back like a rodeo clown, stabbing him in the neck and shoulders and screaming, "Yee-haw!" while he tried in vain to buck her off.

The men in white seemed harmless, though, so Fancy stabbed the antelope boy since they were thoughtfully holding him still for her. But his ribs *also* deflected the knife. Stabbing people in the heart was much more difficult than she'd ever imagined it would be. And the antelope boy wouldn't stop screaming. In a fit of pique, Fancy stabbed him in the throat just to stop the noise, but when she pulled out the knife, blood sprayed everywhere.

Fancy skipped back to avoid the mess and landed on her butt in the grass. She glared at the boy, who was making a horrible gargling racket. She knuckled blood out of her eyes and screamed, "Can't somebody shut him up?"

One of the men released antelope boy and snapped his neck. The silence was luscious.

Fancy regarded the men thoughtfully as they let the boy drop to the ground and stood at attention. They wanted *her* attention. "Thank you," she said generously. "Breaking their necks is much neater than stabbing them. And then getting blood in your ears." She got to her feet, tilting her head to the side and waggling her earlobe. "Amazing, all the orifices that blood can seep into."

"And out of," said Kit, coming up behind her, watching the men with great interest. "Who're they?"

"I dunno. Minions. Isn't that what you call a person who does your bidding? A minion? Minions, bow to my sister."

They bowed and Fancy laughed. "See?"

"Your *bidding*?" Kit said, mockingly. "Look at the little raja."

"Rajas are boys. You must address me as maharaja, if you please." Fancy looked around the garden, counting the bodies scattered here and there in the warm sunshine. "There's one missing," she said. "Where's the one with the tattoo?"

"Through those hedges, I guess," said Kit. At some point during her wild ride with Longhorn, she must have lost the aviator glasses. She bounced in place like a sprinter before a race starts. "Wanna go run him down?"

"No need. Minions!" Fancy snapped her fingers. "Find the tattooed boy and bring him here at once."

The minions disappeared through the hedges that separated the garden from the rest of the happy place, and Fancy grinned ear to ear. "How cool is that?"

Kit seemed to find it more freaky than cool—she had stopped bouncing. "Who *are* those guys?"

"Happy-place people. And happy-place people have to do whatever I want. Watch." Fancy stared hard at the hedges, and moments later people entered carrying armchairs and a pail full of ice and drinks. They weren't dressed in white like the minions; they were just ordinary people, women and men and even a small kid, who looked pleased at the chance to offer Fancy any assistance they could. As she directed them to set up the chairs on the headless statue platform, she noticed that, unlike her and Kit and the dead bodies lying upon the ground, none of the happy-place people cast a shadow. Neither did the statues.

"You can go now," Fancy told them, trying not to feel spooked as they hurried silently past her and left the garden.

"Wow," said Kit, looking gratifyingly impressed as she sat with her bottle of lemonade. "This is the life."

Fancy sat in her own chair and clinked bottles with her sister, glad to see her in such a good mood after all her whining about her inability to "connect" with other people. Whatever that meant. "Did you get any more ears?" she asked.

Kit gasped and nearly choked on her lemonade. "I forgot! Wait here." Kit hurried off the platform, switchblade in hand, and Fancy watched her flit from body to body collecting ears like a bee collecting pollen. Kit returned with four ears stacked in the palm of her hand.

"I don't wanna put them in with *him*," she said when Fancy removed the jar from her pocket and unscrewed the lid. She wagged her finger at the old man's ear. "You'd like being surrounded by the flesh of young boys, wouldn't you?"

Fancy grimaced at the stench rising from the jar. "We gotta bury this thing. It's disgusting."

"I considered preserving it, but decomposition has its own beauty. Don't be such a girl."

One of the elevated, stone-bordered circles of earth that separated each statue drew Fancy's eye.

She walked to it and sat on the stone, trying to shake the old man's ear out and onto the dirt. The ear, however, was stuck tight to the bottom of the jar, so she buried the whole thing, lid and all, pressing it into earth so spongy she didn't need to dig.

She looked for her sister, and then rolled her eyes. "Kit, stop molesting that statue and bring the ears over."

Kit poked her head out from under the loincloth of one of the male statues. "You know these things are anatomically correct?"

"*Kit!*"

"All right, all right. I'm coming."

She gave Fancy the ears and watched her bury them in a ring around the spot she'd buried the jar. Moments later the minions reentered the garden.

"Lemme go, lemme go!" screamed the tattooed boy as the minions hauled him forward. He was battered and bruised as though he had put up quite a struggle, but he was otherwise unharmed.

The sisters left the platform and joined the minions on the ground.

"Lemme go!" he screamed again.

"Let you go where?" asked Kit. "Back home so you can beat up other people just because they're different? What did you call that boy at the park? A freak? You wanna shake hands with a real freak?" She showed him her switchblade.

"I'm sorry!"

"I bet you are."

"I mean it. We grew up hearing these stories about y'all." He was talking fast, eyes on the knife. "We didn't know they were true!"

"Stories?" Kit exchanged a look with Fancy. "About us?"

"About Porterenes. About Portero. About how there's monsters and doors to other worlds." He looked around and the fight seemed to go out of him all at once; he started crying. "I didn't know it was true. Please let me go. I'll go back and tell everybody I know it's the truth."

"Like Scrooge," said Kit, amused. "You've seen the error of your ways and now you'll do nothing but good deeds all the rest of your days?"

"Yes, I swear!"

"What do you say, Fancy?" Kit gave her a strange look.

"Stab him."

"Really?" The strange look deepened. "You don't wanna set him free? Like with Franken?"

"I said stab him!"

The strange look was replaced by one Fancy knew all too well—annoyance. "I'm not one of your minions, *maharaja*. You stab him."

"I'm sick of stabbing things." Fancy threw the steak knife, and the tattooed boy yelped as it landed between his feet. "I know." Fancy smiled at the boy and snapped her fingers.

Half a dozen happy-place people entered the garden, rolling a huge and colorful circular contraption on a stand. A wheel of death, like knife throwers used to entertain people at the circus.

Kit laughed and put her switchblade back in her pocket. "You are so *twisted*, Fancy Pants."

Fancy had the minions strap the boy to the wheel, and one of the happy-place people presented Kit with a metal box full of knives with handles as pink as cotton candy. After Fancy sent the happy-place people away, she said, "Age before beauty," and gestured for Kit to make the first throw.

Kit chose one of the knives and expertly skewered the tattooed boy's thigh.

"Good throw!" Fancy exclaimed, and then took a turn. Both sisters were very good at this game; despite their spinning target, very rarely did they miss.

"You know why people scream when they're in pain?" Fancy asked at one point, after her knife buried itself in the tattooed boy's hand.

"So that if there's friends nearby, they'll come to the rescue," said Kit reasonably, hitting him once again in the thigh—she had made an almost perfect line from the top of his thigh down to his shin.

"I don't think so," said Fancy. "I think screaming's a self-destruct mechanism. The person who's causing the pain gets so irritated by all the noise that she'll do anything to silence it." Fancy threw the knife, and it was a perfect throw. "Anything at all. What do you think?"

"I think you're right," Kit said, watching the boy go round and round on the wheel, silenced by Fancy's knife in his throat. Instead of throwing her own knife, she gave it to her sister and grabbed another bottle of lemonade from the pail on the grass.

"Five bucks says I can get him right between the eyes."

"I think he's dead, Fancy." The strange look was back on Kit's face.

"So? It'll still be a neat trick." She threw the knife, but it stuck, quivering in midair several feet before her. She felt a moment of confusion until she saw the knife wasn't in midair, but in the dashboard. Just as she recognized what was happening, as she felt an inescapable pressure folding her, forcing her to sit, the dashboard became more solid and the knife became less so until it disappeared completely and the Escalade reappeared around Fancy, the kinetoscope in her lap as it had been before. The truck was now empty of boys, but Kit was beside her in the backseat attempting to look unaffected, as if she popped in and out of the world every day.

In the kinetoscope the minions stopped the wheel and let the tattooed boy drop to the ground. The flamingos converged on him and began pecking around the knives poking out of his body.

"Bird food," Fancy said. "Such a sad way to go."

Kit laughed and swiped at her sister's face. "Real sad. You look like you're crying blood."

"What?" Fancy scooted forward and looked at herself in the rearview mirror. "Crap! *Evidence!*" The sisters scrambled out of the truck.

"It's their blood, not ours," Kit said as Fancy fished out some wet wipes and scrubbed the door handle free of prints. "People'll just assume something vicious climbed into the truck and wasted 'em."

"I don't think you're vicious."

The sisters whipped around and saw the scrawny boy still in

the handicapped space, bleeding and sweating in the sun, his face swelling like a balloon even as they watched. He tried and failed to pick himself up off the ground; it looked like he had been trying and failing for a long time.

"Great," said Fancy. "A witness."

"Not a witness." Kit went into bubbly-mode and helped the scrawny boy to his feet. "More like our best friend, right? Seeing as how we just saved your life."

He seemed slightly dazed, possibly due to having been kicked in the head several times. "I didn't dream that, did I?"

"Nope." Kit let him lean on her as she helped him into the shade near the Escalade. "You got your ass kicked in real life, son. You should know better than to walk around town all alone. What if those transies had been a pack of cacklers?"

"I know." He looked chagrined. "I was supposed to meet my friends, but that's not what I meant. You *disappeared* with those transies. I mean, where are they?"

"Someplace they can't hurt anybody anymore," Kit told him.

"Bill?" A group of people in tennis whites—or rather, tennis blacks—hopped the low fence separating the park from the parking lot. They were covered in scratches and blood and looked almost as bad as the sisters. But it was their friend they seemed concerned about. "What the hell happened to you?"

"Fucking transies, man," he said, holding his ribs as he toddled into his friends' collective embrace.

"Better transies than cacklers," said a girl with a blue headband. "We got jumped by a whole pack of 'em on the way over here."

"See?" Kit told Bill.

Bill's friends looked at her and Fancy, at the blood coating them rather liberally. "They get y'all, too?" asked the girl with the headband.

"They're such a menace, aren't they?" Kit answered noncommittally as she grabbed her sister. "Well, have a nice day, y'all!"

The sisters left Bill in the care of his friends and pedaled home.

"What if he tells his friends the truth, Kit?"

"That we sent a gang of assholes through a door?"

"And came back soaked in blood."

"Transy blood. Nobody cares about stupid transies, Fancy. And the people who will care, like their families, won't believe the truth. That we took their kin to another world and stabbed them to death."

"What's wrong?" Fancy asked, baffled by Kit's tone. Kit had

been so happy before, and now she clearly wasn't. And that strange look was back.

Kit sighed. "What happened in the happy place . . . it wasn't what I thought it would be."

"Didn't you have fun?"

"Yeah, at first, but then . . . it felt like we were the bullies."

"*Us?*"

"That last guy? He kept begging us to stop."

And now Fancy recognized the look. It was pity. *Pity.* For transies who had shown none to the scrawny boy in the park. "Next time we'll use a gag," said Fancy as pitilessly as possible, to show Kit how it was done.

Fancy scratched at her blood-caked inner elbows, feeling grimy and itchy all over. "*Look* at me. If you're gone pity somebody, pity me. How disgusting am I?"

"You look fine," said Kit. Pitilessly. At least she was learning.

"We gotta figure out a way to do this that's less messy. I mean, how can you stand it?"

Kit regarded her, eyes big with surprise. "I'm not sure."

Fancy sat on the back porch at Madda's feet eating peach ice cream and staring at the pictures in *Budget Travel* magazine.

One photo in particular had caught her eye: a laughing woman splashing in the surf in Cancun. Fancy desperately wished she had a huge chilly body of water to splash in. It was so still and hot, she could almost hear the grass smoldering in the sun.

A handful of peas landed on Fancy's magazine. She looked up and saw Kit working her way through a mountain of pea pods and scowling at her. Fancy brushed off the peas and turned the page. She saw an even better photo of a man ice fishing in Russia.

Another rain of peas interrupted Fancy's reverie; little green dots peppered her ice cream. When Fancy just ate around them, Kit exploded.

"Why does she get to eat ice cream while I'm sitting here working like a slave?"

"You know she gets overheated, Kit," said Madda calmly. "Don't be mean."

The phone rang inside the house, and when Madda got up to answer it, Fancy poked out her tongue at Kit.

"You're such a faker."

"I *am* hot," said Fancy.

"It's frigging summertime in Texas, stupid girl," Kit informed her, and then stole her bowl of ice cream. "Everybody's hot!"

"Girls!"

The sisters went inside and saw Madda at the kitchen counter packing a picnic basket with food: peanut butter, her persimmon preserves, half a loaf of homemade bread, and leftover chicken and pasta salad.

"Kit, I need you to go to the square and deliver this food to the Darcys."

"Why can't the Darcys cook their own food?" Kit asked, eating the remainder of Fancy's ice cream.

"Something crashed through their kitchen window." Madda crossed herself. "They chased it out but not before it destroyed nearly everything, including their kitchen appliances. This is just until they get on their feet."

"It's too hot to ride our bikes to the square," Fancy said.

"Fancy, you don't have to go just because Kit is going."

"It's okay if *I* die from heatstroke, just as long as precious Fancy gets to stay home and eat ice cream in the—"

"Oh, fine!" Madda snatched the car keys from her pocket. "Take the car, but hurry back for dinner."

"We will!" promised the sisters.

Kit hooked her arm around Fancy's shoulders and hustled her outside, laughing. "I get to drive the Honda! I get to drive the Honda! After we drop this off"—she tossed the basket into the backseat—"we can go to the record store."

"Or Mexico!" Fancy closed her eyes and imagined herself in the surf.

"And be back in time for dinner? Maybe next time, *mamacita*."

Arriving at the Darcys' muted the sisters' good mood a bit. Stepping onto the lawn was like stepping into a war zone. The lower wall of the two-story house was punched through, as though a car had driven out of it. The sisters could see the remains of the kitchen from the yard. A hairy six-legged beast was strung up in the tulip tree near the walkway, dripping yellow blood into the grass. Fancy assumed that was what had burst out of the house, though it didn't look strong enough or big enough to have caused so much damage.

They found a woman near the tree thanking everyone and falling all over herself in gratitude. She was very teary, but Fancy couldn't tell what was setting her off: her destroyed house, the outpouring of help she was receiving from her neighbors, or the creature that had been hanged in her tree. "It's so barbaric," she kept saying.

She got even tearier when Kit gave her Madda's basket of food.

"She sent her persimmon preserves!" Mrs. Darcy exclaimed. "I always knew Lynne was sweet, thinking of my troubles when she's got so many of her own."

She hugged both of the sisters. Her tears smeared against Fancy's cheek, and when Fancy finally pulled free, the side of her face felt as though it had been licked.

"Ma?"

A girl near Fancy's age, maybe a few years younger, wearing overalls and an engineer's cap came forward to tug on Mrs. Darcy's arm. "What is it, Jessa? Girls, this is my daughter."

"Hi," said Jessa perfunctorily before tugging once again on her mother. "I'm gonna help Pop board up the hole in the wall. Okay?"

"You are not." Despite all the crying, Mrs. Darcy didn't seem to be a pushover. "You stay away from all this dust and asbestos and who knows what all. You know how your lungs are. Now go get these girls a cool drink from the cooler out back."

"No thanks, ma'am," said Kit as Jessa pouted. "We're on a tight schedule. Madda's expecting us back in time for—"

"Kit?"

Gabriel came up behind them, pushing an empty red wheelbarrow to a stop beside Kit. He was wearing a gold cross similar to the one he'd given Kit at Cherry Glade. Probably he had a drawer full of crosses that he passed out to silly girls like candy. He was wearing a T-shirt that read 1 TIMOTHY 1:15, some high-minded bit of biblical wisdom, Fancy was certain, but the look he gave Kit wasn't at all Christian.

Gabriel hugged Kit as though they were old friends, and Kit greatly disappointed Fancy by not punching Gabriel in the face for his presumption. Instead she just giggled like an idiot.

"You were great in class yesterday," he said. "Your jazz improvisation was the best one, just real natural."

"That's because Fancy's been making me listen to a lot of Depression-era crap lately."

Since Kit had referred to her, Gabriel finally acknowledged Fancy's presence with a quick nod. "So y'all came to help Miz Irene?"

"Yes!" Kit answered.

Fancy elbowed her.

"Just for a little while?" Kit was practically begging. "Just long enough to help haul some of this junk away?" Kit took her sister's long-suffering sigh as an affirmative, and pretty soon Fancy found herself hauling trash in the hot sun, desperately wishing for an ice-fishing hole to fall into.

A little while had turned into forty-five minutes, and after Fancy rolled Gabriel's red wheelbarrow of broken house to the curb for the millionth time, cursing Kit and her hormones for the trillionth time, she heaved the wheelbarrow onto its side. It hit the ground with a cold, satisfying *clang*. She then went in search of Kit, and if her sister still wasn't ready to leave, Fancy was fully prepared to drag her away kicking and screaming.

Inside the Darcys' house, Fancy went upstairs and, through the doorway of a spare room full of camping equipment, saw Gabriel kneeling over a girl on the floor. Kissing her. And the girl wasn't Kit.

Fancy must have made a noise because he looked up and said, "I have more kisses." His voice made her skin crawl. "Plenty of kisses for you, too."

Fancy recoiled from the ugly expression on his face, ready to disbelieve she'd seen that level of ugliness on such a pretty face.

Almost.

Fancy ran downstairs and searched until she found Kit in the backyard with Mrs. Darcy. Fancy grabbed her sister and dragged her inside the house, Mrs. Darcy right on their heels demanding to know why Fancy looked so upset. When they reached the room where Gabriel was, he was no longer kissing the girl. He was pushing down on her chest.

"Oh my God!" Mrs. Darcy screamed. "Jessa!"

Before she reached her daughter's side, Jessa started gasping and coughing, and Gabriel sat back. "Finally, kid. That took forever."

Mrs. Darcy squeezed her daughter to her chest. "What happened?"

Gabriel said, "Mr. Darcy sent me up here to find a tarp, and I saw her passed out on the floor, not breathing."

"I *told* that girl to mind her lungs." Mrs. Darcy gave Jessa a good shake. "Didn't I tell you?"

"I just wanted to help," Jessa said.

Mrs. Darcy gave her another big squeeze. "My poor baby. We gotta get you to a doctor."

Jessa said, "I don't need a doctor."

"Shut up!" Mrs. Darcy beamed at Gabriel. "But first thank this young man for saving your life."

"Thanks," said Jessa shyly.

He waved away her thanks, as modest and bashful as if he hadn't just had his tongue down her throat moments before. While she was unconscious.

"He's a real treasure," said Mrs. Darcy to Kit, who was also beaming at Gabriel. "I'd keep a good eye on him if I was you."

She took the words right out of Fancy's mouth. Fancy understood now why Ilan was so mean to his brother. Gabriel was beyond weird—he was dangerous.

"'I have plenty of kisses for you, too.' And he was looking dead at me when he said it."

Kit bumped Fancy aside with her hip and then mopped the bit of floor where her sister had been standing. "So what?"

"So he's disgusting, that's what. Hitting on me while he's making out with an unconscious girl."

"He was reviving her, not making out."

"Then why would he say what he said?" Fancy hopped onto the dining table, out of her sister's way. She picked a strawberry from the fruit bowl, a breeze blowing in from the open door. Madda had left for work, and now that the sun was gone, it was much cooler.

"He was probably just trying to freak you out," said Kit. "I do stuff like that to people all the time." Kit scowled at Fancy, who handed her the uneaten green part of her strawberry, expecting her to get rid of it. "Especially obnoxious people."

"I'm not the obnoxious one," said Fancy, scowling right back. "Why didn't you tell me Gabriel was in your music class?"

"Didn't I?" Kit's face was carefully blank as she threw away Fancy's strawberry remains. When she saw her sister reaching for more fruit, Kit pulled her off the table and jabbed the mop at her feet. "Stop snacking and go do your own chores. I know you haven't even watered the garden yet."

"Fine," said Fancy, her dirty feet leaving tracks on the wet floor. "Be that way." She stepped through the back door and recoiled with a squeak from a girl coming up the porch steps, dragging a boy behind her.

"Sorry," the girl said, not sounding like she meant it, posing in the porch light like it was a spotlight. She was athletic and wearing a backless unitard and shorts, the sort of thing Kit would wear, only this girl had much better posture and infinitely more grace. "Are you Fancy?"

"Who wants to know?" Kit answered, joining Fancy at the door.

The girl pushed the boy in the back. "Go to the nice girls, Mason."

"Okay," said Mason, and he came to a stop before them, docile as a sheep. A glazed look dimmed his eyes, but otherwise he looked normal: tall with brown, gel-sculpted hair and a rather homely face. Under his unremarkable jeans and T-shirt, though, was an amazing body—headless-statue amazing.

Kit looked him over, appreciative but confused. "What is this?"

The girl cocked her hip. "God, do you need me to say it? I want him dead. Right now."

FROM FANCY'S DREAM DIARY:

Daddy was lying in the road. He wasn't dead but he was a big bloody mess, like a car or truck had run over him. He wanted me to help him to his feet, but I'd just had my bath and didn't want to touch him.

CHAPTER THIRTEEN

"I can't believe you want us to kill him," Kit said, poking the boy, Mason, in the stomach. "He's got such great abs."

The girl on their porch, the one who wanted Mason dead, put her hands on her hips. "It would be nice if you'd take this seriously. I don't aim to be here all night."

Kit gave Mason's abs one last poke before giving the girl her full attention. Fancy would have just slammed the door in the girl's face—who needed to deal with that kind of attitude?—but Kit always did have an unhealthy interest in people. "Who sent you here?"

"Don't worry," the girl said. "I drove myself. And I parked down the road so no one would see me pulling up to your house."

"I mean how do you know about us? Did you get a letter?"

"What letter? It's all over town what you did for Bill, rescuing him from a bunch of transies. Transies who are now missing. So now I need you to make *Mason* disappear." It was like she was ordering them to take out her garbage.

Fancy and Kit looked at each other, communicating silently.

All over town?

Town schmown. No one can prove anything.

Kit turned to the girl on the porch, and repeated it aloud to her: "No one can prove we did anything."

"What am I?" the girl said. "A lawyer? I don't need proof. I know what I know."

Kit got right in the girl's face. "That guy, Bill, was being beaten. Did you know that? We don't make people disappear without a reason."

"Don't give me that. You're the Bonesaw Killer's daughters. You don't need a reason. Everybody knows that psycho stuff is genetic." For a girl who thought the sisters were psychos, she seemed remarkably unconcerned about being alone with them. "But don't do it right away," she said. "Give me an hour to get to Ryan's house, to see and be seen, and then you can do it."

When the sisters just stared at her, she huffed. "Do you want money? Here." She rummaged through her hobo bag and fished out a wad of bills rolled together. "Four hundred bucks," she said, "and worth every penny."

Fancy had to take the money because Kit had turned away from the girl and was poking the boy, Mason, in the abs again. His only response was to smile at her.

"What's wrong with him?"

"I drugged him," the girl said impatiently. "It was the only way to get him here. His grandma died, and he was babbling about having to go out of town for the funeral. But I need this taken care of now. Tonight. I won't be able to focus on the audition with this hanging over my head. Do you dance?"

Kit seemed startled by the random question. "I can't even touch my toes."

"Too bad," the girl said, looking relieved. "You have the body for it."

Kit regarded the girl for a moment and then seemed to come to a decision. "What's your name?" she asked, in full bubbly mode.

"Call me Claudia." Fancy could almost see the neon lights surrounding the girl's name just from the way she said it.

"That's my stage name: Claudia Cresswell. It's much more stylish than my real name."

"Oh, I couldn't agree more," Kit chirped. "Fancy, go get Claudia a cool drink."

When Fancy came back with a tray of iced tea, Claudia and Kit were sitting on the porch. Tin pails full of flowers lined the steps, and Claudia sat next to a pail of Indian blanket. She plucked the red flowers bald, as though she was nervous or just instinctively destructive. The boy kept vacant watch over them, mannequin-still and smiling for no reason.

"So we're both auditioning for it," Claudia was saying. "I'm a great dancer, but Mason's family runs the Cultural Advisory Board, so he's a shoo-in to get the part, even though he doesn't work half as hard as I do. I'm sick of being passed over just because he's rich and I'm not."

"Thanks, Fancy," said Kit as Claudia took a glass of tea from the proffered tray. Kit brought Fancy up to speed while Claudia sipped her drink. "Seems like Mason here is holding Claudia back as a dancer, and so if we kill him, that'll make Claudia's life way easier."

Fancy set the tray aside and rolled her eyes.

"My sister agrees." Kit placed a comforting hand on Claudia's shoulder. "Your case is superimportant to us, so come along, please, and allow us to give you the help you so richly deserve."

"Come with you where?" she asked, allowing Kit to pull her to her feet.

"To the cellar."

Claudia froze. "The Bonesaw Killer's cellar? No way."

"That's where we'll do it," Kit insisted, "and we need you there so that just in case you ever feel like going to the cops, you'll have to explain why your fingerprints and"—she grabbed a handful of Claudia's hair and yanked—"your DNA is at the crime scene."

"Damn it!" she yelled, rubbing her head and staring at the long strands of dyed red hair in Kit's fist. "I just got my hair done!"

"It looks very nice, by the way," Kit assured her, leading her and Mason into the cellar, with Fancy bringing up the rear.

Claudia's star power dimmed considerably in the small gray space. The sisters cornered her and smiled at each other when Claudia backed away.

She cut her eyes at Mason, who was smiling at the kinetoscope, and said, "I don't wanna be here when it happens."

"Right," said Kit, tossing her handful of Claudia's hair on

the cellar floor. "You wanna be at Ryan's house establishing your alibi."

Fancy bumped Mason aside and looked into the kinetoscope. A tent materialized on the screen, a big billowing tent on the big hill by the sea. "Gonna have to get a new alibi," said Fancy, cranking the kinetoscope.

"So you *can* talk," said Claudia, startled. "I heard you were mute."

Fancy found the idea of people coming to stupid conclusions irritating. "I ain't mute, and you ain't going to Ryan's stupid party."

"Why not?"

"Because the show's about to start." Even as Fancy spoke, the happy place came to life around them, overrunning the entire room.

Claudia gasped and backed up against the wall . . . only to find she'd gone through it. She nearly fell but was graceful enough to keep her balance. The change from gray and dank to colorful and warm had flummoxed her, but only momentarily.

"How'd we get here?" Claudia asked, and then didn't wait for an answer. "Was there a door? I didn't even see a door! Bill was right." As she wandered to and fro on the platform of the headless statues, taking in the sights, her shoes clicked rhythmically against the stone, almost like she was tap-dancing. "This is how y'all made those boys disappear, isn't it? You can open doors."

"She can," said Kit, flicking her switchblade. "I'm just the muscle." But when she moved behind Claudia to jam the blade in her neck, Fancy stopped her and pulled her back. "No. *They're* the muscle."

The same two men in white, the minions, stepped out of the hedges and entered the garden. They joined the sisters on the platform, and their hands were big and ungentle as they grabbed Claudia.

"Escort her and this gentleman to the stage." Fancy pushed Mason toward the minions, and they grabbed him, too.

"What stage?" Kit asked, irritated, though Fancy didn't understand why. This was the fun part.

"The stage in the Pavilion. For the dance-off."

Kit gave her a puzzled look. "Pavilion?"

"Dance-off?" Claudia interrupted, trying to jerk away from the minions but unable to. "I don't . . . You're supposed to kill Mason, not get him work!"

Fancy eyed her coolly. "You say you're a better dancer. If you're right, we'll kill him. If you're wrong, we'll kill *you* for wasting our time over some pointless rivalry."

Claudia harrumphed. "I can outdance him any day of the week."

"Yeah, now that he's drugged." Fancy stood before Mason and looked him over, trying not to let his weird smile rattle her. "What did you give him?"

"Yes-man," Claudia admitted, not the least bit embarrassed. A person on yes-man would do anything anybody said, and was usually associated with the worst sort of freaks. "I got it from a boy named Carmin. He knows how to make all kinds of drugs. I had to practically sign over my firstborn, though. That stuff is *not* cheap."

"Why didn't you just tell him to jump off a building or drown himself?" Fancy asked.

"If they find that drug in his body, they could trace it back to me. With you, there won't be any body. Though I might have made other plans if I had known I'd have to jump through all these hoops." Claudia tried and failed again to escape her minion. "Why can't you just kill him and be done with it?"

"She's got a good point, Fancy," Kit said. "Why can't I . . . you know." She jabbed the switchblade in Claudia's direction.

Fancy ignored her; she'd had more than enough of stabbing

things, thank you very much. "Where did you inject him?" she asked Claudia.

"His neck."

When Fancy saw a faint pinprick near Mason's jugular, she squeezed it like a zit until the drug seeped from the injection site and rolled whitely down his throat.

Mason's pupils shrank to a more normal size, and awareness came back to his face; the smile shut off like a light switch. The first thing he said was, "My folks're waiting for me in San Antonio. My grandma. I have to—"

He started to run, but couldn't, not with the minions holding him. He looked around. "Where am I?"

"In the happy place," Kit told him. "We brought you here through a door."

"*Why?*"

"Your friend wants you dead."

He followed her pointing finger. "Annie?" He seemed more shocked that his friend wanted him dead than that he was in another world.

"I need to nail that audition," said Claudia defensively. "It's not like you need the work." She turned to Fancy. "Tell this goon to let me go!"

"You asked them to kill me?" Mason's minion had to get a firmer grip on him to keep him from tackling Claudia. "Over a *job*?"

"All the jobs, Mason! I can't have you taking what's mine."

"It's not my fault that I'm better than you, Annie!"

"It's Claudia!" she screamed, her face as red as her hair. "Claudia Cresswell, and no one is better than me!"

"That remains to be seen," said Fancy calmly. She snapped her fingers. "Minions! Prepare them both for the dance-off."

It was no contest. Mason and Claudia seemed evenly matched in the beginning, both standing onstage in tap shoes performing increasingly difficult steps. And Claudia was good, even masterful as she wowed the audience with her complicated spins and syncopations. But Mason began to show his true colors, matching and then surpassing every step she made. He not only had more skill than Claudia, but more of a sense of fun, letting the crowd in on the joke, inviting them to laugh at the absurdity of a girl with such joyless, textbook moves trying to outdance him. He literally danced circles around her, and the audience ate it up.

When it was over, a panel of judges that included Fancy

and Kit awarded the points. On a scale of one to ten with ten being the highest, Claudia averaged an eight, while Mason scored a perfect ten.

"That's not fair!" Claudia screamed, her voice booming from the stage, breathless from her exertions. She shoved Mason in the chest. "Why does everybody always choose you over me?"

"Because you suck!" Kit screamed from her place at the judges' table. The audience cracked up.

When Fancy climbed onto the stage to award Mason his well-deserved trophy, Claudia snatched it and tried to run, but the minions were there in the wings and quickly dragged her back to the stage. Mason snatched back his trophy. Eventually. He had a tough time prying it from Claudia's grip.

To console her, Fancy said, "We have a prize for you, too," and presented Claudia with a pair of bright red shoes. "We'd like you to dance for us one last time."

"*Go to hell!*" Claudia yelled. She had to be held down while Fancy strapped the shoes to her feet. Finally they left Claudia alone on the stage. She stood there trembling, rooted to the spot—by the shoes or by fear, no one could tell—until the audience began to clap.

When they clapped, Claudia's toe began to tap. And then she

began to dance, a much more inspired routine than she'd given previously. Only this time she was screaming in agony. The more she danced, the brighter the shoes became, until they were lava red and smoking. Claudia danced until she burst into flames.

The crowd surged to its feet and cheered, and didn't stop until Claudia danced herself into ashes.

"Why didn't you just stab her?" asked Kit as the crowd left the Pavilion. "I mean, that was entertaining and all, but—"

"Why should I get *my* hands dirty?" Fancy admired her snowy nails. "And you know I hate having to scrub off other people's blood."

The minions approached the judges' table, where the sisters were sitting, one of them bearing all that was left of Claudia: a blackened set of car keys and the bright red shoes brimming with her ashes and a few bits of bone. Mason stood behind them, holding his trophy with only his thumb and forefinger, as if it felt dirty.

Fancy took the keys and the shoes and said to the minions, "You may leave."

"Maharaja," Kit muttered.

As Mason and the sisters walked back to the Headless

Garden, Fancy noticed that several trees had sprouted on the platform between two of the statues. Kit noticed it too.

"Isn't that where we buried those ears?" she asked.

"Yep." The middle tree was a wizened thing with a pale, bulbous trunk and skinny, grasping branches from which hung enticing red fruit. It was ringed by four much smaller trees, which seemed withered and lank and buried beneath the bigger tree's shadow.

Fancy hopped onto the platform and stopped at a different earth-filled stone circle. She held up the ash-and-bone-filled shoes. "I wonder what'll grow from these?" she said, and tipped the shoes into the earth. The soil yielded beneath them like water and they sank into the ground like capsized boats, the soil settling smooth and still over them.

Fancy knelt on the edge of the stone and dipped her head into the earth—it really was just like sinking into water!—and saw the shoes floating below her, drifting in the earth as worms converged on them.

Fancy pulled out, shaking the dirt from her hair, eyes, and ears. "There's worms nibbling Claudia's bones," she said, laughing. "Look!" She pulled Kit down to kneel beside her.

Kit bent forward as Fancy had, but the happy-place soil

wouldn't yield to her, and her head rebounded off solid earth. "Figures," she said, rubbing her forehead. She looked at Mason. "This place always did like her more than me."

Mason didn't speak.

"You okay?" Kit asked.

He set his trophy on Claudia's stone circle. "No." He looked nothing like the vibrant performer who had wowed them such a short time ago. It was like he'd been drugged again, only with something that made him frown instead of smile.

"Don't tell anyone what happened to your friend," Fancy warned him, "unless you wanna know what it's like to dance in high heels."

"She *was* my friend." He burst into tears. "Fuck that. She was like a *sister* to me. I can't believe she would do that to me!"

"A real sister would have killed you herself instead of farming it out to strangers. What?" Fancy said when Kit gave her a speaking look.

"Don't cry," Kit said. She stood and gave Mason a big hug. "Hey! Do you wanna try some horny-old-man fruit? I bet that'll perk you right up. Fancy, go get him some fruit."

"I'm not going anywhere near that tree."

"Just do it!"

Fancy walked off in a huff to get the fruit, and then stopped short with a jerk. "Ow!" She rubbed her nose and scanned about, but saw only air. No, not air. A dim gray wall. Four gray walls that quickly coalesced around the sisters and Mason, and in a blink they were back in the cellar.

It took them a moment to readjust.

"So that's it," said Mason in a small voice, still in Kit's arms. "Annie's really gone."

"Looks like," said Kit.

"It's a day for death," said Mason.

Fancy snorted. Like that was some big revelation. As if people didn't die every day.

"First my grandma and now—" He started crying again, and Kit gave him another big squeeze.

Fancy remembered how the Mortmaine had hugged her and, even through her irritation, felt slightly wistful. But she didn't know how to make strangers feel safe. She wasn't Mortmaine.

Kit let go of Mason and reached into Fancy's pocket for Claudia's wad of cash. When Fancy tried to take it back, Kit smacked her hand and gave the money to Mason. "Get your grandma some nice flowers. On us."

"Thanks," he said.

"Well, go on," Fancy said when Mason just stood there sniveling. "We can't spend the whole day fooling with you. Claudia's car is parked down the road." She gave Mason the keys. "If anyone asks, say she lent you her car to drive to your grandma's, and that was the last time you saw her."

"Thank you," he whispered—to Kit, not her—and then fled the cellar.

After Mason had gone and the sisters were heading back to the house, which was shining like a lantern in the darkness, Fancy said, "You don't think he'll tell like that idiot Bill did?"

"It doesn't matter." Kit kicked at a rock as though she hated it. "As long as there's no proof, none of this matters."

"Then what's wrong?"

"Why would he thank me when I didn't do anything? All that stuff in the happy place. It was fun, but not . . ."

"Satisfying?" Fancy threw her arm around Kit's shoulder. "Next time I'll let you stab someone. To death, if you want."

"Okay," said Kit, but not with her usual enthusiasm.

FROM FANCY'S DREAM DIARY:

I was walking down El Camino Real through the woods. After almost every step, a light would shine on me from the trees. A flashlight. When the light hit me, I couldn't move until it shut off. I could hear them whispering in the woods. They were whispering my name.

CHAPTER FOURTEEN

On Sunday, Madda put on a pair of her good shoes, the black leather ones with the ruby red heels. Because she spent most of her life in unattractive Dickies, whenever Madda went anywhere non-work-related, she tended to dress up. "Fancy, you wanna come to the square with me?"

Fancy was dusting the tiger paintings that Big Mama had given Madda and Daddy as a wedding present. "Okay," she said, happy to quit her chores. Fancy hurried to the door and paused. "Kit?" Her sister sat pounding at the piano. "Come on."

Fancy waited, but Kit just waved her hands. "Y'all go on. I wanna practice."

Fancy allowed Madda to pull her out of the house and into

the car, positive that Kit was joking and would run out and say, "Ha-ha, fooled you!" and jump into the backseat. But as Madda drove off their property and into the forest, Fancy realized she had to face facts: Kit had abandoned her. She was still numb when Madda parked in the square and led her in and out of the shops on Seventh Street.

"Okay," said Madda, consulting her list, arms laden with shopping bags. "Oh shoot, I didn't put foil and paper towels on the list. Remind me to—oh, look at those!"

Fancy bumped into Madda, who had stopped to admire a pair of black shoes with pink bows on the toes in the window of Ducane's Department Store. "Those would look cute on you."

"I don't like heels." Kit loved heels. She loved buying useless crap with Madda. Why hadn't she wanted to come?

"Nobody likes heels, but if you're a woman, that's what you wear. It's high time you started dressing your age."

Fancy thought of Claudia bursting into flames in her dancing shoes. "No, thanks. If I start wearing heels, boys will whistle at me when I walk by."

Madda found that hilarious. "Do boys whistle at girls? I've only ever seen that happen in the movies."

"Me too. Still, I'd better not risk it."

"You wouldn't like to be whistled at? I would. Just to see what it's like."

"Not me."

"Not even if Ilan whistled at you?"

Fancy saw his reflection in the window, superimposed over the shoes, so faint and ghostly she doubted Madda could see him. He was playing the guitar, and he was alone. Fancy wondered if he missed Gabriel when he wasn't around, and if he did, how did he cope? Maybe it was the music, she thought, watching his fingers travel over the strings. Maybe if she set fire to Kit's piano, her sister would stop neglecting her.

"Fancy!"

She turned, stupidly hoping it was Ilan, even though she'd just seen him in the window and knew he was inside somewhere.

A boy with a black eye and various lumps and bruises hurried away from his friends and crossed the street to stand before Fancy. She recognized him from the park.

"That's your name, right? Fancy?"

She leaned into Madda's side.

"I'm Bill. Do you remember me? You and your sister saved me from those transy assholes. I still don't know how you did it, but—" He threw his arms around Fancy, who squeaked. He was hot and sweaty and a horrible hugger. Fancy's nose was squished against his chest.

Madda pulled Bill away from her daughter by the ear. "Boy, what do you need?"

"Nothing, ma'am." When Madda let him go and pulled her daughter protectively to her side, he backed away to a more respectful distance, beaming all the while at Fancy. "Just to say thank you. I wish . . ." Suddenly inspired, he dug in his pockets and came out with a few folded bills. "I have money."

Fancy snatched it from him and then retook her position at Madda's side.

Bill grinned wider and moved toward her again, but Madda's quelling look stopped him in his tracks. "Anytime you need a favor. Anything at all, just ask. Cuz that was awesome, what you did."

Fancy shrugged and watched him go back to his friends. Watched them pointing at her and whispering.

"What did you do to that boy?" Madda dragged her down the street, away from Bill. "And why did he pay you?"

"People are weird. I can't explain why they do stuff."

"He said you saved him. From what?"

"Some transy boys were beating on him, so me and Kit ran 'em off. Me and Kit . . ." Fancy sighed.

"You and Kit what?"

Fancy took some of Madda's bags so she could hold her hand. "Why're you so upset? I thought you wanted me to get close to people."

"Not some stranger." Madda looked over her shoulder and grimaced. "There's no need to be indiscriminate. And if he's a stranger, you shouldn't take money from him, no matter what you did for him."

"If I didn't, he'd've just followed us up the street, thanking me over and over. And then I would've had to push him *into* the street, preferably in front of a truck."

Madda blinked, startled. But then she laughed. "You don't talk much, but when you do, heaven help me."

Fancy couldn't bring herself to share in Madda's amusement. Without Kit, laughter was much too depressing.

Monday afternoon, as the class waited for Mr. Hofstram to finally stumble in, Fancy noticed everyone looking at her. Ilan didn't speak to her like he normally did. So she looked straight ahead at her empty canvas, feeling exposed, an itching beneath her skin urging her to run. She'd had misgivings about letting Mason go, but like Kit had said, he couldn't prove anything.

The girl sitting on Fancy's right, one of those stylish popular girls who never had anything to say to Fancy or Kit, turned to her and smiled.

"Mason said to give you this." She held out an envelope.

Fancy took it, wondering what Mason had sent her. The envelope was full of cash. She must have looked stunned, because the girl added, "It's okay. He feels like he needs to say thanks. He said everything happened so fast."

Someone asked, "What happened?"

"Annie tried to kill Mason over a dance audition; can you believe it?"

"Annie Snoad?" said a different girl. "Yeah, I can believe it. I lived next door to her. She wanted to be in the school play, so to get the lead she told everybody I had gonorrhea in my throat and couldn't sing." She smiled expectantly at Fancy. "So what did you do to Annie?"

Everyone had stopped whispering to eavesdrop.

"She opened a door," said the stylish girl when Fancy didn't answer. "And sent Annie through it."

"Well, good riddance."

As everyone broke into a discussion of whether it was even possible to get gonorrhea in the throat, Fancy felt a slight tug on her ponytail. "Mason, huh?" Ilan whispered. "I didn't know you had friends."

Fancy jerked her hair out of his hand, though her roots tingled as though his fingers were pressed against her scalp.

He put his arm across the back of her chair. His arm no longer bothered her; it was actually the least bothersome thing about him.

"I always figured *we'd* be friends."

Fancy clipped a scrap of newsprint to her canvas and wrote, *I don't have friends.*

Ilan's hand covered hers briefly as he plucked the charcoal from her hand and wrote beneath her words, *You have me.*

Fancy came home from class to find a watermelon the size of a small car on the front porch, with a thank-you note taped to it from Bill, signed *Always your friend.*

"I do not have friends!" Fancy screamed, but she wasn't Kit—the forest paid her no mind, chirruping happily despite her upset.

She stormed into her room and looked at the bit of news-print. *You have me.* The words seemed to mock her. She should have thrown it into the forest and let the birds build their nests with it and lay eggs on it, but she didn't. She shoved it between the pages of her dream diary and refused to think about it anymore. She made a gallon of lemonade in the milky-white pitcher and waited for Kit to come home.

She didn't have to wait long. "Did you see that monster watermelon?" Kit asked, bounding into the room. She tossed some sheet music and a pile of letters onto her bed and stripped out of her sweaty clothes. "I guess Bill figures if we eat all that, we'll be too full to come after him for squealing about us all over town. Smart, huh?" She sat at the tea table in her under-wear, some lacy pink stuff that Fancy had never seen before. She turned on the phonograph and played an old Ray Charles record. She poured herself some lemonade and then frowned when Fancy continued to lie motionless on the bed.

"Don't worry, Fancy. Even if Sheriff Baker came sniffing around here, he wouldn't find a damn thing."

"Don't say 'damn.'"

Kit breathed a sigh of relief. "Okay. Just making sure you're still breathing. Why you just laying there?"

"My head hurts." Fancy had changed into her sleep romper and decided to stay in bed until the day was dead.

"Well, I got just the cure for headaches. Look what I found in the mailbox." She grabbed a letter from the stack on her bed and crowded into Fancy's bed with her. She sat against the pillows with Fancy's head on her stomach as she removed a handwritten note inside an envelope.

Kit read it aloud:

"'Hi. My name is Selenicera Woodson. You said tell if I have a problem. I do. My sister wants me dead. She is poisoning me. She mixes it into my food. She had to let me go to school once when my brother took her to court, and I remember how real food tastes. Not like the stuff she feeds me. I don't want to kill her, but if I don't, she'll kill me first. I don't know why she hates me or why she keeps me in this room and won't let me go outside when I want to. Please help me. I would ask my brother, but when he went to court to get custody of me, he lost. He used to beat people up when he was a kid, and he got in trouble a lot. But that was only because he was sad when our parents died. That was a long time ago, when I was still a baby. He doesn't get in trouble anymore, and I don't want him to, but I know that if he goes to jail for killing my sister, they won't let me live with him.'

"Man," Kit said, putting the letter back inside the envelope. "Little kids sure are idiots. *Obviously* they can't give custody rights to a felon."

"But it's a good one," said Fancy against her stomach. "I knew we'd get a reply."

Kit stroked Fancy's hair from her damp face. "You wanna do it right now?"

"Later. It's too hot."

"Fancy, what's wrong with you? And don't give me any crap about a headache."

"I do have a headache. People not acting like they're supposed to always gives me a headache."

Kit harrumphed, massaging Fancy's temples. "You don't always act like you're supposed to either, you know."

Fancy pretended not to hear. "Play 'I Got a Woman.' That's the only Ray Charles I like."

Kit's hands stilled. "I . . . oh, who knows where that record is."

"In the crate?"

"I don't feel like looking through all that."

"They're in alphabetical order."

"Fancy, shh. With your headache you shouldn't be listening to music anyway. Sleep now. We'll call on Selenicera tomorrow morning, when it's nice and cool."

Fancy knew they'd have to wake up superearly to enjoy truly cool air, but the next day Kit woke Fancy before it was even light out.

Fancy rolled over. "Whuzzit?"

Kit was already dressed in her trademark leggings and T-shirt. "Rise and shine!" she hollered, drill-sergeant-like. "On your feet! We have to go help that girl."

"It ain't even six in the morning." Fancy buried her head under her pillow and almost stabbed her eye out with the pencil she kept under there. It was so early she hadn't even dreamed anything yet.

"So we know she's not at work." Kit knocked Fancy's pillow to the floor and dragged her out of bed. "Besides, we gotta finish up before Madda gets home. Let's go!" She pushed Fancy into the inner room.

"Grow one pair of wings . . . ," Fancy muttered as she wandered into the bathroom. A quick, cold shower woke her up and put Kit's angelic tendencies into a new light. If the sheriff did come around, he'd never believe that such a sweet girl could murder anybody.

Fancy came back into the sleeping porch in a sleeveless babydoll dress. The early dawn light glinted off the jars of squirrel organs. Kit was sitting at the tea table with the phone book and the cordless phone.

"Who you calling?"

"Wooding, Woods, Woodson!"

"The girl in the letter?" said Fancy, separating her hair into two low ponytails. "It's too early. She won't even be—"

"We have to set up a meeting and talk strategy." Kit spoke as though she had been doing such things her whole life. After three irate hang-ups, she struck pay dirt on the fourth call. "Hi, is this Selenicera?" Her eyes widened, and she put her hand over the phone. "It's the sister!"

"Hang up. *Quick.*"

Kit thought about it. Then said into the phone, "Is it true you aim to kill your kid sister?"

"*Kit.*"

Kit slapped Fancy's hands from the phone. "This is Kit Cordelle."

"*You told her your name?*"

"No, she said you're trying to kill her," said Kit into the phone. "Are you? Well, you know me. I can't hardly point fingers, considering my own situation. Yeah, *that* Cordelle. Well sure, I mean, kill her if you want; she's your sister. I just figured you'd want some help. We've seen our old man in action, after all." She winked at Fancy after uttering that complete lie. "We could offer any number of tips. We know where you live. Yeah, *we*. Me and my own kid sister, Fancy. We're a team. No problem."

"What'd she say?" said Fancy, the minute Kit hung up.

Kit grinned. "She wants us to come over right away."

FROM FANCY'S DREAM DIARY:

KIT WAS FLYING ABOVE OUR HOUSE, THE WIND FROM HER PINK WINGS BENDING THE TREES. EVERY TIME HER SHADOW PASSED OVER ME I SHIVERED.

CHAPTER FIFTEEN

The sisters biked to the address, the kinetoscope propped awkwardly in Fancy's basket as they twisted down Torcido Road,
only a few miles from El Camino Real.

"Think it's a scam?" Fancy asked, veering behind Kit as a
car passed them on the road. Cool, slightly damp air rushed
against them. The sun rays slanted intermittently between the
thickening clouds. "Or a setup?"

"Probably."

"She knows we know what she wants to do to her sister,
so . . . be on guard."

A few minutes later the sisters rode onto the Woodsons'
property and walked their bikes up the stony path.

The Woodsons lived in a nice neighborhood in a peach A-frame house. It was an area where the home owners had trained the wisteria to decorate the outer walls of their homes and not eat them alive, very unlike the sisters' own home.

"Now we know where she's getting the poison from," said Kit as the sisters tiptoed their bikes almost respectfully past the fragrantly gorgeous toxins in the front yard.

"Even destroying angels," said Fancy pointing out the delicate white mushrooms growing around the holly in the yard.

"She can't be using those, or her sister would be dead already."

The sisters leaned their bikes against the front porch. Fancy lifted the kinetoscope from the basket of her bike.

Kit ran her hand over it. "It looks weird in broad daylight, doesn't it?"

It didn't, but Fancy knew what Kit meant: that the kinetoscope was a cellar dweller like them, and out of its element among the bright beauty of the Woodsons' flower garden.

They went up to the front door, and Kit rang the bell.

"What'll you say?" asked Fancy, trusting Kit, as always, to speak for the both of them.

A woman—the older sister, they presumed—opened the

door before Kit could answer, a willowy, freckled blonde with a pink mouth and weird, jittery eyes that couldn't seem to rest on anything longer than a second, including the sisters. She had a white-knuckled grip on a bottle of water, which she held to her chest like an amulet to ward off demons.

"Did we talk on the phone?" she greeted them.

"Sure did," said Kit, in full bubbly mode. She tipped her newsboy cap. "I'm Kit and that's Fancy."

"I'm Datura." She pointed her water bottle at the kineto-scope. "What's that? A camera?" She looked vaguely upset at the idea—vaguely because she wasn't looking at the kineto-scope in particular, but rather at everything. Her restless violet eyes were giving Fancy motion sickness.

"They don't make cameras out of wood anymore. Der." Kit laughed in a way that invited Datura to join in, but Datura didn't. "That's what we're gone use to solve your problem. After you let us inside?"

Datura only hesitated a brief moment before she stepped back and waved the sisters indoors.

As she passed, Fancy noted Datura's strong, sweet smell, as if she herself had been plucked from her own poisonous garden.

Datura's house was clean and orderly, the living room as bright and steamy as a greenhouse.

Datura waved the sisters to the couch by a glass coffee table piled with books on night-blooming plants.

"What beautiful flowers," Kit chirped as Datura fussed with a vase of bright red oleanders on the end table. "And what a beautiful garden! I told Fancy outside that I never seen such a beautiful garden. You should give us the name of your gardener."

"I'm the gardener." Once she was done with the flowers, Datura smoothed Fancy's hair off her shoulders and shoved a pillow behind her back, as though Fancy were a wilting flower in need of extra support. Fancy gripped the kinetoscope and shot Kit a freaked-out look.

Kit ignored her. "Oh my God, you're so lucky! I wish my thumb was as green as yours."

Satisfied with the sisters' arrangement on the couch, Datura guzzled from her water bottle. "Y'all thirsty? Want some tea?"

"We love tea! Thanks!"

When Datura disappeared into the kitchen, Fancy said, "Like, oh my God, Kit! I wish I was as full of it as you are!"

"I'm not full of it. I'm full of *shit*. That's why she likes me. Gardeners adore fertilizer. She seem weird to you?"

"Did you not see her fondling me? That lady sailed past weird a long time ago." Fancy looked into the kinetoscope, but saw only the happy place.

"What're you looking at?"

"Not *at*. For." She leaned forward and shoved aside one of the books to clear a surface on the coffee table. She stared into the glass, and the Woodson kitchen materialized.

"What're you looking *for*?"

"That." She pulled Kit forward. "Look." The sisters watched Datura chop her deadly destroying angel mushrooms into a teapot.

Kit cried, "Well, that won't taste good!"

But when Datura brought them their tea, the sisters were all smiles.

"Old family recipe," said Datura, clearing a space on the coffee table for the tray. "It'll probably taste a little weird at first."

"Can't be *too* many in your family," said Kit, "if y'all sit around drinking destroying angel tea all day."

Datura froze, sugar tongs in hand.

"Why you trying to kill us?" asked Kit, in a wounded tone. "I told you we're here to help."

She sat across from the sisters, her eyes skating drunkenly around the room. "My sister's growing strangely. She don't thrive in sunlight like I meant her to. She sneaks out of the house *in sunlight* even though she knows it ain't good for her. I don't understand it. I tried to alter her so she'll thrive in the light, to cross-pollinate her with something really hardy and sun-loving, like a sunflower, but it ain't working."

Fancy and Kit exchanged a confused look. Beyond weird was right. Datura was insane.

"I was ready to give up and toss her on the compost heap," she continued, "but then you called." She smiled at Kit. "So I figured I'd kill the two of you and then cremate your bodies. Human ash makes excellent fertilizer. Selenicera might thrive in it."

Kit elbowed Fancy. "Gardeners and fertilizers, see?" Then she sat forward and pinned Datura with her most earnest gaze. "Look, we came here to help you kill your *sister*, remember? If the kid's as bad as you say, she's too far gone for any last-minute Hail Mary fertilizer. Know what I mean?"

Datura swiped a fresh water bottle from the tea tray and drained half of it in one gulp. She wiped her mouth so hard she tore the skin of her lip. "You're right," she said, a bright bead of blood trembling on her pastel mouth. "I have to face the fact that she's more fungus than flower. Follow me."

The sisters followed Datura to the back of the house, where the smell of earth and plant life grew ever more pervasive. She ushered the sisters into a low-lit room with a dirt-covered floor, a room with plants growing weird and pale in the gloom—up from the earth, down from the ceiling, and along the walls. One of the plants wasn't a plant at all, but a little girl, maybe six or seven, sitting in a corner in a white nightie, dirt covering her feet to the ankles.

She was albino pale, her white hair creeping over her shoulders like spiderwebs, but her eyes were violet and surprised to see the sisters. Surprised and hopeful.

Kit's bubbliness fled as she took in the girl's condition. "You're Selenicera?"

The girl nodded.

"Doesn't she look horrible?" Datura waded through the soil to the girl and poured the dregs of her water bottle over Selenicera's head. "So pale and sickly?" Selenicera flinched from the touch of the water, wiping it from her eyes like tears.

"She's the horrible one? How can you treat your own sister like a . . . a *toadstool*? Crazy bitch." Kit whipped out her switchblade and darted forward, as out of control as the lichen growing over the window.

"Kit," said Fancy, sharp enough to stop her sister in her tracks. "There's no need for that, remember?" She held up the kinetoscope.

So Kit held up her knife, her rage replaced with frustration. "But you said next time you'd let me—"

"I don't feel like scrubbing that woman's blood out of my clothes, like I had to do with those transies and the old man. It took forever. And think of all the evidence you'd leave behind if—"

"Fine. Do what you want." Kit put the knife away with an ungracious amount of swearing as Fancy cranked the kinetoscope and sent them all into the happy place.

Datura and Selenicera stared around the garden from the platform with the statues, disoriented and wide-eyed— Selenicera kept patting the cobbled platform, feeling for the dirt she'd been buried in. The confusion soon gave way to admiration; Datura and Selenicera knew a thing or three about gardens, after all, and the headless garden was in fine form today.

"The kinetoscope's gone!" Kit exclaimed.

"It doesn't come over, Kit." Fancy said. "It never has."

"Why not?"

"I dunno. It's not like Cherry gave me a manual."

While the Woodsons were busy gaping, Fancy's minions entered the garden and made a beeline for Datura, and to her displeasure, dressed her in a straitjacket.

"What's going on?" Datura demanded, her jittery eyes flitting toward the sisters and then away. "What are you doing? Why're they manhandling *me*?"

Fancy spoke up as Kit helped Selenicera off the ground, helping her stand on her spindly legs. "Just a precaution. I aim to test what you said. See if the kid can thrive in the light. If she can't, then we'll kill her. And if we do kill her, I wouldn't want you to suddenly turn on us and try to take revenge."

"What do you mean?" Datura turned to Kit. "What does she mean?"

But Fancy was too busy watching the sky to answer. Under her gaze the clouds parted and sunlight fell on them, as gently as a warm shower.

Selenicera began to grow taller and sturdier. Her thin, lank hair thickened and flourished, and roses bloomed in her milky cheeks. She laughed to see the changes in herself, running her hands through her hair and twirling on her suddenly strong legs. Fancy realized as she watched Selenicera becoming healthier that she must be closer to nine or ten; life with Datura had stunted her growth.

Unlike her sister, Datura began to weaken in the sun. Her skin shriveled and dried; her hair began to fall out like leaves from a dead tree; she squirmed in her straitjacket, gasping for water.

Fancy told her, "It's not the kid who can't handle the light; it's you. Imagine that."

"Please." The minions had to hold her upright. "Water."

"So by your own reasoning," Fancy continued, ignoring her pleas, "you're the one who needs to be killed. Right?"

Datura bared her teeth. One of them fell out and clattered on the stone. "I should've followed my first mind and cremated you."

"But then we wouldn't be here having a swell time," Fancy exclaimed, as Kit scooped up the tooth and put it in her pocket.

Fancy snapped her fingers, and a flood of happy place people poured through hedges carrying garden furniture and trays of food. Not muscle, just regular people, who smiled and bobbed their heads when they entered Fancy's presence.

Within moments they had set up a table and chairs and furnished tea and sandwiches and cakes enough for high tea with the queen.

"Selenicera, do something," said Datura during the commotion. "Don't let them treat me like this. Not after all I've done for you."

Selenicera stopped spinning and looked at her sister, took in the straitjacket, seeing her as though for the first time. "It's because of what you did to me that we're even here." She turned to Fancy to speak, decided against it, and turned to Kit instead. "Where *are* we?"

"The happy place."

"How'd we get here?"

"Remember the wooden box with the crank Fancy was carrying? It's a kind of door."

Selenicera got it then. Porterenes understood all about doors that led out of the world. "What you gone do to Datura?"

Kit laughed humorlessly. "Ask my sister. She's the one 'handling' it."

"Don't be like that," said Fancy sharply. "Killing her in her house would have left evidence behind; I told you. We're kinda trying to avoid that, remember?"

"Well, we're here now, so why can't I—?"

Fancy snapped her fingers again and all the happy-place people came to attention. "You may leave." After they trooped away—all except Fancy's personal minions, who were still holding Datura—Fancy extended her hands to Kit and the Woodsons. "Please. Have a seat."

They all sat at the table, Kit on Fancy's right, Selenicera on the left, and Datura several feet away at the opposite end of the long table, the two minions flanking her.

Fancy smiled, enjoying her role as gracious host. "Now let's e—"

"Kit!"

Franken loped up behind Fancy's chair and stopped beside Kit. He'd gotten clothes from somewhere: a long-sleeved turtleneck and pants, both black. He was much thinner than when they'd first met, and his hair was in his face, like he was hiding behind it. But his stitches were still prominent, bulky and black. They'd need to be taken out at some point. Fancy could order the minions to do it. Or she could just leave it. Who cared what Franken looked like?

"Hey, Franken!" Kit pulled him down and kissed his scarred face. Kit obviously didn't care.

He gestured at the spread. "Room for one more?"

"What the hell?" said Kit as Franken crowded next to her at the table. "The more the merrier, right, Fancy?"

"If you say so. That's Franken," Fancy told Selenicera, whose eyes bugged out of her face as she took in Franken's patchwork visage. "Kit's old playmate."

Selenicera waved shyly.

"I need a drink!" Datura yelled, startling everyone, straining helplessly toward the teapot, rattling the buckles of her straitjacket.

"She looks real bad," Selenicera noted. "And thirsty. She's always really thirsty."

Fancy swished the tea in the teapot around a few times and then poured everyone a cup. The tea was as silver as the teapot and rippled in the pink china cups like a liquid mirror.

"What kind of tea is this?" asked Franken, taking the proffered cup.

"My own blend," Fancy answered, handing one of the minions a cup for Datura. "Brewed in Datura's honor."

While Datura gulped her tea with the help of one of the minions, Fancy slid a tray of cakes to Franken.

"Try one of the cream cakes," she said, and then watched intently as Franken chose one.

He bit into it and then filled a saucer with them. "These're awesome!" He spoke with his mouth full. "Tastes like—" He slumped forward onto the table, his cheek squishing his saucer of cakes.

Kit tsked at her sister. "What'd you do?"

"Nothing much."

Kit raised Franken's arm, then let it go. It dropped limply to the table. "Then why is he passed out?"

"Maybe he's tired from obsessing over you."

"You are cold-*blooded*," Kit said admiringly, ignoring Franken as she filled her saucer with finger sandwiches. Fancy was glad to see that whatever fascination Franken had held for Kit in the cellar was now broken. Perhaps she'd been silly to worry.

"I feel funny," said Selenicera. Before she had finished speaking, wings tore out of her back and ripped through her nightgown—not Kit's angel wings, but butterfly wings. Emerald ones with matching antennae wagging atop her head. The sisters laughed at the sight of her.

Fancy held up an empty silver tray so that Selenicera could see herself. "Look."

"I'm a butterfly?" She seemed more astounded than upset.

"It's cuter than what you were," Kit said. "A mushroom growing down in the dark."

"Much cuter," Selenicera agreed, taking the tray from Fancy so she could admire herself at her leisure.

But Datura didn't look cute. She swelled and puffed and changed from white to greenish-brown. Her mouth thinned and widened until she looked like a toad. She screamed like one too, croaky and guttural, as she ordered the minions to bring her more tea—that unslakable thirst that the sisters had first noticed in her still evident.

Kit eyed the Woodsons, amazed, then grabbed another tray and looked at herself. "Why haven't we changed?" she asked, disappointed.

"The tea's meant to show what they're like on the inside. So Datura can see for herself who's good and who's not."

"We drank it too."

Fancy shrugged. "This is who we are."

"So then, we're good?" Kit paused, as if listening to what she'd just said. "Is that possible?"

"*She's* good." Fancy nodded her head at Selenicera, who was waggling her antennae and stretching her wings.

"I think that goodness could be flexible enough to include

the two of us," Kit insisted. "I think it's possible. *We* didn't turn into toads."

"That doesn't mean we're saints."

"It's not about being saints or sinners or good or bad, Fancy. It's about being both. You know? About being complete."

"Can I fly?" asked Selenicera, either asking permission or asking whether it was possible.

Fancy nibbled one of the tiny sandwiches. "Try it and see," she said absently, wondering why Kit was so fixated on goodness.

Selenicera shot into the air with a whoop, but Datura's tongue whipped forth NASCAR-quick all the way from the end of the table and caught Selenicera in the chest, her gluey tongue holding her sister fast. Kit reached out, casually, and severed the link with her switchblade.

Once she was free, Selenicera shot into the air, laughing, flapping around the table, fanning the sugar out of the bowl.

Datura reeled in what was left of her bleeding tongue, knocking over teacups and tracking blood over the finger sandwiches. She cried for more tea, so obsessively thirsty she didn't seem to care that the drink she was begging for had turned her into a toad.

The happy-place people returned briefly to clear the spoiled food—and the severed tongue, which was so gross not even

Kit wanted it as a trophy—and replace it with more sand-wiches and cakes. Selenicera alighted in her chair and dug in, but Datura only wanted tea.

"Come on," Kit coaxed around a mouthful of cherry tart. "Even common criminals get a last meal. It's only right."

"I'm not hungry." Datura's severed tongue made her words sound strange.

"What if I gave you a special type of fruit?" said Fancy. "It can only be found here. You like plants. Look at those trees over there."

Datura studied the trees growing between the statues. The dancer's tree had grown tall in the sisters' absence and sported leaves of fire. But it was the old-man tree with its blood fruit that caught Datura's eye.

"What kind of tree is *that*?" she asked.

"The horniverous oldmandia," said Fancy.

Kit snorted into her teacup.

"The fruit of that tree stimulates an unholy appetite," Fancy told her. "Wanna try it? You'd be the first."

"I'll get it!" Selenicera shot up, her emerald wings blowing Fancy's hair this way and that, and flew to the tree and picked the fruit. She flapped to Datura's end of the table and giggled as her sister ate as tamely as a dog.

After consuming the fruit, Datura immediately began eating everything the handlers held before her. They all ate in earnest, but shortly thereafter Datura began to moan and swell. Alarmingly. Her features stretching and rounding like a balloon.

"Is she gone change into something else?" asked Selenicera, nibbling a scone and watching her sister attentively.

Kit looked to Fancy for an answer, but though Fancy had great fun dreaming up murderous scenarios and setting them in motion, she never knew exactly how things would turn out.

"She gets any bigger," Selenicera said, "she gone float away."

But Datura didn't float away.

She popped.

The damp explosion knocked the minions off their feet and blew the girls away from the table. They hit the platform hard, and it took several moments before they recovered enough to pick themselves up off the ground. Selenicera had regained her old skin, the blast having stripped away her winged form. The only thing left of Datura was the gore covering her sister.

Selenicera spoke first, wiping a glob of Datura from her mouth. "I'm officially full now." She flung the glob away, and when it stuck to the air two feet away, she jerked back, startled.

"It's nothing," Kit told her. "Just means we're going home."

A few seconds later the walls of Selenicera's strange garden room closed around them.

Fancy noticed the kinetoscope on the floor and picked it up, petting it like a faithful dog.

"Did all of that happen?" Selenicera wrapped her arms around herself as though she was cold. "Did my sister really explode?"

"Yep," said Kit. "Are you okay?"

"I'm good. But this?" She looked at the goo coating her. "This ain't so good."

Fancy shrieked with frustration when she saw her clothes, having just realized that Selenicera wasn't the only one covered in gore. "This is really starting to irk me out."

"Let's go get cleaned up," said Kit, her lighthearted manner at odds with the wads of skin matting her short hair.

Selenicera showed the sisters the bathroom, much more subdued than she had been in the happy place.

"That's a huge tub." Kit put her hand on Selenicera's head. "Since it's your house and all, we'll let you shower first, kid."

"I don't like showers. I don't like . . . being watered."

Kit slid her hand to the back of Selenicera's neck. "You don't have to bathe if you don't want to. I could drown you instead."

Selenicera shook her head vigorously.

Kit laughed. "Your head says no, but your eyes say yes. Don't they?" She turned Selenicera to face Fancy, who was watching her sister with growing concern. "Look at her. Doesn't she look miserable?"

"Of course. Her sister just exploded all over her."

Fancy went to the sink to scrub her hands clean. "What's the point in helping people, just to kill 'em afterward?"

"You wanna know what the point is? The point is, I have *no fucking idea* why you brought me along!"

Fancy was so stunned by her sister's outburst she didn't even chide Kit for swearing.

"You promised that this time I could stab someone," Kit continued, "but here I am! Covered in blood and yet completely unsatisfied." She considered Selenicera, who'd once again wrapped her arms around herself. "But I don't have to stay unsatisfied. How long do you think this kid'll survive, all alone with no family? I'd be doing her a favor."

"I have a brother," Selenicera said in a small voice. "He'll take care of me. He said he would."

Kit smiled at Selenicera reassuringly. "I could make it so that it wouldn't hurt, if that's what you're worried about. You wouldn't explode or—"

"Please." She was shaking her head, shaking all over. "He's got a den. He said I could stay in it."

Fancy pulled her sister away from Selenicera. "Kit, I told you, there's no need for that. We can kill people without stabbing them or getting our hands dirty."

Kit held her bloody hands in Fancy's face.

Fancy grimaced. "I just gotta work out some kinks."

Kit looked at herself in the mirror. Fancy had no idea what her sister saw, but whatever it was seemed to depress the hell out of her.

"I guess there *is* no need to stab people anymore." Kit took Datura's tooth from her pocket and tossed it in the garbage pail by the toilet, but Fancy hurried forward and fished it out.

She waggled the tooth in Kit's face. "There's also no point in having the happy place if you're gone leave evidence out like Christmas cookies for anybody to find!"

Kit sighed all the way from her toes and sat on the edge of the tub. Then she smiled at Selenicera, who was eyeing the two sisters nervously. "No worries, kid. I won't kill you. I've decided to quit while I'm ahead." She looked down at her own gore-streaked body appreciatively. "Be a shame if all this good stuff turned into a toad."

FROM FANCY'S DREAM DIARY:

MADDA TOOK US TO A CEMETERY FULL OF DADDY'S VICTIMS. KIT GOT MAD EVERY TIME ME AND MADDA PUT FLOWERS ON THEIR GRAVES. SHE KEPT SAYING, CAN'T YOU HEAR THEM SCREAMING DOWN THERE?

CHAPTER SIXTEEN

The sisters made it home fresh and clean and just in time to have breakfast with Madda. They'd brought Selenicera with them, since it was on the way to the bus station, and hid her in their inner room while they visited with Madda and picked at a breakfast they didn't want. After Madda finally bedded down for the day, they snuck Selenicera out of the house and walked her about a mile down El Camino Real to the bus station, a tired wooden building that was more of a hut than a station. After Selenicera called her brother in Houston and told him to meet her at the bus station there, Kit paid for her bus ticket and even gave her extra cash in case she wanted to buy a snack on her way to her brother's house.

The sisters would have left then, but Selenicera had about an hour to wait. She was a different girl from the one they'd rescued from Datura's weird garden room: a butterfly—even without the wings—healthy, but scarily fragile. So without saying anything, the sisters settled on a bench to wait for the bus. Kit went into the station and bought a pair of pink hair ribbons and passed the time playing with Fancy's hair while Selenicera amused herself by hopscotching in and out of the sunlight.

When a dusty bus finally wheezed to a stop before the station, Selenicera hurried onto it. Fancy wasn't surprised that she was in such a hurry to quit them, but she was surprised when Selenicera opened a window and leaned out to say thanks.

"You're welcome." Kit shuffled her feet, a sheepish grin on her face. "Sorry about trying to kill you back there. Nothing personal."

"I know," Selenicera said gravely, turned slightly toward the sun. "You're like rottweilers—they protect you from burglars, but nothing protects you from them."

Fancy found that hilarious, but Kit didn't.

"A rottweiler?" she exclaimed as the bus pulled out of sight through the trees. "Is that how people see me?"

The sisters ditched the road and took the long way back

down Sayer's Trail through the woods so they could eat the ripe, shiny blackberries that grew along the path.

"You're more like a golden goose than a dog," said Fancy. "Letting everybody get rich off us."

"Huh?"

"We shouldn't be shelling out money, paying our clients' expenses—"

"Clients?"

"We provide a service." They had to walk single file over the wooden bridge that spanned the creek below as squirrels dashed across the branches over their heads. "*We* should be getting paid."

"Forget money, Fancy. We're supposed to be helping people."

"Doesn't mean we have to end up in the poorhouse. And that's another thing: Why'd you take all that money from the treasure chest?"

Kit's steps faltered guiltily.

"You think I wouldn't notice that we're short over *two hundred dollars*? What'd you spend the money on?"

"Just some . . . music stuff."

"Music stuff like what? The Dallas Symphony Orchestra?"

"It's my money too."

"*Our* money. And I got my own plans, you know."

Kit snorted. "You still trying to sail the seven seas?"

"The *South* Seas. And shut up." They left the bridge, Fancy in front, wishing it was always as easy to lead Kit.

Behind her Kit said, "Maybe instead of sailing we could do something normal. Like get after-school jobs."

Fancy whirled and walked backward to watch Kit in disbelief. "Doing what?"

"I could teach piano and you could . . . what *can* you do?"

"Kill people. Same as you."

"Maybe it's time to do something else."

Fancy tripped over her own feet and fell backward into a patch of gory Annas. Kit had already knocked all the wind out of her, so the fall was anticlimactic. As Kit came forward to help her up, the ground exploded in a billowing cloud of petals. A pair of hands bloomed in the middle of the path like grisly flowers—more grisly than the gory Annas themselves, which resembled flaring white skirts with red dots like blood at the hem—and latched hold of Kit's bare ankles.

Kit screeched and tried to skip backward, but the hands were holding her too tightly, were in fact climbing her legs hand over hand, as though she were a rope dangling from the school gym ceiling. As the corpse rose, Fancy noted more details. Its bones were visible in places, and the flesh that remained was a mottled gray color. It was wearing a tattered black dress.

Fancy scrambled forward in the dirt and grabbed the corpse to try to pull it off her sister, but couldn't. Instead she came away with a handful of dress, which crumbled to dust in her fist. She grabbed the legs but let go in disgust, rubbing her palms on the front of her jumper. The corpse's skin had felt wet and somehow loose.

Kit, however, after that initial screech, stood oddly silent in the literal grip of a nightmare. The corpse was standing, holding her by the shoulders. Its fingernails were painted a glittery blue. It looked Kit in the eye, although the corpse's own eyes were gone. It opened its lipless mouth and spoke:

"Will you ease my pain?" A ghostly feminine voice soughed in the woods, as if the air itself spoke instead of a corpse whose lungs some animal had long since nibbled out of existence.

Kit had to swallow before she could answer. "Yes."

"My mother doesn't know where I am. She cries for me." The wind blew its dress to dust and made Fancy cough.

"What's her name? How do I find her?"

"Amelia Dandridge. 824 St. Teresa. Tell her where I am. Tell her I didn't run away."

"I will."

As though Kit's promise were magic words, the corpse sank back into the ground. Fancy thought of the spongy earth in the Headless Garden and felt a moment of surreality. "We didn't accidentally wander into the happy place for a few minutes and then wander back out, did we?"

Kit laughed, a skittering sound that revealed that she wasn't as calm as she seemed. "I should be the one asking you that." She collapsed on the path, rocking herself and smothering her giggles until tears stood in her eyes. Fancy knelt beside her, not liking to kneel over the corpse but having no choice. "Kit, shh. It's okay."

"I know it's okay. Remember what Madda said? The thing Big Mama could do? What Cherry herself could do? Me! I can do that. Did you see that? I settled a corpse. I laid her to rest." Simple amazement overcame her giggling fit. "I did it. I mean, I'm about to. As soon as I tell her mother. Damn. I didn't ask what her name was."

"Greenley." The ghostly voice seeped from the ground.

Fancy shot to her feet and would have taken off except that Kit stayed on the ground and laughed.

"She's dead, remember? She can't hurt us."

"You don't know that."

Kit untied the ribbon she'd put in her sister's hair and then drove a sharpened twig into the ground.

"Why did those bones grab you?" Fancy asked, her black hair floating willy-nilly about her face. She felt willy-nilly too, as though Kit had undone some stabilizing cord between them. "I walked over that same spot and nothing grabbed me."

Kit tied the ribbon around the stick in a jaunty bow. "You can see things in glasses of water and I can't. Same thing." She pulled her sister along the path, her hand gritty with dust and dirt. They left the beribboned twig behind like a girly grave marker.

"Why're you grinning like that?" asked Fancy, skipping to keep up with Kit's loping stride.

"Cuz I'm not useless."

"Who said you were?"

"And cuz I can do something you can't."

Fancy stopped skipping. "You don't have to be all happy about it."

"Sorry!" cried Kit.

Happily.

*　*　*

That afternoon the sisters went to the square where Amelia Dandridge lived—St. Teresa Avenue to be precise. On the corner of St. Teresa and Third, a boy running a dark peach juice stand called out, "You girls need luck?" The dark peaches that grew downsquare were notoriously lucky, so dark peach juice was always popular. The boy wore an Uncle Sam hat and had a crowd of people lined up, waiting in the hot sun.

The juice was warm and almost medicinally sweet, but dark peach juice wasn't popular because of its taste. Porterenes didn't believe in magic, but they believed in having all the good luck they could get.

Kit stopped before the stand and smiled at the boy. "What do you say, Fancy?"

Fancy shrugged and rolled her eyes, knowing that Kit wouldn't have felt so in need of luck had the boy not been cute.

"Fancy?" said the boy, handing out plastic cups of pale golden liquid with one hand and snatching dollars with the other. "And Kit? The Cordelle sisters?"

The crowd of people stilled and stared. "Yeah?" Kit said as the sisters braced themselves for an attack.

"Y'all need more than luck," he said solemnly, handing the sisters their drinks. "Y'all need a miracle. Your old man's toast. Too bad he couldn't be more like y'all."

Kit, who had been on the verge of exploding, was shocked out of her anger. "Like *us*?"

"We heard about Mason," one of the waiting customers told her. "And Selie."

"You know Selenicera?"

"She took ballet with my kid until Datura . . ."

"Went apeshit?" Kit suggested. She exchanged a look with Fancy, who couldn't believe that instead of screaming for the cops, everyone was *smiling* at them.

"On the house, ladies," said the peach juice boy after the sisters drank up. "With any luck you'll find out you were adopted."

"With any luck," said Kit, "you'll realize you're an asshole. That way strangers won't have to constantly point it out to you. Thanks for the drink!"

They walked their bikes down St. Teresa, past the cathedral of the same name where a couple of Blue Sisters conversed on the steps in their grayish-blue habits. "You wanna go back and get him?" Fancy said under her voice as they passed the sisters.

Kit frowned. "What for?"

"For saying that about Daddy. We could take him to the happy place. Really put the fear of God into him."

"Fuck him."

Fancy glanced back nervously at the sisters, but they didn't seem to have heard. "You almost killed a little girl for less reason than he just gave you."

"I can't show up at a stranger's house covered in blood—I wasn't raised in a barn." Kit was distracted, searching the house numbers for 824. "Besides, it's like you said: If we went after every rude person, we'd have to go after everybody in town."

"I say a lot of stuff you never listen to."

"Well, I'm listening now." A group of kids raced by, waving tiny American flags and sparklers. "After I do this thing with Amelia, you wanna go to Fountain Square?"

"What for?"

"To hang out, dummy. It's the Fourth of July." When Fancy just stared, dumbstruck, Kit huffed, "Forget I said anything."

Kit stopped at a row house that had been converted to apartments. When Fancy tried to follow Kit up the stoop, Kit put up her hand.

"You should go on home."

"It's too hot for jokes, Kit. Let's get this over with so we can leave."

"It's over right now, Fancy, for you."

Kit was wearing Madda's *my way or the highway* expression, and that's how Fancy knew she was serious. "Why do you wanna send me away?"

"You freak people out, Fancy," she said in the reluctant tone used to inform someone she had bad breath. "The way you sit all quiet, hating everybody. I can put Amelia at ease a lot easier without you there *looking* at her."

"But we do everything together! You came to the happy place with me."

"Because you *asked* me to. Now I'm asking you to go home."

"Why wait until I'm all the way out here to say that?"

"I didn't wanna hurt your feelings."

"But now it's okay?"

Kit turned her back and went into the building. Didn't even apologize, didn't even pretend to feel bad about ditching her own sister. That Kit could care about a stranger's feelings over her own blew Fancy's mind.

"Fine. Don't include me. See if I care." As soon as the door closed behind Kit, Fancy yelled. "And don't say 'fuck'!"

FROM FANCY'S DREAM DIARY:

Kit was running ahead of me through the woods on a path made of pink glass. I tried to keep up but my legs weren't as swift as hers and the glass broke under the weight of my feet, bloodying them, but Kit still wouldn't slow down. When I fell, the glass shattered all around me and cut me into seventeen pieces.

CHAPTER SEVENTEEN

Madda was so thrilled that Kit was carrying on the family tradition of settling the dead that she made her special red velvet cake with cream cheese frosting. To Fancy it tasted like creek mud.

"You're quiet tonight," Madda said, finally noticing her. "What's wrong?"

"She's always quiet," said Kit.

"Quiet*er*." Madda put her palm against Fancy's forehead. "Are you sick?"

Fancy nodded and let Madda put her to bed.

Kit came in some time later and sat next to Fancy in the dark. "You woulda been bored. Amelia just cried a lot and hugged me. It was all very emotional and tragic—you woulda hated it."

"I hate *you*. I'm sick with it. I'm gone die in this bed hating you. Just like Uncle Miles."

"Uncle Miles died of the flu, not hate. Stupid girl. You won't die. You're way too evil and ornery, but if it'll make you feel better, I'll watch over you."

"All night?"

"I'll be here." Kit climbed into bed with her and pulled her close, rubbing her back in slow circles.

Fancy fell asleep listening to Kit's heartbeat. Her dreams were strange and blackberry scented, and every time she woke up, Kit was there, watching her.

But the next day, Kit was gone. Fancy opened her eyes to late-morning sunshine and two notes on the nightstand:

Sorry I missed you at breakfast.
Feel better, sweetie.

And:

Watching you sleep is like watching
paint dry. Gonna find something
exciting to do. Be back soon.

Exciting?

Fancy rolled out of bed and looked into the vanity mirror and saw Kit riding her bike, face turned up to the sun, a smile on her face like she was happy. Even without Fancy by her side she was happy. Fancy got dressed and left the house. If Kit wanted to be happy without her, she'd find a way to be happy without Kit.

Fancy rode her bike into the square and stopped at the music store, secretly hoping to see Kit there, but Kit was nowhere in sight. Fancy rifled listlessly through scratched vinyl records.

"Hey, Fancy."

It was the shop owner, an older lady with wavy hair, a hippy skirt, and rings on her toes. Kit knew her name, but Fancy didn't—she'd never paid attention. "Someone donated a bunch of Louis Armstrong LPs, if you're interested."

Fancy went to where the shop owner was pointing.

"Is it true that you went mute after Guthrie was put away?"

The shop owner was watching her, but Fancy didn't mind— she had a nice face and weird taste in music, which Fancy always appreciated. Fancy gave her a scornful look.

The shop owner laughed. "People have lots of theories, don't they? Do you get hate mail?"

Fancy looked up, surprised.

"So do I. I was married ten years to a child molester, and no one believes that I didn't somehow know that he was hurting children. He does the crime; I get all the hate. They always take it out on the wrong person. All the sympathy gets used up on the victims, and so there's never any left over for innocent bystanders."

"I'm not innocent," said Fancy without thinking, moved by the shop owner's lurid confession. "Maybe that's why they hate us. For reminding them that innocence is just an illusion, and that if you scratch the surface, we're dark and maggoty all the way down to the bone. We're animals, and we're guilty— every one of us."

Fancy brought a record up to the counter—Louis Armstrong's version of "On the Sunny Side of the Street"—but the shop owner wouldn't take her money.

"On the house. Isn't your sister gone meet you?" She looked out of the shop door as if a line of beasties were waiting out on the sidewalk for Fancy to exit. "You shouldn't go around alone."

Fancy wished there were beasties. "I don't care if I get eaten."

"Kit would care," said the shop owner, as if she knew anything about Kit's feelings. "Did y'all have a fight?"

Fancy shrugged.

"It's okay to fight, honey." She grabbed a bag for Fancy's record. "If you don't fight, you never realize how much the people you love mean to you. She'll come to her senses. You come back soon, huh? It's nice to talk to someone who appreciates the joys of utter despair."

Fancy thought about this. "Okay."

She left the store, marveling at how easy that had been, how almost natural to walk away from an encounter with someone without wanting to hurt or maim.

How strange.

When Fancy got home, Kit was sitting at the piano, playing softly and singing into the phone cradled between her face and shoulder. Fancy recognized the song—they had the record in the crate beneath the phonograph. "I Wanna Be Loved by You" by Helen Kane.

Kit sang it giggling into the phone, but then the words took on a deep meaning, her voice full of longing. When Kit saw Fancy glaring at her, though, she straightened, nearly dropping the phone. "Uh, I'll call you back."

Kit stood, put the phone in the charger, and followed

Fancy into the sleeping porch. "Hey. Where you been?"

Fancy raised the bag with her record inside. "What about you? You find something exciting to do?"

"Not really."

"Who was that on the phone?"

Kit sat at the tea table. "Nobody."

"You were singing to nobody?" Fancy put her new Louis Armstrong on the phonograph and decided to smash the Helen Kane record later.

"I wasn't singing *to* him. I was just . . . singing."

Kit could barely look Fancy in the eye. "Let's read the mail."

"Slim pickings today." Fancy skimmed the letters, disappointed. There was still hate mail, although they didn't get nearly as much as they'd used to. But no one had written to them for help, at least not the kind of help the sisters were offering.

"Just means ain't that many people who aim to see someone dead. At least not today."

"I'm really sorry for not letting you come with me to Amelia's."

"Here's one," said Fancy, as though Kit hadn't spoken.

"'Dear sisters, I think there's a monster stalking me. It's green and feathery and has long red teeth. I'm scared to go outside anymore. Could you help me?'"

"It's just, you get so weird whenever I pay attention to other people." Kit was staring at the tea set as though she'd never seen it before, as though she had been taken over by a replicant.

Fancy wrote, "Sorry, Gayle. *Human* monsters we understand. *Monster* monsters are out of our league. Be safe, and good luck not getting eaten."

Kit stroked Fancy's hair, petting her as though she were a cat. Though Fancy tolerated this, she wasn't anywhere close to purring.

"There's gone come a time when I meet somebody and you won't be able to just whisk him away to la-la land—"

"It's the *happy place*. It was. I'm not happy anymore."

Kit stopped touching her. "I'm sorry."

"You apologize so much about so many different things that the words don't even make sense anymore."

"What do you want me to s—"

A knock sounded at the door. The sisters regarded each other quizzically—the Cordelles rarely received visitors.

They answered the door and found a little boy, about eight years old, standing on the front porch. He was dressed in fall clothes—long-sleeved shirt and pants—so of course he was monumentally sweaty and breathing sharply as if he had run all the way to their door.

"I'm Doyle. You sent me a letter."

Kit stepped forward. "Oh, yeah?"

"Yeah." He had thick, dark eyebrows that made him look fierce. "I want you to kill somebody for me."

"I guess I spoke too soon," Kit said to Fancy as she waved the boy inside and led him to their sleeping porch, where she sat him at the tea table.

"Who needs to die?" Kit asked as Fancy poured the iced tea.

The boy drank it in one gulp. "My godfather. Kent Butterman. He beats me."

Kit tugged at the boy's sweaty shirt. "Let's see."

The boy removed his shirt. He was a kaleidoscope of colors: blacks, blues, yellows, greens. And not just his chest and back. He raised his pant legs and showed them additional colors painting his legs up to his thighs.

Kit whistled appreciatively while he straightened his clothes. "You must be a tough little kid."

"Not tougher than Godfather." He slouched on the mushroom stool like a grim gnome. "He been beating on me for a year, ever since Daddy went to jail." He gave Kit a knowing look. "My daddy's in jail too."

He jumped at the sound of the screen door slamming shut. He and Kit watched Fancy hurrying across the yard to the cellar.

"Where she going?"

"To get something to help you. She's good at this sorta thing." Kit put "Beans and Corn Bread" on the phonograph. "Why's your dad in jail?"

"He tried to rob somebody. It was on the news. But then I saw this other thing on the news, about this kid. He was six. His neighbors heard him get beat every night, but they didn't do nothing, even the night the kid died. At least Godmother tries to do something, but then he beats on both of us, 'stead of just me. I'm not gone sit around and wait for him to just beat me to death." As if to illustrate his point he shot off the stool.

The sight of Fancy coming back to the sleeping porch reminded Kit of something.

"How much money you got, Doyle?"

"Seven bucks." He handed over the crumpled bills.

Kit pocketed the money as Fancy came in with the kineto-scope. She poured Doyle another cup of tea. "Go out on the front porch and wait for us."

After Doyle exited through the inner door, Kit turned to Fancy and handed her the money. "You don't need me to go with you, do you?"

"How can you ask me that?"

The bedsprings creaked as Kit sat. "This is your thing. We both know that. At the tea party? At the talent show? What did I do? Nothing. You don't need me." The words hung in the air, buzzing and stinging like wasps.

"I got something planned for this godfather of his, and I *do* need you to pull it off. You'll be center stage."

"I don't need to be center stage; it's not about that."

"Yeah, it's about whether or not we're a team. Me and you against the world, remember?"

Kit didn't answer, and the buzzing grew louder: *You don't need me.* Fancy turned her back on it.

"But if you'd rather abandon me *yet again*—"

"Don't gimme that shit, Fancy! You're the one who won't accept my apology."

"Talk is cheap." Fancy held open the door to the inner room and waited for Kit to walk through it.

When Kit did walk through, a wave of relief washed over her. She hurriedly shut the door on those buzzing, hateful words, but their sting—that she couldn't shut away.

The sisters followed Doyle through the woods to his house, which was about a mile or so down El Camino Real and then another half mile through the woods. Dandelion fluff had turned the air into a snowy tableau. Doyle led them down Mission Trail, past the old ruins of one of the first missions to be built in Texas. Kids from upsquare haunted the ruins on the weekends, and when the wind was right, the sisters could hear their drunken revels from the sleeping porch.

As Doyle walked, he sang the first line of "Beans and Corn Bread" over and over until Kit told him to shut up. He did for a while; then he asked, "What're you gone do to Godfather?" They left the path and waded through a patch of gory Annas. "Shoot him?"

Kit laughed at the hopeful note in his tone. "Whatever we do we won't do here. We're gone take him somewhere else."

"Can I watch?"

"Please yourself, kid. We don't c—" Kit stumbled and nearly smacked face-first into an elm tree. She looked at her feet and heaved a sigh. "Not again." But she didn't seem particularly put out, unlike Doyle and Fancy, who stood frozen by the sight of the hand gripping Kit's ankle.

The corpse climbed Kit, as the first one had done, and when it was free of the earth and face-to-undead-face with Kit, it asked, "Will you grant my plea?"

"Yes."

"Then get me outta these stinking woods! I don't feel safe here. He said I'd never feel safe anywhere, but you have to find somewhere for me."

Kit was patient with the babbling. "Where would you feel safe?"

"*Anywhere* else. Anywhere he can't get me."

"Okay."

"Promise me."

"I promise."

Instead of collapsing back into the ground as the first corpse had done, as soon as Kit finished speaking, this one disappeared.

"What'd you do?" Doyle asked.

"I think I sent her to heaven." She was looking at Fancy, who looked back, awestruck.

"How?"

"I don't know." Kit took Doyle's hand, and then as an afterthought took Fancy's hand as well. Fancy pulled away, uninterested in being anybody's afterthought.

"I was thinking of paradise, something afterlifey like that."

Doyle stared openly at Kit as they walked. "Are you a witch?"

"Ain't no such thing."

"I know. But are you?"

"What do you think?" Kit asked him.

Doyle decided to keep his opinion to himself. "Is it easy to kill?"

"Yep."

Her quick answer seemed to trouble him. "I put a knife to Godfather's throat while he was asleep," said Doyle, "but I couldn't do it."

"Didn't say it was easy for everybody. If it was, everybody would do it. You leave the killing to pros like us."

Doyle nodded thoughtfully. "Do dead bodies always come to life around you?"

"Lately, yeah."

This was news to Fancy. Kit looked away, guiltily.

"I can't cross the street without 'em grabbing at me. I was

thinking I'd be smart like Big Mama and just stay out of graveyards, but there's so many bodies buried all over. I can feel 'em. Even the ones that don't rise. When I pass over 'em, my legs start to shiver like they're full of electricity."

"Is she a witch too?" asked Doyle, pointing at Fancy, swinging Kit's arm like a regular kid instead of one with murder in his heart.

"If I am, she definitely is."

"What can you do?"

When Fancy didn't answer, Kit squeezed Doyle's hand. "You'll see when we get to your house."

"There it is." Doyle pointed out a tiny red house with a swing in the yard and pinwheels in the flower bed.

Before they even reached the front door, a woman came out to meet them, to meet Doyle, as if she had been waiting for him. "Doyle." Her voice was barely audible. "He's looking for you."

She said "he" like a Christian too frightened to speak the name of God for fear of the wrath it would bring.

"Who's she?"

"My godmother, Steffie."

Kit stepped forward, all smiles. "Hey, Miz Steffie. We came over to hang out with Doyle. That okay?"

Steffie had a young face, a whisper-thin body, and a caged expression. She regarded the sisters nervously, as if they were the problem and not the man she lived with.

"He don't like being disturbed in the afternoon."

"What's the holdup, Steffie?" boomed a voice from within the house, less like God's voice and more like a cranky child's.

Kit pushed past Steffie and went inside, Fancy, Doyle, and Steffie following in her wake. They entered a den—a smallish room, Fancy was happy to note. It was cigar-smoke sweet and paneled with dark wood, neat and tidy except for the large man sprawled across a leather recliner, a newspaper spread over his lap, reading glasses perched on his nose. He removed the glasses when he saw them. He had striking eyes: golden irises like a cat's, with large, dark pupils that stood out like pebbles caught in amber. He did not look happy to see them.

"We're the holdup," burbled Kit, standing before him.

"Whatever it is, I ain't buying." He refolded his newspaper and shot Steffie a cold look.

"We're not selling, Godfather." She giggled. "Godfather. I feel like I should kiss your ring." Kit knelt before the recliner, startling the godfather, and took his hairy-knuckled hand. "No rings. Not even a wedding ring, huh, Steffie? But lots of bruises. Why is that? You been knocking some sense into the kid?" She glanced at Doyle, who was leaning back in Steffie's arms. "Looks like he needs it. I can read that smart-ass look from all the way over here."

Godfather seemed to enjoy the sight of Kit at his feet holding his hands. A smirk spread across his face like slime mold. "It's done with love."

Kit's eyes widened. "What's it feel like to get punched with love? Does it feel like this?" She leaned forward and kissed the godfather on the mouth. Fancy watched, appalled, as Kit did a very thorough job.

Kit pulled away from the kiss and punched the godfather in the balls.

"Is *that* what it feels like?" Kit asked him as he doubled over in pain.

As the godfather struggled to catch his breath, Kit stood and spoke to Steffie, who was watching her man with a greedy look in her eyes, as if she was enjoying his every grimace of pain, savoring it as if it were nutritious.

"Hey!"

Steffie snapped to attention and focused on Kit.

"I said, why don't you go into another room? We don't

want you along." Kit glanced at Fancy. "Do we?"

Fancy shook her head, wondering how had Kit learned to kiss like that? Like some sexpot in the movies?

"Along where?"

"Never mind where."

"I'll be okay," Doyle said, pulling away from her. "They're the good guys."

When Steffie wavered too long, Kit snapped, "Go on!"

Steffie was schooled to follow orders and didn't question further. "Okay, but we eat at six."

When Steffie had gone, Kit sat on the arm of the recliner and clapped her hand on the godfather's shoulder. "You know what you're gone do?" she asked Fancy.

Fancy knew exactly. The godfather, still doubled over, turned away from her, as if Fancy's expression alone were more painful than his balls. Kit patted his shoulder, sympathetically. "Don't be scared; she only gives that look to the bad guys."

"He *is* the bad guy!" Doyle cried, afraid Kit had missed the point.

"He is?" she said in surprise. "Well, then." She put her mouth to the godfather's ear as Fancy turned the crank. "Go ahead and be scared."

FROM FANCY'S DREAM DIARY:

Uncle Miles was a real tiny little boy, but he was smart. He taught me how to unlock a doorway that would lead me to Daddy. But when I stepped through, the flesh of my leg fell off. Uncle Miles looked confused and said, Daddy, Death; I always get the D words mixed up.

CHAPTER EIGHTEEN

As they entered the happy place, the minions whisked the godfather away, and the sisters and Doyle followed after. They left the Headless Garden and went down into the village, the sea breeze so refreshingly cool Fancy wished she could bottle it and take it back with her to Portero.

A crowd had gathered in a field around a boxing ring, and Fancy, Kit, and Doyle arrived just in time to see the minions taking the godfather into a small tent nearby.

"Somebody's gone beat up Godfather?" exclaimed Doyle, ecstatic at the idea.

"This is hilarious." Kit laughed. "Who did you get to fight him?"

"You," said Fancy. "He's Beans, you're Corn Bread."

"Me?"

She clapped Kit on the back. "If you can give yourself wings, why couldn't you give yourself some boxing skills? You could whup that turkey even without extra skills. *You're* not a little kid. In that other tent is a change of clothes for you. Good luck, not that you'll need it."

"True." Fancy watched Kit's shoulders go back and her spine straighten. "I can take this guy."

Doyle kicked his foot awkwardly after Kit left. Sometimes Fancy wished she had Kit's easy way with people, especially around little kids. She didn't like it that Doyle was scared of her. She tried to take his hand as Kit had, but he shied away.

"Let's sit down," she snapped, annoyed with him and with herself for caring that he preferred Kit. Didn't everyone?

As Fancy and Doyle took their seats in the front row, Kit came out of the tent in shiny pink boxers and a tank top and climbed nimbly into the ring. The announcer, a woman wearing a mask made of peacock feathers and a sparkly evening gown, introduced the contestants, speaking into an even sparklier microphone.

"In this corner, at six feet and weighing two hundred

seventy-five pounds, is Kent 'the Godfather' Butterman!"

The crowd erupted into boos. Doyle booed more loudly than anyone.

The godfather, in his yellow trunks, was solidly built, only a little flabby around the middle. He was spoiling for a fight, and so of course he turned his anger on the weakest person there: Kit, who was waiting on the other side of the ring.

"And in this corner, at five foot four and weighing a hundred and seven pounds, is Christianne 'Kit' Cordelle!"

The crowd surged to its feet, cheering. "Get him, Kit!" Doyle yelled.

Neither the godfather nor Kit wore gloves. Kit pranced around, shaking out her long arms and legs, blowing kisses first to the crowd and then to the godfather, who was yelling at her and trying to attack her. There was no referee, so the announcer had to keep him distracted until the bell sounded, signaling the beginning of the match. The announcer fled the ring, and Kit had to deal with the angry godfather on her own.

He immediately grabbed Kit by the throat and choked her, much to the crowd's dismay. Their dismay didn't last long. Kit stepped back and left her neck and head in the godfather's hands. He wrung her neck several moments before he realized

Kit's body was several feet away, tapping her foot impatiently.

The godfather did a double-take when Kit's head blew a raspberry at him, and he yelped and flung her head away. Kit caught it and placed it on her shoulders, then bowed to the appreciative audience. Then she ran forward and punched the godfather in the mouth.

Kit had somehow made her fists larger than normal, like sledgehammers, so he flew six feet through the air, then dropped to the mat like a bomb. Though the godfather somehow climbed to his feet, he didn't stand a chance against Kit's new fists. When she was done with him, he looked like a man who had been stung by the residents of an entire beehive. Kit did a little Mexican hat dance all around his swaying figure, to the merriment of the crowd, who shouted, "Olé!" When she was done, she bowed again and accidentally on purpose knocked her butt into the godfather, laughing as he dropped, unresisting, to the mat. He didn't get up again.

As he lay on his back, Kit knelt at his feet and, starting at his toes, began to curl the godfather as if he were a tube of toothpaste and she were determined to get every last drop. Doyle was actually standing on his chair, cheering deliriously along with the rest of the crowd. After Kit finished literally squeezing the life from the godfather, she stood and tucked his rolled hide under her arm. The sparkling announcer reentered the ring and slipped in the godfather's remains as she thrust Kit's arm in the air and declared her the champion.

After that it was pandemonium. The crowd went wild, stamping and clapping and photographing Kit using old-fashioned cameras with huge, noisy flashbulbs. Tuxedoed men and décolletaged women rushed the ring to be the first to congratulate Kit, Doyle included. Doyle was little enough to dodge through miniscule gaps in the crowd. Fancy tried for a while, then gave up and went back to her front-row seat. Let Kit have the attention; she liked that sort of thing.

Kit wasn't out of place among all the finely dressed happy-place people. Even in her boxing shorts, she looked natural and, most of all, comfortable. Fancy had always thought Kit was pretending when she acted bubbly and *how do you do* with everyone she met. But it was no pretense. Fancy didn't want to suck up to people the way Kit did, but it seemed unfair that Kit should be so much better at it.

While people clamored for Kit's autograph, Fancy waited it all out in her seat alone. Alone until Franken plopped beside her, his scars livid against his pale skin.

"Why do you keep coming around?"

"I'm surprised I can, seeing as how you're so bent on killing me."

Fancy couldn't believe that the boy who'd been locked in her cellar was now mouthing off to her.

"I know you poisoned that cake."

"All it did was make you sleep," she said. "But if you want me to poison you—"

"Why do you hate me so much?" He had been in the happy place for such a long time, and yet he still looked incredibly miserable.

"I don't feel any way about you. Neither does Kit. It's best you get on with your life."

"Without her?" He looked downcast, gently petting his stitches as though each one were precious to him. "Could you?"

"She's my sister."

"You can't get any closer to her than I can."

Fancy frowned at the crowd hiding Kit from sight.

A woman wearing a sequined gown stood at the edge of the crowd directly in front of Fancy, so she concentrated on the sequins, and soon Kit's image in the ring came into focus along the woman's back and rear end.

As the cameras snapped in great blinding flashes, Kit posed next to a young man with no head. He had a head, but he was holding it in his arms, like Kit had done in the ring, only for him it was permanent.

"Who's that with Kit?" Fancy asked.

"Lorne," said Franken. "One of the headless."

Fancy saw them fanned behind Kit, a crowd of gorgeous people carrying their heads in their hands, sharing the spotlight with her. Their heads had not been severed—there was nothing gory or ghoulish about them. They had simply been born in two pieces.

"They're like celebrities," Franken continued, watching them stroke their own heads with a fawning affection typically reserved for spoiled lapdogs. "Like models. People are always wanting to paint them or photograph them."

"Or sculpt them," said Fancy, thinking of the statues in the happy place. The headless people were beautiful in a way real people never were. Even models had to be airbrushed. The headless were beyond even the idea of flaws. Unless their headlessness could be considered a flaw.

"Lorne's one of the more sought-after ones," said Franken. "A real hit with the ladies."

What amazed Fancy was that Kit wasn't sizing up Lorne or anyone else as a potential victim the way she usually did; she was just having a good time, was actually *flirting* with him. When Lorne held his head up to Kit's face, she kissed his ear and then laughed as everyone around her went wild whistling and snapping photos.

Fancy shot out of her seat, and when the camera flashed again, Lorne's brown eyes exploded.

The silence lasted one shocked second, and then Lorne screamed, holding his head to his chest, ruining his tuxedo shirt, and feeling the damage done to his eyes with his free hand.

Fancy lost the view as the sequined woman turned to face her. *Everyone* was looking at her, stunned and silent. When Fancy stood, they parted before her until the ring was visible and Kit's shock plain to see. Fancy joined her sister in the ring.

Kit pointed to Lorne's empty sockets, her hand trembling. "Why did you do that?"

"Why should he see you when I can't?"

"Take it back!"

"No."

"I can't help it if people like me!"

"*I* can help it. Where do people get off liking you anyway? They don't even know you."

"Fix his eyes, Fancy."

"With what? I don't have an extra pair of eyes in my pocket."

Doyle stepped between the sisters, referee-like, and reached for his godfather's rolled skin, still tight under Kit's arm. He peeled back the godfather's swollen eyelids to reveal those striking gold irises. "Do you want these?" he asked. "You can use 'em. He don't need 'em no more."

Fancy didn't want to do anything nice for Lorne, but she didn't like the way Kit was looking at her—like she was rabid—so to prove she could be reasonable, Fancy plucked the eyes from the godfather's head and pressed them into Lorne's empty sockets. After they'd popped into place, Lorne blinked and, cradling his head to his chest, wiped the residue of his old eyes clear. He was even more beautiful than before. The other headless gathered close, exclaiming over the pretty change in their friend.

"You want any other alterations?" Kit asked, noting how pleased he seemed, even as she glared at her sister. "You deserve it after what Fancy did to you."

"No," Lorne said quickly, glancing nervously at Fancy.

"Though I am thankful for the replacements—an improvement, some would say." The crowd murmured its agreement, fully aware that Fancy had hurt him. And yet in awe of her too. The way everyone here behaved around her no matter what she did. Unlike Kit, who had never before disapproved of her.

"You can go now," Fancy announced, sick of their toadying. "All of you."

The crowd cleared away so fast it was as if they'd never been there.

The sisters and Doyle left the ring and passed the one person who'd stayed behind. But Kit stalked past Franken without speaking to him, and Franken was too crestfallen to call after her.

Fancy trailed behind Kit and Doyle as they made their way back to the garden. Once there, Kit tossed the godfather skin at Fancy without looking at her. That was fine with Fancy; she didn't particularly want to look at Kit, either. She took the skin to one of the stone circles, grimacing at the empty, floppy feel of it, and tipped it into the soft soil, wondering what manner of tree the godfather would produce.

"I thought you said *she* was the witch," Doyle said to Kit as they sat together on the platform. "How did you make

Godfather curl up like that? And how'd you make your head come off and your fists get so big?"

"I just think about it and it happens."

Doyle looked at his own hands, thinking furiously at them to no avail. Kit demonstrated, her fists growing to the size of catcher's mitts. The extra weight tipped her forward onto her face. When she rolled over, her hands were again normal-sized, and Doyle fell next to her laughing, the light, giddy sound of a boy without any threat of violence hanging over his head.

Before long, the den in Doyle's house reappeared around them. Kit made Fancy give Doyle back his seven dollars, and then Kit gave him another twenty and laughed when he ran into his godmother's waiting arms.

"Never gone get to the South Seas if you keep giving our money away," Fancy muttered when they were back in their room, bugs bumping against the screen.

"Why you wanna leave?" Kit sat in front of the vanity, applying deep red lipstick. "When there's so much here to stick around for now?"

"So much of what?" Fancy flopped onto her bed and grabbed Bearzilla from the shelf overhead. "Headless boys and wicked old men like the godfather? And what's up with you kissing every boy you see? You're so . . . indiscriminate."

Kit touched her fingers to her mouth and stared at her red lips in the mirror. "You know what I think, Fancy? I think we need to spend time apart."

"Apart?" The word was so foreign and strange, Fancy had to say it again. "*Apart?*"

"Yes. That way when I'm indiscriminate with people, you can't *make their eyes explode!*"

"I didn't mean to do that," she said, wondering what Kit's problem was. The old Kit would have giggled at the sight of a boy's eyeballs exploding. "It doesn't even matter. Happy-place people aren't real."

Kit said nothing, just continued to bury the old Kit under cosmetics and crap. "Don't forget to turn the oven down to three-fifty at six o'clock."

"Why do I have to remember?"

"Because I won't be here."

"But it's almost dinnertime!"

"Madda knows about it."

Fancy squeezed Bearzilla to her chest. "Where you going?"

"Amelia Dandridge wants to take me to dinner to thank me for telling her about Greenley."

"About who?"

"*Greenley.* The first corpse I raised. But really, I just think Amelia's lonely and wants to talk or something."

"And you're the shoulder to cry on?"

Kit looked offended. "What's wrong with my shoulders?"

"What did I just say about being indiscriminate?"

"Amelia's a real person, Fancy. Or can't you tell the difference anymore?"

"You know what I mean."

"I worry about that," Kit said, staring at Fancy in the mirror, her eyes sad. "About how one day you won't be able to tell the difference between real and unreal. Because that'll be a bad day, Fancy. A bad, bloody day."

FROM FANCY'S DREAM DIARY:

I saw a tree full of bright red fruit. I picked one to take home and share with Kit, but I couldn't resist taking a bite just to see if it tasted as good as it looked. It did. But the loud crunch attracted a pack of dogs. I hid the fruit in my pocket but the dogs surrounded me, sniffing me and nipping my hips and my thighs, so I broke free and ran. But they caught me, and when they bit into me, I made a crisp juicy sound.

CHAPTER NINETEEN

Kit sat at the tea table in a pink slip, flipping through Fancy's sketchbook, a studious frown marring her forehead. It was the most attention Fancy had gotten from Kit in a while. Since the godfather incident Kit had been gone a lot, and even when she was home, she was often preoccupied, and she'd developed an annoying fixation with love songs—"Mr. Sandman," "Earth Angel," "I Only Have Eyes for You"—the sappier the better. But today she seemed almost normal.

"What do you think?" she asked when Kit had finished mulling over the India ink and watercolor renderings of fruit bowls and articulated dummy limbs.

"You got an eye for color. There's a certain intensity." Kit shook her head and closed the book. "But mostly you suck. I can't even tell what half this stuff is. Maybe you should get glasses or something."

"Thanks." Fancy threw Bearzilla at Kit's head and then finished writing in her diary, admiring the neat penmanship. Usually she wrote her dreams while she was still half asleep, and the words scrawled all over the page and all over each other and she had to work really hard to decipher them. But this one she'd remembered clearly upon awakening, her thighs still tingling from the dream bites.

"What did you dream about?" Kit asked, as Fancy shoved the dream diary under her pillow.

"Dogs chasing me."

"I dreamed *I* was being chased. Not by a dog, though. By a boy." Kit smiled in a way Fancy hated. "He had laser eyes, and even in the dark I couldn't hide. Wanna know what happened when he caught me?"

"Wanna watch me puke all over myself?"

"Why write down your dreams anyway?"

"Dreams are a reflection of one's inner landscape."

"You get that from a fortune cookie?"

Fancy was unamused. "It's important to know what you're like on the inside."

"What're you like?"

"Weird."

Kit laughed. "I coulda told you that."

"I might not stay weird."

"Is that what you hope? That one day you'll start to dream about the prom or getting married or . . ." A folded page fell out of the sketchbook. Kit unfolded it and gasped. "What is this? Is this you and Ilan? *Kissing?*"

Fancy would have hidden under the covers, but it was too hot and she had long since kicked the covers from the bed. She had to settle for busying herself with the phonograph, grabbing the first record to hand: "Hello Stranger."

"Ilan had to do that for an assignment."

"And you had to keep it? He draw this from memory?"

"No!"

"Still never been kissed."

"No," she gritted, prickling at Kit's patronizing tone.

"You should take Ilan for a test spin. Looks like he'd be good at it."

Fancy snatched the drawing from Kit and then refolded

it carefully and shoved it back into her sketchbook.

"I'm not surprised you'd pick a guy like Ilan. You're a lot alike. Ilan pushed Gabe down a flight of stairs once; did you know that? His own brother. Broke both his legs and put him in traction for almost three months."

"How's that make him like *me*?"

Fancy remembered how creepy Gabriel had behaved with the severed head and with the girl he'd given CPR to and found that she wasn't at all surprised that Ilan would break Gabriel's legs; *she* wanted to break his legs. Kit was the only one who didn't seem to have seen Gabriel's true colors. "How's that make him like *me*?"

"Just seems like something you'd do. To me. You always hurt the one you love. Who loves me more than you?"

"How do you know that about Gabriel?"

"I told you we have a class together. Sometimes we talk."

Kit stopped her playacting and began to fiddle with the tea set.

Fancy couldn't help but notice how her sister, who had always been able to look her in the eye, now seemed unable to. "You'd tell me, wouldn't you?" The words were so soft, Fancy could barely hear herself saying them. "If you were seeing him?"

"So you could put me in traction too? I don't think so."

"I wouldn't hurt you like that," Fancy said over the skip-hiss of the phonograph, the sound of finality. Fancy was sure that skip-hiss was what everyone would hear at the end of the world. "You're the one who hurts me, always abandoning me for other people. You're the one—"

Kit kissed Fancy on the mouth, knocking over the teacup. She kissed her cheek and then her ear. "I love you. Do you know that?"

"I know," Fancy said as Kit squeezed her tight.

"That's the only thing that matters," Kit was whispering. "Please remember that." Kit whispered in Fancy's ear for a long time.

Anything to avoid looking her in the eye.

In art class their assignment was to paint a childhood memory. Fancy had painted a whiskered catfish. She looked at that catfish and remembered the first time Daddy had taken her and Kit fishing on the Sabine River, how cool it had been to look over the water clear into Louisiana, and how patient Daddy had been with her and Kit, helping them thread their hooks and telling them fairy stories to keep them from noticing how long it took the fish to bite. The catfish represented all of that to Fancy, but Mr. Hofstram didn't get it.

"What is this hideousness supposed to represent?" he exclaimed, dabbing his face with a hankie.

"A fish."

"A fish!" Mr. Hofstram yelled, his hankie over his nose as though her painting smelled. "What are all those angles? There should be three dimensions. Three! Not twelve."

"I draw what I see, sir," she said, resisting the urge to skewer Mr. Hofstram with the business end of her paintbrush. "It ain't my fault you don't get it."

"It *is* your fault. An artist's job is to *make* people get it."

"I'm not an artist."

"You'll get no argument from me, madam." Fancy ignored the tittering of the other students as Mr. Hofstram turned his attention to Ilan's work.

Ilan had used oil paint, which gave his work the wet reality of a photograph. A crime-scene photograph—he'd painted the inside of Fancy's cellar. It gave Fancy a slight chill that he'd gotten so many details right, flawlessly recreating what it had looked like three years ago: the tall metal shelving unit, the cot, even Daddy's mirror that once hung on the wall—

because of the blood that had been smeared on it, the deputies had taken it away as evidence. The dense grayness of the room itself had been exaggerated so that the room appeared to have been created from heavy fog.

In contrast Mr. Turner's body was almost clinical in its depiction, strewn about in naked, bloodless pieces like a disassembled cadaver. Mr. Turner's head sat high on the metal shelf, one of his muscular arms lay across the cot, and both his legs, like dark, hairy drumsticks, had been propped carelessly against the wall. In one shadowy corner of the cellar curled something that could have been a mouse . . . or a penis.

Mr. Turner's head, though severed, didn't wear an expression of death but of awareness, pulsing with life as he stared out of the picture, his expression both beautiful and horrified—beautiful because all the Turner men were beautiful and horrified because, despite the bonesaws bleeding in the middle of the floor below Mr. Turner's head, he didn't seem to understand what had happened to him.

Even though Ilan had taken liberties in his painting—only Mr. Turner's severed arm had been found in the cellar—Mr. Hofstram didn't have to ask what memory it represented. Everyone knew what had happened to Ilan's father, and enough had been written about the Bonesaw Killer's infamous cellar that even people who had never seen it could describe it.

"Interesting approach to the afterlife, Ilan," Mr. Hofstram murmured, with none of the contempt he used whenever he had to address Fancy. "To put him in that cellar in pieces instead of on a cloud somewhere."

"In heaven? I don't believe in that stuff."

"Art as therapy. You might try putting him on a cloud. It might make you feel better." Mr. Hofstram moved on to the next pair of students, circling them like they were a large fairy ring. Maybe he'd circle one too many times and disappear through a door.

"Maybe I don't wanna feel better." When Fancy tore her eyes from Ilan's father it was to find Ilan staring at her, a streak of red on his cheek like war paint. But his expression had nothing of the warrior about it. He looked young and sad. "I'm not afraid of pain. Are you?"

When Fancy didn't answer, he said, "I know you can talk. You talked to me at Cherry Glade, remember?" When Fancy still didn't answer, he took her hand, and with his red paintbrush he wrote *please* into her palm.

Fancy looked at the word a long time, frankly stunned by

his boldness in even touching her, let alone begging for favors. She closed her hand over the word as if it were alive and frag-ile. "How do you know what our cellar looks like?"

"Photos."

"Death ain't really like that," she told him. "Beautiful like that."

"What *is* it like?" Ilan asked, giving her a sly look. "A dance contest or a tea party? A boxing match? Seems to me like you don't wanna face the reality of death any more than I do."

"You don't know what I want. I don't know what people are saying about me, but don't get to thinking you know me."

"I do know you, Fancy. All about you. The problem is, you don't know about me."

Fancy's day was made even more unnerving when Kit didn't show up to read the letters. The ringing bell brought Fancy racing to the front door, until she realized Kit wouldn't be ringing the bell like some stranger.

When she peeped out, she saw that it was only Ilan and opened the door.

"You know you got a fruit basket out here?" The smell of rain was on the wind.

He picked it up off the porch, a giant thing almost taller than Fancy. It was addressed to her and Kit from Doyle and his godmother. Ilan stepped past her into the house.

"Wait—"

"Where do you want me to set it?"

"I can carry a fruit basket."

"Just being helpful." He set it on the coffee table. He wore black wristbands wrapped in silver chain, like he'd broken loose from a dungeon. Fancy was sure that if she chained him, he wouldn't break free.

"So what's up?"

"Nothing."

It was too dark, so she opened the shutters to brighten the room. Ilan followed her as she went from window to window, reminding her of one of the velvet tigers on the wall, stalking her, circling her, and looking her over in a way she couldn't hide from. In a way that made *her* feel chained.

"You alone?"

"Madda's here." He wasn't even that tall, but he seemed to take up too much space. She was embarrassed suddenly by the ripe-rotten smell of blue statice, which Madda liked to decorate the house with because the flowers "died so beautifully." It was especially embarrassing because Ilan smelled so nice, like sweet clover and paint.

He stopped in front of her. She could see the pulse beat in his throat. "Is it okay that I'm here? Your ma has all these notions of what kinda stuff you're ready for. Maybe you ain't ready to be alone in the house with a boy."

"I'm not alone."

"Unsupervised," he amended.

His lips looked slightly moist, as though he had licked them recently, but she didn't remember seeing his tongue. She would have remembered that.

"I'm not five."

"Then why are you dressed like that? In that teeny dress? Don't you have anything that fits? The straps are cutting into your shoulders, probably cutting off your circulation."

"Are not." They were, sort of. He illustrated by trying to wiggle his finger under her strap, but he couldn't.

Fancy moved away from his hand and sat in the wicker chair.

"If I cut that dress off you, I'd be doing you a favor." He pulled up an ottoman and sat in front of her, determined to crowd her. "Saving you from gangrene or something."

"I'm not scared of you. It's funny you think I would be."

"Is that the problem? You think I'm holding a grudge? Looking to hurt you? What happened between our families . . . I don't blame you."

"That's what you told Madda. That you don't blame her."

"I don't even blame your pop. I tried that. It didn't bring 'em back, you know?"

"Anybody did to my family what Daddy did to yours, I'd kill 'em. Or die trying."

"You get mad. You get violent. But nothing changes."

"You one of those goody-goody types?"

"No. I don't know. Maybe. You like goody-goody types?"

"No. I don't like anybody except my family."

"Even your dad? Even after what he did?"

"Everybody does bad things. What's that got to do with love?"

"Now who's goody-goody?"

"Why're you in my house?"

"To pay back the money for the amp." He stood and dug in his back pocket. She caught a flash of his lower stomach. He had an outie. "Frigging Tony destroyed it in a tantrum. I weaseled it out of Gabe, where the money came from."

"Amp?" She stared at the crisp folded bills he held out to her.

"We needed a new amp so we could audition for the battle of the bands, and we only just got paid today, so thanks." He pushed the money into her hand when she wouldn't take it and sat back down. "I woulda given it to you in class, but I figured it'd be easier for you to talk to me if nobody was around."

Fancy took the money with fingers that felt numb. Counted it. Two hundred dollars. Exactly what had been missing from the treasure chest. Maybe her dress *was* cutting off her circulation—she felt dizzy.

"Kit's cool for helping us out like that. I told her she should be in charge of the band's finances."

"You . . . see her?"

"Gabe brings her by the house most days after her music class. It's always weird to see her without you. Even now. Y'all have such a stranglehold on each other usually. I told Miz Lynne those classes'd be a help."

"*You* told Madda?"

"I didn't *tell* her, like I'm her boss. She was asking about classes, and I told her about the ones me and Gabe are taking. Y'all got it easy, though. We take three each, plus we have to work. The band's the only thing I got to look forward to. That and art class."

"Where's Kit now?" She could barely hear herself speak over the roaring in her ears. "At your house?"

"Probably. You okay?"

"I wanna go to your house."

"Fancy." His voice compelled her to look in his eyes. He was worried about her. "Is something wrong?"

He ought to be worried about his brother.

"Let's go."

The ride to Ilan's house downsquare was awkward. Ilan tried to make conversation, but Fancy blasted the radio to shut him up. She had to concentrate on filling her mind with hope. Hope that Kit's only interest in Gabriel was how to kill him and not get caught.

The Turners lived with their grandpa in a shotgun shack down the street from St. Michael's Church. They entered to find Ilan's grandpa dozing on the couch in front of the TV. He mumbled something about "devil's music" as Ilan walked past, but both Ilan and Fancy ignored him. Ilan led her to the back of the house, through room after room, until she heard Kit laughing behind a door.

When Ilan opened it, Fancy saw Kit and Gabriel lying together on a fuzzy brown coverlet, so caught up in each other they didn't notice Fancy and Ilan.

Kit was laughing as Gabriel made smacking sounds against her neck and telling him she had to go, but not seeming in any big hurry to actually do so.

Fancy looked away from Kit's expression. The mirror on the wall behind her, above the dresser, showed her the happy place. But it wasn't soothing her.

"Gimme twenty more kisses and I'll let you go."

"Twenty? Where?"

"Lady's choice."

"Your spleen."

Fancy looked back at her sister, hopeful.

"Huh?"

"Your liver. Your thyroid glands. I think about it all the time, opening you up and kissing you on the inside."

"You are inside. Right here." He touched his heart.

"I love you." She kissed his mouth. His cheek. His ear.

Fancy stormed into the room, hooked her arm around Kit's neck, and dragged her from beneath Gabriel. She felt like she was outside her own body watching the arm around her sister's neck tighten. She had just wanted to get Kit away from Gabriel, but now she was afraid to let go. What if Kit ran back to him?

Gabriel scrambled off the bed. "Don't be mad at her, Fancy. I'm the one—"

"Don't talk to me like you know me!"

Kit clawed at the arm Fancy had at her throat, leaving long, red scratches that Fancy didn't feel. Her veins felt full of Novocain.

Gabriel's hair, normally corralled into artistic squiggles, was free and sprouting all over his head in black crinkles. He looked like a clown. A clown with his fly undone.

Kit got her feet under her and broke free of Fancy's hold, pushing her back into the wall. "Fancy, calm down."

"I am calm."

"No, you're not. Remember what I said? I love you. I know you think there ain't room enough for you and other people, but there is. I swear. Gabriel's a good guy. He even goes to church! But he's not scared of me or freaked out by me. He loves me, Fancy. And if a boy like Gabe can love me, there must be something in me worth loving. Something good in me."

"And you think I'm so evil and tainted that my love doesn't count?"

As she spoke, the happy place seemed to ooze out of the mirror, sliding along the walls.

"Fancy," said Kit. "What're you doing?"

"All of a sudden I'm not good enough for you? Why can't I be enough for you?"

"Because I don't wanna *be* with you! Don't you get that? I wanna be with Gabriel!"

Fancy looked away from Kit, the realization that she had been making a scene in front of strangers heavy in her mind. Ilan and Gabriel. Staring at her like she was a particularly good show on television. She saw the Ray Charles record on the dresser. "I Got a Woman." The one she'd been looking all over for.

"I loaned it to him," said Kit, following her gaze. "Fancy, look at the walls. Are you doing that? Without the scope? How is that—"

"You loaned it to him because you wanna be with him. Give him things. Even my things."

"Our things."

"*My* things!" Fancy broke the record against her knee. And hurled the pieces at Kit. "You wanna *be* with him? After I take his head, you can keep it in a jar and have him all to yourself and be with him *all the time*."

The happy place took over the room, consumed it.

FROM FANCY'S DREAM DIARY:

I died. I don't know what of. I was in a crate in the Pikachu costume I wore for Halloween when I was seven. Kit was dragging me from house to house trying to get somebody to take me in and bury me, but nobody would.

CHAPTER TWENTY

The happy place was almost unrecognizable. Clouds hung low and heavy and reddish like blood clots in the sick-yellow sky. The light that colored the clouds also touched the statues with a red glaze, so their heads seemed to have been lopped off in some bloody massacre. The trees creaked in the wind, only the creaking sounded like shrieks of pain. A smell of rot soured the air, wafting from the flamingos lying dead on the grounds.

It was as if they'd entered an alternate world where the happy place was run by a lunatic instead of a young girl. A sweet young girl with a wicked, deceitful, faithless sister.

"What did you do to this place?" Kit whispered, staring wide-eyed at the garden.

Fancy reached into Kit's pocket and grabbed her switch-blade. Then she leaped on Gabriel and brought him to the ground. "After I cut his head off, you can keep it in a jar and have him all to yourself and be with him *all the time*." She released the blade and went for Gabriel's neck.

People were screaming, but Fancy felt more calm than she had ever felt. Her purpose in life had been reduced to one simple goal: remove Gabriel's head.

Someone grabbed her arm and kept her from jamming the blade into Gabriel's throat, so Fancy leaned forward briefly and then whipped her head back hard. Ilan groaned and dropped to the ground beside her. Fancy didn't pay him any mind, too busy jabbing the knife toward Gabriel's—

Fancy was yanked to her feet, the switchblade snatched from her hand. "Have you lost your fucking mind, Fancy?" Kit pushed her aside and helped Gabriel to his feet. Stay away from him. Stay away from *us*."

Fancy tried to grab the knife again, but she tripped over Ilan's unconscious body. As she stumbled Kit caught her, and this time, she slapped Fancy across the face.

"Slap me again," Fancy said. "Might as well get all that anger out now, cuz Gabriel's *dead*. I'm going to kill him, and you can't stop me." Fancy waited, but Kit didn't hit her again.

"I don't wanna hurt you."

"Too late!" Fancy screamed, and it was too late. She felt like one big bruise from head to toe.

A stone circle, full of earth, pushed up through the ground near Kit and Gabriel, causing them to stumble into each other. The circle was right in the center of the platform, a showcase spot. And Fancy knew exactly what she wanted to showcase there. She was sure Gabriel would make an especially handsome tree.

Fancy ran forward and shoved Gabriel backward into the dirt, and smiled when it swallowed him up.

"No!" Kit dove into the stone circle, but instead of bouncing off the dirt as she had before, she sank into it, disappearing the same way Gabriel had.

"Damn it." But despite her annoyance Fancy felt a warm curl of pleasure that Kit was finally beginning to accept that the happy place was just as much hers as it was Fancy's.

Fancy held her nose and then jumped in after her sister. She swam through the moist cakelike earth, batting the worms away, and crashed into a dark coffin. She ripped open the lid, struggling to keep her hair and the earth out of her eyes and throat, but when she saw Gabriel lying inside the coffin, looking at her with a nervous grin, her focus narrowed to just one thing—choking that grin right off his face.

Fancy reached for him, but Kit shoved her away and slammed the coffin shut; she floated over it protectively.

Fancy tried to push Kit aside, but Kit would not be moved.

"I'm not one of your happy-place subjects, *maharaja*. How many times do I have to tell you that you are not the boss of me? Now get outta here."

"I'm not leaving you down here alone with that—"

"GET OUT!"

Fancy shot out of the grave, the force of Kit's anger lifting her so high in the air that she could have touched the neck of one of the statues. So high that when she finally hit the ground, Fancy was sure she would break against it like an egg. But this was her place. When she hit the ground, it made itself as soft as down. So unfair that the ground cared more about her than Kit did.

When someone stumbled over Fancy's ankle, she sat up. The platform was full of mourners in black, weeping. She hadn't authorized this.

Fancy shoved through the crowd, a sick feeling in her stomach as she reached the center of the platform, where she'd raised what she'd meant to be Gabriel's grave. Instead of a tree sprouting from it as she'd planned, a tombstone jutted from the soft earth with an inscription that read:

CHRISTIANNE CORDELLE	GABRIEL TURNER
1995–2011	1997–2011

DIED IN THE BLOOM OF THEIR YOUTH
BECAUSE CHRISTIANNE'S HORRIBLE SISTER
REFUSED TO LET THEM BE HAPPY.

The headless people filed into the garden in a long, sad line. One by one they each placed a single flower on Kit's fake grave. Fancy watched angrily. How could they play along with Kit's idiot fantasy?

"I can't believe she's gone." Franken stood beside Fancy, tears in his eyes, scars bled white with shock. "I was so sure I'd go before she did. I thought she'd see to it."

"You're all a bunch of idiots."

The mourners started weeping. Lorne looked at her nervously

with the godfather's old gold eyes and switched his head to the crook of his other arm, out of her reach.

"We've only come to pay our respects," he said, "but if you don't wish it—"

"What do I care? Dance on her grave, if you want. *Break*-dance on it."

They stared at her as though she'd cursed in church. She felt the sacrilege more than they did. "Just get out of here. Get out before I throw all of you down there with them!"

Everyone left the garden except one person.

Ilan, his forehead bloody, walked dream slow toward the stone circle, as if he didn't trust each step to land him on solid ground. His eyes crawled over the tombstone inscription.

"It was the mirror," he said. "It brought us through. Just like . . . You opened a door." He was trying to digest everything, but it was sitting hard inside him, hurting him. He looked at Fancy. "You did this. You killed my brother."

"Your brother's not dead. Him and Kit are down there snuggled up, laughing at me." She put her mouth close to the stone. "I hope you get eaten by maggots!"

"You're *crazy*."

Fancy straightened up and smoothed down her hair in an

effort to look less insane. "Kit, come up so Ilan'll stop thinking I killed you and his disgusting brother!"

The tombstone inscription changed.

SORRY, BRO.
IF YOU WANT, YOU CAN HIDE
DOWN HERE WITH KIT AND ME.

"Gabe?" Ilan put his hand to his head, maybe feeling the urge to smooth away some of his own craziness. "Is that really you?"

SOMETIMES WHEN I WAKE UP SCREAMING,
YOU SING "CARAVAN OF LOVE"
UNTIL I GO BACK TO SLEEP.

"How are you doing that?" Fancy yelled at the tombstone, at Gabriel. "How are *you* able to change things? Kit! Are you the one changing the tombstones?"

GABE DOESN'T NEED ME TO SPEAK FOR HIM.
UNLIKE **SOME** PEOPLE.

"Gabe," Ilan said, shoving Fancy aside so he could get closer to the stone. "I know you and Fancy don't get on, but this is stupid. Come up and let's just deal with this."

I AIN'T COMING UP TILL YOU CALM
THAT CHICK THE HELL DOWN.

"*I don't need to calm down.* This is my happy place, and I can do what I want, including not calming down!"

"Fancy, wait a minute, okay? This is freaking me out." Ilan no longer looked ready to kill Fancy. He no longer looked ready to do anything except lie down and take a nap. "We need to talk about this."

"I don't wanna talk." Fancy screamed at Ilan. "You think you can tell me what to do? You're nobody in here. Just another victim. You hear that, Gabriel? Stop hiding under my sister's skirt and come face me, or I'll send your brother down to you in pieces!"

YOU THINK YOU CAN
HURT MY BROTHER?
HA HA HA.

Fancy didn't move—*couldn't* move, she was so furious—but a pack of dogs entered the garden through the hedges. They were lean and pale, even in the bloody light suffusing everything. They leaped onto the platform and closed in on Ilan as swift and eerie as ghosts, their jaws open, growling.

Ilan's reaction to the dogs was surprising—impatience instead of fear. "Look," he told Fancy, "I decided a long time ago not to let anybody push me around. Not ever again. I'm not that person."

"Who are you, then?"

He eyed the salivating dogs. "Tastiest boy in the world, looks like." Ilan held out his arms to them, as if for a hug. "Want a piece? C'mon." The dogs rushed him, snapping. He stayed still while they bit him, grinning in the face of such ugliness, a horrible grin that masked something even uglier. It flickered in his eyes like downed power lines no one could get near enough to fix.

The dogs bit him, and he *let* them, grimacing but not swatting them away. Fancy felt weirdly jealous of the dogs, at the intimacy Ilan was allowing them.

Until one by one, the dogs stopped biting him. They backed away, first whimpering, then foaming at the mouth, then puking, then dying.

"Who else?" Ilan was bloody and ravaged. And grinning. He walked past the dead dogs, offering himself to the ones still left. "I could do this all night. Any takers?" The remaining dogs looked at one another and whined.

Ilan lowered his arms. "Smart."

He removed a few wet wipes from his pocket and not only wiped away the blood from his wounds, but the wounds themselves. Fancy was beyond impressed. He could change things too, the way Kit could. As though a part of this place belonged to him, too. The thought didn't upset her.

"How did you do that?"

"You're asking me?" Ilan said. "You said it was a happy place. I thunk happy thoughts." Ilan squatted and petted one of the dogs. "Good boy. I know I look good on the outside," he told the dog. "But on the inside? Pure poison."

The dog licked his chin and rested its head against Ilan's chest when Ilan leaned back and propped himself against one of the dead dogs behind him. Ilan stared at the bloody sky as the other dogs crowded close to him.

Fancy entered the circle of dogs and sat before Ilan and really looked at him for the first time, noted the dark, smiling weirdness behind his eyes. He let her watch, not bothered by her.

"This is where you do it," he said. "Where you kill people. I been hearing that you and Kit were helping to rid Portero of bad guys on the sly. But it's not about that, is it? It's about *you* and how you need to control everything, who lives, who dies, who your sister can hang out with. Even trying to control your own development"—he batted one of her pigtails—"like hair ribbons'll keep you young forever."

She shrank from him. "You don't know anything about it."

"I know a spoiled brat throwing a tantrum when I see one."

"Fine. I'm a brat and I wanna control everything but I can't cuz I snap over the littlest thing, right?"

"Right!"

"Like losing my sister to a boy so worthless his *own brother* pushed him down a flight of stairs?"

He didn't even look guilty about it. "You know about that?"

"*All* about it."

"So you think you know me?"

She found herself wanting to fill the silence with an apology, but what was the point? Cordelles + Turners = Disaster. Daddy had solved that equation long ago.

"Why would you try to kill me with dogs anyway?" Ilan

asked. "Seems like if you really wanted me dead, you'd do it yourself, with your bare hands, chop me into pieces, like you said."

"I didn't want to get your blood under my fingernails. It would have made me feel bad." It seemed silly not to be truthful with someone you had just tried to kill. "Gabriel's blood under my nails, though? I wouldn't mind that at all."

"Would it be worth losing your sister?"

She looked toward the grave where Kit was hiding. "I already lost her."

Ilan's head smacked against the floor.

"Ouch!"

The dogs had gone, and they were back in Gabriel's room. Fancy hadn't even noticed the change.

"We can only stay in the happy place for a little while," Fancy explained, as Ilan picked himself up off his brother's bedroom floor.

"What about Gabe and Kit?" he said. "How're they getting back?"

"How would I know? I don't even care. Kit'll look after your brother."

Ilan drove her home and she made him park well away

from the house, just in case Madda was awake. As he walked her across the yard, he paused before the cellar doors.

"You wanna see?" she asked. Everybody was curious about the cellar.

Ilan nodded, so she threw open the doors and led him down the steps. As he looked around she imagined him on the shelves in neat, labeled pieces like the painting he'd done of his father, and felt an urge to pull at him, to make sure he wouldn't come apart like monkey bread. She dug her nails into her palms to keep her hands in check.

"Where're the bonesaws?" he asked. "Those old-fashioned ones. What'd Guthrie call 'em?"

"Osteotomes," she said, marveling at how normal he made it all feel. "Cops took 'em as evidence years ago. Haven't seen 'em since. And they're really old and valuable, too. Daddy loves all those really old devices."

Daddy had used those old devices to dismember his victims, usually while they were still alive. He'd then hide the blood-less, individually wrapped pieces in random places around town. By the time Daddy had gone to trial, all the victims had been accounted for, but not all their parts. Since Daddy hadn't been able to remember every hidey-hole, several of the victims had been buried without hands or toes or buttocks. Only last month a kid hunting for pretty bird eggs had found Mrs. Edith Burleson's forearm wrapped in butcher paper inside the knothole of an oak tree.

Unlike with the other victims, Daddy hadn't told the cops where the rest of Mr. Turner was hidden. When asked, he'd only say, "You're lucky to even have his arm."

Most people thought that he must have eaten Mr. Turner and that's why he hadn't been found. Fancy thought it highly unlikely, though it bugged her that she couldn't rule it out as a possibility. Daddy was mysterious.

Ilan sat on the cot and ran his hand along the thin mattress, perhaps imagining his father lying there. Perhaps imagining too well because he shot off the cot and wiped his hand on his pant leg. "Has Guthrie ever talked about that night?"

"He said he didn't do it." Ilan was still scrubbing his hand against his leg. He didn't seem to notice he was doing it. Fancy hoped he stopped soon, before he scrubbed all the skin off. "It's what he told Madda when she caught him. 'Caught in a lie? Deny till you die.'"

Ilan stopped scrubbing. "Do you agree with that?"

"*I* like to know the truth, but I lie to Madda all the time. Some people can't handle the truth."

Thunder rumbled outside, and the distant smell of rain poured into the cellar through the open doors. "You better go," Fancy told Ilan. "Summer storms are the worst."

"Yeah," he agreed, and then just stood there.

"Or"—Fancy couldn't believe she was about to say it—"we could go to my room."

Ilan smiled at her, and even after all this time it still hit her like a kick to the chest. "Okay."

Fancy led him out of the cellar and took him across the yard, past the riotous flap of the laundry sheets billowing like sails on the clothesline, clean and white against the dirty gray sky. She let him inside the sleeping porch, and saw right away that he didn't belong there. He didn't fit.

Ilan wasn't the tallest boy in the world, but he looked like a giant at the tea table, his knees jutting up twice as high as the tabletop. And though Fancy was shorter than Ilan, she was a giant too; she'd never noticed before. She tried to continue not noticing as she turned on the phonograph out of habit and turned the volume low when "My Baby Shot Me Down" began to play.

Madda was baking bread; she could smell it. Cranberry

bread. Daddy's favorite. Kit's, too; it was a shame neither of them was home to enjoy it.

"All of a sudden," said Ilan, watching her closely, "you look more sad than angry."

"Maybe I caught my sadness from you."

"I'm usually better at hiding it," he said, not bothering to deny it. "Sorry."

"Be sad if you want. I don't care."

"I know you don't," he said sadly.

But Fancy didn't want to think about Ilan's bad feelings, not when she had so many of her own. "I don't know what to tell Madda about Kit."

"Kit'll be back," Ilan said, as if he had any say in it. "I know Gabe will; he's gotta work tonight."

"They won't leave the happy place unless I *let* them. And I don't think I will."

"You're such a brat," he said, annoyance overpowering his sadness. "But it's no wonder you act the way you do." He slid off the pink mushroom stool and pushed it away, crossing his legs on the floor. "Your room looks like it was decorated by a demented kindergartner. Which is what you look like. Don't you have any big-girl clothes?"

"I could see you getting on me about trying to kill you and Gabriel, or the way my daddy killed your daddy, but . . . my furniture? My clothes?"

"I can't change who you are, who your people are, or what they did. But tables and dresses, that I can change. Maybe if I keep at you for long enough, you'll let me undress you."

Fancy surprised herself by laughing out loud. She quickly put her hands over her mouth.

"I mean, and then dress you in something more appropriate. You make me feel like a dirty old man looking at you in those little-girl clothes. You know what I mean?"

Fancy couldn't believe she was having such an inappropriate conversation. "Madda keeps telling me to get different clothes. I just don't want people looking at me. More than they already do."

"People are gone look at you regardless. Hot people always get looked at."

"Do you like being looked at?"

"You think I'm hot? No, that's good," he said when she stammered. "I finally got your attention. Too bad I had to nearly die for it."

"I'm sorry. I'm just . . . going through something right now."

"I can see that." He leaned forward, elbows on the table. "What do *you* see?"

"Why did you push Gabriel down the stairs?"

He leaned back. "Because I love him. And because pain is relative."

She thought of Kit. "Pain is *relatives*."

Ilan laughed. "It's always family, right? What else could fuck up a person as much as his family?"

She touched his hand. "Don't say 'fuck.'"

He turned his hand over beneath hers, and their palms touched. Fancy understood what it must be like to get struck by lightning. She felt as if her hair were standing on end.

"Fancy!"

Fancy started at the sound of her sister's voice.

"Let us out!"

"Do you hear that?" Ilan asked, staring all around the room.

"It's just Kit," Fancy said. "Begging for help that she's not going to get."

"Fancy, I'm serious. Let us out. Gabe says he has to work. Besides, the happy-place air is giving him a headache."

"Yeah." It was Gabriel. "My nose is starting to bleed."

"Good."

"Was that Gabe?" Ilan sat up. "Where the hell are they?"

"In the teapot."

Startled, Ilan stared down at the table, and at the bottom of the pink teapot half full of cold chamomile, stood Kit and Gabriel. They were on the platform in the happy place where their graves had been, staring up at Fancy and Ilan.

"What the hell?" Ilan poked his finger into the teapot. "Gabe?"

"Ow!"

Ilan jerked his finger away, but his brother was laughing. "Just kidding."

"Don't pay any attention to them," Fancy said. "They won't be so amusing after I flush them down the toilet."

"Please don't, Fancy," Ilan said as he sat back against the screen, "because if I see one more weird thing today, my head'll explode."

"Listen to him, Fancy," Kit said from the teapot. "I don't know how to get us outta here."

Neither did Fancy. But . . . she had sent them all to the happy place without using the kinetoscope, possibly breaking all the laws of physics. But that's what laws were for—breaking.

Fancy concentrated on Kit and Gabriel, their bodies rippling under the tea. Concentrated on Kit, who waited so patiently to be saved even though she'd betrayed Fancy so egregiously.

Fancy grabbed the teapot and tossed out its contents, and along with the expected splash of tea, Kit and Gabriel also hit the hardwood floor with a resounding thud.

Ilan looked away from them and said to Fancy, "See? Now my skull's splattered all over the room. Are you satisfied now?"

Fancy wouldn't have minded seeing Ilan's skull—she was sure it must be very handsome. She remembered what Kit had said about wanting to see Gabriel on the inside, but even though she suddenly understood what Kit must have been feeling, it didn't make her any less angry.

"Girls?"

Everyone held their breath at the sound of Madda's voice outside the door of the inner room. "What was that noise?"

"Our old steamer trunk tipped over," Kit called. "Sorry. Did we wake you up?"

"No. I'm just about to shower. When I'm done, y'all help me take in the laundry, okay? Before the storm hits?"

"Yes, ma'am!" cried the sisters in unison.

Gabriel jumped to his feet and helped Kit to hers. They were both remarkably clean and dry for people who had just returned from the inside of a grave by way of a teapot. "I can't believe you got us outta that place."

"*I* got you out," Fancy snapped and then glared at her sister. "Why do people always give you the credit for everything?"

"It's good to see you still alive, Ilan," said Kit, ignoring Fancy. *Ignoring* her. Like some stranger on a street corner. "Good, but troubling, because if I know my sister, she didn't plan on you and your brother coming back alive. I had better alert NASA. I just know that Fancy not getting her way for the first time in her life has opened up a wormhole in time and space."

"Maybe we oughta go, Ilan," said Gabriel, eyeing Fancy uncomfortably, unlike his brother, who looked more entertained than nervous. "Miz Lynne'll be done with her shower any minute."

Kit ruffled his wild mane of curly hair. "She won't care."

"I care!" said Fancy.

"I think Gabe's right," said Ilan, in a *let's keep the peace* tone as he got to his feet. "We'd best get while the getting's good."

Gabriel kissed Kit rather sloppily in his haste and waited for his brother by the screen door.

"I'll call you later," Ilan told Fancy. He said it like a threat, but Fancy understood that he didn't mean it that way, so she nodded. Her hand still tingled from when he'd held it.

When the brothers were gone, Kit glared at Fancy, like Gabriel's lousy kissing was her fault. She said, "You *do* like Ilan. I knew you did. Notice how I'm not running after him trying to chop off his head?"

Fancy threw Kit's favorite T-shirt to the floor and used it to mop up the spilled tea. "You don't care about me the way I care about you. You never did." She picked up something that looked like a compact from the floor. She shook the tea off it, but before she could open it, Kit snatched it from her.

"What's that?"

Kit opened it and breathed a sigh of relief. "Thank God they didn't get wet."

"What didn't?"

"My pills." Kit waved the little compact or whatever it was proudly. "I'm on the Pill."

"Why?"

Kit gave her sister a sardonic look.

"*You're having sex with him?*" As she said it she knew it was true. People said that you couldn't see a difference, but Fancy could, now that she was looking. Kit had the same pixie hair and skinny limbs, but there was a certain ripeness, a ruddy glow beneath her brown skin. So ripe she'd been plucked while

Fancy still hung green and bitter on the vine. "Of course you are." Fancy laughed humorlessly and tossed the wet T-shirt onto Kit's bed. "With Franken, too? Was Franken the first?"

Kit burst into tears, a shocking explosion. Kit often pretended emotion, but not this time. "Gabriel was the first, the only, no matter what you think about me."

"Was it bad?" Fancy went to Kit. "Did he hurt you?"

"*Of course he hurt me!*" Kit pushed her away and scooped Kleenex from the box on the vanity. "It always hurts the first time. But it was beautiful."

"Only you would think pain and blood and . . . bodily fluids were beautiful," Fancy snapped. "Stop crying!"

"Why should I?" Kit threw the box of Kleenex at Fancy's head. "Because you never cry? Because you don't know how? Because you never felt anything real your whole life? Well, I have, and I'll cry all I want—!"

"Over a stupid boy!"

"Over how I can't share something so beautiful with an unfeeling bitch!"

"*I'm* unfeeling?" Fancy grabbed a jar of squirrel brain and brandished it. "When you go all psychotic on your precious Gabriel and start doing surgery on *him*, you ask me again who's unfeeling. You're not any better than me. I know you *wish* you were—"

"You're the one who thinks you're better than *me*. That I'm an animal because I don't mind gutting people or get prissy whenever I get a little blood under my nails. But it doesn't matter. I don't have to be better than you. I don't have to be anything like you. Gabe likes me for who I am."

"A killer." Fancy put the jar back on the shelf with all the other jars.

"He knows about me," said Kit defensively, as though she were ashamed of who she was. "I told him everything, even about the happy place. I wanted him to know before we did it. And I *love* doing it with him. It used to be only stabbing people made me feel connected with them, but . . . it's so weird. When I'm done with Gabe, he's not dead or cut up. Just sweaty and whole and in love with me. And I like that. *He's* the good one, not me. He's an angel."

"So is Satan. And he's in hell now. Maybe Gabriel'll join him there."

Kit froze. "You'd better not do anything. I mean it, Fancy; you better not touch him!"

"*I* won't have to." She slammed out through the screen door.

FROM FANCY'S DREAM DIARY:

Kit was pregnant and I was helping her pick out a crib. I picked up a pot instead and asked her if she thought babies preferred being boiled or baked. She snatched the pot out of my hands and said, neither. I snatched it back and said, we'll see.

CHAPTER TWENTY-ONE

As Fancy parked her bike outside the Standard before class, she saw Ilan sitting below the deserted ticket stand. She figured he'd be sitting on the bench at the curb on any normal day instead of on the ground, but the bench was inexplicably covered in blood and flies. Fancy sat next to Ilan.

"What happened over there?"

He glanced at the bench, then went back to his sketchbook. "Dunno. It was like that when I got here."

Fancy looked at what he was drawing: a series of broken mirrors. Just a sketch, but even his sketches looked like they should be hanging in a museum. A face stared out of the shattered mirrors: Ilan's own face. His eyes in one of the glass shards were a rabbit's eyes, scared and trapped.

"Why're you sitting in the heat?"

"Cooler out here than upstairs."

"Were you waiting for me?" He did that sometimes, but not so often that she took it for granted.

"Nope. But it's nice to see you. Especially when you ain't trying to kill me."

It couldn't have been too nice to see her; he hadn't looked at her once. "I wanna talk to you."

He finally looked at her, and his real eyes, unlike the drawing, were anything but scared. Just the same ironic gaze he always gave her.

"So talk."

She stared around the street. "Not here."

"Where then? Someplace public, I hope."

"You pick, if you don't trust me."

"I don't." He crumpled the drawing and tossed it into a nearby garbage can. She felt a pang to see such beauty so casually disregarded.

When class was over, Ilan drove Fancy to Smiley's for cheese fries. Tons of kids were squeezed into booths not big enough to hold them all, or standing at the counter shouting their food orders.

They snagged one of the tiny, couple-friendly tables by the windows. As she ate, Fancy hummed along to "Sh-Boom" playing on the jukebox.

Ilan frowned at her humming, half amused and half irritated. "You like that crap?"

"It's not crap. It's historic."

"You like history?"

"No. Just songs from history. They're soothing."

"I guess a girl as full of rage as you needs tons of soothing."

"I'm not full of rage."

When he just looked at her, Fancy sighed and said, "Yesterday was . . . unfortunate. I'm not like that, usually."

To her embarrassment the happy place materialized in Ilan's water glass, still as foul-looking as it had been when she'd . . . misbehaved.

"Sorry."

Ilan peered into the glass, his lip curled at the sight of the rotting flamingos. "How're you doing that?"

Fancy shrugged. "Just happens. It's a coping mechanism."

"What're you coping with? Trying to kill me and my brother?"

"This isn't about you or your stupid brother. This is about me and Kit and how . . ." Fancy faltered, her stomach burning and not from the cheese and jalapeños she'd just swallowed. She pushed her cheese fries away and took a sip of her milk shake. "She won't even talk to me anymore."

"Can you blame her?" Ilan helped himself to her cheese fries. "Trying to kill off the love of your sister's life is always a dumb-ass strategy."

"What about you? What kind of strategy involves pushing your brother down the stairs?"

"It seemed like a good idea at the time."

"Why'd you do it? Is he horrible?"

"No."

"So he's a perfect angel?"

Ilan polished off her fries and said, "There's a middle ground between horrid and angelic. If I swallow my water, am I gone swallow that flamingo too?"

Fancy was about to tell him not to be ridiculous when she remembered tossing Kit and Gabriel out of the teapot. So she took a deep breath and made herself calm down, and after a few seconds, the happy place disappeared from the glass. She didn't bother answering Ilan's question, though, because she didn't know the answer. She didn't know herself at all anymore.

"What's the worst thing Gabriel ever did?" she asked, trying to sound casual. Maybe she didn't know herself, but she was about to know absolutely everything about Gabriel.

"Why?" Ilan asked suspiciously, and rightly so.

"I'm curious."

"About *Gabe*?"

"About why Kit likes him."

"It's a Turner thing. We're all charming as hell."

"I saw you slap him," she reminded him, lest he get too full of himself. "That day we bought the dresses."

"He was sleepwalking," Ilan said, infuriatingly unapologetic about his behavior.

"You said you wanted to strangle him."

"The way you strangled Kit? Yeah, all the time," he admitted cheerfully. "Especially when he gets all holier-than-thou."

Fancy gave up trying to shame him, as it appeared to be an impossible task. "He got any friends?"

"Guys from school. Bandmates. Except Tony. About to fire his ass anyway. Tony Castle," he elaborated, on seeing Fancy's blank expression. "He's our bassist."

"Why you gone fire him?"

"Don't even get me started." It was nice to see that she wasn't the only person in the world who irritated him.

"But why don't Tony like your brother?" she asked, storing the info away.

"Tony only likes himself." Ilan leaned back in his chair and crossed his arms. "Is this why you wanted to be alone with me? To talk about other guys?"

Fancy decided to back off. For now. "What do you want to talk about?"

"You. And me. All these things I wanna say to you. And then do to you."

"What things? Like torture?" Fancy was astounded he would admit to such a thing. "Cuz I could torture you a lot better than you could torture me."

He gaped at her as though a unicorn horn had sprouted from her forehead. "I'm not talking about *torture*."

"What, then?"

"Drink your milk and maybe I'll tell you when you grow up."

"Milk *shake*. Don't treat me like I'm five."

"I thought you liked being babied," he said, his eyes wide and innocent. "That's how Miz Lynne treats you."

"It's Madda's job to take care of me. I don't need that from you." To show him how adult she could be, she decided to make a peace offering. "You want this?"

He looked where she was pointing. "Your cherry?"

"I don't like maraschinos." She plucked it off the top of her milk shake. "Do you want it or not?"

Ilan took the cherry, carefully wiped it clean, and put it in his shirt pocket.

"You're saving it?"

He smiled, a secret smile that annoyed her; she wanted to know his secrets. "Not ripe enough yet. Soon, though. Okay?"

"Okay." Fancy found herself smiling with him—even though his smiles hurt her chest, they were very infectious smiles—but she had no idea what she'd just agreed to.

Fancy biked through the rain Thursday morning. Tony, like the sisters, lived upsquare, but in the less wooded, more suburban and cookie-cutter part of upsquare, near Torcido Road, in a two-story split level that was more garage than house.

She checked the address against the one she'd copied out of the phone book, parked her bike, and rang the bell. A boy much more vibrant-looking than his house answered the door.

"Are you Tony Castle?"

"Yeah." He looked her up and down, lingering on her chest.

"I wanna talk to you." It felt strange not to have Kit speaking for her. She had to shove each word in the back to get it free of her mouth. "Can I come in?"

She passed through a mudroom into the living room, nearly tripping on an umbrella. She stopped, wide-eyed, at the state of the living room: the lacy white bra under her shoe, the overturned furniture, the beer bottles rolling and clinking together.

"Pardon the mess." He stretched, his jeans low on his hips. He noticed her staring and smiled. "Had a beer bash last night."

"Where're your folks?" Fancy couldn't even imagine what Madda would do to her and Kit if they wrecked their house the way this boy had.

"No folks. Just me and the old man. He's offshore this week." He opened a box on the coffee table and removed a tightly rolled joint. "You do this?"

"No." She'd smoked with Kit once, but she wasn't about to get high with some stranger. "Why don't you like Gabriel?"

"Gabe Turner? He's the one don't like me. Cuz of your sister. He don't like the way she looks at me."

"Y'all fight over girls?"

"Girls fight over me. The band thing. The looks. The gold stars in my eyes. See?"

He did have gold stars flashing against the brown irises of his eyes. But so what?

"Hm." Fancy withdrew from the rancid green cloud surrounding him. "What's Gabriel really like?"

Tony sat back. "I dunno. He was cracked for a while. He'd get in these weird moods. Like, we'd be onstage and he'd start crying for no reason." He laughed. "Like a bitch. I know he was young, but still. This one time he even ran away from home. Course, that was after his pop got killed."

"So he's not like that anymore?"

"Nah. After he got religion, he calmed way down, like church was some kinda weird-ass shock treatment for him. Speaking of weird-ass, I hear you been taking care of people"—he mimed shooting himself in the head—"around town. Putting bad guys in their place."

"Yeah?"

He sat next to her. "Think you could take care of something for me?"

"What?"

"This." He took her hand and pressed it against his crotch.

"You know how, right?" He sat back, getting comfortable. "I know your sister does."

Fancy lifted his bass from the floor, gripped it like a baseball bat, and swung it at Tony's head.

"Did *that* take care of it?" she asked, sometime later. But Fancy didn't expect an answer.

Not from a corpse.

Kit was in bed reading a biography of Tori Amos when Fancy got home. "Still haven't figured out how to kill without getting dirty, huh?" she said, taking in Fancy's bloodstained clothes.

She checked the time and put her book aside. "Madda's gotta be up by now. Get cleaned up and come help me with dinner."

Fancy couldn't imagine chopping onions or straining pasta or grinning at Madda like everything was cool. "You want my help?" Her voice shook. "Are we *helping* each other now?"

"Go take a bath, Fancy, and calm down."

"Is that your answer for everything? To send me away? You said nothing would ever split us up."

"We're not split up. I'm here!"

"To make dinner? To run off and screw some boy when I

need you? I *needed* you, Kit. If you had been with me, I never would have killed that boy!"

"Stop yelling before Madda comes in here and sees you looking like that."

"I don't care what she sees!" The walls began to flicker as the happy place projected onto them. In the stone circle where Fancy had buried Tony, a green shoot had already started to sprout.

Fallen fruit from the old-man tree rolled into their room, and Kit picked it up.

"Look what you're doing. I told you one day you wouldn't be able to separate real and unreal."

Fancy pressed her hands to her eyes, and when she looked again, the fruit was gone from her sister's hand, and the walls had returned to normal. But Kit was no longer her Kit, and that was just wrong.

Kit reached for her, but Fancy slapped her hand away. "Don't touch me. Go touch that little creep you like so much, but don't ever touch me again!"

Fancy ran out of the house and into the rainy remains of the day with no destination in mind, but she ended up at Bony Creek.

She sat on the edge of the water, the rain washing Tony's blood from her skin and mixing it into the mud beneath her. The rain sizzled against the creek's surface, and every now and then Fancy saw a flash of Daddy's face peeping out at her. She wished for him with an almost painful longing. Maybe one day she would miss Kit in the same way, not because she'd been arrested, but because Kit had simply walked away from her. Fancy didn't understand why people found her so easy to leave.

A flash caught her eye. A single, shining raindrop hung suspended over the creek. It grew bigger as she watched, open-mouthed, expanding until it was a beach ball of water. Daddy's head appeared within the gigantic raindrop, huge and distorted. Like a view in a fishbowl. He smiled at her. "Fancy?"

She put her head back and let the rain fall into her eyes. She blinked.

"You're not seeing things." Daddy was so matter-of-fact that she had to believe in what she was seeing. "Why're you so surprised? You do it too. I've seen."

"You been watching me?" The idea didn't embarrass her. The upside of having a serial killer for a father is that no matter what you do, it's never as bad as what he's done.

"I watch all of you."

"I can't do that," Fancy said, gesturing at the raindrop, impressed despite herself.

"Yet. You'll find yourself doing all kinds of tricks in no time. I did, when I was your age."

Fancy nodded. "Is that how you got rid of Mr. Turner's body? Some trick?"

She could only see his face, but he looked around as though he wasn't alone. "I didn't do anything to his body."

"You chopped off his arm. Madda saw you."

"Not everybody who gets his arm chopped off dies from it."

"So you chopped off his arm and then let him wander off and then somebody *else* killed him?"

"We live in a crazy world, Fancy Pants. Y'all plan on visiting me before they sic the firing squad on me?"

"I dunno. Kit always wants to see you. Do you visit her like this?"

"No. I popped in on Lynne one night, and she made me swear not to do it again. But you were looking in on *me*, so . . . You won't tell Lynne, will you?"

"No, she hates it when we talk about you."

"Do you hate me?"

"Kinda. You messed everything up when you got caught. You messed all of us up."

He nodded. He didn't have the hardened look of an inmate, wasn't wild and unkempt. Even in his mug shot he'd looked serene and caring, the way Jesus would look in a mug shot.

"What I did," he said, "had nothing to do with how I feel about you and Kit. And Lynne. I love you."

"So what? You think you can just say 'I love you' and make everything okay? *Nothing's* okay."

"Nothing was ever okay. We are who we are, Fancy. Nothing can change that. But if there's enough love, sometimes you can ignore how . . . tumorous the rest of the world is."

"I must not have enough, then. Cuz I *clearly* see that everything sucks."

She threw a rock at the water ball and burst it. There was only the rain and silence. And loneliness.

FROM FANCY'S DREAM DIARY:

Kit told me I sucked at being a real girl. She said fake girls were easy to spot because they couldn't say I love you. Every time I tried to say it, my jaw fell off.

CHAPTER TWENTY-TWO

Friday, after Mr. Hofstram dismissed them from class, Fancy found herself walking with Ilan. Not with him, exactly, but it was so easy to fall into stride with him. And so when he stopped before the entrance doors in the lobby of the Standard, she stopped too. And waited.

He was unhappy with her. He hadn't put his arm on the back of her chair during class; he hadn't even spoken to her. He'd wanted to, though, she knew. He'd kept opening his mouth to say something, but then he would snap it closed and just sit there glowering at his easel.

But now in the lobby he spoke:

"What did you do to Tony?"

"Who?"

"Tony Castle. Don't play dumb. He disappeared right after I told you about him."

"Oh. Him." Through the porthole-shaped windows on the entrance doors Fancy could see the street, see the bench out front, where a group of tweens sat, probably waiting for their ride. Sitting where days before there had been a mess of blood. And that was how it went: You cleaned up the mess and you moved on.

"Did you visit him?"

"Yes."

"Did you kill him?"

"Yes."

"Cuz of what I said about not liking him?"

"No. Because he was an asshole. And I don't use the word lightly. He's in the happy place now."

"How can you say that? How can you tell me that?"

She found it strange that he seemed more upset that she'd confessed to it than that she'd done it.

Boys were weird.

"I saw how you were with the dogs. The way you kept yourself safe. You decided you would be, and so you were.

You have to be strong to bend the world to your will, even a made-up world. Anybody that strong wouldn't be afraid of the truth."

He waited until a group passed through the doors, and out of the building into the bright afternoon before saying, "I wanna see Tony. Will you take me to him?"

"Fine. But only because I'm bored. Not because I wanna hang out with you."

He pushed through the doors, and Fancy went with him, marveling again at how easily they fell into step with each other.

The happy place looked especially pretty today. Fancy stood with Ilan on the platform, admiring the view. Jewel-colored birds twittered in the trees; the grass was spit-polished to a high gleam; the flamingos were gone, but fluffy pink rabbits had taken their place and bounded playfully around the stone circles. It was nothing like the way it had been when he'd come before. But Fancy might as well have brought him to a vacant lot. All of his attention was focused on the guitar in his hands, a thick wooden instrument with a black signature scrawled along the body.

"This was Tony's," he said. "He loved this thing. He got frigging Prince to autograph it. Tony gave it to me and asked me to keep it safe for him. He knew that if his dad found it, he'd pawn it or lose it in a bet or something. Every time he missed rehearsals or pissed off a bandmate or showed up to gigs so high he'd fall off the stage, I'd look at this thing and decide to give him one more chance. Tony didn't have anyone to keep him safe."

He gave Fancy a look like he wanted her to respond. But she had nothing to say. Tony's home life didn't interest her.

He turned away from her like she was the uninteresting one. "So where'd you bury him?"

She pointed to a tree growing in one of the stone circles.

"Under that tree?"

"He is the tree."

He looked more closely and saw that instead of leaves the tree was covered in mini people, who were dewy and all looked alike, like clones.

"Tony?" He gaped at Fancy. "What did you do to him?"

"I buried him, and he grew into a tree," said Fancy, as though repeating it for the millionth time.

The mini Tonys were nude and cute and hung from the

tree like fruit. Fancy had read somewhere that in China people grew pears in the shape of Buddha. The Tonys were like that, only alive, blinking their starry eyes and kicking their wee legs.

Ilan stepped beneath the tree and plucked one of the Tonys, and it wailed so sharply that he dropped it like a hot coal. The Tony hit the ground and rolled onto its back, then stilled, legs and arms curled up like a dead spider.

Fancy kicked it away and sat down on the dark, rich soil, and after a slight hesitation Ilan sat next to her. He played something slow and sad on the guitar, his hands trembling.

"Play something I know."

"I'm playing Tony's favorite song," he snapped, not looking up from the guitar strings. "You mind if I play Tony's favorite song at his own fucking funeral?"

"Is that what this is?"

"It's the only one he'll ever have." Ilan continued playing, and as he did, the Tonys began to sing.

Ilan gazed openmouthed at the fruit above him, at the sweet tone issuing from their throats. As they sang, the happy-place people came into the garden wearing their best funeral garb. Fancy waved them closer, and they circled the tree and wept for a boy they'd never met. It was all fake, just as fake as when they'd stood and cried for Kit, but Ilan seemed to like all the fuss. Seemed to need it.

"I can't help who I am," she told him, feeling the need to explain. "I try to keep it in check. I try real hard. But sometimes I fail. I know he was your friend, but . . ."

"He wasn't my friend. You're right; he was an asshole. The worst thing about Tony dying is that people'll be like, 'I knew he'd come to a sorry end one day.' Because he was wild. Because his dad is a gambler and on drugs. People have this attitude . . . like they can't stand anyone to come out of a bad situation and survive it."

"People say that about me and Kit all the time. That it would be better for us to have never been born than to have a serial killer for a father. There's worse things to have, I guess."

"Like morals?" He came to the end of the song, and though the Tonys stopped singing, the weeping continued.

Fancy said, "Morals complicate things." She snapped her fingers, and the weeping ended abruptly, as if switched off. "You may leave," she told the mourners.

They dispersed through the hedges, but two people remained behind—Franken and a woman with shiny hair and the long, unsturdy legs of a colt. Franken no longer had scars;

his skin was as whole and fresh as it had been when the sisters first met him. He was quite handsome. Annoyingly handsome.

"What happened to your scars?" said Fancy with unnecessary force. People were looking good when they were supposed to be hideous, mourning the death of an asshole when they should have been celebrating. Everything was topsy-turvy.

Franken looked nervous. "After Kit died, I felt like I needed a new start. So I got a new skin from the godfather tree."

He pointed at a tree a few yards from where she sat: thick and squat with pale, skinlike leaves and fruit that looked like golden eyes. "Everybody's gotta fly the coop sometime, right?"

Fancy winced, wondering if people would be throwing those words back in her face for the rest of her life.

"I figured you wouldn't care," Franken continued.

"I *don't* care."

He brushed his hand across the smooth skin of his face. "I could take it off."

"I said"—Fancy clenched her fists—"I don't care."

The woman with him put her hand on Franken protectively, as if Fancy couldn't wipe the both of them out of existence just by snapping her fingers.

"This is Gloria."

"Nice to see you again." The woman smiled at Fancy.

"Again?" Her voice sounded familiar.

"I remember you from the woods. Where's your sister?"

"She's busy. *Sinning.*"

"Too bad. I wanted to thank her for sending me here. To paradise."

"*This* is paradise?" said Ilan, as though the idea that people might actually enjoy the happy place were ridiculous.

"It is for me," said Gloria. "Especially after the last place. I was kidnapped. By some guy. He kept me in a cellar for two years. Never once told me his name." Like that had been the worst part.

"The cellar she was kept in was way worse than mine," said Franken apologetically, as though to spare Fancy's feelings.

"You were kidnapped and tortured too?" Gloria exclaimed. "We have so much in common! I mean, it's really amazing. I was glad when my guy killed me, because I thought now I can finally be free, but that wasn't what death was like for me. I still felt trapped. I think it was being in those woods, all the roots twining around my bones, like shackles. I'm from the Panhandle, and I'm just not used to being hemmed in by all those trees. But now I'm free." She turned to Fancy. "Thanks to your sister. I never thought I'd owe my life to a psycho."

"She wasn't that bad," said Franken, loyal to the end. "She let me go."

"*I* let you go. If I had left it up to Kit, you'd be buried under our front porch!"

They backed away from Fancy's outburst, clutching each other like frightened children.

"*So leave!*"

They fled so quickly Fancy could almost see the smoke churning up from their feet.

"You tortured that guy?" said Ilan. *He* didn't look ready to flee. He'd already proven himself to be more fight than flight.

"We barely even touched him." Seeing him unafraid and waiting for her to talk to him calmed her down.

"You tortured him and then set him free." Now that he was paying attention to her instead of that guitar, she almost wished he weren't. He had such an intense gaze, like light concentrated through a magnifying glass. "Why couldn't you have done that to Tony? You could have at least thought of me and my band. You could have at least waited until I found a replacement. Now *I'm* gonna have to be the front man, and I'm not half as good as Tony."

"You're a hundred times better than him," she said, refusing to believe that Tony could be better than Ilan at anything. "I'm not sorry I killed him," she said, and then whispered, "but I'd take it back if I could."

"That's the thing about killing," he said. "It can't be undone. Even if you could take it back, why waste it on Tony when you could bring back my pop?" He smiled, but it was so full of pain she had to look away. "Now *that* would be useful."

"Kit is the one who can raise the dead, but even she can't bring them back to life." She thought of Gloria. "At least, not in the real world."

"If I had the power to resurrect, I'd use it on you." Now he was the one whispering. "There's an important part of you that's dead: the part that cares." He brushed the back of his hand over her breast, over her heart. His fingers shook in time to her heartbeat.

Fancy couldn't believe he was touching her like that. Couldn't believe she was letting him.

"I'd give just about anything if I could make you care," he said. "Especially about me."

Under his touch something sparked.

FROM FANCY'S DREAM DIARY:

KIT WAS PAINTING MY TOENAILS WITH SOMEONE'S BLOOD—
I COULDN'T TELL WHOSE—AND DESCRIBING THIS WEIRD
SEXUAL POSITION THAT SHE LIKES. KIT TOLD ME THAT THE
TRICK WAS TO PUT YOUR HEAD ON BACKWARD. LIKE THIS,
SHE SAID AND CRANKED MY HEAD AROUND TO THE BACK.
THAT'S WHEN I SAW ILAN SITTING BEHIND ME IN THE
WINDOW. I ASKED HIM WHAT HE THOUGHT HE WAS DOING IN
MY HOUSE AND HE SAID, I'M HERE TO HELP YOU GET YOUR
HEAD ON STRAIGHT. THEN HE UNZIPPED HIS JEANS.

CHAPTER TWENTY-THREE

Fancy woke up Saturday afternoon, sweating, her hand sore because she was squeezing the pencil she used to write her dreams and it had snapped in half. The broken points left red marks in her palm. She sat up and read what she'd written, as she always did after awakening. She looked wildly about the room, half expecting Ilan to be watching her through the screens, half annoyed that he wasn't.

Fancy kicked free of the linens and went into Madda's room. The window air conditioner was at full blast, and it felt like the inside of an igloo. Fancy hurried into Madda's bed. Madda rolled over and looked at her sleepily.

"What's wrong?"

Fancy cuddled next to her. "It's too hot in our room."

"I thought you girls thrived in the heat."

"Kit's not there."

"Where is she?"

"I don't know. She never talks to me anymore. Not now that she's got her precious *Gabriel*."

"You'll get a boyfriend too."

"I don't *want* one. How could she want one?"

"Don't be such a little girl, Fancy. You can't be everything to Kit."

"I used to be."

"Things change."

"Change sucks. Almost as much as Kit's disgusting boyfriend."

"She's not gone stop loving you just because Gabe's in her life. She's your sister."

"And Daddy's your husband. You stopped loving him."

"No, I didn't."

"You don't even talk to him. Or about him."

Madda rolled onto her back, her arm over her eyes. "Know why?"

"Cuz you found out he's a killer and now you hate him."

"It's because I found out he's a liar." The AC was so loud Fancy could barely hear her. "If he had told me about the people he'd killed ... maybe I would have left him, maybe not; that's not the point. The point is, he didn't trust me enough to give me a choice. It's a big risk to show someone the real you. It takes a lot of courage, the kind of courage a woman could admire. But he chose not to show himself to me. I had to catch him in the cellar with that poor man's arm and then hear about it on the goddamn news. I can't forgive him for that."

Silence, and then Fancy asked: "Do you know the real me?"

"You're fifteen. I don't know if there is a real you. Not yet. But when you find out, I hope you'll know you can trust me. You and your sister."

Fancy listened to Madda's breath even out as she slipped back into sleep. She did know who she was. Knew exactly. She wished she were brave enough to let Madda see it.

Fancy awoke in Madda's bed. It was dark, nearly ten o'clock according to the red numbers glaring in the dark. Fancy couldn't believe she'd slept all day. Or maybe she could. She'd read somewhere that excessive sleeping was a sign of depression.

That's how she felt—deflated and low. Fancy turned on the lamp.

Old jam jars decorated nearly every surface in the room, full of things like loose change, bright yellow esperanzas, even goldfish. Fresh Dickies were folded on the cabbage-rose-printed chair, out of place in the feminine room. On the nightstand beside Fancy sat a crystal decanter of bloodred strawberry wine, a half-empty wineglass, and a bottle of Tylenol PM.

As Fancy drained the wine from the glass, she saw the note on the nightstand near the clock: *Kit loves you and so do I. Remember that.*

Kit had wanted her to remember it too. Her and Daddy. But what was the point of love if it didn't keep people from leaving you?

Fancy got up to get some water, shuffling along the cool floor. She came to a sudden halt in the living room, where she found Gabriel and Kit nude and intertwined on the couch.

Madda had gotten rid of the TV after Guthrie had been arrested and replaced it with the fish tank. The glow of the aquarium washed over their bodies, over the tangle of clothes littering the floor before the couch. The dragon fish was hiding in his cave, possibly traumatized by whatever he had witnessed.

Gabriel moaned like even in his sleep he and Kit were . . . Fancy hurried to the toolshed and rummaged until she found a pair of shears. When she turned around, Gabriel was there. Stark naked.

"What're you doing here?" he had the nerve to ask.

"Looking for these." She snapped the garden shears. "Cuz I'm gone cut off your wiener. Good thing you brought it with you."

"You think I'm scared."

"You should be."

"I'm so used to you after all these years. When you bleed, I feel it. When you eat the flesh of the young, I taste it. I know your dreams."

While she tried to process what he was saying, he snatched the shears. She reached for them, but he took her by the throat.

"I knew you'd come out sometime. And I'd get my hands on you. And I'd show you what it feels like to have someone crawl inside you."

He shoved her to the ground, falling on her heavily. "There's space just behind your amygdala. Just enough room for me to nest." He tried to kiss her, but Fancy head-butted his mouth and scrambled away.

He grabbed her foot and hauled her back beneath him. He

snapped the shears, which made a horribly sharp sound. "It doesn't have to be kisses," he said, smiling despite his split lip. "There are other ways."

"*Kit!*"

He used the shears to cut open Fancy's nightie, the rusty blade cold against her belly. "There's no one here but me. And when we join, there won't even be that. Just . . . we."

He put the point at her belly button and pushed.

"Gabe." Kit appeared in the shed like an angel of mercy, her pink gown floating around her like mist. She took the shears from Gabriel's suddenly slack grip. "That's not the right way to kick someone's ass, remember?" Kit tugged him off her sister and kissed him gently and patted his cheek. "Wake up, Buttercup."

"*Wake up?*" Fancy clutched her gown together. "You think he's *asleep?*"

"He sleepwalks. Gabe." Kit slapped his face the way Fancy wanted to, only Fancy wanted to use a two-by-four.

Gabriel put his hand to his head and squinted at Kit. "What happened?"

She ran her hand over his wild hair and looked at Fancy. "You were sleepwalking."

"The hell he was! He tried to gut me with the shears."

He looked at the shears Kit had set aside and rose to his feet so he could back away from them, from Fancy. "I'm so sorry."

"The hell with sorry!" Fancy tried to kick his balls, but she was still sitting on the floor and the angle was bad.

"Fancy, let him alone." Kit pulled him out of the shed.

"He tried to kill me!"

"You tried to kill him first, in the happy place," said Kit unsympathetically. "Now you're even."

She tried to help Fancy up, but Fancy smacked her hand away.

"I told you not to touch me!"

Fancy stood on her own two feet and ran into Madda's room; she locked the door and shivered for a long time. But once the trembles worked their way out of her system, she picked up the phone.

"Your brother just tried to kill me."

Ilan said, "I'm on my way."

Fancy was sitting on the back porch steps when Ilan arrived. A guy in a pickup truck dropped him off. She heard Ilan say, "Thanks, man," before the driver disappeared down the road.

Fancy hurried to Ilan as he approached the front of the house.

"Is my brother still alive?"

"So far." Kit and Gabriel were back in the living room, murmuring in the dark, so Fancy led Ilan to the back porch so she wouldn't have to hear them.

"What'd he do?" Ilan asked when they were seated on the steps.

"My sister."

"Well, you knew about that."

"They were on the couch! I have to *sit* on that couch. After I saw them, I went to the toolshed to . . ."

"To get a weapon. And?"

Fancy was silent a moment, surprised that Ilan could read her so well. Surprised and irritated. "He's the one who jumped all over me, so don't make me out to be the bad guy." She told him what happened.

"He gets like that sometimes," Ilan said, as though they were discussing a case of the sniffles. "If it was anybody but you, I'd be worried."

"I was lucky Kit came out. Or he'd've cut me open. You don't even care, do you?"

"I care. But karma's a bitch, Fancy."

"That's all? You came all the way out here to tell me that what goes around comes around?"

"No." Ilan hopped off the porch and held his hand out to her. "Come walk with me."

Fancy looked at his hand a long moment before she took it. The pads of his fingers were very rough, but the rest of his hand was baby soft.

"Look at that." He pointed across the backyard, at the moontree in bloom. Fancy looked up and saw a full moon, its bright white light mirrored in the moonflowers. Ilan squeezed her hand. "You know it's bad luck to tell lies under a moontree?"

"Der. But you can ask me anything. I got nothing to hide. Not from you." Fancy was surprised that she meant every word. But Ilan was nothing if not discreet.

"Must be nice to be such an open book," he said as they neared the moontree. "I think God made me out of secrets."

"God made me out of steel."

"You don't seem that tough to me."

"Well, I am." Fancy let go of his hand and marched through the mahonia bushes ringing the tree. "Tough as—"

Ilan followed behind her. "Tough as what?"

"Cacklers." But even as she said the word, Ilan saw them himself beneath the moontree, outlined in the moonlight.

They were short, only four feet tall when they stood upright. These were on all fours and had looked up at Fancy's intrusion. They were thin and had fat round heads that were almost cute, but their many rows of teeth were less cute, as were their screaming laughs, the sound they made whenever they spotted prey. They weren't laughing, though; they seemed more startled than hungry, their normally pink eyes red in the moonlight. But when Ilan and Fancy didn't leave, they reared onto their spindly hind legs and rushed Ilan and Fancy in a mad, cackling run.

Fancy remembered the advice the Mortmaine had given her, about how she should never run because only prey ran . . . but she ran anyway. And was tackled from behind. She fell into the bushes, and something poked her in the back—fangs?— but almost as quickly as the weight had landed on her back, it vanished.

Trying to outrun a cackler was pointless; they were speedy and tireless. But they were much lighter than humans, and their big pumpkin heads were their weak spot. Ilan had pulled the cackler off Fancy, and once he had the writhing creature on the ground next to its dead companion, Ilan beat against its head with his boot.

It fought back, clawing Ilan's arms with its horny nails and its teeth. Fancy tried to help with the stomping, but it snapped at her bare foot and nearly bit it off. Fancy decided to stay out of it, but Ilan kept up the attack until the thing's head was a pulpy mess and it lay still.

Ilan dragged the carcasses away, deeper into the woods, and then came back and sat next to Fancy beneath the moontree, breathing hard and cleaning goo off his boots. "You can sit up now, scaredy-cat."

"I'm not scared of anything. Except monsters."

"But you're made of steel, Fancy. Remember? So why would you be scared of one measly cackler?"

"There were two, and I *am* made of steel. And shut up." Fancy continued lying on the grass, fighting a weird urge to fall asleep. "They were so busy fighting each other, I'm surprised they even bothered attacking us. They probably wouldn't've if you hadn't come barging in and spooked 'em."

Ilan hauled her upright, and Fancy let him, marveling at his sturdiness as she snuggled next to him. "Fancy, it's mating season." It sounded like he was trying not to laugh. "They weren't fighting. Why'd you think yours had a boner?"

Fancy remembered the hard spike that had been jabbing her in the back. "Puke. And stop laughing at me. Excuse me for not being fascinated by monster genitalia, unlike *some* people."

"I never said I wasn't a pervert."

"I guess it runs in your family."

Ilan froze beside her.

"Well, he is a pervert. How would you feel if a perverted maniac was dating *your* sister? Wouldn't you do whatever it took to protect her?"

Ilan kept quiet.

"You're sitting under the moontree," she reminded him. "You have to tell the truth." She reached up and plucked a sweet moonflower, holding it before Ilan's mouth like a microphone.

"Gabe would never hurt your sister."

"Of course he would. And it wouldn't be the first time he hurt someone he loved. Would it, Ilan?"

Ilan scooted away from her. "What's that supposed to mean?"

"It means I know one of your secrets."

"Gabe loved Pop. So whatever crazy thing you're thinking—"

"That Gabriel's the one who went crazy and killed Mr. Turner, not—"

"—stop thinking it!"

Fancy knew she should have been put out by him raising his voice, but there was something . . . exciting about the way he yelled.

"Even if Gabe killed him," he continued, oblivious to Fancy's thoughts, "even if Gabe killed a truckload of people, who are you to judge him?"

Fancy decided to back off, not because she was afraid of Ilan's anger, but because she could hear beyond the anger, hear the hurt underneath it all. "Pain is relatives," she said, almost to herself.

He sighed away his anger in one long breath. "You have no frigging idea."

Fancy didn't want to hurt him. But she didn't mind teasing him. "I know some things."

"Like what?"

"I know what you want to do to me. I had a dream. . . ." Fancy remembered something—Ilan framed in the window— but then lost it. She reached out and touched his face, saw the moonlight flash in his eyes. There wasn't nearly enough light for what she wanted to see, which was everything. "Or maybe you're so upset about the whole *I hate Gabriel* situation that you don't want me anymore?"

"I still want you." Ilan touched her face the same way she was touching his. "I don't love Gabe *that* much."

Fancy laughed, relieved and slightly in awe that such an understanding boy could want someone like her. "You still have my cherry?"

"Nope." She felt his cheeks stretch into a smile. "Ate it. Couldn't resist."

"How was it?"

"Sweet." He leaned forward and kissed her.

"Wait." Fancy pushed him back, cursing the dark that hid his face.

"Still not ripe?" he said, giving her space, disappointed but not surprised.

"I do want you to kiss me," she explained. "Just warn me first. So I can pay attention."

"Okay," Ilan said, laughing but taking her seriously. "Ready. Steady. Go." When he kissed her that time, she didn't push him away.

He tasted sleepy. Like a dream. She kept her hands on his face, thinking that if she stopped touching him, he would vanish and she would wake up kissing her pillow. She caressed his lips as they moved against hers, was just getting used to the press of them when his tongue got involved and made it harder to pay attention. "I like that," Ilan said, and touched the tip of his tongue to her upper lip, delicate as a hummingbird. "The way you taste."

"What do I taste like?"

"Pancakes."

Fancy laughed, and the fact that she was laughing during her first kiss made her laugh even harder. She'd always thought it would be . . . different. That there would be roses and violins somehow. But here she was in the bushes with the smell of cackler blood in her nose and a boy she couldn't even see who thought she tasted like breakfast.

Ilan laughed with her. "You know those pancakes on a stick? Swear to God, that's what you taste like." He kissed her again, and the urge to laugh dissolved. She tried to decide what he tasted like, but could only think of rain. Something fresh and wet like that. Summer rain.

When he stopped again, she was on her back and he was on top of her, though she had no memory of lying down. He was panting, a sound so unromantic she had to laugh again. "You must really like pancakes on a stick."

"I *love* those things."

Fancy felt pressure on her hip and gasped. "Just like that cackler!" She reached down and grabbed his crotch.

Ilan did some gasping of his own and scurried off her.

"Not quite mating season for us yet. It won't be if you get the hell on indoors."

"Don't talk to me like that."

"Would you please get the hell on indoors?"

"No." Fancy sat up and wrapped her arms around him.

"Damn it, Fancy."

She kissed his ear. "Don't be mad."

"I ain't mad. I can't even blame you. You *told* me you like to torture guys."

They kissed again, and she wondered if she would ever stop being startled by his tongue.

A door slammed.

Fancy let him go, reluctantly, and he peered through the mahonia bushes. "That's Gabe," he said. "I better go catch up." But when she tried to follow, he stopped her. "You wait till we're gone."

"Why're you trying to protect him?" she said, feeling an intriguing mix of arousal and irritation. "He tried to kill *me*."

"He's only like that when he sleepwalks. You're like that all the time. So stay here." He pulled her in for one last kiss. "I'll call you, okay?"

"Okay."

"Bye." He ran through the mahonia bushes. "And be sweet, for Christ's sake!" he called over his shoulder.

"I'll try!"

Fancy watched a surprised Gabriel relinquish the driver's seat to Ilan and decided it had been a sort of romantic first kiss. Didn't the full moon make everything romantic?

She reached up and picked another moonflower. She would be sweet tonight like Ilan thought she was. Pancake sweet. And tomorrow? Pure poison.

FROM FANCY'S DREAM DIARY:

I looked at my garden of trees in the happy place. The dancer, the old man, Madda, Ilan. They were all there and growing. The only problem was Kit. She was stunted and gray and a weird fungus was growing up her trunk. She begged me to chop her down. I just laughed.

CHAPTER TWENTY-FOUR

Fancy was lying in bed, snuggling with Bearzilla, sulking about Gabriel, and staring at the ceiling. It was painted sky blue to discourage insects, but a pale green luna moth fluttered against it. Fancy wanted to smack it and put it out of its misery, but it was too hot. Besides, it was bad luck to kill anything green. She had to settle for intense glaring.

She started at the tap on the screen door and cheered a bit when she saw it was Ilan.

He came inside and sat on her bed, just made himself right at home. "What's the matter with you?"

"Nothing. I'm bored."

"Aw, do you want a glass of juice? Or maybe a coloring book?"

Fancy stopped feeling cheerful that he had come. "I told you to stop babying me."

"Then stop acting like a baby." Ilan snatched Bearzilla from her arms and then did a double take. "What the hell is this?"

"Bearzilla."

"But . . . what *is* it?"

Fancy snatched it back, not liking the way Ilan was staring at her toy like it was a freak. "It's the head of a dragon sewn onto the body of a bear."

"Why would anybody . . ." Ilan remembered who he was talking to and didn't bother to finish the sentence. "Why don't you go find some people to help if you're so bored?"

"What's the point? It doesn't make me happy."

"So you think happiness is gone fly in here and give you a hundred bucks?" Ilan batted the bear/dragon out of her hands and hauled her to her feet.

"Bearzilla, no!" Fancy exclaimed as her toy hit the floor.

"You and Bearzilla can terrorize major cities *later*. Now stop whining and come with me. I wanna show you something."

Fancy let him drag her outside to his sand-colored Oldsmobile. In the front seat sat a little boy with a bloody bandage wrapped around his forehead. "You do that to him?"

"Ha-ha, funny girl. That's not what I wanna show you." She followed him to the back of his car, where he unlocked the trunk. A different boy was bound and gagged inside, glaring at them and blinking sweat from his eyes. "*That's* what I wanna show you," Ilan told her, as proud as if he'd brought home a deer for dinner. "I brought him for you."

"Like a present?" Fancy asked, touched.

Ilan scuffed his foot against the driveway. "You don't seem like the flowers and candy type."

Fancy gave him a hug, which seemed an inadequate expression of what she was feeling. Kit would have known the right way to respond to such a great gift. "It's really sweet," she said. "But I don't think killing will make me feel better."

Ilan laughed at her. "Then don't kill him. You don't have to kill *everyone*. Sometimes the worst thing you can do to someone is to let him live. With the pain and guilt."

Fancy thought about this and then went back to the passenger window and studied the blood encrusted all over the little boy's face. "Did the boy in the trunk do that to you?" she asked, pointing at the bandage.

The boy nodded and frowned into his lap.

"What's your name?" Fancy asked.

"Egbert."

"Egbert?" Fancy gave the boy a pitying look, taking in his dork haircut, potbelly, and short pants. "That's too bad. So what? Did he get bored of pantsing you on the playground and putting Kick Me signs on your back?"

"Nobody puts Kick Me signs on me," said Egbert, offended. "Everybody likes me. I don't know why George doesn't."

"George is the boy in the trunk?"

Egbert nodded. "Can you make him take back what he did? Ilan said you could."

"What did he do?"

Egbert unwrapped the bloody bandage. Carved deeply into the boy's forehead was the word "faggot."

She helped Egbert rewrap his injury and walked back to the trunk where Ilan was waiting expectantly. "Still bored?" he asked.

Fancy frowned at George. "All of a sudden, I'm feeling real lively."

Fancy and Ilan were sitting beneath the Tony tree holding hands and listening to the mini Tonys sing "Why Do Fools Fall in Love" when Egbert ran up to them grinning ear to ear.

"How was it?" Fancy asked after she'd dismissed the

minions who had escorted Egbert to his appointment.

"Great! It didn't even hurt."

"Now that George is taken care of, let's take care of your forehead." Fancy stood and went to the godfather tree.

"How *did* you take care of George?" Ilan asked.

"Can I show him?" Egbert was practically imploding with the need to show someone.

"Hold on." Fancy studied the skinlike leaves until she found the right one for Egbert. She plucked the leaf and placed it over the word on Egbert's head. The leaf matched his skin tone and adhered so well it could have been the boy's own perfectly unmarked skin.

"*Now* can I show him?"

Fancy shrugged and smiled, and Egbert ran to Ilan, turned, and pulled down his shorts.

Ilan laughed. He laughed for a long time. "They tattooed a picture of George on his ass?" But Ilan's laughter stopped abruptly when the tattoo began to move.

"That's not a picture," Fancy told him. "That's George."

George rippled colorfully across Egbert's pale butt cheek. Only the left one—he couldn't seem to cross the great divide to the other side. Within the space he had to maneuver, he flitted this way and that, like a trapped fly butting its head against a window.

"Pull your pants up, pervert," Ilan said after the cellar walls suddenly closed around them. "We're in the real world now."

Egbert pulled up his shorts with a satisfied sigh and touched the smooth skin of his forehead. "Is it still on?"

"That's your skin now," Fancy said. "Of course it's on. Just remember, Egbert. If you decide you don't want George on your butt anymore, let me know, and I'll remove him and set him free in the happy place."

Egbert smiled at Ilan. "Thank you for coming to my rescue." Then he turned to Fancy. "And thank you." He reached in his pocket and brought out three quarters and a dime.

Fancy took the money automatically, but then wavered. "That's okay," she said, giving him back his change.

After Ilan got Egbert settled into his car, he went around to the driver's side, where Fancy was waiting for him. He put his arms around her. "I can go hunting for you again, if you want. Or we could even go together."

"Okay," Fancy said, feeling inadequate. Ilan always knew just what to say to make her feel . . . perfect. But she never knew what to say back.

"That was sweet, what you did."

"You mean what I *didn't* do."

He kissed her and smiled against her mouth. "Yeah. Pancake sweet."

The pancake sweetness lingered a surprisingly long time. Fancy felt so sweet that the idea of being mad at Kit no longer made sense, and so Wednesday, after class, she decided to make peace.

Kit was in the living room practicing scales when Fancy sat next to her on the piano bench and held her Daisy Duck compact before Kit's face.

She hit a discordant note and stopped playing. "Daddy?"

He was in an orange jumpsuit, sitting in his single-person cell, reading a book—*Bleak House* by Charles Dickens.

"Is that really him?"

"If I was making it up," said Fancy, staring into the mirror, "I'd make up something a *lot* more interesting."

"Yeah, you would." Kit laughed and watched the unentertaining spectacle of Daddy reading for several minutes as though it were the most fascinating thing she'd ever seen.

Kit tapped the mirror as if trying to get Daddy's attention. "I know he hurt all those people, but how can somebody just decide that you and me don't deserve to have a father anymore?"

Fancy considered this. "You'd think the least they could do is provide a replacement."

Kit bumped her shoulder. "Nobody could replace Daddy. Unless it was, like, Bill Cosby or something."

"I been thinking about going down to visit him."

"Really? I don't know if I could watch it. I know we're allowed, and that lethal injection is painless, but I don't know if I wanna watch him die. Besides, it's only seven minutes long and he won't even twitch or anything, so what's the point?"

"I mean visit him *before* he gets killed."

"You think Madda'll let us?"

"*She* wouldn't want to go, but she wouldn't keep us from going. Long as you promise not to drive like a maniac."

"Let's go next weekend! A road trip, Fancy, just like in the movies. With boys! You think the boys'll go with us?"

"Boys?" Fancy's enthusiasm for the road trip died almost as soon as it was born.

"The Turner brothers. You don't think they might want to come and confront Daddy? Maybe get some closure?"

Fancy slammed the compact closed so forcefully they both

heard the mirror crack. Fancy shot off the bench and fled across the room, taking refuge by the credenza.

"It's like you never want it to be just me and you anymore. Like you'll use any excuse not to be alone with me."

Kit looked as though Fancy had punched her in the gut, which wasn't fair because that's how Fancy felt.

"It's not just you and me anymore. Gabe is a part of my life now."

"But—"

"And that's it! I'm not having this conversation again."

"If you wanna joyride all across the state with that sleep-walking weirdo, count me out!"

Kit turned back to the piano and played a D-minor scale. "We'll send you a postcard."

"Girls?"

Madda came out of the hallway that led to the bedrooms wearing a deadly serious expression, the same expression she'd worn when she'd told them Daddy wasn't coming home ever again. Even worse than her expression was the letter in her hand. The sisters looked at each other and held a silent conversation with their eyes:

Didn't you get the mail?

I thought you *did.*

Madda paused behind Kit and looked at each daughter in turn. "Why am I getting letters about your 'contributions to Portero'?"

The sisters were speechless.

"'Your daughters have handled problems before,'" Madda read, "'and I was wondering if you could ask them to handle one of mine. My ex-husband is trying to win custody of my child, but he is a drunk and doesn't deserve to raise her. You are a mother and understand what it is to have a horrible husband. Could you please ask your girls to take care of this for me? Thank you.'"

Madda smacked her hand against the letter as if it were someone's face. "Y'all have something to tell me?"

The sisters hovered on the brink of a precipice, and neither wanted to be the one to tip them all over the edge into the abyss.

Madda turned her gaze on Fancy. "I told you how I feel about finding things out secondhand."

"You haven't found anything out, Madda," said Kit blithely. "Fancy, come turn the pages for me."

Fancy went back to her sister's side, happy not to have to

stand alone against Madda. She stared at the sheet music for a song called "Strange Fruit," the notes meaningless black specks that gave her something to focus on besides Madda's darkening expression.

"I wanna know what's going on around here," Madda said, the words falling brokenly from her mouth as if she had to speak around something sharp lodged in her throat. "I keep hearing all this talk, this crazy talk about you girls, but . . . after everything we been through with Guthrie, y'all wouldn't just . . . you wouldn't—"

"We ain't like him, Madda." Fancy turned the sheet music, her hand shaking, as Kit played on, neither of them daring to look back at their mother.

Madda reached between them, startling them, and snatched the sheet music from the piano. They turned then and watched her rip it and the letter she'd received into pieces. "You're just like him."

"No, Madda."

"You know how I feel about being lied to!"

Fancy turned away, hating the look on Madda's face, that look of betrayal and heartbreak. She faced forward and let Kit deal with it.

"We know, Madda, and we're not lying. There's a reason there ain't a mob with pitchforks and torches standing outside our door, and the reason is we're *not* like Daddy. You can trust us."

"Okay." Whatever Madda heard in Kit's tone seemed to calm her. Slightly. "I gotta get ready for work. You girls be good," she added fiercely. "You hear me?"

"Yes, ma'am," said the sisters in unison.

Madda stalked back the way she'd come and slammed the door to her room.

The sisters looked at each other. "We are so fucked," said Kit.

Fancy nodded. "Completely. What're we gone do?"

"Tell her the truth."

"She'll hate us! Not like the way we hate each other sometimes. But, like, real hate. The way she feels about Daddy. We can't trust her with this."

Kit dropped to the floor and began to gather the ripped sheet music and puzzle it back together. Fancy went into the kitchen and scrounged up a roll of Scotch tape. When she came back into the living room, Kit was staring off into space.

"What is it?"

"Just imagining if Madda stopped loving me." When she looked at Fancy, her eyes were wet. "I think it'd hurt, the way torture hurts."

"Kit."

"No," she said, when Fancy would have come to her. "It's fine. I learned a whole lot this summer. And one of the things I learned is that I don't have to depend on Madda for love. Other people love me. *Gabe* loves me."

The name "Gabe" shivered in Fancy's belly like a poison dart.

"Still," Kit continued, "if Madda could ignore the murder and mayhem and love me anyway, I think I'd have everything I want."

Fancy threw the tape at Kit and nearly hit her in the eye. Instead it sailed past her and disappeared into the shadows of the shuttered room.

"Nobody gets everything they want. Why should you be any different?"

FROM FANCY'S DREAM DIARY:

It was raining and I could see Daddy's face in all the raindrops.

CHAPTER TWENTY-FIVE

That Friday, after Kit and Gabriel had left on their trip, Fancy was hanging the laundry in the backyard when a police car pulled into the driveway. She tried not to panic when Sheriff Baker got out and approached her. He wore a brown uniform and hat and always reminded Fancy of Smokey the Bear, only less friendly.

"Fancy." He tipped his hat to her. Cops didn't salute people they were about to arrest, did they?

"I heard about what you been doing."

Fancy dropped the clothespins.

"About those transies. About Datura Woodson. About

Annie Snoad." Sheriff Baker picked up the clothespins and helped Fancy pin the bedsheet she was fumbling with to the line. "That's real good of you."

"*Good?*"

"If your pa had been of a mind to be as helpful as you and your sister, I could have worked with him, maybe got him a different outcome. Of course what I'm telling you is strictly between us."

"Everybody keeps saying that," Fancy exclaimed, "that everything's a secret. That they'll never tell anyone, but . . . everybody *knows* everything!"

Sheriff Baker chuckled. "You know better than to try to keep a secret in a small town. We're all like one big family here." He mopped his brow with a red handkerchief, and she noticed the last two fingers of his right hand were gone; deep teeth marks were grooved into his remaining flesh. "That's what I never could stomach about your pa, that he could hurt his fellow Porterenes that way. We have enough trouble keeping safe in this town without worrying about our neighbors hacking us into pieces. Anyway, I thought I'd come over and pay you a visit. Let you know I'm watching your back." He gave her a sly look. "And if *I* should run across any unsavory characters who need to be taken care of away from the eyes of the law . . ."

"I'll watch your back?"

"Atta girl." He clapped a hand on her shoulder and steered her away from the laundry. "Come walk me to my car so I can give you the batch of muffins my wife made specially for you."

As they walked to the car Ilan pulled up in his Oldsmobile. After he jogged over, Fancy let him grab her and kiss her cheek, but she wouldn't allow anything more, gesturing toward the sheriff, who watched them openly.

"Hey, Sheriff."

"Ilan." The sheriff looked as if he couldn't decide whether to handcuff Ilan or shoot at his feet to run him off the property. He turned to Fancy. "Your ma still at work?"

"She's at the store."

Sheriff Baker handed her the plastic-wrapped plate of blueberry muffins and said, "Well, you two stay outdoors, then. Ain't right for boys to come sniffing around young girls when they folks ain't home."

"Yes, sir," said Ilan, struggling to appear innocent. And failing.

"Enjoy those muffins," the sheriff said to Fancy, after giving Ilan a final warning stare. "I'll be seeing you."

As soon as the sheriff's car was out of sight, Ilan kissed Fancy as non-innocently as possible and said, "Please don't tell me you were about to kill the sheriff."

"Ha-ha." She pushed away from him. She liked kissing him, but it was too hot for long embraces. "He just wanted me to know that he knew about all the killing," she said. "And that he doesn't mind so long as he can get in on it."

"Nice. It's kinda hot watching you do good deeds," he said as she led him to the stairway leading down into the open cellar, where the cool underground air could waft toward them. "I oughta buy you a fairy-princess wand so you can really get into the part." He sat awkwardly on the steps, his knees bent as if he didn't want his legs to stray down into the shadowy pool at the bottom of the cellar.

Fancy unwrapped the muffins in her lap. "I got seven wands. I'll let you borrow one sometime. Kit don't like playing fairyland anymore. But *we* could play, if you want."

Ilan laughed like he thought she was joking. But his laughs were as contagious as his smiles, and she laughed with him, fiercely glad all of a sudden that he was there with her and not down in Huntsville.

"Why didn't you go with Kit and Gabriel?" she asked.

"Gotta work this weekend."

"Where?"

"Pinkerton. I'm a bellhop." He stole a bite of her muffin. "Why didn't you go?"

"Same reason I skipped class today: I hate everybody."

"Even me?"

"No. But when I'm mad . . . I didn't wanna accidentally do something to you. Or Kit. Or *Gabriel*."

"I'd rather you hurt me than Gabe. I'm responsible for that little punk. But just stab me or something quick. I'd rather not live on somebody's ass cheek the rest of my life." He waved down into the cellar. "Or disappear into your version of hell or wherever."

"It's not hell," said Fancy, indignant. "It's nice, usually. I just been in a bad mood lately. You wanna go over?"

He ducked his head, trying to see all the way down the steps but unable to because the angle was bad. "I dunno."

"I'll take care of you."

"You mean that in a nonmurderous way, right?"

"Do I really have to answer that?"

"Yeah, you really do."

"I promise I won't—"

"I'm kidding. I trust you."

"You do?"

"What the hell. You decided to trust me when I didn't let your dogs kill me. You trust me enough not to lie to me. So I decided to trust you back." He frowned when she looked down at the plate of muffins in her lap. "I can trust you, can't I?"

Fancy shrugged. "Sure. I won't do anything." She stood and waved him down into the cellar and watched as he descended.

"Not to you," she whispered.

"Is that a new tree?" Ilan asked, walking to one of the stone circles on the platform.

The moonflower Fancy had taken from her backyard and planted in the happy place after Gabriel had attacked her had grown into a tree with yummy-smelling fruit in the shape of tiny white crescents.

"Yep. It's the only tree here that wasn't grown from a corpse." She plucked one of the crescents. "Try one."

She fed the crescent fruit to Ilan and laughed when he nipped her fingers. "How is it?"

"Great."

She stilled then, as his dark eyes became as milky white as the moonfruit and his gaze as blank as a doll's. She grabbed his hand; even his hand felt fake. Plastic. "Can I ask you something?"

"Anything."

"Why did you really push Gabriel down the stairs?"

"Because I love him."

"That's not the only reason." She shook him when he didn't answer. "Is it?"

"No."

"You were mad at him, weren't you?"

"Yes."

"Tell me why."

"Because of what he wanted to do." Even his voice was wrong, more like the recording of a voice, rather than a real one. "He was just a dumb kid."

"So you helped him cover it up?"

"It wasn't Gabe's fault. I just wanted to protect him."

"You can't protect him forever, Ilan!" Fancy yelled at the white-eyed thing standing before her. She wanted *her* Ilan back, the real one, but maybe he wasn't coming back. Maybe she'd . . . broken him. If she had, she at least wanted to hear the truth.

"I know what Gabriel wanted to do," she said. "What he did do. Admit it—you pushed him down the stairs because *he's* the one who killed your dad."

FROM FANCY'S DREAM DIARY:

GABRIEL KEPT EXPLAINING TO EVERYONE HOW HAPPY HE WAS. HE TOLD ME EVEN HIS NAME MEANS HAPPY. BUT ILAN CALLED HIM A LIAR. HE SAID "ILAN" MEANS HAPPY AND "GABRIEL" MEANS LIAR. GABRIEL CRIED CRIED CRIED. AND HIS TEARS WERE SORDID AND THICK, LIKE HE WAS SO ROTTEN INSIDE, HE WAS LEAKING.

CHAPTER TWENTY-SIX

Ilan blinked. "What?"

"I asked you about Gabriel."

"What about him?" He spat as if he had a bad taste in his mouth and sat on the stone circling the tree. When he looked up at Fancy, the white had cleared from his eyes and they were pale brown again. Fancy was so happy he'd shaken off the effects of the moonfruit, so happy he was aware and real and not broken, that she almost didn't care that he hadn't answered her question.

Almost.

She sat beside him. "You don't remember what I asked you *five seconds ago* about Gabriel?"

"Why you always wanna talk about other guys when I'm with you?" When she just stared at him, half irritated, half relieved, he spat again. "That aftertaste is killer." He popped an Altoid and offered her one. And then he studied the fruit growing over his head.

"So what's in that fruit? Truth serum or something?"

She nodded and sucked on the Altoid, marveling at Ilan's Kitlike ability to brush her games aside like cobwebs. Sometimes it was hard to remember that she hadn't known him for years. "Looks like it takes more than one moonfruit to keep people under long enough to get anything useful outta them. Live and learn." She cut her eyes at him. "Are you mad?"

"No," he said, after such a long pause she wasn't sure she believed him. "If I were you, I'd want answers too. But don't ever drug me again."

"Or what?" asked Fancy, honestly curious. "You wouldn't push *me* down the stairs, would you?"

"I might. If I had to." That she believed. "Does that scare you?" he asked in a faux-creepy voice.

"Nothing scares me. Except monsters. I'm just very protective of my family. I hardly have any left."

"I know the feeling. But trust means not drugging people

in order to get answers from them. Trust means giving people a chance to come clean on their own."

Fancy understood then that Ilan wasn't mad; he was hurt. His *feelings* were hurt.

"I'm sorry," said Fancy, unsure what to do about his feelings.

"Promise not to trick me again and I'll forgive you."

She crossed her heart. "I promise not to trick you again."

"Now give me a kiss so I'll believe you."

She kissed his ear. That's what Kit liked whenever her feelings were hurt. But Ilan seemed disastrously unmoved. So she kissed him the way she had that night in her backyard.

When she pulled away, he was grinning ear to ear. "See? Kiss me like that, and I'll believe anything."

Fancy filed the information away for future reference. "Wanna see the rest of my happy place?"

"Is that code for . . . ?" He laughed at the blank look on her face. "Never mind. Lead the way."

"Baron von Big Ears can give the tour." She took a pink, elephant-shaped finger puppet from her pocket and put it over her index finger. "Daddy made it for me before he went away." She made the puppet kiss Ilan on the ear, but Ilan didn't seem to like ear kisses from Baron von Big Ears any more than from her. "Would you like a grand tour, kind sir?" said Fancy in Baron von Big Ears's slow, deep voice.

Ilan looked askance at Baron von Big Ears. "O-kay."

Fancy let Baron von Big Ears give a tour of all the happy-place hot spots: the big hill overlooking the beach, the sailing ships, the Pavilion. But when Baron von Big Ears pointed out the carnival rides near the beach, Ilan began to laugh.

"What's funny?" said Fancy in her own voice.

Ilan leaned back against the base of a carousel to catch his breath. "It's so childish. This place. You."

"I'm not childish."

"I thought you were kidding about the fairy wands. I bet you still play with jacks and jump ropes and shit too, don't you?"

"It's not shit. And it's not childish!"

Ilan leaned forward and snatched Baron von Big Ears from Fancy's hand. He slipped the puppet over his own finger and made it speak. "Why do you like carousels, little girl?" he said, doing a passable Baron von Big Ears impersonation.

Fancy stared at the puppet, disconcerted by the idea that her once-friendly toy was now mocking her. "I like to ride the horses."

"Going up and down with something sturdy between your legs," said Baron von Big Ears wisely. "All girls like that. It's how they practice."

"I don't know what you're talking about."

"Oh, yes you do." Baron von Big Ears dove headfirst into her cleavage.

"Stop it." Fancy snatched the finger puppet from Ilan and said it again to his face. "Stop it!"

"I can't." He used his own voice. "And neither can you. None of your little toys are gone keep you from growing up." He tried to grab the finger puppet, but Fancy hid it behind her back. Instead of reaching for the puppet, Ilan grabbed Fancy's elbow and dragged her onto the carousel, past the horses, and brought her to a stop before the bright metal column around which the carousel spun.

As soon as Fancy saw herself, she stopped struggling, the shock of her reflection paralyzing her. She was sure the metal had distorted her image into the fun-house creature she saw staring back at her, that oversize girl in the undersize dress—a baby face, yes, but with eyes full of dark understanding.

"Do you see?" Ilan asked, letting go of her arm.

Fancy nodded, watching the girl in the mirror nodding,

wondering why no one had ever told her how ridiculous she looked, how sad and deluded.

"Do you trust me?" said Ilan gently. He put out his hand. "You said you did."

She set the finger puppet in his palm and felt a pang as he shoved it unceremoniously into his pocket. She followed him off the carousel, tugging at her dress. Had it always fit so tightly?

"Now whyn't you let all this go?" Ilan said, waving his arm at not just the carousel, but the entire carnival. "Just to see what it's like. Just to see what's beyond all this kid shit."

She looked at the rides, which had been so much fun once upon a time, but now made her feel ashamed. The Ferris wheel fell over onto its side with a rending crash, the chains holding the swings to the whirligig snapped, and the carousel horses grew old and gray and withered like overripe fruit on their poles.

"Now what?"

"It's up to you!" Ilan exclaimed, as though not knowing who you were was exciting. He surveyed the wasteland the carnival had become with an almost gleeful satisfaction. "Think big. What's the one thing you can't wait to do when you grow up?"

Fancy didn't have to think about it very hard; she knew exactly what she wanted to do when she was old enough.

A happy-place citizen popped up on the other side of the ruined carousel and nailed Ilan in the face with a tomato.

"When you grow up," Ilan said in a surprisingly calm voice, a tomato stuck to his forehead like a hideous, mutant zit, "you wanna throw food at me?"

"No. I wanna travel." More people came forward from all over the happy place, hands full of tomatoes, faces full of mischief.

"There's this thing in Spain called La Tomatina," said Fancy as a tomato war exploded all around her. "People get together on the streets and have a huge tomato fight like this, for no reason at all except that it's fun." One of the wizened carousel horses nearest Fancy broke open, and a flood of tomatoes spilled free like bright red candy from a burst piñata.

Fancy knelt and scooped up the tomatoes, but froze when she heard Ilan behind her laughing, swiping the tomato off his forehead. Laughing at her. Still.

"I guess this ain't exactly grown-up either," she said, letting the tomatoes fall from her hands.

"Nope," Ilan agreed, retrieving her tomatoes for her and

then grabbing a few for himself. "But it's important not to grow up too fast."

She kissed his cheek when he stood, tasting the tomato on his skin, but he wasn't paying attention; he was too busy giving the massive happy-place crowd the evil eye.

He bounced a tomato in his hand. "Let's go kick some Tomatina butt."

Some time later Fancy and Ilan stood in her backyard taking turns hosing tomato sauce off each other.

"Why can't I ever stay?" Fancy complained as she circled Ilan, spraying water over his chest and back. "It's my place. Why do I keep getting kicked out of my own place?"

"Maybe when you create something," said Ilan, taking the hose from her, "you can only enjoy it as an outsider, like God. I mean God doesn't hang around Earth, and back when he did, it was only for little pieces of time. So maybe it's like that for everybody."

Fancy thought that over as she yanked the pink ribbons from her hair and tossed them away. "How come every time you get the hose, you keep it aimed at my bubbies?"

"Cuz they're tomatoey. Like, *really* tomatoey."

"But look at all the tomato on my legs. In my shoes. And I still feel it in my hair."

"You're right," he said, watching her strip off her patent leather shoes and ruffled socks and toss them into the woods. "You're a mess. Why don't you just strip down all the way? I don't see how else I could possibly get you clean."

"You can start by aiming that hose somewhere besides my bubbies!"

"I want to," Ilan explained, regretfully, "but I can't. See, the wetter I get your dress, the better I can see through it. And since you're refusing to strip for me, well, you do the math."

Fancy tackled Ilan to the muddy ground, laughing. "You're a big, fat pervert, Ilan Turner."

Ilan was laughing too. "Yup. And you rolling me around in the mud ain't really helping the situation." He rolled her onto her back and kissed her.

"Why do we always end up with you on top of me?"

"You ask the best questions, Fancy." He rolled them over again and put her back on top, astride him.

She sat up and bounced a few times, experimentally. "This *is* better than a wooden horse."

"Whoa, there, cowgirl." Ilan pushed her up a bit and

unzipped his pants, and Fancy had a weird feeling that Ilan had unzipped his pants for her before, which was ridiculous. It became even more ridiculous when he removed a cherry tomato from his boxers.

Fancy laughed and clapped her hands, as though he'd just performed a magic trick for her. "What else you got in there?"

"One or two things," he said modestly.

She reached into his boxers to see for herself. "*Three* things," she shrieked, as he squirmed beneath her. "Maybe." She squeezed. "Does this count as one or two?"

"Fancy, is that you?" Madda appeared in the kitchen window. "I been calling you—" Madda stopped at the sight of Fancy and Ilan frozen on the ground.

Fancy was prepared for anything. Ever since the letter incident Madda had been snappy and cross with her and Kit, but Fancy wasn't prepared for Madda to smile at her.

"Your hands cold?" she said, pointedly staring at Fancy's hand burrowed inside Ilan's pants.

"I'd turn the hose on you," Madda said, nearly laughing as Fancy scurried off Ilan, "but looks like you beat me to it. Turn that thing off and stop wasting water."

Fancy shut off the hose. "We were just—"

Madda waved her hand. "I'm not so old I need to have *that* explained to me. How you doing, Ilan?"

"Great, Miz Lynne." He was on his feet, readjusting his pants and looking everywhere except into Madda's eyes. "Fabulous, really."

"Don't you think you oughta be getting your fabulous self on home now?" she asked.

"Yes, ma'am. I was just thinking the same thing."

Fancy stood beside him. "I'll walk him to his car."

"You do that."

Fancy and Ilan slunk off toward the driveway, faces burning. Madda's good humor about the situation should have been a relief, but Fancy found it inexplicably irritating.

"I'm *never* gone live this down," she said after they reached the Oldsmobile.

"Aw, let her enjoy herself. Her baby's all growned up." Ilan plucked at her wet, muddy dress and sighed wistfully, looking her up and down. "I know *I'm* enjoying it."

That Saturday, Fancy stepped out onto the roof of the Pinkerton Hotel. The rain had stopped, but the clouds still hung ominous and low in the sky. She walked to the edge of the roof, past big metal vents and whirring fans, the black shirtdress she'd stolen from Madda's closet molded to her figure by the wind. She leaned her elbows on a wide, damp ledge and looked out over Fountain Square.

Low, towering clouds made the houses below look like toys. Here in the flatter, comparatively treeless part of Portero, Fancy didn't have to look up through trees to see the sky—it was all around her.

Ilan had told her to wait for him up here. Kit was still on her road trip with Gabriel, but would be back tomorrow. Fancy was glad Ilan had called her and wanted to see her. Otherwise she would be moping at home. Madda had been right. Having friends did come in handy sometimes.

In a little while Ilan showed up with a dinner cart that he had swiped from the kitchen. He was still in his red bellhop uniform, a welcome spot of color in all the gray.

"You're gone get fired."

"Please." He smoothed her ribbonless, windblown hair from her face and kissed her. "I've got the dirt on too many people at this hotel. Did you know the manager gets high with the laundry staff? It's like a soap opera in there. Me sneaking food up on the roof to my girlfriend won't even register."

Fancy's eyes went wide at being called his girlfriend so casually. But she didn't say anything. "What did you bring?"

"Fruit. Sopaipillas. Tomato salad. Mint julep."

"Really?" Fancy had never had mint julep before.

"They *call* it mint julep." He sat beside her and poured them each a glass. "But look at it. It ain't supposed to be bright green like that."

Fancy tried hers. "Oooh, it's good, though."

They sat with their backs against the ledge of the building and drank and nibbled in silence a few moments before they began talking. Light things at first, like whether the rain would hold off, but they quickly moved on to heavier topics, sinking into them with a sense of relief.

"I don't understand how all these people are so thirsty for Daddy to die, just because he killed their people, like they think it'll restore a balance. Like how people burned women in the old days whenever a cow got sick or whatever? One person's life can't replace fifteen or however many other lives. One person's life can't even replace *one* other person's life. People ain't interchangeable like that."

"If you like people so much and think they're so precious, why do you kill them?"

"I didn't say they were precious; I said they're not inter-changeable. Like if I wanted to kill you, killing Gabriel wouldn't satisfy that. Or if I did kill you, and then Gabriel killed me in revenge, it wouldn't satisfy him, because he wouldn't want to kill me. What he'd really want would be to bring you back to life, and killing doesn't create life. That's all I mean. If you're gone kill somebody, you should at least know why you're doing it."

"Why do *you* do it?"

"To feel whole. Kit said that once. That it wasn't about being good or bad—it was about being complete. She was right." Fancy shrugged. "That and sometimes I just get mad. Either way."

"You don't want to kill Gabe anymore, do you?"

"Not all the time."

Ilan made her look at him. "It's like what you were saying. Killing Gabe won't give you your sister back. It'll probably drive her even further away. You gotta let her do her own thing."

"I don't get why Kit doing her own thing means she's gotta shut me out."

"People always shut off parts of themselves, even from people they love. Some things should never be seen. Unlike your bubbies."

Fancy laughed. "Why you wanna see *them*?"

"Oh, the questions you ask, Fancy."

"They're not even interesting. They just jiggle around."

"Jiggling is interesting."

"No, it's not." She pressed her palms against her breasts, reassuring herself that they were nothing special. "Sometimes when I get the curse they swell like balloons, and then when I touch my nipples it hurts."

"Do you touch your nipples a lot?" asked Ilan, more intrigued than ever.

"Sometimes. Kit's nipples only poke out when she's cold. Mine poke out *all the time*. Not sure how to make 'em go down. It's more stupid than interesting."

"Do you know what the word 'interesting' means?" Ilan asked, unbuttoning the shirtfront of her dress. "Because I don't think you do."

Fancy suddenly remembered her dream. "What does 'Ilan' mean?"

"Tree." He gasped. "A front-snap bra? For me? You're so thoughtful, Fancy." She giggled as he moved behind her so that she could sit between his legs with her back against his front.

"*Happy* tree?"

"Just tree," he said, and then his hands were on her.

Fancy closed her eyes. "My doctor touched my bubbies once. She stroked them like that. I can't remember why."

"She probably thought they were interesting." She felt his smile against her temple. "What about Fancy? What's that short for anyway? Frances?"

"Francine. Means free."

"And happy?"

"Not usually. I kind of feel happy right now, though. Tree and free."

A drop of rain fell on Fancy's mouth. She licked it off. She felt akin to the clouds, the trouble brewing within them, the darkness. The rain that fell on her made her shiver, like extensions of Ilan's hands, tickling her knees and smacking her toes.

"Fancy . . ."

"Um?"

"*Are* you happy? Like, way down?" His hands drifted down to her belly as if to illustrate.

Fancy shook her head, unable to remember the last time happiness had infiltrated that deeply inside her. Had it ever?

"I think that's why I like you." He kissed away a drop of rain from Fancy's neck. "I see you and think, if anybody's more unhappy than me, it's her. If anybody would understand and not judge, it'd be her."

"Not judge what?"

"I'll tell you one day. When you like me more than you do now."

"If I liked you more, I'd explode."

He put his mouth against her ear. "You wanna explode?" he said, sliding his hands farther down her stomach, past her belly button, past her—

Fancy grabbed his hands and made him stop.

"Don't be scared," Ilan said, holding his hands before her face. "They're harmless."

Fancy pressed her palms against his. "I don't know how to do all that stuff."

"Sure you do. You had all that practice with those carousel horses, remember?"

Fancy rolled her eyes at his complete goofiness and turned to face him. "Are you as much fun as a wooden horse?"

"You tell me." He helped settle her onto his lap so they were face to face. He was all smiles as he slid his hands under Fancy's dress.

"Giddy up, cowgirl."

FROM FANCY'S DREAM DIARY:

Kit ran into the kitchen and showed Madda and me Gabriel's heart dripping all over the floor. She said Gabriel gave her his heart for Valentine's Day and that she needed to frame it. When I gave her a wooden picture frame, she yelled at me and said she wanted gold. So I went looking for a gold frame and saw Gabriel lying dead in the hallway. I asked him if it was worth it. He couldn't answer because he was dead, but I caught him smiling anyway.

CHAPTER TWENTY-SEVEN

Kit made it home in time for Sunday dinner. The sisters had parted in such a cold way, with Fancy refusing to even say good-bye, that both girls were startled by their mutually enthusiastic reunion, hugging and laughing and crying all over each other as though they had been separated for years instead of just the weekend.

"I missed you so much," Kit said into her ear, as they stood on the back porch. "The whole way down there I kept thinking, what if I crash and die with Fancy hating me?"

"I don't hate you. Even when I hate you, I don't ever really hate you." She squeezed Kit so hard Kit winced and pushed her away, her hand hovering over her chest, as if actually touching it were out of the question.

"What's wrong?"

"It's not you," said Kit, tears still dripping down her face, but not *happy to see you* tears. Not even tears of pain. At least not physical pain. Kit looked miserable.

"Is it Daddy?" Fancy whispered.

"Come on inside!" Madda yelled. "What're y'all waiting on?"

Kit wiped her face and hurried into the kitchen, the *everything's fine* smile on her face sitting easily and naturally due to many years of practice. "Want me to set the table?"

"You just sit over there and relax," said Madda, setting Kit's bag out of the way. "And tell us all about Huntsville."

"Oooh, sopaipillas!" exclaimed Kit, practically diving facefirst into the basket.

Fancy took one for herself, and the light, sweet smell took her back to the roof, to the meal she'd shared with Ilan—the meal and other things. Ilan hadn't gone all the way with her on the roof, but he'd used his hands on her and taught her how to use her hands on him. He'd used that word "teach" as though his penis were an especially difficult trigonometry problem, like it would require years of lessons to master instead of . . . how long had he lasted . . . five minutes?

But it had been a very educational five minutes.

He *could* have gone all the way. After she'd rolled off him, she'd just lain on the rooftop spaghetti-legged and pleasure-dazed, so he could have done anything he'd wanted. Instead he'd rested his head on her breasts and made her laugh by singing the theme to *Two and a Half Men* in time with her heartbeat.

"How was he?" Madda asked, startling Fancy, who thought she was talking to her.

"I don't know."

Fancy squeezed into Kit's chair. "They didn't let you see Daddy?"

"We didn't go to Huntsville. We went to Houston instead."

"Why?"

"It felt wrong to go without Fancy."

Madda smirked. "You sure this wasn't some elaborate scheme you cooked up just so you and Gabe could be alone all weekend?"

"Me?" said Kit, oh so innocently. "Scheming?"

"What exactly did you and Gabe get up to in Houston?"

"Hardly anything, really."

Even Fancy had to laugh. Until she noticed Kit's mask slip a little, enough to see the misery again. She squeezed Kit's hand. It must have been hard for her to pass up a chance to see Daddy. For the first time Fancy felt bad for not going, felt as petty and childish as Ilan had accused her of being.

"I'm so glad you girls are out there in the world getting involved," Madda said. "At the beginning of the summer did you ever think you would be where you are now?"

"No way."

"I've been very worried about y'all. But maybe I'm wrong to worry so much. You're involved in the community. People talk about you in town. In a good way, for the most part."

"What do they say?" asked Kit.

Madda grimaced. "It doesn't matter. What matters is that you used to hate being around people, and now you're driving across the state with a boy. And you"—she pinched Fancy's cheek—"never even wanted a boyfriend, and I catch you and Ilan making out on the lawn."

Kit squealed. *"What?"*

"I caught her red-handed with her hands down his pants."

"You did not," Fancy told Madda sternly, with as much dignity as she was able. "It was just *one* hand."

After dinner the sisters went into the inner room to get ready for their baths, the same as always, except that Kit wouldn't undress in front of Fancy.

"Why're you acting so strange?" Fancy tossed her shorts and top on the bed. "All shy and unhappy?"

Kit sighed and sat next to Fancy's discarded clothes. "I didn't want to say anything in front of Madda, but me and Gabe broke up. I mean, *he* broke up with me after he did this."

She slowly removed her shirt. Fancy froze at the sight of her bruises. Her chest looked swollen and green, almost gangrenous.

"He *beat* you?"

"In his sleep. You know how he gets. Just . . . crazy. It was like he was trying to smash his fist through my heart. He kept saying that he wanted to live inside me. I said that to him once, that I wanted to crawl inside him. It's like he was mocking me."

"I doubt it. He said the same thing to me in the shed. What a weirdo. How'd you get him to wake up?"

"I kneed him in the balls."

"Good! Serves him right."

"He was so ashamed." Fancy had never thought of misery as an active, ravenous thing, but it seemed to claw at her sister, to distort her so that she hardly seemed recognizable. "He said that he goes to church every day to pray about it, but it doesn't work. He told me"—Kit's breath caught as she tried and failed to choke back a flood of tears—"he said he can't risk anything like that ever happening again. That he couldn't stand hurting me again. He said we have to stay away from each other."

"You're better off." Fancy got toilet paper from the bathroom and brought it to Kit. "Don't cry over him. He was just a—"

"I know you hate him," Kit interrupted, sad and defeated. "But I don't need to hear that right now."

"You don't have to hear it from me." She thought of the moonfruit. "We can go to his house, and you can hear it straight from his own mouth how he—"

"Fancy." Gabriel's cross shone in Kit's palm. She turned it this way and that as though it were a tiny gadget she had no idea how to operate. "Will you do something for me? Will you come to church with me?"

"Church?"

"I wanna pray for him. God would listen to a prayer for Gabe."

"Why do *I* have to listen?"

Kit let go of the cross and reached for her sister. "Because I don't have anybody else."

Fancy sat next to Kit and embraced her, careful of her sore chest. "Told you so," she whispered.

The next day, inside St. Teresa Cathedral, Kit and Fancy stood before a long, ornate altar full of candles. Fancy held on to Kit's hand, feeling small inside the icy, echoing space. Even the altar outsized the sisters, burying them in flickering candlelight.

Kit studied several of the unlit candles, a frown puckering her brow. "Which one of these candles are we supposed to light? Does it matter what row they're on or—"

"You're asking me?" Fancy snorted. "I can't even remember the last time we went to church."

"Big Mama's funeral. That was the last time." She lit a candle next to a statue of Mary, the only statue either of the girls recognized.

Kit lowered herself onto the kneeling bench to pray, and then froze, eyes wide, hands knotted together. "I don't know any prayers." She looked panicked. "The only one I can remember is 'Good food, good meat, good God, let's eat.'"

"This is stupid." Fancy looked around and spotted a couple of Blue Sisters chatting near the confessionals. "See them? Go ask them to pray for you."

Kit stood and rubbed her knees—the padding on the kneeling bench had worn thin. "You think they will?"

"Der. It's their job. Go on."

Kit put a Sacagawea dollar in the donation box before she approached the sisters, who, though on the small side, managed to loom like holy skyscrapers in their grayish-blue habits. The oldest-looking sister smiled a bright Pollyanna smile, like she thought the world was awesome. "You girls look lost. Can we help you with something?"

Fancy had to poke Kit in the side to get her to speak. "Do you know Gabriel Turner?"

"Yes," said Sister Pollyanna somberly. "But we haven't seen him in a while."

Kit shook her head as though shaking water out of her ears. "Gabe hasn't been coming to church?"

"Not for weeks."

"But he said he—" Kit grabbed her cross. Fancy thought

she was going to yank it off, but she didn't. Just squeezed it so hard the veins in the back of her hand began to visibly throb.

"I think he wants to come, dear," said Sister Pollyanna gently. "I see him ghosting about on the steps most days, but he never comes inside. Not anymore. No matter what we say to him."

"He's a liar. Or he's crazy. Or both." Kit swallowed hard. "Either way, I was hoping you'd pray for him. Maybe you can help him. I don't think I can."

"Of course we'll pray for him. If you should see him—"

"I won't. Come on, Fancy."

The sisters fled outside and, joke of all cosmic jokes, ran into Gabriel on the cathedral steps.

Kit froze as Gabriel joined her on the landing. His hair was in braids again, no longer wild and curling this way and that, but there was something wild in his eyes as he faced Kit. Fancy moved closer, fully prepared to kick him down the stairs if he tried anything.

He said, "What're you doing here?"

"You don't own church," Kit snapped. "I can come here if I want."

"Gabriel!" Sister Pollyanna stood in the doorway behind them, oblivious to the tension between him and Kit. "We were just talking about you. Come on inside!"

"I can't." He looked at Kit. "I want to, but—"

"But I'm here? You don't wanna occupy the same space as me? Fine. It's all yours." She walked behind him and kicked his butt so hard that he stumbled forward past Sister Pollyanna into the cathedral.

"It's okay," Kit told them as the nun gasped at the sight of Gabriel sprawled at her feet. "He's the one who taught me the proper way to kick a—" Fancy pinched her arm. "Butt. The proper way to kick butt. Stop pinching me!"

"Kit," Fancy hissed. "*Look* at him."

Gabriel lay just past the threshold of the chapel doors, writhing and screaming. He kicked his legs against the floor, and one of his flailing hands touched one sister's black-stocking-covered ankle. He snatched his hand away, hissing as if burned, and grabbed his head. The Blue Sisters came forward, their shin-length blue habits rustling as they dragged him into the building. Kit ran forward to help. Fancy was happy to have so many witnesses. Perhaps they could provide the testimony necessary to have Gabriel put away in a facility somewhere. He was obviously a basket case. Or sick. Or both.

Sister Pollyanna examined Gabriel. "Is this what I think it is, Sister Judith?"

Fancy noted the excited concern in the sisters' eyes. "Only one way to be sure. I'll fetch the holy water."

"Gabriel?" Sister Pollyanna knelt by his face and tried to force him to look at her, her eyes full of the calmness that comes from knowing that no matter what happens, you can just blame it on God. "It's me, Sister Maggie. Assuming you still remember me. We haven't seen you in church in months, you bad boy."

"You told me you came every Sunday," Kit said, frowning at him. "Have you been lying to me about everything?"

"Don't blame him, child. He has a demon."

"A demon?" Kit brandished her switchblade, scanning Gabriel's body as if it were something she could cut out.

"Put that away, child," said Sister Maggie. "That won't help."

"Can you help him?"

"I can if you stand back." Sister Maggie didn't wait for Kit to move, just pushed her into Fancy's arms. Sister Judith came back with a clear vial full of water and knelt on Gabriel's opposite side to help hold him steady.

Fancy put her arm around Kit, wondering if she had been wrong about Gabriel. He didn't look crazy; he looked like he was in pain—excruciating pain.

Sister Maggie poured some of the holy water into Gabriel's right ear and then began to speak the Lord's Prayer into it. By the second recitation Gabriel was howling, and on the third a tiny gray blob began to swell from his left ear. The blob shot free and landed on Sister Judith, who let go of Gabriel's head and grabbed it, holding it up like a newborn. It screamed like one, but it looked like the end result of a love affair between a man and a widemouthed bass, a shiny, wriggling thing with muddy eyes on either side of its head.

"How marvelous!" cried Sister Judith, delighted. "I've always wanted to see one up close and personal!"

The creature's head exploded all over her.

Sister Maggie laughed at the horrified expression on her fellow sister's face. "Doesn't get more personal than that."

Kit broke free of Fancy's grip and ran to Gabriel; she put her arms around him. "Are you okay?"

"I guess." He held his hand over his bloody ear, as if to

keep anything else from shooting out of it. "What *was* that thing?"

"An imp," said Sister Maggie brightly. "A young one." She dabbed at Gabriel's ear with a tissue she'd pulled from her pocket. "You're lucky it was only about three months old. If it had grown any bigger, that would be your head sprayed across Sister Judith's bosom. Imps transfer spawn into other hosts, usually by way of kisses." She looked at Kit and shook the vial of holy water. "You'll need this too."

"*Me?*"

"You're the girlfriend? Been sharing kisses?"

"And other stuff."

"Shut up, Fancy." Kit exchanged an embarrassed look with Gabriel until Sister Maggie bent her forward and tilted her head to the left. "We use birth control." As if Sister Maggie would be impressed by that.

Sister Maggie poured the holy water into Kit's right ear, but the brown ooze didn't shoot from her left ear. It shot out of her nose and hit the floor with a splat. It wasn't fully formed the way Gabriel's imp had been; it was just a blob that sizzled and burned against the white cathedral tile.

While Kit squealed and rubbed so vigorously at her nose

it nearly detached from her face, Sister Maggie looked around the cathedral and sighed contentedly. "The power of Christ himself. Best birth control in the world."

When Sister Judith tittered, Sister Maggie rolled her eyes.

"I mean against imps."

Fancy sat in the backseat of Gabriel's, or rather Ilan's, Oldsmobile in the parking space down the street from the cathedral, glowering at Kit and Gabriel, who sat in the front shamelessly making out.

"So all this bad stuff," Kit was saying, between kisses, "the sleepwalking and trying to kill people, was because of the imp trying to spawn?"

"I guess so," said Gabriel. "I . . . oh no!" He slapped his head. I'm gone have to send Jessa to the Blue Sisters."

"The CPR girl?" said Kit. "Fancy *said* she saw you kissing her."

"Yeah." Gabriel looked deeply embarrassed. "And Cici. And Madeline. And Alysha."

"Did you just go around kissing every girl in Portero?"

"No, just those four," said Gabriel quickly. "I hate that it was even one. And I oughta chop my hand off for hurting you the way I did." Kit let him pull her back into his arms.

"I'll do it for you," said Fancy, watching his offensive hand moving along her sister's chest.

They froze, as if they'd forgotten she was there.

"I'll do it," she repeated, "and not just for hitting my sister, but for being a liar. Sister Maggie said that imp was only three months old. *You* been sleepwalking for years."

"But not hurting anybody," Kit said, her hand resting protectively over Gabriel's hand, as if she thought Fancy had an ax in her pocket. "The way he hurt me, the way he tried to hurt you, *that* was the imp."

"You can't blame every horribly horrific thing you've ever done on that imp, now can you?"

Fancy noted the guilt in Gabriel's eyes.

"What're you talking about?" Kit said, looking from one to the other. "What horribly horrific thing?"

"Get out, Kit," Fancy said, not looking at her sister. "Me and him need to talk."

"About what?"

"Personal stuff between me and him," snapped Fancy, irritated by Kit's hesitation.

Kit squeezed Gabriel's hand and left the car, reluctantly.

He turned to face Fancy. "I'm real sorry about the toolshed thing and—"

"Don't get nervous," Fancy said. "The only thing I want from you is the truth. Assuming you even know what that is anymore."

"Is this the part where you give me the moonfruit?"

"Ilan told you about that." Fancy would never have guessed they were the sort of brothers who talked and shared secrets.

"He trusts me." Gabriel sighed and looked away. "With certain things. Anyway, you don't have to bother. I did it."

Fancy leaned forward. "You did what?"

"I killed my pop." The admission seemed to cost him, and it was a long time before he could speak again, his voice low and full of tears. "I killed him and then blamed it on Guthrie."

"Why?"

"My pop . . . He touched me." Gabriel shook his head, distancing himself from the words, even as he spoke them. "And I snapped."

"How did Mr. Turner's arm get in our cellar? Did you plant it there?"

"No. I don't know how Guthrie got Pop's arm. Unless he was following us when we hid the body."

"Ilan helped you cover it up."

"He's been helping me outta jams for years."

"Where's the body?"

He told her, and Fancy smiled.

"You're not gone tell Kit, are you?"

"You should be the one to tell her."

Gabriel looked relieved. "Thanks, Fancy. I will. Soon. I'm just waiting for the right moment. I hope she'll take it the way you have."

"I hope she does too," said Fancy, inwardly cavorting, but trying not to show it. "I'll go get her."

Kit was a ways down the street, standing in a narrow clump of gory Annas growing outside a beauty parlor.

"Sometimes a flower is just a flower," Fancy said, after she'd caught up with her.

"And sometimes a flower is a signpost of the living dead." Kit stepped out of the flower bed and eyed her sister suspiciously. "What did y'all talk about?"

"This and that. Life, love, all that stuff. And Dog Run."

"What about Dog Run?"

"Well. They're having the battle of the bands up there real soon. And since Ilan and Gabriel's band is playing this year, and since you have this fantasy about us double-dating . . . Well . . . do you want to?"

Kit crushed Fancy in a back-breaking hug and tried to dance her around in a circle. Instead they crashed into the bike rack and knocked all the bikes off true.

"I been *dying* for the four of us to do something together!" Kit exclaimed. "It'll be so much fun. I can't wait!"

"Me either." Gabriel was staring at her from the car window, and when she smiled at him, he flinched. "I have a feeling it'll be interesting."

FROM FANCY'S DREAM DIARY:

Daddy pulled me to the side and showed me his monster. It was red and had weird elbows, and he kept it in his pocket. He said I had to figure out how to shrink my own monster down enough so that I could hide it better. When I told him I didn't have a monster, he pointed behind me so I turned and saw this thing that was as big as St. Teresa Cathedral but way less holy. And slimy. And all mine.

CHAPTER TWENTY-EIGHT

The sisters had never been way downsquare before, in the low, swampy area of Portero. Luckily, Dog Run was relatively swamp-free, encompassing flat, treeless acreage covered in gramma needles and buffalo grass. And the dog-run cabin, of course, from which the land got its name, a sagging bit of wood that looked as though a tornado had dropped it from the sky.

But today the house was barely visible because of the hundreds of people crowded around a makeshift stage. Groups from all over Navarro County—from Castelaine and Charter, as well as Portero—had come to compete for a cash prize and bragging rights. The sisters stood in the midst of the crowd, gaping as Ilan and Gabriel performed their brand-new song, "My Girlfriend Put My Head in a Jar (and I Liked It)."

"You would too!" Ilan screamed, grinning maniacally as he thrummed his guitar. "You better! Cuz now she's coming after YOU!"

The sisters exchanged baffled looks as the crowd went wild all around them.

"Is that supposed to be about us?" Fancy screamed into Kit's ear.

"Gabe claims we inspired them!"

"They're inspiring me!" said Fancy as Gabriel beat the drums as if they owed him money. "They're making me want to *kill* somebody!"

"I know, right?" yelled a boy Fancy didn't know, who slammed into her and knocked her to the ground.

Kit helped Fancy to her feet, but before she could rip the body slammer a new one, a crowd of unamused Porterenes wedged themselves between the sisters and the boy and did all the ripping themselves. The Porterenes were easy to spot because they were the only ones not wearing bright *notice me please and then eat me* clothes, unlike the transies.

Fancy felt warm and protected as Kit led her out of the

fray; for the first time she understood what Sheriff Baker had meant, what Madda was always saying. Whether it was against bullies or transies or monsters, Porterenes stuck up for one another.

When the concert was over, and each band lined up on the stage so they could determine the winner based on audience applause, Fancy clapped the hardest and screamed the loudest for all the Portero bands.

Unfortunately, the girl doo-wop group from Castelaine kicked everyone's ass. However, Ilan and Gabriel's band, Pig Liquor, got an honorable mention.

"That and two bucks'll get me a guitar pick," Ilan said later as they hung out in the cabin. But he was smiling. Ilan, Fancy, Kit, and Gabriel sat on the floor of the dog run—the long outdoor passageway linking the two sides of the cabin—with their other bandmates and assorted groupies, the breeze playing over them as they shared a bottle of Southern Comfort. The sweet peach taste reminded Fancy of Big Mama. The bodies pressed to hers made her feel plugged in, like Kit had once explained, as though electricity were zipping their bodies to hers. It was nourishing, in a way, being able to feed off other people's energy, like social cannibalism.

Ilan tried kissing Fancy, but she was too fired up to relax into it. "Why all this tension?" he said into her ear, hand on her backside. "Music is supposed to soothe you."

"Not your music," said Fancy.

"You didn't like 'My Girlfriend Put My Head in a Jar'?" He looked genuinely upset. "I wrote it for you."

Fancy considered what she could say that wouldn't hurt his feelings. "Your band name is interesting. I like the way you scream—you have a good yelling voice. And, um, I liked when you took your shirt off—that was fun to watch."

"The girl's got no appreciation for the arts, man," slurred one of Ilan's bandmates.

"What would be really fun," Ilan told her, "is if you took your shirt off and screamed for me. No?" he said when Fancy just laughed and slapped his hands away from her shirt. "Well, then kiss me, and we'll call it even."

As Fancy kissed him a flash went off in the darkness. Kit had taken Fancy's picture with Gabriel's phone.

"I'm gone have it framed," she said, giggling so much that Fancy wondered how much Southern Comfort she'd had. "Maybe give it to Madda for her birthday. Then she'll stop being so grumpy and suspicious."

"Grumpy and suspicious about what?" Ilan asked.

"Us. She doesn't know what we do. Everybody else in town knows, but not her. She doesn't want to know." Kit looked like she was about to break into a million pieces, but she kept smiling. "Listen to me going on and on. Or better yet don't listen. Let's not talk about sad stuff."

"But it *is* sad," Fancy said, "when people are that afraid of the truth. Right, *Gabriel*?"

"I guess." He took his phone from Kit and started playing with it so that he wouldn't have to look at Fancy.

"Will you take a picture of me and Kit?" Fancy asked him.

"Sure!" Gabriel said, relieved and grateful, as though she had changed the subject for his sake.

"Not here," she said, when Kit tried to squeeze next to her and Ilan. "Outside, while there's still some light."

The four of them climbed over all the bodies and left the dog run. It was still incredibly crowded at the back of the house, not only with people, but with parked cars, so they circled around to the front of the house, where it was relatively calmer.

"What looks like a good spot?" Kit asked. "Ain't nothing but grass for miles."

Fancy scouted about, and far from the cabin, about a football field's length away, she found what she was looking for. "How about over there? In that patch of gory Annas?"

"No," said the Turner brothers in unison, wearing identical expressions of horror.

"Why not?" Fancy asked with her most innocent expression.

"Yeah," said Kit. "We might as well take at least one picture over there. I'm going anyway." Kit wore her skinny pink heels and was managing to walk in the grassy field admirably well. "Everybody knows gory Annas grow near corpses. Maybe whatever's buried there wants to talk."

Gabriel caught up with her. "Can't you just skip it for once?"

"That's not very Christian, *Gabriel*," said Fancy, serenely following her sister.

Ilan grabbed her arm and held her back. She'd never seen him look so panicked, not even when she'd sicced the dogs on him. "Fancy. Stop her. Please?"

She watched Kit moving ahead with Gabriel at her side talking very fast and trying ineffectually to steer her away from the gory Annas. "She has the right to know. She's the only one who doesn't."

"When Gabe told me you helped save him from that imp, I thought you were past this . . . pettiness."

"The Blue Sisters saved him from that imp, not me. See? He can't be truthful about *anything*. Don't look at me like that, Ilan. It's nothing personal. Just family stuff. You know how that is." She broke free of his hold and caught up to Kit just as she stepped into the gory Annas. Almost immediately an arm shot up through the white flowers, and bony fingers encircled her sister's shin.

"Quick, Gabe," Kit said, striking a faux-frightened pose, as the corpse's skull broke free of the earth. "Take the picture! Otherwise my children will never believe how awesome I was when I was young." She dropped the pose when Gabriel just stood there, staring at the corpse that was using his girlfriend as an anchor to drag itself out of the ground. "Gabe?"

Gabriel looked sick, like he had come down with the flu. Ilan placed a hand on the back of his neck, holding him steady. Or keeping him from fleeing. Ilan didn't look any better than his brother, of course. Fancy hated involving him in this, but Kit deserved an introduction to the real Gabriel.

Once the corpse was fully free, it released Kit and put its hand over the hole where its ear should have been. It only had the one hand because its right arm was missing. "God," said the corpse, using the air around it to make speech. "What horrible fucking music."

"You want me to make it stop?" asked Kit, breezy as ever. "Is that your wish?"

"No, that won't give me peace."

"Then what will? Tell me. I'll give you anything you want."

The corpse turned to Gabriel and Ilan, who stood beside Fancy on the edge of the flower patch. It had no eyes, but its gaze was intense nonetheless. Intense enough to drive Gabriel back several steps. "My sons. I need them to be with me, the way I'd always intended. I don't see why death should keep us apart."

"What do you mean?" Kit frowned. "I can't bring you back from the dead. Nobody escapes death."

"But you can bring them to me," said the corpse. "Especially the one who killed me. It's only fair."

"Who killed you?"

"My son." But the corpse didn't point his lone, bony arm at Gabriel, as Fancy expected.

He pointed at Ilan.

FROM FANCY'S DREAM DIARY:

Kit and Madda and me threw a party for Daddy's victims down in the cellar but only one of the guests showed up and he was kind of a jerk. He said it was too cold in the cellar and the music was too slow to dance to and why had we used Christmas decorations when it wasn't even Christmas and he was real mad cuz there wasn't any food. Even after I pointed out that he was dead and didn't need to eat, he still wouldn't let it go so we kicked him out and locked the doors against him.

CHAPTER TWENTY-NINE

"No." Fancy darted forward and slapped the corpse's pointing finger so hard one of the knuckles snapped off. "Don't point at him. *Gabriel* killed you. Not Ilan."

"*Mr. Turner?*" said Kit, her face almost blank with confusion. "Wait a minute. Daddy killed Mr. Turner," she told Fancy. "Everybody knows that."

"Guthrie didn't want to kill me. He wanted to kill my son. My Gabe." Mr. Turner stretched his hand to Gabriel, imploringly.

Gabriel looked at the broken, skeletal hand as though it were a spitting cobra and shoved his hands into his pockets.

Mr. Turner lowered his hand and said, heavily, "I had hoped

he'd go back for you so we could finally be together, but—"

"Don't talk to him!" Ilan stepped between his father and Gabriel.

"Ilan." Fancy caught his eye, but only briefly; he couldn't hold her gaze. "*You* killed Mr. Turner?"

"Ilan was always jealous of his brother," said Mr. Turner, "the attention I gave him. He used to poison my Gabe. Did you know that? Even pushed the poor boy down the stairs once. But I forgive him."

"You forgive *me*?" Ilan yelled.

"Jealousy is just a sign of devotion. I understood that, even then."

Ilan launched himself at Mr. Turner, who grabbed him and held him so tight Fancy heard the creaking of bones—whether Mr. Turner's or Ilan's, though, she couldn't say.

"I know you didn't mean it," Mr. Turner hissed into Ilan's ear. "I know you'll make it up to me."

"Let him go!" Fancy tried to pull Ilan free, but Mr. Turner's bony grip would not loosen.

Kit pulled Fancy out of the way and spoke to Mr. Turner. "If Ilan's the one who killed you, why do you want Gabe, too? He didn't do anything."

"You said I could have anything." The darkness in his voice stood Fancy's hair on end. "You promised."

"Well, I take it back!" Kit shouted, unaffected by Mr. Turner's voice. "There's no way I'm—"

Mr. Turner let go of Ilan and shoved Kit to the ground by her face. He knelt on her, his knees in her belly, and put his hand over her heart, over that empty space that was not as empty as she'd thought. She was full of life, and Mr. Turner was sucking it out of her.

"No!" Fancy screamed, watching her sister decay, shriveling and cracking like a mummy, like something that had crawled out of the ground with Mr. Turner. Fancy fell on him and dislocated several of his ribs, but she couldn't pull him off her sister. Gabriel and Ilan tried to help, shoving and pulling at their father, but he wouldn't budge. He didn't have to budge. Kit had broken her promise.

"Kit," Fancy said. "Quick! Take back what you said."

"No." It was just a small croak from her dried lips. Small, but decisive. She'd obviously lost her mind and didn't know what she was saying.

For the first time in her life Fancy would have to speak for her.

"Leave her alone!" Gabriel cried, dropping to his knees

beside his father. "Please. Kit's the only one here who's really innocent—she didn't know the truth!"

Despite the dire situation Fancy couldn't help but roll her eyes at Gabriel's use of "Kit" and "innocent" in the same sentence. Fancy shoved Gabriel out of Mr. Turner's reach.

"He's not gone kill Kit," Fancy said, calm and in control. Maybe Mr. Turner was sucking the life from Kit, but *she* wasn't what he was hungry for. "If he does, he won't get what he wants." She stared into Mr. Turner's empty eye sockets. "*I* take back what Kit said."

That got everyone's attention.

"Me and her are practically the same person," Fancy continued. "So this time I'll speak for her. If you fix what you've done to her, you can have your sons."

"*What?*"

Fancy held up a hand to silence Ilan, but continued speaking to Mr. Turner. "You can take them far from here, far from this horrible music. You can—" She gave Ilan a quick look. "You can take them to paradise, and Ilan can introduce you to the cute little dogs that live there."

The look of outrage on Ilan's face was replaced with understanding.

Mr. Turner heaved himself off Kit and stood. Ilan put a hand on Gabriel's shoulder, and Fancy heard him whisper, "I'll take care of you. I always have."

Before Gabriel could say anything, Mr. Turner slung his arm around both their necks and pressed their faces to his splintered ribs.

"I've wanted so long to hold you both," he said, and then turned his skull in Fancy's direction. "Now, keep your word."

Fancy shot an embarrassed look at Ilan, relieved that his face was smashed against his father's ribs and he couldn't see her removing bubble solution from her purse. She blew a bubble so big that all three Turners fit inside it. There were no gory Annas in the bubble with them. Only the stone platform ringed with the headless statues.

Mr. Turner was no longer a corpse, but was as fully alive and real as Franken's girlfriend had become after Kit had sent her to the happy place. Though he was still missing his right arm, he was tall and handsome and strong and dressed in the suit he'd been buried in.

When she stopped blowing, the bubble popped, and the Turners disappeared.

"Fancy?"

Kit groaned behind her, no longer shriveled and horrible, but groggy as she sat up. "Where's everybody? Where's Gabe?"

"I let Mr. Turner take him. Both of them."

Her grogginess cleared up instantly. "How could you let that happen?"

"Don't worry. They're just in the happy place."

Kit noticed the bubble solution. "Show me Gabe. Quick!"

Fancy tried, but the bubbles she blew were all black. Before Fancy could apologize, Kit punched her in the mouth, bloodying her knuckles on Fancy's teeth and spilling the bubble solution all over the ground.

"I thought you didn't want to hurt me," Fancy said, trying to dodge Kit's fists, her mouth stinging.

"You took everything else." Kit pushed her. "What's left but this?" She slapped Fancy. "And this!" She slapped her other cheek. "Don't just stand there, you heartless bitch!"

Fancy wasn't just standing there, but Kit was stronger and quicker than her. She couldn't win in a real fight, so she fought with words. "Not heartless, *sensible*. Sensible enough to fall for a guy who can take care of himself. Unlike your whiny, horrible—"

"Whiny, horrible, and *innocent*!" Kit shoved her again and

then backed away from her, as if she couldn't stand to touch her anymore, not even to fight. "You set this up, didn't you? Just to break up me and Gabe. Why do you have to be like that? All jealous and scheming?"

Fancy swallowed the blood in her mouth and rubbed her slap-swollen cheek. "It's ridiculous for you to care so much what Gabriel thinks of you, when he's no better than we are."

"Well apparently he is. *Ilan* killed Mr. Turner."

"Well, if Ilan did it, he must've had a really good reason."

"Gabe couldn't've had a reason?"

"Like I can believe anything he says! He told me he killed Mr. Turner and buried the body at Dog Run. See how devious he is, mixing in the truth with his lies?"

"Oh, shut up, Fancy. Maybe he does feel responsible for Mr. Turner's death. I felt responsible when Daddy got arrested, and I didn't have anything to do with that. Kids always blame themselves for shit their grown-ups get involved in." Kit glared at Fancy. "Or maybe Gabe told you what Ilan *made* him believe. Mr. Turner said Ilan used to poison Gabe. Maybe Ilan poisoned his mind, too."

Fancy went cold at the idea that Ilan would treat his brother that way. It was one thing for him to hate Gabriel—Fancy fell in and out of hate with Kit all the time—but it was another thing entirely to mess with his brother's mind, to make him believe horrible things about himself.

"We have to get the boys back," she said after a long silence.

"How?"

"We go to the happy place and *get* them. I didn't promise Mr. Turner he could keep 'em for all eternity. If he didn't read the fine print, that's not our problem. We have to find out the truth, because if Ilan's been blaming Mr. Turner's death not only on Daddy but on his own brother this whole time—"

"What?" Kit said. "You'll kill him?"

"Yes," Fancy said, and then burst into tears. "And then I'll kill myself. I'd have to."

Kit listened to her sister cry for a long time before she nodded. "I guess you ain't that heartless after all."

"I wish I was," Fancy said, practically clawing the tears from her face. "Love sucks."

FROM FANCY'S DREAM DIARY:

I WENT TO MADDA'S ROOM AND ASKED HER IF SHE WANTED TO GO ON VACATION WITH ME AND KIT. SHE SAID, WHERE ON VACATION? I SHOWED HER THE HAPPY PLACE IN THE MIRROR ON THE WALL. SHE TOOK THE MIRROR DOWN AND HID IT UNDER HER BED. SHE TOLD ME SHE DIDN'T LIKE VACATIONS.

CHAPTER THIRTY

Kit drove them home from Dog Run in Ilan's Oldsmobile. Since Madda was usually awake that time of day, they parked back in the woods and then snuck into the cellar, and from there entered the happy place.

"You been busy," noted Kit once they'd made it past the hedges of the Headless Garden, taking in the changes since her last disastrous visit. "Didn't there used to be a carnival over there?"

Fancy looked where Kit was pointing, down near the beach. A massive forest had sprouted where the carnival ruins had been, dark and heavy and out of place in the breezy seascape.

"I didn't do that," said Fancy. "But I bet I know who did."

As they marched toward the forest, Kit said, "Gabe told me something once about how his dad liked to go camping in the woods. Gabe always made his childhood sound so . . ."

"Idyllic?"

"Yeah! All this stuff about his dad taking him to the fair and out fishing—"

"Like Daddy did for us?" Fancy snorted. "*We* had a great childhood. Now we're going into the woods to rescue two murderers from their dead father. Great childhoods are overrated."

"One murderer." Kit took Fancy's hand in an instinctive, big-sister way, as they threaded past the first line of trees.

"Gabriel knew about it. And helped cover it up. That makes him responsible too."

"You just refuse to give Gabe a chance."

"If he dropped dead tomorrow, I'd dance at his funeral."

"Fancy!"

"But as long as he's alive," she shouted, forcing herself to say the words, "and as long as you wanna keep him, I promise not to hurt him or try to run him off. Okay? Is that better?"

"I don't love him more than I love you, stupid girl!"

"You almost died for him at Dog Run."

"I knew you'd figure something out. You're smart."

"Not that smart!"

"You are." Kit helped Fancy over a fallen log in their path as they entered the forest. "I'm still here, aren't I? The thing about a boyfriend is, it's easy to show him how you feel. When you feel love for him, you can just throw him down and nail him."

"You should write Hallmark cards."

"But when you feel love for your sister," Kit asked, ignoring the sarcasm, "what can you do? You can be real obvious with a boyfriend, but with a sister you have to be more subtle."

"Like promising not to kill her boyfriend?"

"Exactly! See, you are smart. I figured—" Kit dropped Fancy's hand and ran forward into a clearing where a campsite had been set up. "Gabe!" She ran around the campfire and ducked into the large canvas tent, but she came out frowning. "It's empty. Where the hell could they—"

A warbling scream silenced her.

The scream was coming their way fast, like an auditory freight train, rushing at them from the thick foliage.

"Gabe?"

"Ilan?"

The sisters drew together. Neither sister wanted the scream

to belong to either brother, but who else, if Mr. Turner was that determined to get his revenge?

But it wasn't the brothers who rushed forward from the trees. It was Mr. Turner.

He no longer looked sure and in control as he had at Dog Run. His suit jacket was gone, his tie askew, his shirt soaked in sweat. He looked scared. Hunted. Prey. He tried to clamber up a tree, but his missing arm made it difficult.

And then the sisters heard it. Barking. Loud and wild and vast. Five or six pale dogs, the same dogs that had once attacked Ilan, came leaping out of the brush at his father. The sight of them gave Mr. Turner the motivation he needed to scramble up the tree, just in time to escape the dogs' slavering fangs.

Ilan and Gabriel came out of the trees, a pack of pale dogs following closely behind them. They came to a stop beneath the spot where their packmates had treed Mr. Turner.

"Come on," Ilan yelled up at his father, over the barking. "It'll only hurt a little and then it'll feel good, right, Pop?" He had that same crazed bubbliness that Kit got just before she stabbed someone in the throat. On Ilan, though, the look wasn't natural; it was hiding something so ugly that all the bubbliness in the world couldn't mask it. "You know I love you, don't you?" he screamed at his father. "Why're you hiding from me up there? Get down here, damn it!"

"How can you treat me like this?" Mr. Turner yelled from his rickety branch. "I've never been anything but good to you. I always gave you everything you wanted. Gabe, talk to him!"

But Gabriel just stood there watching his brother, his face etched in misery.

When Mr. Turner refused to come down, Ilan picked up a rock and hurled it at him. It smashed into his skull and knocked him neatly from the tree. He hit the ground in just the wrong way, and his leg snapped underneath him. His resounding scream rang in the woods.

Ilan ordered the dogs away from his father, who he grabbed by the scruff of the neck. "You wanna go in the tent with me, Pop? Let's go. All of us together like you always wanted."

"Please don't. I can't."

"You can. You will."

Ilan dragged him into the huge tent, unconcerned for his broken leg, so focused on his task that he walked past the sisters without acknowledging them. Gabriel followed close behind, stricken and dazed, and closed the tent flap behind him.

Fancy and Kit sat back-to-back on a stump before the campfire and watched the tent. The dogs ringed it, and when Mr. Turner began screaming, they howled as if in mockery.

After awhile Kit said, "Why does Ilan hate Mr. Turner so much?"

"He's hurting Mr. Turner, so Mr. Turner must have hurt him."

"There's a difference between hurting and killing."

A light was on inside the tent, and the sisters watched the shadows streaking about. One of the shadows had an ax. Fancy smiled. "Bet Mr. Turner wishes he'd *stayed* dead."

"Too bad there's no popcorn," Kit said, as blood sprayed the thin tent walls. A few seconds later the minions entered the campsite, carrying not only a big bowl of buttery popcorn and a pitcher of lemonade, but a small table and two lawn chairs.

"I told you this was just as much your place as mine," said Fancy, shoveling popcorn into her mouth.

"I made them do that?" Kit looked very pleased with herself. "You may leave us," she told the minions grandly, after they'd finished setting up the chairs.

The sisters sat, and Fancy said, "Now who's the maharaja?"

"Me, of course." Kit leaned back and waved her hands theatrically at the tent, which, to Fancy's marveling eyes, unfolded and grew, stretching into a rectangle like a movie screen. The Turners were still silhouetted on the other side, intent on their dark deeds.

"Are you doing that?" Fancy asked, impressed.

"I am the maharaja," Kit said, "and the maharaja wants to know what happened that night." She laughed at her own foolishness. "And so do I."

"I can't see the past, Kit. I told you that."

"This is our place. Who's gone tell us we can't see the past here if we want to? Don't you want to?"

Fancy passed her the popcorn. "Definitely."

So they stared at the tent screen Kit had created, and an image suddenly projected onto it, playing out the way a movie would.

Ilan, at around age twelve, entered a bedroom, a child's room with bunk beds and glow-in-the-dark stars on the ceiling. He held the door open for Mr. Turner, who passed inside, a ten-year-old Gabriel limp in his arms. Mr. Turner placed him on the lower bunk bed, and Gabriel turned over on his side, fast asleep. Mr. Turner sat next to him on the bed and reached for his shirt.

Ilan stepped forward. "I can take care of him now."

Mr. Turner paused, hands hovering over the hem of Gabriel's *Iron Man* T-shirt. He gave Ilan an innocent look. "I'm just going to—"

"I said I'll take care of him," Ilan repeated, sharply.

Mr. Turner heaved a deep sigh. "Fine. Come get me when he wakes up."

Ilan waited until the door was shut behind Mr. Turner before he undressed Gabriel and put him in his pj's. Then he removed a dark brown bottle from his pocket and knelt on the floor beside his brother and whispered, "Sorry I have to keep making you sick, but he won't do anything if you're sick." He tried to feed his brother whatever was in the bottle, but it was empty. He looked at the bottle as though it had betrayed him. "Damn it."

Ilan stood and dropped the bottle into a nearby garbage pail. Then he went into the bathroom and rummaged desperately through the medicine cabinet, until a *thump* sent him running back into the bedroom. "Gabe?"

But Gabriel was no longer in bed.

He was halfway through the mirror on the wall opposite the bunk beds, his legs kicking violently.

"Gabe!"

Ilan raced forward and grabbed him around the hips, just in time to be yanked forward with his brother, his head vanishing into the mirror, which didn't reflect the room. It was more like a window, which looked out onto a gray cellar and the slight man with a kind face who stood inside it, holding Gabriel by the arms. The man was dressed in blue Dickies, with the name GUTHRIE stitched over his heart. He seemed surprised to see Ilan, but not unhappy.

"Two for the price of one," he said. The sound of his voice coming through the mirror was muffled. And so was Ilan's.

"I don't know who you are, mister, but you can't have my brother. I been trying all my life to keep him safe, and I ain't fixing to just hand him over to some stranger. If you need a boy, take me."

"If you take your brother's place," Guthrie said, "who'll protect him from your dad?"

Ilan went still and didn't speak for a long time, while Guthrie gave him a knowing look.

"I've seen you through the mirror. You and your dad."

"Then why don't you take *him*!" Ilan yelled, his voice so loud and anguished that Guthrie winced.

"Take your dad?" Guthrie tsked. "Why should I do your

dirty work? If you hate him that much, *you* kill him."

"Daddy?" The voice was thin and girlish, crackling as though spoken through a walkie-talkie. "We're ready to go. Where are you?"

While Guthrie was distracted by the intercom on the wall behind him, Ilan braced his leg against the wall and hauled himself and Gabriel free of the mirror. The brothers hit the floor with a force that rattled the furniture.

"What's all the noise?" Mr. Turner called. Moments later he stood in the doorway.

Gabriel was wide awake now and shaking as Ilan helped him to his feet. "There was a man in the mirror!" But when he looked, all he saw was his own frightened reflection.

Mr. Turner pulled Gabriel into his arms and rubbed his back. "You were just dreaming."

"Let him go."

"Ilan, hush. I'm trying to make him feel better."

"Well, don't. He's sick."

"I'm not," said Gabriel, plaintively. "Just thirsty. Wasn't there a man, Ilan? A bad man?"

"Yeah," Ilan said, trying to pull Gabriel away from Mr. Turner. "A very bad man."

Mr. Turner shoved Ilan toward the door so hard Ilan smacked his shoulder against the door frame. "Go get your brother some water," he said.

"*You* get it."

"I want Pop to stay," Gabriel said, holding on to Mr. Turner as though he were a giant teddy bear. The sight seemed to pain Ilan.

"You heard him," said Mr. Turner, something smug and dark in his tone.

Ilan raced downstairs and poured a glass of water. While he stood at the sink, he spied a butcher knife on the draining board. He took it, and when he got back to the room, he was glad he had. Mr. Turner's hand was in Gabriel's pajama bottoms.

The glass of water smashed against the floor, but the knife remained firmly in Ilan's grip.

"No wonder you want him dead," said a muffled voice.

Guthrie was back in the mirror, watching them, eyes bright with amusement. Mr. Turner snatched his hand free of his son's pants.

"The man!" Gabriel screamed, and scrambled behind Mr. Turner. "Pop, it's him!"

Guthrie was looking at Ilan. "But what did you *think* he'd do when you got to be too old? At least my way your brother would've been spared."

Ilan said nothing, merely stared at his father with such hatred that his eyes seemed to glow red.

Mr. Turner, oblivious of his son's wrath, gaped at the man in the mirror. "Who the hell are you?"

"A student of human nature," Guthrie told him. "I find it fascinating what goes on in the most average households. But what will you do when they grow up? Have more children? Or will any child do? Or are you only attracted to them because they're yours, and fucking them is like fucking yourself? Narcissists have always intrigued me."

Mr. Turner charged up to the mirror and smashed his fist into it, but instead of his fist breaking the mirror into a million pieces, his fist—and consequently his arm all the way to the shoulder—passed into the mirror. And Guthrie caught it.

He held on to Mr. Turner with his left hand, and in his other hand he held a bonesaw. He brought it down on Mr. Turner's arm at the shoulder, and in a surprisingly short amount of time Mr. Turner fell away from the mirror and hit the floor, minus one arm.

Ilan stepped toward him, the knife still in his hand. He watched blood spurt from his father's shoulder and pool on the wooden floor.

"I softened him up for you, kid." Guthrie was watching Ilan, expectantly. "Why don't you take it from here?"

"Guthrie? Have you changed yet? The girls want—"

Madda, with long hair, ruby red heels, and a shocked expression, stood at the top of the cellar stairs, staring at the severed arm in Guthrie's hand.

He tried to hide it behind his back; he looked more shocked than Madda did.

"Sweetie, I . . ."

Her screams drowned him out.

"Lynne!" he shouted, and then the mirror went momentarily black before it regained its natural state and reflected the room: the bloody man on the floor and the boys who watched him, wide-eyed and silent.

Ilan dropped to his knees beside Mr. Turner, and the silence ended, abruptly. Mr. Turner had not screamed when Guthrie cut off his arm. He had whimpered and pleaded and called to his sons for help, but he had not screamed.

Now he screamed. Not at the sight of his bloody stump, but

because Ilan had driven the butcher knife into his groin.

"Don't worry," said Ilan, adopting his father's gentle, loving tone. "It'll start to feel good in a little while. I promise." He continued hacking away long after Mr. Turner's screams devolved into grunts of pain and then . . . eternal silence.

"Ilan?" The sound of Gabriel's voice finally stopped his assault. "Why isn't Pop moving?"

Ilan stood and backed out of the pool of blood. So much blood. "Cuz he's dead now. You don't have to worry about him anymore."

"But I don't want him to be dead." Gabriel had wrapped himself in a cocoon of blankets.

"You don't have to be scared anymore," Ilan said, and stripped the covers from the top bunk. He unwrapped Gabriel from his cocoon and took those as well. "I'll make sure nobody ever hurts you again."

Ilan wrapped his father's body in the bedclothes to keep it from leaking and then dragged the body through the house to the garage. He wrestled it into the trunk of the Oldsmobile and got into the driver's seat.

Gabriel climbed in beside him, uninvited. "Where're we going?"

"I gotta bury him." Ilan clumsily adjusted the seat to fit his twelve-year-old frame.

"Where?"

"Dog Run. Where they have the battle of the bands." Ilan squeezed the steering wheel and stared blankly out of the windshield. "Pop hates music; it'll serve him right to have to choke on a big fucking concert every year." He started the car, and when the lights came on, they shone on a pile of tools leaning in the corner of the garage.

"Go get that shovel over there," he told his brother. "We'll need that."

Gabriel didn't move.

"What?" Ilan finally looked at him.

"What Pop did?" Gabriel's face was small and miserable. "While you were getting the water? It didn't hurt."

Ilan burst into tears. He lowered his head to the steering wheel and hid his face in his arms. "Yes, it did, Gabe." His voice was so distorted by tears and shame it was barely recognizable. "Yes, it did."

The image of Ilan and Gabriel sitting unhappily in the Oldsmobile disappeared in a wash of gray.

Fancy blinked her eyes to clear them, only to realize the grayness was just the walls of the cellar closing around her. Around everyone. Kit, Ilan, and Gabriel huddled together with her on the floor, which was barely wide enough for all of them.

"That was some movie," said Gabriel, deadpan.

"You saw it too?" Kit asked.

"How could I miss it? Y'all made that screen big enough for Martians to see it. I *hate* thinking about that night." He realized he was yelling and visibly forced himself to calm down, but he couldn't calm the despair that flared in his eyes when he looked at Ilan. "I hate thinking about what must have been happening to you all those years."

Ilan, unlike his brother, was truly calm, even serene. But then he was covered in his father's blood. And Fancy knew firsthand how therapeutic killing could be.

"I wanted at least one of us to grow up ... without ..." Ilan sighed. "I'm just sorry I had to hurt you to do it, breaking your legs, giving you poison to make you sick all the time. But he would have hurt you worse. And bones heal; other stuff not so much. Maybe not ever."

Gabriel lowered his head and spoke to the floor. "I feel like I should have done something. *I* should have been the one who—"

"Don't talk like that." Ilan slid closer to his brother and

kneaded the nape of his neck in an easy, unstudied way that held an air of ritualism. "I wanted to keep you safe more than anything."

"But . . . it's like you blame me. You get pissed at me for being useless and weak."

"Not useless—damaged. And I don't blame you. I know it's my fault you started sleepwalking and seeing things and acting crazy. It's because I did all that in front of you. I tried so hard to keep him off you, so you wouldn't go through what I did, but I ended up putting you through something worse. I didn't know how to keep you safe from that. From your own head. Sometimes you end up fucked, no matter what you do."

Fancy reached over and slapped the back of Ilan's head. "Don't say 'fucked.'"

After a moment of dumbstruck silence Ilan laughed, and then everyone did. Not heartily, but it was something.

"I'm sorry I blamed it all on your dad," Ilan told the sisters.

"Well, Daddy started it," said Kit, magnanimously. "What's one more body to him? Since we're apologizing"—she nudged Fancy—"you have something you wanna say to Gabe?"

Fancy looked Gabriel in the eye. "I don't like you."

"Fancy!"

She flapped a hand at her sister. "But since Kit and Ilan seem to think you're so great, I promise to stop trying to ruin your life."

Gabriel leaned over and kissed Fancy on the cheek. "Apology accepted."

"Puke," she said, but her heart wasn't really in it. She thought about everything she had learned about Gabriel. "Why'd you tell me *you* killed Mr. Turner?"

"Cuz I didn't want you to hate Ilan, especially since he likes you so much. I figured once I admitted it, you'd let it go. And since you hate me anyway, well, you couldn't hate me *more*. And Dog Run is huge. I never even thought about how those gory Annas might give away where the body was, or that you'd let your own sister summon a corpse to get rid of me."

"People underestimate me all the time," Fancy said. "That's why I'm such a successful predator."

"Did it feel good," Kit asked Ilan, "killing Mr. Turner a second time?"

"He didn't die," Ilan said. "He was still wriggling when we got kicked outta paradise."

Fancy stood and looked into the kinetoscope. "There he is. Still in pieces."

Ilan came to look over her shoulder. Her minions were at the campsite, piecing Mr. Turner back together like a jigsaw puzzle.

Fancy leaned in to Ilan's side, impressed. "What did you do to him?"

"There was an ax in the tent, just lying there waiting for me."

"The happy place is like that," said Fancy. "It knows." She kissed him, and when she tasted blood, she sighed, realizing she would have to once again clean blood out of the cellar. But she was so happy to see Ilan safe and away from his horrible father that she couldn't really mind.

"How long will he stay there?" he asked.

"How long do you want him to stay?"

"Just a little while longer." Ilan wasn't as serene as he seemed, not if the quaver in his voice, in his body, was anything to go by. "Just until I get it outta my system."

"Let me go!"

Fancy and Ilan jumped at the sound of Mr. Turner's voice. Fancy was especially shocked. She had never before heard any sound from the kinetoscope. But Mr. Turner was dead. Maybe the rules were different for dead people.

"This is not the deal we made!" Very different. Mr. Turner was staring directly at Fancy, somehow able to see her. His bloody head was half split from the ax, and his eyes were very far apart as he looked at her. "This is *not* the way this day was supposed to end!"

She decided that Daddy had been right about Mr. Turner; he was completely self-centered. "You made a deal with the Bonesaw Killer's daughter," Fancy told him. "How did you *think* this would end?"

Fancy took Ilan's hand and led him out of the cellar, Gabriel and Kit close behind. The sun was low in the sky. Gold light shone through the treetops and threw leafy shadows across the lawn.

"Anytime you wanna visit him," Fancy said to Ilan, "just let me know. I'll even help, if you want."

"You don't have to help. Guthrie was right. I can't let other people do my dirty work."

"People do my dirty work for me," said Fancy, loftily. "Daddy doesn't know everything."

"Neither does Madda." Kit said. She stopped beneath the persimmon tree, and they all stopped with her. She was looking at Madda, who was weeding in the little kitchen garden. They could hear her singing tunelessly as she worked, something about mighty people of the sun.

"We should talk to her," said Kit. "If Daddy had been honest with her, she wouldn't have freaked and run to the sheriff."

Fancy thought of Madda screaming on the cellar stairs, the fear and disgust on her face as she realized exactly who she'd married. "Madda says she wants to know the truth, but people always say that. What if she can't handle it?"

"She loves us," Kit insisted. "When you love someone, you can put up with anything, even murder. I mean, look at us."

The four of them studied one another and tried to get pumped about the idea of the truth setting Madda free. No one seemed convinced it was a good idea, Fancy least of all. But Kit was already stalking toward Madda.

She turned as the four of them drew near and their shadows fell on her.

"Hey, kids!" She looked so happy to see them together. "How was Dog—" She gasped as she got a good look at the blood decorating Ilan and shot to her feet.

"What happened? What's all this blood? Was it hogs? *Cacklers?*"

"No, ma'am," said Ilan. He looked to Fancy for a clue on how to respond, but she only shrugged at him and took hold of her sister's hand, nervously. "We were just down in the cellar. There was an ax, and lots of blood and . . . unpleasantness."

"An ax?" Madda froze and turned to her daughters. "Y'all did this to him?" she said. "Cut on him? With an ax?"

Kit looked shocked. "If we had used an ax on him, he wouldn't be walking and talking, that's for sure. Give us some credit."

"What was it then? A bonesaw?" Madda was almost screaming. Fancy remembered how Madda had been smiling at them not moments before, and wondered if she would ever see that smile again. "All the gossip I been hearing about what you've done to all those people. It's true isn't it? You're just like your father."

Tears were pouring down her face. Fancy had never seen Madda cry before. She hadn't reacted this badly when she'd caught Guthrie in the cellar. Fancy would have rather seen disgust in her face instead of this . . . wretchedness.

"Madda, listen—"

She flinched from Kit's hand and nearly knocked over the snow-pea trellis. She ran into the house, the sisters on her heels.

"Where're you going?" Fancy cried.

"I can't do this again," Madda said, barely able to speak past her sobs. She snatched up her car keys from the kitchen counter.

"You're not leaving us." Kit snatched the keys from her hand.

Madda tried to grab them back, but while she and Kit tussled for the car keys, Fancy noticed that each tear that dripped from Madda's face turned into a cherry as it hit the floor.

The cherries rolled across the tile, such a flood of them that Madda and Kit forgot about the keys as the sour-red fruit, before everyone's stunned eyes, aligned themselves into letters on the snow-white floor: *you wished for this.*

Madda slumped against the counter. Her daughters joined her, bookending her, wishing they knew how to erase the devastated look from their mother's face.

"I did wish for this," said Madda, defeated. "At Cherry Glade. I wished to know what y'all got up to when I wasn't around. And now I know, but how can I—"

"You can't run away," Fancy told her. "If you go, who'll give me advice on how to manipulate men? Who'll make red velvet cake on my birthday? Who'll give me strawberry wine to drink when I feel bad?"

"I never gave you strawberry wine," Madda said.

"We need you here to be nice to us," Kit said, jumping in before Fancy could further incriminate herself. "Chapter one in the mommy handbook specifically says you have to be nice to your children and never abandon them."

"Ma abandoned me," Ilan said as he and Gabriel came into the kitchen. "And I turned out all right."

Fancy kicked him in the ankle. "That's not helping."

"If she kicks you out," Ilan said, rubbing his ankle, "you can come live with us. There's plenty of room."

"My daughters are not moving in with you and that kook grandfather of yours." Madda's spirited reply gave the sisters hope. "They're too young." She really looked at her daughters, her eyes crawling over their skin like lasers, like she was seeing them from the inside out.

Gabriel looked from the cherries to the Cordelles and said, "Maybe we should go."

"No," said Madda. "Y'all seem to know more about my daughters than I do. I want y'all to tell me the truth. Everything."

So they told her. Kit and Fancy told her about how they'd started dissecting animals after Daddy had gone away, about taking Franken hostage, about the old man. They told her about how the town had gotten into it and asked for the sisters' help.

And then Ilan and Gabriel told the part about Daddy and Mr. Turner and how Ilan had been the one to kill him.

"That's why you told me you didn't blame Guthrie," Madda said to Ilan.

"I'm sorry I let him take the blame," he said. "Especially when he was cool enough not to bring up what really happened that night."

Kit said, "Daddy has a warped set of values, but a warped set of values is still, you know, *valuable*. Isn't it?"

She directed the question toward Madda, who didn't look interested in having a philosophical discussion. Madda only shrugged and said, "Guthrie wouldn't've been caught if it hadn't been for what happened to your father. She smiled tiredly at Ilan. "If you ask me, they both deserved exactly what they got."

Fancy pressed against Madda's side. "What do you think we deserve?"

Madda took hold of her daughters' hands. "I can't be the judge of that."

"I don't care about going to hell," said Ilan. "Been there, done that. Been to paradise, too." He winked at Fancy. "Think he's healed yet? Is it too soon to go back?"

"Y'all are not going back to that cellar," Madda said sharply. "Not till after dinner. You boys staying? We're having pork chops."

But while the boys washed up at the sink, Madda stayed on the floor. She didn't seem inclined, or even able, to get up. She kept looking at her daughters' hands, as if she couldn't believe the things they'd done with them.

"Are you okay?" Kit asked her. "Or are you not looking us in the eyes because you hate us now?"

"I could never hate you," Madda said quickly. "I just want you to be happy and healthy. That's the most any mother can reasonably hope for. I just wish—"

"Be careful what you wish for, Madda," Fancy reminded her.

"You're the ones who need to be careful." Madda looked at them, and there was only sadness in her eyes. And a steely determination. Suddenly she was squeezing their hands so tightly that Fancy heard Kit gasp in pain. Madda was staring at them, looking back and forth, tears shivering in her eyes.

"You girls *be careful*. Promise me."

"We will," said the sisters as one.

ACKNOWLEDGMENTS

First and foremost, here's a special hello to Jeremy West, just like I promised. How does it feel to have your name immortalized on the printed page? Pretty groovy, huh?

Speaking of groovy, here's a big hug and thanks to my groovilicious work peeps Sylvia Nordeman and Allison Jenkins for keeping my secret so well (until we got busted; oh sad day!) and never making me feel awkward about being weird for a living.

I'm so happy to be able to thank the Tenners this time around. Yay! Jackie Dolamore, Chelsea Campbell, the Berkinator, Steve the Breeze, to name a few—where would I be without my writer peeps to keep me sane? I shudder to think.

I also want to say howdy to my number one fan—whether she wants to be or not—Kay Fraser! And also her grandma Luisa Zorilla. People who love their grandmas are okay with me.

Big, big thanks to my agent, Jamie, who has no idea how cool I think she is, and a big hug to my editor, Emilia, for being so patient while I sweat blood all over this manuscript. Also thanks to Karen S. for her awesome copyediting skills and to the crackerjack team at Simon Pulse, whom I've met and know for a fact are too cool for school. Especially Mara Anastas, whose children really do love her (ha ha, you thought I forgot).

Last but not least, thanks to my family—all nine billion of you. I love and fear you all in equal amounts. Peace.